Summer Storm

A Novel of Ideas by
James A. Warren

Published by

VERITAS PUBLICATIONS

Bringing Hidden Truths to Light

This is a work of fiction. The characters and events in this book are products of the author's imagination. Any resemblances to real persons or events are entirely coincidental.

Esse quam videri.
To be, rather than to seem.
North Carolina State Motto

Acknowledgments

I am grateful to Alex McNeil for his careful editing of this book. His sound editorial suggestions sharpened the wording, removed inconsistencies, and fleshed out several points related to the Shakespeare authorship question.

I also want to thank Hank Whittemore for friendship and encouragement rare in this world. Chris Pannell, Bill Boyle and Gary Goldstein read parts of the book at important junctures and provided critical comments that helped me develop the story lines and increase their prominence. And I want to thank Bill Boyle for his work on the cover design.

I am grateful to all of them for their willing to provide encouragement and critical input even though none of them agreed with all the controversial beliefs held by characters in the book. Needless to say, I alone bear responsibility for the final contents.

Contents

PART I

SATURDAY, MAY 30

1

"How do you know that?" Alan asked, doubting that he would receive an explanation that made much sense.

"Well, everybody knows that," Diana said. "In all the time we've been married, have I ever not had a good reason for what I know?"

With his wife about to board a plane for the 24-hour journey to Taiwan, there was no point in saying that "everybody" might be wrong. Besides, she had enough to think about with both her mother and her father not well.

They were at the Raleigh-Durham airport in North Carolina, near their house and Cary University, where Alan had been teaching English literature for a dozen years. Before that, he'd taught at a university in Taipei for a decade. Diana had been a student of his there before they'd married.

"Look at this," he said, showing his wife a new report from the American Council of Trustees and Alumni. "Only four of fifty-two top colleges and universities require English majors to take a course on Shakespeare. What a shame."

"Don't forget to feed the dog while I'm gone," she responded.

"Thank God I work for a university that recognizes just how indispensable Shakespeare is as a foundation for understanding English language and literature, even though it no longer requires students to take a course on him."

"And don't forget to change her water every two days. Last time mold was growing in the bowl when I returned."

"I think I'll see what's new at the airport bookstore," Alan said. As he crossed the walkway, dodging people of all ages staring into small rectangular devices as they walked, he wondered if he and Diana would ever be able to hold a conversation on any intellectual subject. He'd never doubted that would be possible when she'd been his student, given her active participation in classroom discussions. But, as he learned soon after they were married, that had only shown that she was good at meeting class requirements, not that she had any interest in intellectual subjects of consuming interest to him.

Glancing at the bookshelves, Alan saw that most books were the kind of novel you read once and then throw away. Any book not worth a second reading, he'd concluded long ago, wasn't worth a first.

He was about to leave the store when a book with the word "Shakespeare" in the title caught his eye. He picked it up. *The Mysterious William Shakespeare*, by somebody named Charlton Ogburn, Jr. Oh, no, he groaned almost out loud while reading the back cover. Not another book by conspiracy theorists who believe that Shakespeare didn't write Shakespeare. He was about to put it back when it occurred to him that somebody should put a stop to that nonsense, and that he was just the right person to do it by writing a review definitively refuting whatever fantasies the author relied on to reach his outrageous conclusions. He bought the book.

As he walked back towards his wife, again carefully avoiding children and adults of all ages staring into small electronic devices rather than watching where they were going, Alan considered his good fortune to have the job security of a tenured professor at a time when many people were either out of work or working in part-time jobs for a fraction of his salary.

Seeing him approaching, Diana picked up her carry-on bag. It was time for her to go through security.

"Have a good flight, dear," Alan said as they walked to the checkpoint. "Say hi to your parents for me. You know I'll miss you."

"I'll miss you, too," she said, giving him a goodbye hug and kiss. "It's been almost a year since I've been back to Taiwan."

As she disappeared from sight after a final wave, Alan sent messages to Delilah and Carson letting them know that their mother had just gone through security and suggesting that they text her. Diana would appreciate hearing from them as she began the long journey to Taipei.

The skies were dark as Alan drove out of the airport. It wasn't raining yet, but occasional flashes of lightning lit up the darkening clouds, each followed by the sound of distant thunder. That's odd, he thought. It had been such a perfect day on the drive to the airport.

2

MONDAY, JUNE 1

2

Alan felt a sense of excitement as he walked through the campus. It was like this at the beginning of every term. Though it was still early morning, the grassy quad was already occupied by hundreds of students standing and sitting in small groups, each charged with the energy that comes with the opening of a new term. That energy affects faculty as well as students, something he'd felt at the start of every term since his academic career had begun more than twenty years before.

After checking his mailbox, he stopped in at the Literature Department office to say hi to the two secretaries. They were surrounded by students with questions, so he merely waved to them before poking his head into the office of Matt Harris, the Department Chair. He'd expected just to say a few words of greeting before heading over to the library. Instead, Matt waved him in, saying he needed to discuss something with him.

Alan sighed, expecting to be asked to sit on yet another faculty committee. He tried to keep those commitments to a minimum to preserve as much time as possible for research and writing. He enjoyed teaching as much as he disliked serving on committees, but he enjoyed most the writing and publishing aspects of his career. Someday, he told himself yet again, he would free himself completely from teaching responsibilities so that he could devote all his time to writing.

A few months earlier he'd begun working on a book on Shakespeare, his first on that subject. Wanting to make progress on it during the summer term was the main reason he hadn't accompanied Diana to Taiwan—that and the income the summer work would provide to help cover their kids' university tuitions. He had titled the book *Shakespeare's Journey* to reflect the intellectual and emotional journey Shakespeare traveled over the course of his life, as shown by changes in the topics he addressed in his plays and by what he said about them.

It seemed to Alan that Shakespeare had moved from being an idealistic young man to a mature man disillusioned about his fellow human beings, and from one with a view of the world as a benign place to one who saw it as hostile to human endeavors.

He hadn't gotten far with the book before becoming stumped about how to proceed. The problem was the gap between what he'd deduced about the brilliance of Shakespeare's mind from reading his works, and the records of the mundane details of his life that had survived. This summer, with his light teaching load, was his chance to make significant progress on overcoming that problem before the fall semester began.

"Great to see you, Alan," Matt said. "Hope you've had a productive break between terms, as short as it was."

They had been friends for more than two decades, ever since they'd been literature students together, sharing the same idealistic view of literature and its importance, and never doubting that the future had great things in store for both of them.

Alan had been largely responsible for Matt's having become Chair half a dozen years before. The Chair's responsibilities had traditionally rotated through senior faculty in the department, and it had been Alan's turn. Instead of accepting the temporary duties, he had proposed that a permanent Chair position be created and that it be filled by someone from outside the department. The idea had been accepted and Matt had been hired to fill it.

"I've just come from a meeting with Mary Wolpuff, the new Dean of the School of Arts and Humanities," Matt continued. "It wasn't exactly a pleasant meeting, Alan. As you know, the Dean was just hired and this is her first term with us. We always expect new Deans to have different priorities from their predecessors. No problem there. But what is a problem—or rather a challenge—are the particular priorities that Dean Wolpuff has.

"She noted that the School of Sciences is a net producer of revenue for the university, while the School of Arts is a net consumer of resources. 'That,' she told us, 'must change.' Wolpuff wants the Department of Literature, and all other departments in the School, to break even at the very least, so that they won't continue to be a drain on university finances. That's her top priority. How do you like that?"

"She isn't serious, is she? Doesn't she understand that the Department of Literature isn't a profit-making business? That its mission is to educate students who are paying tuition to study here?"

"She does, Alan. She also said she understood that the School of Sciences is able to engage in activities that wouldn't be feasible for the School of Arts, such as operating laboratories that provide training for employees of local corporations, and conducting research that sometimes results in patents that generate revenue streams.

"But here is the kicker. She wants the School of Arts to develop the equivalent of the School of Sciences' labs, training programs and patents. She doesn't know what those equivalent activities would be, but she expects us to find them and develop them to the extent that the School would no longer be a consumer of University resources. And she was pretty damn insistent about it."

4

Neither of them spoke for a moment. Finally Alan said, "Well, good luck with that, Matt. I sure am glad I'm not the Chair of the Department." He stood up to leave.

"Not so fast, Alan. I don't have much of a clue as to how to create revenue producing programs within the Department of Literature. That's something outside my range of experience. I'll be turning to you and other senior professors in the Department for ideas. Think about this, and let's discuss it at the faculty meeting on Thursday."

Alan looked back at him from the doorway and said, "Well, that's a hell of a way for the term to begin."

3

"Good morning, everyone. I'm Dr. Alan Fernwood. Welcome to English 240: Shakespeare in His Own Words."

Some of the students responded with a "Good morning" of their own, others with a smile or a nod.

With only six students, the class was meeting in one of the smaller classrooms reserved for seminars that had one large square table in the middle of the room. Alan was at one of the sides, with two students on each of the other three.

"As you know, a course on Shakespeare is no longer a requirement for a degree in English or literature at Cary University. So, I assume that all of you are here voluntarily because you enjoy reading the works of Shakespeare and believe that he has things of value to tell you in them."

He paused and looked at the students in the class. Six is a good number for a seminar, he thought. Enough to bring in a variety of viewpoints, but not too many for everyone to be involved in the discussions. It was also just above the minimum needed to keep the course from being canceled.

"In this course, the focus will be on trying to understand what Shakespeare had to say on subjects that were important to him. This isn't always easy because the English language has changed a lot in the 400 years since he lived and wrote. Still, once you master Elizabethan English, you will find it not as difficult as it might seem at first.

"Understanding Shakespeare's intentions and reasons for writing each particular play is also difficult because the modern practice is to read into older works modern concerns. That's just what we won't be doing in this class. As the course title indicates, we will be seeking to understand 'Shakespeare in His Own Words.' We'll focus on specific situations or character traits or issues that were important to him. For the purposes of this course, we'll assume that the issues that he returned to again and again in his works were important to him personally.

"T. S. Eliot once said of Henry James that he had 'a mind so fine that no idea could enter it.' That might sound like an insult, but it wasn't. It was praise of the highest kind. What Eliot meant was that James wrote novels about realistic people and situations, and that his plots developed organically. The same could be said of Shakespeare.

"The opposite of that approach is the production of works of fiction intended to portray an ideology—political, economic, social or even sexual in nature. In such works, characters and plots are consciously constructed to portray certain ideas.

"I don't believe that Shakespeare wrote that way. His aim was more to portray the world as he found it than to shoehorn his characters and plots into predetermined ideological straitjackets. He sought to capture in fictional form important aspects of the world as it appeared to him.

"Any questions so far?" Alan asked, looking over the group of students. "No? Then let's introduce ourselves. A seminar like this consists mostly of discussions, which will flow more freely as we get to know each other.

"You've probably read my bio on the university website, but I'll add a few details to it. I've been teaching literature here for more than a decade. Initially, I taught literature originally written in English from the mid-sixteenth century onwards, but a few years ago I began to specialize in Shakespeare.

"In this course, I hope to give you a real sense of why Shakespeare's works are important for us today, of why they're not mere historical documents that belong in museums. I hope you'll conclude that much of what Shakespeare had to say is directly relevant to the lives of people living in modern society in the twenty-first century.

"And now on to all of you." He motioned to the student on his left.

"Hello, everyone. My name is Nancy Kramer. I'm a business major, studying organizational management, and need another humanities course in order to meet graduation requirements. I enjoyed the lower division course in Shakespeare that I took a couple of years ago, and want to learn more about his works. So here I am!"

The next student's situation was similar. "I'm Dave Camacho. Shakespeare's works are so famous, and I want to know why. The first course I took on Shakespeare a couple of years ago didn't quite show me that; I'm hoping this class will.

"In fact," he said, turning to Nancy, "I think we might have been in the same introduction to Shakespeare course. But it was so large that we never got to know each other."

"Oh, I remember having seen you somewhere before but couldn't remember where," she replied. "That must have been it. It was a very large class."

"Good morning. I'm Lisa Newton," said the first student at the opposite end of the table, with a bit of a laugh. "I also had one previous course in Shakespeare, but I felt lost most of the time because it was so hard to understand Shakespeare's English and the actions of many of his characters. I'm studying accounting and like everything to be lined up nice and neat, but there were messes in most of the plays we read. I didn't really enjoy the first course, but know that Shakespeare is important so am taking a second course on him."

"I'm majoring in psychology," the next student said. "My name is Patrick Compton. But you can call me Pat." He smiled as he looked at each of the other students. "I'm interested in many subjects and want to learn more about how people think and why they act the way they do. So I have found psychology and literature courses to be the most interesting because of the way they reveal people's motives, sometimes motives they didn't even know they had. Shakespeare does that, though I agree with Lisa that it's not always easy to understand what he's saying."

"Hello, everyone. I'm Doug Jordan, and I'm studying film. Film and TV. Broadcast media." He turned to Pat. "I also like to understand how people think, and how people with different ideas might act differently in the same situation. It's interesting how many TV sitcoms have episodes that begin with similar plots that are then resolved differently due to the different personalities of the characters in them."

"And I'm Amelia Mai," the last student said. "I'm a Fulbright student from Vietnam. I'll begin a master's program in linguistics in the fall, but now am enrolled in an orientation program for students from other countries who have received Fulbright scholarships. This is my first time in the United States, and I am eager to learn more about American life before my academic program begins."

That's interesting, Alan thought. She must have a real interest in literature. It was unusual for foreign students to take a course in the humanities. Most studied technology, the hard sciences or business to acquire skills that would get them good jobs once they returned home. Some also studied English, but only the teaching-English-as-a-second-language aspects of the subject.

The Fulbright Program, Alan knew, was funded by the U.S. government and provided scholarships for students from other countries who had, in the opinion of the Program, the potential to become future leaders in their home countries.

"I decided to enroll in this course in addition to the orientation program because of the movie *Anonymous*," Amelia continued. "It portrayed William Shakespeare as a front for the real author, Edward de Vere, Earl of Oxford. Ever since watching it I have wanted to know who really wrote Shakespeare's works." With everyone now staring at her, she became a bit flustered. "Well, the movie did present a plausible scenario for Oxford as the author. Have any of you seen *Anonymous*?"

Two or three of the students had.

Alan wasn't sure how to respond. "Um, Amelia, *Anonymous* was only a movie. It wasn't any truer to life than movies that take place on Mars are. It was purely fiction. In fact, I'm just about to begin writing an article on the authorship subject identifying the flaws in the evidence and reasoning of those who doubt that William Shakespeare wrote the works attributed to him."

He then explained a bit more about the course requirements, noting that although he would introduce and moderate some of the sessions, each of them would take on those roles for one session in the first half of the course and two sessions in the second half.

As he watched the students leave, Alan regretted that the authorship issue had come up in the first meeting. It usually arose at least once during the term, and students were always eager to discuss it. But he knew of no colleagues who doubted that Shakespeare wrote Shakespeare. He would have to write his review of Ogburn's book soon in order to skewer once and for all doubts about Shakespeare's authorship.

4

Alan gathered up his books and papers and walked through the campus toward the coffee shop. It was lunchtime, and the quad was even more crowded with students than it had been earlier.

As he walked under the American elms lining the sidewalks that crisscrossed the quad, he recalled how surprised he'd been by his increasing interest in Shakespeare's works a few years ago. Maybe it's a midlife crisis, he smiled to himself. But whatever the cause, he was glad that his renewed interest had led to his becoming Cary University's Shakespeare specialist.

He was now looking forward to some down time in the coffee shop. He wanted to think about how to structure *Shakespeare's Journey* to highlight the changes in Shakespeare's outlook. He also wanted to think through what he'd heard from Matt Harris about Dean Wolpuff's priorities. It wasn't the subject itself that interested him as much as it was wanting to find a way to help his friend meet the challenge he faced.

"Professor Fernwood!" Alan heard his name called as he picked up his coffee from the counter. He turned and saw the foreign student from his Shakespeare class standing by a table near a window.

"Professor Fernwood," she said again as he walked over to her table. "I am so glad to see you."

"Oh, hi, uh, Amelia, isn't it?"

"Yes, it's me, Amelia Mai, from your Shakespeare class this morning. Might you have a few minutes to help me understand some things?" Alan noted how startling it was to hear English spoken with a British accent by someone of Asian origin.

"Uh, sure, Amelia," he said, as they both sat down.

"You will find that I am always full of questions," she said, smiling. "You know, I have not read many of Shakespeare's plays. Only about a dozen, and I do not think I understood much of what I read. It is so hard to understand English written so long ago. Why couldn't Shakespeare just have said what he had to say in simple words so that he could be easily understood? After all, he wrote for the public theater, didn't he, for people who were mostly illiterate?"

"Actually, there is growing evidence that some of the plays were written for performances at private theaters, for audiences with higher levels of education and understanding, even if the plays were later performed in public theaters. Don't worry if you don't understand everything you read. Shakespeare is difficult even for people who speak English as their first language. There are passages that I still don't understand.

"But tell me why you have read so many of Shakespeare's works, Amelia. The dozen you've read is probably twice as many as most students. I can't imagine that reading so many would have been required in any courses you took in Vietnam."

"I read the ones with titles I came across in other books that I read. They were mostly the best-known plays—*Hamlet, Romeo and Juliet*, and so on. I always try to learn more about things referred to in books I read."

"Well, I wish a few more of my American students had the same curiosity and degree of interest in Shakespeare that you have. What's that book you're reading now?"

"Oh, this book is from my Fulbright orientation class. There are a dozen students in it, from countries all over the world. The class helps us understand American people and society, and also helps us understand what will be expected of us as graduate students. It is all a bit terrifying.

"The book is *American Ways: An Introduction to American Culture*, by Maryanne Datesman. It has a lot of information about American history and institutions. Our professors said that the course and book will help us improve our reading and critical thinking skills so that we can understand what we read faster and better."

"Yes, I know the book," Alan said. "It's an excellent introduction to thinking and writing about American history and society. But for understanding the everyday American culture that you see around you, you might also want to see another book with a similar title, *American Ways: A Guide for Foreigners in the United States*, by Gary Althen. I think I have an extra copy that I can bring in for you."

After a pause, he asked, "How long have you been here, Amelia?"

"Oh, only one week. Just long enough to get over jet lag and walk around the campus a few times, and find out where to buy food and get my apartment set up."

"What do you think of us—of Americans—so far? Are we much different from people you've met elsewhere?"

Amelia laughed. "My first impression is that Americans are so causal. They dress so informally, and their manner is equally informal. It is as though they do not understand how to dress and behave properly. Back home, no one would attend a class at the university wearing a T-shirt and short pants, and no would ever have dared to call a professor by his given name. I was kind of shocked to hear that as I walked by a few other classes."

Alan sighed. "You've touched on a subject that has irritated me for years. Americans seem to have lost the sense of public decorum, of knowing how to dress and behave in public. You might have seen pictures of American society from sixty years ago, a time when everybody dressed up to go out in public. Most people wore a hat even to see a movie or attend a baseball game. It's not like that anymore, I'm happy to say. But I still like the formality of having students call me by my title, either Doctor or Professor Fernwood."

"But I have also noticed that in some ways Americans are very rule bound," she continued. "They follow rules that it is hard for me to understand. For instance, they arrive right on time. They wait at crosswalks until the 'walk' light appears, even when no cars are coming. They stand in straight lines rather than crowding up at the counter. And when they buy a newspaper from a vending machine, they take only one paper even after the machine is open and they could take all of them. All these things are surprising to me."

"Well, I suppose we are distinctive in some ways, just like people in every country are, in their own way. But you are right about Americans making a point of arriving on time. I must be going," he said as he stood up. "Don't worry if you don't understand everything you read, Amelia. If you did there wouldn't be any need to take a course on Shakespeare."

TUESDAY, JUNE 2

5

Elvin Alvarez walked through the newsroom of the *Cary City Herald* early Tuesday morning. He approached his cubicle with a degree of confidence, feeling that after three months in his position he had mastered the craft of reporting on STEM issues: science, technology, environment and medicine. It was now rather easy, he thought, to determine which new developments were most worthy of being covered in his twice-weekly articles. He'd just handed in the article for the Saturday edition, and had several days to digest the latest scientific developments before the next article was due for the Tuesday paper.

He was about to put his feet up on his desk and begin reading through the latest reports, when Jennifer, the reporter in the next cubicle, appeared. "Oh good, you're here. Ed was just looking for you. He wants to see you right away."

Jennifer had joined the paper about three months ago, taking over the subjects of education and academia that Elvin had covered before moving to STEM issues. They'd gone out a few times for drinks or dinner after work before concluding that their initial mild attraction for each other wouldn't develop into anything more.

Elvin instinctively glanced at the clock. It was only 9:15. "Did Ed say what he wanted to see me about?" Edward Perkins was the new Special Topics Editor, and Elvin's boss. Reporters hadn't yet figured out what his priorities or work style would be like.

"Nope, just that he wants to see you right away."

"Well, I guess I'd better go see him."

Elvin walked past his row of cubicles, turned right and walked past a row of offices until he reached Ed's. Before he had time to knock, Ed looked up and waved him in.

"Come in, Elvin. Glad to see you here so early. How are things going?" He continued without waiting for a response. "Although I have been here only a few weeks, I have seen that you have a good sense of which new scientific developments to write about. You seem to be on top of STEM issues as they arise."

"Yeah" Elvin said, sitting down. "I finally feel as though I have a solid grounding in the issues and can see quickly which new developments are most important."

"I was hoping that was the case, because I think it's time to make some changes in the focus of your articles. We need to approach scientific issues in a more aggressive way to create more interest in them. You're doing a good job covering the scientific aspects of new developments, but you treat new reports as if they are isolated events. They aren't, though. Each report comes on the trail of many previous studies on the same subject.

"I would like your next articles to highlight how new reports conflict with those issued previously. That will add a bit of controversy to the articles—and controversy will increase readership. For instance, in the next articles I want you to highlight the new guidelines just issued by the Dietary Guidelines Advisory Committee. One issue is trans fats. After decades of recommending them, the Committee is now banning them. This is a major change. Another issue is salt. A new report clears salt of being harmful, again contradicting decades of previous guidance from the same Committee. Contrasting new reports with previous studies won't be a problem, will it?"

"Absolutely not. I'll get on this right away."

"Good. I have seen your latest article, the one about the report highlighting the dangers of lithium batteries. Take another crack at it from this new more skeptical stance. The report you cited described the possibility that planes could crash because of fires onboard caused by exploding batteries. You accurately covered the contents of the report but didn't make much effort to ask whether the report itself was accurate. For instance, you could have sought out FAA statistics on how many crashes have been caused by lithium batteries.

"You could even make the article more personal by noting that practically every passenger on flights you've been on was carrying a laptop or notebook of some kind, all powered by lithium batteries, but you've never seen a fire started by any of them. You could note that practically every customer at Starbucks is staring into a laptop or notebook or cell phone, yet you've never seen any burst into flames.

"In fact, I would like to see a more personal approach to all your articles. I have described this in a prosaic way, but you can use the flair you have in writing to highlight the contradictions between the reports and everyday common sense by citing personal experiences. You get the point?"

"Indeed I do," Elvin said, nodding. He sighed as he walked back to his cubicle. He knew that Ed's ideas would result in more interesting articles. He also knew that they would require a lot more effort than merely reporting on new developments. Well, he sighed again, I have heard this before—that I have a certain facility in writing but that I have often taken the easy way out, that I need to put more effort into my work.

At the same time, Elvin was struck by the beginnings of a sense of challenge, even excitement. Ed really does have a good idea; this is an approach I can sink my teeth into, he thought as he sat down at his desk.

6

Alan sat back in his chair and looked around his home office. Since the kids had moved out, the entire basement had become his office. Books lined all four outer walls. On two of them, bookcases went up almost to the ceiling, seven shelves high. On the other two, shelves stopped halfway up, leaving wall space on which he'd hung prints of paintings he especially liked. His collection of Shakespeare books, 800 strong, was located against the wall directly across the room from his desk, where he could easily see and access it.

His thoughts turned to the opening day of the summer term. It was off to a good start, with all six students having some background in Shakespeare, and all having good reasons for wanting to take the course. He shuddered when he recalled the student last term who'd said he'd enrolled because he liked famous things. Shakespeare, Gucci, Prada, lululemon, Nike; he liked them all because they were famous—and many of the other students in the class had nodded in agreement.

Part of the joy of teaching, Alan felt, was showing students that there is so much more to Shakespeare than merely a name they'd heard before, that the name was justly famous for serious reasons. But that had been a particularly difficult class in which to make the case. He was relieved that his students this term appeared to be genuinely interested in Shakespeare. It was just such students as these that he—and every teacher—dreamed of having in class.

The best part of the summer term this year was that he was teaching only one course, which gave him time to move forward on writing *Shakespeare's Journey*. He was about to do just that when he recalled the Fulbright student's comments on *Anonymous*, the movie portraying Shakespeare as a front for the real author, the Earl of Oxford. That thought led him to recall the book he'd purchased at the airport, *The Mysterious William Shakespeare* by Charlton Ogburn, Jr. and his idea of reviewing it in order to crush the authorship issue for all time.

As always, Alan had an almost visceral response to the entire question of whether William Shakespeare wrote the works attributed to him. Whenever the subject arose he felt angry and impatient that anyone would waste time on such nonsense. He wondered why his reactions were so strong, because he was usually rather even-tempered.

The first such occasion had occurred during a Knowledge Bowl he participated in decades ago, at the end of his junior year of high school. One of the questions asked was "Which member of Queen Elizabeth's court has been proposed as the real author of Shakespeare's works?" He'd been the only one able to answer the question because he'd read an article on the subject of Sir Francis Bacon's authorship in *Time Magazine* a week earlier. But even then he had little patience with what had become known as the Shakespeare Authorship Question (SAQ).

Alan decided to delay work on his own book long enough to glance through Ogburn's and write his review of it. There it was, resting on the top of the stack of books he'd bought recently but hadn't yet had time to read. It was, he thought, just about the biggest book he owned that wasn't a reference book. Leaning over to pick it up, he had to use both hands to lift it up to the desk.

Looking at the dust jacket, he noticed what he'd expected to see: "facts" about William Shakespeare from Stratford-upon-Avon presented in a way to make his authorship seen unlikely—that he was barely literate, that he was a glover's son, that he lacked knowledge of Italy, the law, courtly pursuits, and other subjects portrayed in the plays. There was also the usual list of famous people who doubted his authorship, including Otto von Bismarck, and Sigmund Freud, who had written that "The man of Stratford seems to have nothing at all to justify his claim, whereas Oxford has almost everything." But they weren't writers, he noted, so how could their opinions possibly matter?

Actors, too, had expressed doubts. Charlie Chaplin, for one, and Orson Welles, who'd written that "I think Oxford wrote Shakespeare. If you don't, there are some awfully funny coincidences to explain away." But what do actors know? They're not scholars.

Alan also noticed the list of highly accomplished writers who didn't accept Shakespeare's authorship, including Walt Whitman, Mark Twain, John Greenleaf Whittier and Henry James, who'd said that "I am . . . haunted by the conviction that the divine William is the biggest and most successful fraud ever practiced on a patient world." More recent writers had also expressed doubts, including Anne Rice, who'd remarked that "I am falling in love with this idea that the real

Shakespeare was Edward de Vere, the Earl of Oxford. . . . It is astonishing what the Edward de Vere camp has turned up in the way of research to explain all kinds of mysteries of the plays and the life of the so-called Shakespeare. Very, very interesting stuff."

Well, Alan thought, they might be *writers*, but they aren't Shakespearean scholars, people who have dedicated decades of their lives to the study of Shakespeare and his works. Their opinions aren't the judgments of well-informed experts.

He then noticed statements from three Justices of the U.S. Supreme Court who doubted Shakespeare's authorship. Justice Lewis F. Powell, Jr. had "never thought that the man of Stratford-on-Avon wrote the plays of Shakespeare" because no evidence exists that he had ever visited Italy, where a dozen of the plays are set. Justice John Paul Stevens had expressed "lingering doubts and gnawing uncertainties" about Shakespeare's authorship, and Justice Harry A. Blackmun even went so far as to say that "If I had to rule on the evidence presented, it would be in favor of the Oxfordians."

Well, that's interesting, Alan thought. It's hard to dismiss the opinions of serious people who recognize the need for evidence and who are well versed in making judgments by applying legal principles to situations with insufficient or contradictory evidence. On the other hand, throughout the history of the Supreme Court decisions had been overturned because justices in the past had misinterpreted the law or misapplied the law to the evidence at hand. And in any event, Justices aren't literary scholars intimately familiar with the details of Shakespeare's life and works.

Alan could see already that before he could write the review of Ogburn's book he would have to study it carefully. The next step would be to find out why so many prominent and accomplished people had doubts about Shakespeare's authorship. But that would have to wait; now he needed to organize his thoughts for Thursday's class.

7

"Hi, Dad," Delilah said, coming in the front door early in the evening.

"Hi, Delilah. Welcome back home," Alan said, giving her a quick hug. She was as petite and as energetic as ever.

She had just finished her junior year at King University, the nearby rival to Cary University where Alan taught. She'd moved into an apartment a year earlier, after living at home during her first two years of study. She'd been eager for more independence then, but now that she'd been on her own for a year she stopped in often to see her parents.

"How's the internship going? Are you enjoying it?"

"It's great, Dad. I really enjoy the chance to do things in the real world. Class assignments, even case studies, always have such an air of unreality about them. And it's great to be around adults, around people serious about what they are doing, rather than students thinking only about the next drunken party. How are you doing with Mom away?"

"I'm fine. She's only been gone a few days. As you can see, I have put my limited cooking skills to use. We're having meat loaf. When I cook, I like to make things that will last for several days."

"Smells good. I also brought some Chinese spring rolls because I didn't know what you were fixing."

Alan smiled, thinking about how much Delilah had liked meat loaf when she was a girl. But now she was so much like her mother, wanting Chinese food much of the time even though she had been only eight years old when they'd left Taiwan.

"What exactly are you doing in the internship?" he asked, while taking the meat loaf out of the oven.

"Well, I'm only in the second week. I will rotate through the three sections of the marketing department over the course of the summer. Now I'm working in the section that seeks to understand what products customers want and what they think about ours. The competition is fierce, with so many other companies producing similar products. We have to try to stay ahead of them by understanding how the needs of the market are changing, then pass that information on to the engineering department to design products that incorporate the features that people want."

"That sounds interesting," he said as they sat down to eat. "How are the people in your section to work with? Are they happy to have an intern in their midst?"

"They are. There are many smaller tasks that have to be done that they don't want to spend time doing. So I'm helping out with those, and by doing them I'm learning what each person in the section does. It's kind of exciting, understanding each step in the process of how customer input is sought, analyzed, and then written up in reports for other sections of the company. Later I'll work in the section that designs advertising campaigns to let potential customers know how our products can help them meet their needs."

"You are already speaking like a true marketing officer, Delilah. Focusing not only on the features of the product, but also on the wants and needs of the market. Focusing not on selling, but on meeting needs.

I think you have natural abilities in that area."

They were quiet for a while, each pondering their own thoughts. While Delilah looked around the room to see if anything had changed since her last visit, Alan wondered whether she was getting a real education or merely training in a specific field. He knew that at her university, as at his, students could graduate without ever having taken a course in Shakespeare, without ever having heard the music of Beethoven or Mozart, without ever having seen a painting by Renoir or Rembrandt, without ever having heard the names of Aristotle or Plato— without having become familiar with the major artistic and intellectual achievements of their own culture. They were, he thought, getting trained but not educated.

Delilah had heard him comment on that point too many times for him to do so now. At least, he thought, she is better off than most because our house is filled with books of literature, history, philosophy and science that she sometimes looked through when she still lived at home. And he'd played a lot of classical music for the family to listen to while she and Carson were growing up. He suddenly realized that he hadn't listened to much music lately. It had probably been a year since he'd heard Beethoven's *Eroica*.

"Oh, I talked to Mom last night," Delilah said, interrupting his reveries. "She said that Grandpa isn't well, and she doesn't know how long she might have to stay in Taipei. She doesn't want to leave until he has recovered."

"Uh, we didn't tell you before she left, but the reason for her trip is that your grandpa isn't just unwell. He has a major heart problem. The doctors are now trying to determine whether open-heart surgery will be necessary. You know how loyal your mother feels toward her family, especially her father. He needs her now to take care of him because everybody else is so busy. She wants to stay as long as she is needed. So this wasn't just another of her usual trips back home.

"We had several long talks about whether I should cancel my summer teaching and accompany her. In the end, we decided that I would stay here because I spent most of last summer in Taiwan, and because this summer I want to complete as much of my Shakespeare book as possible before the fall term begins. I need to be near my library for much of my research."

"Gosh, I hadn't known that Grandpa was so unwell. I'll have to call Mom again to get a fuller update."

"Yeah, I think I'll call her, too. It will soon be morning there."

"I haven't heard much from Carson recently. Have you heard from your brother?"

"Not much. Just an occasional text message."

"Well, I'm sure he is doing well." Alan was silent as he thought about the wonderful experience his son was having in Europe. He was proud that Carson had been the only undergraduate intern selected to accompany a group of architectural faculty traveling to several countries to study medieval and early modern cathedrals. Their focus was on the types of knowledge that the builders must have possessed to have built such impressive structures that still stand after 600 years.

At the same time, he worried about Carson a bit. This was his first extended trip away from home since they'd moved here from Taiwan. He recalled how difficult it had been for all four of them to adjust to life in the United States. Still, he reasoned, Carson is there only for two months, and he's part of a group, not off by himself. The professors are surely looking after him.

"I'm just glad that both of you have interesting internships this summer, activities from which you will learn a lot. And get paid, too. How's Robert these days?"

"I'm not seeing him any more," Delilah said firmly. "Earlier, when I mentioned students with short-term vision—those not serious about what they're doing but only looking forward to the next party—well, that was Robert. I'm relieved we have gone our separate ways."

"Oh, I'm sorry to hear that, but happy you were able to get out of a relationship that wasn't right for you." Alan would have liked to have offered more guidance to her, the way that Polonius had advised Ophelia in *Hamlet*, but he couldn't find the right words.

They talked a bit more as they washed and dried the dishes. Then Delilah left, returning to the life she was building for herself. Alan watched her go, wishing that he could have back, even for just one minute, the little girl who had run through the halls of the house not so many years ago.

THURSDAY, JUNE 4

8

"Good morning, everyone," Alan began.

It was the second meeting of Shakespeare in His Own Words, and the six students were all seated, looking at him expectantly.

"The theme of today's discussion is that of the importance of critical moments of decision in Shakespeare's plays. Many of them are built around decisions that characters must make. Their choices often determine much of the action in the rest of the play.

"In selecting this theme, I have drawn on the work of John Alvis, who made this interesting observation: 'The subject which for Shakespeare subsumes all others and which appears to be the distinctively human province is the activity of making choices. His characters deliberate toward choice, implement their decisions, and reflect upon the consequences of having chosen one possibility in preference to another. Every play builds towards, then moves from, an important act of choice which stands as a fulcrum transferring momentum of complication to momentum of resolution.'

"Do any of the plays on our reading list have such moments?"

"Well, *Hamlet* certainly does," Pat offered. "Hamlet must decide how to respond to the death of his father, which he discovers was actually the murder of his father by his uncle."

"And *King Lear* begins with such a moment," Amelia noted. "He has decided to abdicate at the beginning of the play, though we don't know why. We do know, though, that he mistakenly thinks he can retain all the prerogatives of a king even after giving up power."

"Yeah, boy, was he ever mistaken!" Doug said.

"From these moments," Alan suggested, "we might infer that Shakespeare himself had to make difficult decisions in his own life. That would explain how he was able to portray so well his characters' uncertainty before, during and after making their decisions.

"To give some shape to our discussion, I'd like to begin by focusing on decisions made in *Julius Caesar*. Consider Brutus. He had to make many important decisions over the course of the play. What is especially interesting is that every decision he makes is wrong. That can't be merely accidental; it had to be a deliberate effort by Shakespeare to show the importance of decisions and the consequences that flow from making bad ones.

"What is so odd, though, is that Brutus is so highly admired by all the other characters in the play. He is widely regarded as 'noble' and 'honorable.' So, here we have a universally admired character who can't seem to make a good decision. We can't help but wonder why this is the case. What is the source of Brutus's bad decisions? Is he a flawed character? If so, then why is he so respected by the others? Nancy, I see that you have some thoughts on these questions."

"Yes, I do," she said. "These Romans were smart. The ones depicted in the play were at the top of the political structure of their society. One doesn't get that far without the ability to read other men well. So I think that Brutus must have done things that others admired him for. He must have made good decisions in the past, though we don't know what they were. The question is why his decisions *now* aren't good. What has changed? If we can answer that, we will have a clue to the explanation."

Lisa then jumped in. "Yes, it's true that Brutus has changed. His wife, Portia, wonders why he no longer confides in her. She is worried about the change in him, and says that whatever is bothering him 'will not let you eat, nor talk, nor sleep, / And could it work so much upon your shape / As it hath prevailed on your condition, / I should not know you Brutus.'"

"Well," Dave said, "it sometimes happens that people under tremendous pressure crack. They can't handle the strain. Maybe that's what has happened here."

"But other members of the coalition setting out to murder Caesar don't crack under the pressure," Doug observed. "Cassius, in contrast to Brutus, appears to make all the right decisions, but he is overruled by Brutus. And the others go along with Brutus because of his reputation as an honorable man."

"Perhaps the reason that Brutus cracks although the others don't," Amelia suggested, "is that he is under more strain than they are. Brutus was widely believed to be a natural son of Caesar, an illegitimate son. If that was the case, then Brutus would have been under tremendous stress as he contemplates killing his own father."

Everyone looked at her, struck by the relevance of that point.

"Is that true?" Lisa asked. "I haven't had time yet to read all the supplementary materials."

"It is, yes." Pat and Dave said at the same time. Pat explained that "Brutus was regarded by many people as Caesar's unacknowledged son," and Dave added that "It was widely known that Caesar often favored Brutus with special appointments."

"Ah," Nancy said. "That explains why Caesar said those famous words, 'Et tu, Brutè? Then fall Caesar.' It wasn't merely because Brutus was his most trusted younger advisor, but because he was his son."

"Let's look at some of the specific examples of Brutus's decisions to try to understand better why he made them," Alan suggested. "We might find a common thread running through them."

Doug was first to offer an example. "Brutus suspects that Caesar is becoming too powerful, that he desires to become a king. He thinks that if Caesar is removed from power, the Republic will endure. He expects that the assassination of Caesar will serve as a warning to other potential dictators. But he's mistaken."

Pat had another example. "Brutus refuses to let Cicero in on the plot. As a respected elder statesman, Cicero might have provided more mature judgment, and the people's respect for him might have helped sway them to support the assassination. All the other plotters were unanimous on this point, but Brutus wouldn't allow it."

Amelia offered the example of allowing Antony to remain free. "Brutus's refusal to kill Antony was a mistake. All leading members of Caesar's ruling coalition should have been wiped out so that they could not regroup and rebuild on the existing power base. Mark Antony, as Caesar's right arm, should especially not have been left alive. Cassius made this point to Brutus, but he didn't listen."

Nancy then hit upon what Alan thought was a key point. "The problem was that Rome had changed. Although it was still a Republic in name, it wasn't in spirit. It had already become an empire or was well on the way to becoming one. And empires need a king, a form of rule from Rome suitable for managing far flung provinces."

"That change in public sentiment is clearly shown by the plebeians calling not only for Brutus, the murderer of Caesar, to live rather than be put to death for the crime, but also to replace Caesar."

"And," Lisa interjected, "not merely to live and to replace Caesar as head of the Republic, but to become king. One plebeian calls out 'Let him be Caesar.' Not 'Let him be leader of the Republic, but 'Let him be Caesar.' 'Caesar' has become a title, not just the name of the assassinated leader. And to make it even more explicit that he would be king, another calls out, 'Caesar's better parts shall be crowned in Brutus.' They wanted a king, and simply didn't understand the dangers of having their desire fulfilled."

"Brutus misread the mind of Antony as well as those of the plebeians," Dave said, moving on to Brutus's next poor decision. "Brutus not only allowed Antony to live, but also to address the plebeians in spite of Cassius's effort to stop him. Cassius had said something like 'Do not consent that Antony speak at the funeral. Know you not how much the people may be moved by that which he will utter?' But Brutus wouldn't listen."

"Antony was clearly a master politician," Pat added. "He knew that he needed the support of the plebeians, and as a master of rhetoric, he knew how to get it. He also used part of Caesar's wealth to buy the people's support."

Amelia then summed up the situation. "At the time of the assassination, Rome was a Republic. Tyranny, which had been only a possibility before the assassination, was, afterwards, a reality. The masses cannot be trusted with power. The first time they get it, they call for a king. Even if Caesar had lived but not been crowned, someone else would have been."

Building on Amelia's comment, Doug added, "Brutus and the other conspirators failed to consider that the cure, the assassination, might be worse than the poison. They hadn't realized that the very act of killing Caesar might release demons in the minds of their fellow Romans, triggering the very dictatorship they feared Caesar would create."

"And that is just what Antony did," Dave observed. "He and others, backed by the power of the mob, drew up lists of those to be assassinated, including Brutus and Cassius. One assassination leads to another and another. Even the poet Cinna is murdered by the unthinking mob, which doesn't care that he isn't the Cinna they were looking for. Mobs become bloodthirsty and any blood will do."

"But still, Brutus might have been okay—" Nancy started to say, but Pat interrupted. "Yes, he might have been, except that he continued to make bad decisions. He insisted on conducting the climactic battle immediately on the plains rather than waiting for a time and place in which his troops would have the best advantage. And even though Cassius once again tried to convince him of the advantages of waiting for the right conditions."

"Well, this has been quite an interesting opening discussion," Alan said. "Let's take our short break now. We'll pick up at this point when we return."

9

"So, how are we to explain Brutus's string of bad decisions?" Alan asked, once everyone was back at the table. "He had good advice from the other plotters, especially Cassius, but he resisted it. Is the strain of having killed his father the only source of the problem?"

Dave had an idea. "In every instance we have noted, Cassius made good decisions and Brutus flawed decisions. Perhaps Brutus felt able to dismiss the advice given to him because he was used to being treated as a golden boy by Caesar. He was used to receiving deference from those who regarded him as Caesar's son. Cassius, meanwhile, had incurred Caesar's suspicion because of his 'lean and hungry look.' Maybe Brutus had absorbed some of that attitude toward him."

Pat proposed that "Brutus might have thought that because he was an honorable man—he thought he was and so did everybody else—that his decisions would be the right ones. He thought that his good intentions—that he aimed at the general good and not at personal advantage—meant that what he proposed would be effective. But he was mistaken, again and again."

"Or," Lisa suggested, "maybe the problem is that Brutus was too noble. He was too ready to attribute noble goals to others, including the plebeians and Antony. That is why he doesn't acknowledge that the mob had called for him to become Caesar, or that Antony had different ideas about how Rome should be governed. He thought that the assassination had changed everything, including the thinking of the plebeians and Antony. In reality, it had only changed everything for himself. He was the one who was now fatherless, and by an act of his own hand."

"Yes," Amelia said, picking up on that theme. "The common thread running through all these instances is that Brutus was a dreamer. His feet were not on the ground. In every instance, that is the cause of the bad decisions he makes. Perhaps before his death, Caesar had kept that tendency in Brutus in check. But now, with Caesar gone and with the added strain of having murdered his own father, Brutus overemphasizes the nobleness of his own actions as a way of explaining away the horribleness of his crime, and also attributes the same noble motives to everyone else, even those not involved in the plot. He fooled himself about what to expect from other people."

"Now we come to the most important question of all," Alan said. "Did Brutus and the other conspirators make the right decision when they assassinated Caesar?"

"That is the hardest question to answer," Lisa responded. "It's also the only decision that Brutus and Cassius agree on—and also Casca, Decius, Cinna and the others."

"But it's not a simple question," Pat added. "On one hand, Brutus says that 'I do fear the people choose Caesar for their king,' and for that reason—'for the general good,' he says—Caesar must be assassinated. But on the other hand, he has so far found no reason to fault Caesar. His fears are only about how Caesar *might* be changed by having a crown on his head."

'Yes, that is the point," Lisa agreed. "His exact words were 'So Caesar may. / Then lest he may, prevent.'"

"It's a legitimate fear," Dave commented. "Someone once observed that 'Power corrupts and absolute power corrupts absolutely.' I have seen it happen many times that when someone gets a bit of authority they are likely to abuse it for the sheer pleasure of doing so rather than using it responsibly on behalf of the organization they work for. So Brutus and the others were right to worry about how Caesar's being crowned would affect him."

"And," Nancy added, "Caesar wasn't entirely free of ambition. He brought 30,000 troops across the Rubicon River and into Roman territory. That was the first time any Roman general had ever violated the law by doing so. Although that potentially intimidating action isn't mentioned in the play, it must have been on the minds of the conspirators and everybody else in the city."

"So Caesar was ambitious," Doug observed, "and the combination of his ambitiousness and the plebeians' call for a king meant the death of the Republic. The fall of the Republic was a tragedy that neither Brutus nor any of the other conspirators could do anything about."

Alan then made final remarks to wrap up the discussion. "The question of whether the conspirators were right to assassinate Caesar has been examined and argued over for 2,000 years. It's interesting to note that if Brutus had been right to assassinate Caesar, that would have been the only right decision he made in the entire play. But if it was a bad decision, it was the only bad decision that Cassius made.

"I hope you have seen how valuable it can be to approach the plays from the standpoint of the decisions the characters make. And I hope you can see that Shakespeare wrote about serious people making decisions about important events in their lives. He didn't write about trivialities, ever. His characters don't consider which flavor of ice cream to order, or whether to go to the beach or the mountains for vacation this summer. They consider whether or not to kill Caesar, or whether or not to abdicate their responsibilities by staying in Egypt with Cleopatra.

"We form our lives through our decisions, Shakespeare seems to say. His characters ponder the choices they must make, and suffer the consequences if they choose poorly. It's the seriousness of the situations the characters face and the necessity of their having to make decisions even when they have no good options to choose from that makes Shakespeare's plays so endlessly fascinating and so true to life."

As the students walked out of the classroom, Alan overheard Doug asking the others if they had seen the movie version. "I think it was called *Julius Caesar, Superstar!*" he said. "They changed the plot, though. Caesar doesn't get killed. Some other guy does."

Nancy, Lisa, Dave and Pat laughed. Amelia looked at Doug and was about to say something, but Dave stopped her. "Don't bother, Amelia," he said with a smile. "Doug's been this way since he was born. It's sad, really, but there's nothing anybody can do about it." And everybody, including Doug, laughed.

10

Just as he picked up his coffee, Alan saw Amelia at the far side of the coffee shop. He walked over to her table.

"Hi, Amelia. I'm glad I ran into you here. During class I forgot to give you the copy of Gary Althen's *American Ways* that I promised you. Here it is."

"Oh, thank you, Professor Fernwood. If you have a few minutes, might you be able to answer a few questions I have about your country?" She purposely steered the discussion away from Shakespeare. After having been through such an intense discussion of his works earlier in the day, she needed a break from that subject.

Alan looked at his watch. "Sure," he said, as he sat down across from her. "I have a few minutes free." He, too, was glad to talk about something other than Shakespeare.

"Well, first, are all Americans as crazy about baseball as the students here seem to be? They seem to be as crazy about baseball as Vietnamese are about football during the World Cup. But I do not understand baseball at all. It seems to be like cricket, with a ball and a bat, but I do not understand that game, either."

"There are a lot of rules in baseball," Alan agreed, "but most Americans grow up playing the game, so it doesn't seem so complicated to us. Baseball is known as the 'great national pastime' because it has been so popular for so many decades. But cricket is very different. I don't understand it at all. In fact, I think one must be born in the British Commonwealth to understand it."

"You know, Professor Fernwood, everyone is talking about the game the Durham Bulls will play on Saturday. I will be at the game! The organizer of my Fulbright program got tickets for all of us."

"That's great, Amelia. You'll enjoy seeing the game live. It's a very different experience from watching it on TV. A live performance gives you a more visceral feeling for what is happening."

"'Visceral?'"

"Oh, sorry. A 'visceral' response is one that you feel with your body rather than something you understand intellectually. If you saw another woman kissing your husband, you would have a bodily reaction to the scene, a visceral response, not a response characterized by reason or logic or even emotion. You might feel like someone had just shoved you."

"Oh, I see."

"I have that word on the brain these days because I'm using it in an article I'm writing about the value of literature. I'm describing why literature is important—how it helps us—in response to those who claim that it's a waste of time and that courses on literature should make way for more courses on science and technology."

Amelia cocked her head, a sure sign that she was interested in the subject being discussed.

"Let me tell you about two of the reasons I'm discussing in my paper. The first is that literature can give us a better understanding of the most important part of our environment—other people—by showing us how people might behave in a wider variety of situations than we have a chance to experience in our own lives.

"And second, literature can help us understand ourselves and other people better than nonfiction or scientific works because it presents situations and characters in such a way that we have a visceral response to them, that we feel as well as understand the subtleties and nuances of what is unfolding on the stage or on the page.

"Here is a statement I'm going to quote in my paper," he said, pulling some pages out of his bag. "Professor R. V. Young, in *A Student's Guide to Literature*, provides an example of how this happens. Discussing *King Lear*, he writes that 'The reader or theatrical spectator who has felt the full impact of *King Lear* has a knowledge more profound and moving than the simple proposition that deceit, betrayal, and murder are never justified; he will gain an emotional and imaginative revulsion at evil dressed up in bland excuse and political pretext. He will have an inner resistance to collaboration with the Edmunds he meets in the world, or to complicity with the Edmund who lurks within each of us.'

"Sorry for talking at such length. Once I get started on the subject of literature it's hard for me to stop."

"I am the same way," Amelia told him. "It is like when I am reading a novel I really enjoy. I don't know what is going on around me. The house could fall down and I wouldn't know it. Unless someone calls my name. I always hear when my name is spoken."

"I know that you are reading a lot of nonfiction about the United States in your orientation class, Amelia, but to get a better understanding of American life today, a more visceral understanding, you might need to read fiction. I'll find a suitable book for you and bring it next week. But now I must get going," he said as he stood up.

"Thank you, Dr. Fernwood. It is so kind of you to help me. I will tell you next week what the baseball game was like."

As he walked to the library, Alan wondered if all Vietnamese were as interested in literature as Amelia appeared to be. And he wondered if all Vietnamese women were as beautiful as she was.

FRIDAY, JUNE 5

11

Ah, it's Friday morning, and I can finally get back to Ogburn's book, *The Mysterious William Shakespeare*, Alan thought to himself. A few days earlier he had noted the names of many prominent and accomplished people who'd expressed doubts that William Shakespeare wrote the works attributed to him. Now it was time to find out why.

After reading just the first few pages, Alan had learned two important facts. First, no one with the name William Shakespeare lived in Stratford or worked in the theater in London at the time Shakespeare wrote his works. The man credited with the authorship was christened Gulielmus Shakspere. Although he and other family members spelled their last name a variety of ways, none ever spelled it Shakespeare. "Shak" and "Shake" were similar, but they had different roots and different meanings. The same was true for "spere" and "speare."

That would mean, Alan concluded, that "William Shakespeare" was a pseudonym regardless of who wrote the works. He would determine from this point on which person was referred to—the man from Stratford or the author—whenever the name Shakespeare was mentioned.

Second, Shakspere of Stratford never claimed to have written any literary works. That's both interesting and disconcerting, Alan thought. If Shakspere was the author, why didn't he ever say so? And if he never claimed authorship, why did people believe he was the author?

Alan read further. No one during Shakspere's lifetime ever claimed that he was the author? How can that be? He'd thought that Shakspere had been widely recognized as the author during his lifetime. This is very odd, he thought.

The more Alan read the more he wanted to read. The question of whether William Shakspere wrote Shakespeare's works was far more fascinating than he'd ever realized, and the information Ogburn provided about Edward de Vere, Earl of Oxford, the man Ogburn believed wrote the works, was so voluminous and absorbing that Alan couldn't put the book down. He continued reading late into the night, and all through Saturday, before finally finishing the book's more than 800 large pages midmorning on Sunday.

SUNDAY, JUNE 7

12

That's funny, Diana thought. I am in the East, yet I'm twelve hours ahead of Eastern Standard Time. I wonder why I never noticed the similarity in wording before.

She was at her parents' compound outside Taipei, sitting beside the pond in the courtyard that separated the main house from the guest house at the back. She was watching the goldfish swim back and forth, and feeling at ease, as though she, like the fish, was in her natural element. It was a feeling she had each time she returned to visit her parents. But that thought was always accompanied by a feeling that she wasn't Taiwanese any more. She was American.

It was almost like having two souls. On thinking further, she decided that she had only one soul that expressed itself differently in two different cultural environments and languages. In Taiwan, she was her parents' daughter with all the obligations and duties that entailed. Each time she visited, she needed to adapt herself to Asian ways of thinking and acting, which felt both natural and constraining. In America, she also had obligations and duties to her family and to her employer, but somehow they didn't seem as confining as being a daughter in a traditional Taiwanese family.

Diana had heard from both Alan and Delilah about how much each had enjoyed their dinner together a few days ago. She hadn't heard much from Carson in Europe, but with him no news was good news. He would surely contact her and Alan if he had a problem.

Diana's mother had recovered, and her father, while not well, wasn't getting any worse. It now looked likely that surgery wouldn't be necessary. So she was able to relax by the pond for a while, with her mind temporarily at ease.

13

"My God!" Alan said out loud as he finally put down Ogburn's book. It had taken him close to thirty hours to finish it. I will never be able to think about the Shakespeare authorship question the same way again, he thought. In fact, I'll never be able to think about Shakespeare's works the same way again.

He shook his head, knowing that he wouldn't be able to write a critical review that buried the authorship question forever. On the contrary, he was even tempted to write a review praising the book and supporting the idea that Shakspere didn't write Shakespeare's works, or at least calling for further investigation into the authorship question.

His head was still clouded from the vast amount of information Ogburn had provided, and he decided to swim some laps to clear his mind. The physical movement and the need to focus on maintaining his form even when growing tired would give his brain a break from the sustained concentration reading the book had required.

Alan hadn't swum many laps before his mind turned to the question of how Shakspere had come to be regarded as the author. The first indication that the man from Stratford and the playwright were one and the same was in the First Folio, the first collection of Shakespeare's works published in 1623, some seven years after Shakspere's death. But there were odd things about it. Perhaps the oddest was its complete lack of biographical material about the author. Not even his coat of arms was printed in it. Another was that the strongest link to the man from Stratford were the references to "thy Stratford monument" and "sweet swan of Avon" in the lengthy prefatory material in the Folio. The Avon, Alan knew, was the river that ran through Stratford-upon-Avon, Shakspere's home town. But why were those two references printed several pages apart in statements by two different people? Why was there no unequivocal statement that the man from Stratford was the author in a large and expensive book that was supposedly compiled to honor him and his works? There were other oddities about the Folio that were too numerous to consider while swimming.

The second indication of Shakspere's authorship was the famous Shakespeare monument in Holy Trinity Church in Stratford. Surely the mention of that monument in the Folio connected the works to the town of Stratford, and thus to Shakspere? There were odd things here, too, Alan remembered. The Folio had actually mentioned a "moniment," not a "monument." In Shakespeare's day a "moniment" meant a body of work, not a structure made of stone to honor the memory of a person or event. The Folio, then, had really instructed the reader to view Shakespeare's literary remains in its pages, not Shakspere's bodily remains in a stone structure in Stratford.

And, he recalled, the monument in Stratford itself was odd. It gave no indication of where exactly Shakspere was buried, nor any indication that whoever was buried there had ever written a word. There was no reference at the monument to any literary works, let alone a statement that Shakspere had written them.

The next event establishing Shakspere as the author in the public mind didn't occur until a century and a half later, when, in 1769, actor David Garrick organized a Jubilee in Stratford to commemorate

Shakespeare. Alan tried to keep all these details straight in his head while swimming, but there was too much to think about. He needed his laptop, which was in a locker inside the club. He swam a few more laps, then stopped so that he could write down his thoughts while they were still fresh in his mind.

Once inside, Alan turned to the question of when and why doubts about Shakspere's authorship arose in the nineteenth century. Not too many years after the Jubilee in 1769, those who sought to gather together his documents found something surprising: There weren't any. Not only had Shakspere himself apparently never sent or received a letter, but no surviving documents from his lifetime contained any reference to the author as a distinct person living at the time the works were written. There were many references to the name "Shakespeare," but no one appeared to have ever stated in writing that he had known or even met the writer.

Even in Stratford, Alan had learned, in the century and a half between the First Folio and the Jubilee, not one person had ever referred to Shakspere as a famous poet or dramatist. Contemporary descriptions of Stratford and its noted inhabitants by such well-known historians as William Camden made no mention of a famous author of plays and poems as having come from that town.

This odd lack of evidence reflecting Shakspere's authorship had led to two startling incidents. At the end of the 18th century, William Henry Ireland forged numerous documents purporting to have been written by Shakespeare. His deception was eventually discovered, but that discovery didn't prevent a second series of forgeries by John Payne Collier in the first half of the nineteenth century.

The effect of these two hoaxes on Shakespeare studies was to create a more skeptical attitude toward Shakspere's authorship, and it was in that intellectual climate that serious doubts about his authorship arose in the second half of the nineteenth century.

New scholarly approaches, Alan had learned, uncovered more details of Shakspere's life. Those details, however, had nothing to do with literary matters. They established that he had been a grain merchant and a money-lender, and that he had sued several fellow townsmen for small amounts. They also revealed that his father, mother and daughters were illiterate. This is too much, Alan thought. It's beyond belief that anyone growing up in an illiterate family—and someone who didn't even bother to ensure that his own children learned to read and write—could possibly have written Shakespeare's works.

The most significant damage to the claim that Shakspere was

Shakespeare was the total absence of any indication how he could have acquired the depth of knowledge in so many areas depicted in the plays, areas such as Italy, the law, horticulture, classical literature, and diplomacy at the highest levels. It was this gap between the biography of the man from Stratford and the learned nature of the plays that had led such literary luminaries as Walt Whitman, Mark Twain and Henry James to express doubts about his authorship.

Alan realized he was hungry. It was time to go home, eat, and relax.

14

After eating dinner and watching part of a baseball game on TV, Alan considered the reasons why Ogburn believed that the Earl of Oxford was Shakespeare. My summary will have to be quick and simple, he said to himself; my brain is pretty much played out for now by the effort it took to read Ogburn's book.

First, he noted, Edward de Vere had been the right age and in the right place to have had the experiences needed to acquire the bodies of knowledge that Shakespeare had. As a courtier, he had been tutored by the most respected scholars of his time. And, although he had been highly praised as both a poet and playwright during his lifetime, no plays and few of his poems have survived under his own name.

Alan felt his eyes closing but quickly noted an interesting event. Ogburn had highlighted the case of a poem of seventy lines put together by professor Louis P. Bénézet of Dartmouth University, taken from verse by the young Edward de Vere and the mature Shakespeare. The poem contained six passages from one author and seven from the other. Bénézet had submitted his finished work to an expert in literature, who expressed the opinion that the poem was "unquestionably" written by one man. Other experts were unable to identify which lines had come from Shakespeare and which hadn't, and several Shakespeare scholars, hearing of the poem, refused even to look at it.

What a difference a weekend makes, Alan reflected as he got into bed. He had begun it fully intending to write the review that would demolish the authorship question for all time. But now he knew that would be impossible. His belief in Shakspere's authorship was shredded, and it wasn't a pleasant feeling. Not all is lost, he told himself; his investigation wasn't finished. He would turn next to how Ogburn's book had been received by others on both sides of the authorship issue. Drifting off to sleep, he wondered when or even if he would ever be able to return to *Shakespeare's Journey*.

MONDAY, JUNE 8

15

"Good job on those nutrition articles, Elvin," Ed told him. "You expressed just the right degree of skepticism by comparing the latest reports with past studies that conflict with them. Readers have posted comments on *The Herald's* blog asking how they could know which reports on other issues are correct, given that they contradict each other. At some point it would be good to write an article or two on how non-experts can make sense of contradictory claims on their own, on issues you haven't written on. I have some ideas on the matter, but let's talk about that later. Now, I have a more important issue to discuss."

Elvin nodded, wondering what it could be.

"I would like you to focus several columns on the issue of global warming. You haven't written on that subject for a while, probably because it has become so politicized. You are our science specialist, after all. Best to leave politics to the political desk. So, when you write on that subject stay away from the political aspects; focus solely on the science of the issue. Compare various reports that contradict each other to create controversy and interest."

"But Ed, I have written on nutrition and other issues because the scientific reports contradict each other. The reason I haven't written on global warming recently is that the science is settled. All the scientific reports say the same thing: that global warming is occurring and that human activity is the main cause."

"Well, that might or might not be the case. Here's a letter signed by a number of scientists saying that the science isn't yet settled."

"They're probably not climate scientists," Elvin responded. "They probably aren't any more educated about the issue than rock stars are about the issues they comment on."

"Thirty-seven thousand scientists have signed the letter, Elvin, and nine thousand of them have Ph.D's. Why don't you investigate to see how many were climate scientists?"

"Thirty-seven thousand?" Elvin asked, surprised. He reached for the document. That can't possibly be right. There can't possibly be that many kooks willing to sign such a foolish statement. "Ed," he asked with a smile, "you aren't one of those global warming deniers, are you?"

"I want you to examine the subject, Elvin. The issue has become too politicized, the rhetoric too hot. I want you to address it in a more folksy way. I'm not saying the conclusion that human activity is causing global warming is incorrect, but that it can be written about in an interesting, even a humorous way. Perhaps by asking if toasters are the cause of global warming. After all, every time a toaster is used it emits heat. Find things like that, that approach the issue in a way that will engage readers' attention. Let's have one of your twice-weekly articles focus on global warming from this perspective, and the other on another STEM issue.

"Take your time to get up to speed on it. Here are a few books with a contrary view on the subject. You might find them useful."

"Thanks, Ed," Elvin said as he picked up the books. "I'll see what I can do." Good grief! he thought to himself as he walked to his cubicle.

16

"Good morning, everyone," Alan began, and the third session of Shakespeare in His Own Words was underway. "Today we'll look more closely at some aspects of Elizabethan society that form the context in which Shakespeare's characters make their decisions.

"The Elizabethan era was a time of great changes in English society. It wasn't change in the form of peaceful evolution of social processes, though, but rather a time of clashes between different ways of understanding the world and the place of human beings in it.

"I realize more fully now than I did a few years ago how much Shakespeare's thinking was caught up in those clashes of values, and how much the fire in the plays comes from portrayals of them by a man with great observatory power who also had a deep facility with language and a flair for creating dramatic structures. What were some of the clashes discussed in your background reading?"

At first, no one said anything. Then Lisa offered an example. "It was a time when the Catholic and Protestant religions clashed, wasn't it? Henry VIII had broken with the Catholic Church and established the Anglican Church. Mary, his successor, was known as Bloody Mary because of the violent way she attempted to return the country to the Catholic fold."

"Yes, that's right." Alan said. "When Elizabeth became queen, she tried to put a damper on the religious issue. Although she was Protestant, she initially adopted a policy of almost turning a blind eye to her people's private religious convictions. That didn't last long, for various reasons, and the religious issue remained so sensitive during Shakespeare's lifetime that he rarely openly referred to it in his plays. It was also a time when many new ideas came in from abroad, wasn't it? Do you recall where those ideas came from?"

"Well, that would have to be Italy," Pat answered. "Shakespeare seems to have been fascinated by that country, and he set many of his plays there."

"Not just Italy, but Renaissance Italy," Amelia added. "The Renaissance had been underway there for a hundred years or more by the time Shakespeare began writing his plays. The ideas of the Renaissance—from France as well as Italy—were brought to England by English travelers who visited those countries."

"That's right," Alan said. "New ideas from Italy and France flooded in, reaching a peak in the 1570s, when Shakespeare was still a boy. They influenced English life so deeply and in so many ways—political, religious, intellectual, cultural, artistic—that the term 'English Renaissance' is used to describe the final decades of the 16th century. Who can tell us a bit more about the earlier Renaissance, the one in Italy and France?"

Nancy spoke first. "The Renaissance was the time when people in those countries rediscovered the great philosophical, literary and historical works from ancient Greece and Rome. Ideas in those works transformed Italian and French societies, just as they later transformed English society."

"But the ideas that reached England weren't just those from ancient Greece and Rome," Doug added. "With them also came new ideas from the Renaissance about man's place in the world. There was a new emphasis on man as the measure of all things. He was no longer just a cog in a fixed, unchanging universe."

"Yeah," Dave agreed. "The new ideas had a dynamism, an energy that conflicted with the passive acceptance of the static nature of the world found in medieval attitudes. I'm thinking here of how the traditional medieval Christian world was described in one of our assigned readings, Tillyard's *The Elizabethan World Picture*."

"I was impressed by that book," Amelia said. "It gave me a very different way of seeing the world. Tillyard describes traditional medieval understandings of the cosmos as characterized by three things: first, an ordered universe with a fixed state of hierarchies and the need to maintain balance and order at each hierarchical level; second, the great vertical chain of being that connects the hierarchical levels, with man in one of the middle regions, lower than the angels but higher than the animals; and third, what he calls a 'cosmic dance' in which men, born sinful, could achieve salvation if their actions were honorable and did not disrupt the cosmic order."

"I can see aspects of the view of the world as fixed and static in some of Shakespeare's plays," Pat said, "and also aspects of the dynamism of the human-centered world in Renaissance thought. The two are very different. I can see why the introduction of the new ideas clashed, not meshed, with the older medieval understandings."

"So Shakespeare sought to portray clashes of ideas in his plays," Alan said. "Who has an example of how he did that?"

Lisa offered one. "Shakespeare depicts two very different concepts of revenge, though he did it in two separate plays. How revenge is regarded in pagan Rome is shown in *Julius Caesar*. How it is regarded in Christian societies is shown in *Hamlet*."

"In *Julius Caesar*," Dave said, jumping in, "revenge was direct and quick. Antony doesn't mess around. He quickly forms an army to hunt down and kill the conspirators, and he and Lepidus draw up a list of people to be assassinated to clear the way for their political ambitions.

"Laertes, too, in *Hamlet*, knows how revenge is enacted in the pagan tradition. He is determined to avenge his father's murder without caring how it might affect his standing in the court or with God. 'I'll not be juggled with,' he says. 'Let come what comes, only I'll be revenged / Most thoroughly for my father.' He will have his revenge even if he must 'cut his throat i' th' church!'"

"And is that how Hamlet acts?" Alan asked, catching Amelia's eye.

"No, Hamlet acts very differently," she responded. "If Hamlet had lived in Rome, he would simply have killed Claudius to revenge the murder of his father. But in a Christian society, Hamlet wants not only to revenge the murder of his father's body but also the torment of his father's soul.

"Hamlet at first thinks like a pagan, with the ghost's commandment in mind. 'If thou didst ever thy dear father love . . . Revenge his foul and most unnatural murder.' He seeks immediate revenge. He will, he says, 'with wings as swift / As meditation or the thoughts of love, / Sweep to my revenge.'"

"Hamlet is ready to do just that," Nancy noted. "When he sees Claudius in a vulnerable position, at prayer, he pulls out his sword, ready to kill him. But then he recalls his father's ghost telling him that he'd been killed so suddenly that he hadn't had a chance to ask God for forgiveness for his sins. He was, he said, 'Doomed for a certain term to walk the night, / And for the day confined to fast in fires, / Till the foul crimes done in my days of nature / Are burnt and purged away.'"

Doug then added that "Hamlet, being a Christian, had two duties: to avenge the death of his father's body by killing his murderer, and to avenge the torment that his father's spirit is suffering by ensuring that his uncle's spirit suffers the same torment. He stops himself from killing his uncle while he is in prayer asking forgiveness, which is what Hamlet thinks he's doing. Killing him then wouldn't have been retribution because his soul would have gone to heaven. Hamlet forces himself to wait for a more opportune time so that he can achieve both goals."

"I think it's worth noting," Pat commented, "that Hamlet is to revenge those two things only. The ghost was adamant that he is not to harm his mother. 'Taint not thy mind, nor let thy soul contrive / Against thy mother aught,' the ghost says. 'Leave her to heaven /And to those thorns that in her bosom lodge / To prick and sting her.'

"Later, when Hamlet appears to have forgotten the ghost's demand in the heat of the moment when confronting his mother, the ghost reappears to remind him not to harm her. It's a good thing that Hamlet confronted his mother at night, or the ghost wouldn't have been able to appear to stop him," he said with a wry smile.

"We have now established the existence of two opposed sets of principles," Alan summarized. "The stage has been set for the clash between them in Hamlet's mind. And this is where Shakespeare shows true fire. He doesn't just have Hamlet choose one or the other of the two options; he remains drawn to both."

"That's one of the things that makes this play so great," Nancy said. "Hamlet is continually drawn to the pagan concept of revenge even as he is drawn to a concept influenced by Christian ideas of reward or punishment after death. He is tormented by the desire for action toward the first goal even as he holds himself back in order also to achieve the second.

"Yeah, he wants to achieve both," Amelia responded. "But at times he questions whether his delay in exacting revenge is due to cowardice rather than self-control. 'Am I a coward?' he asks himself. He then compares his not having acted when he has great cause to act with Fortinbras and the Poles, who are going to fight over a worthless piece of soil in Poland."

"And with that tension between the two values continuing in Hamlet's mind, we must take our break," Alan said.

When the class resumed, he turned the discussion to a second clash that arose during Shakespeare's lifetime, one between older chivalric ideas of honor and newer mercantile or commercial values. "In the traditional medieval Christian roots of Elizabethan society, honor was derived from the status of one's family. Titles given by the king were important. Wealth was acquired through licenses and monopolies issued by the king to favored courtiers through a patronage system designed to strengthen support for the monarchy.

"During Elizabeth's reign, merchants and trading companies—and raiders such as Sir Francis Drake—began to make their fortunes in ways independent of the monarchy. The commercial values inherent in their independent activities clashed with the older ideals of the nobility. Shakespeare, well aware of those clashes, portrayed them in several of his plays."

"When I was younger," Dave said. "I read many adventure stories about Sir Francis Drake and Sir Walter Raleigh, about their raids on Spanish ships carrying treasure back from the New World."

"Hey, I did too," Doug interjected. "One book described how dangerous it all was, out on the open seas in small ships. But it was exciting, too. At that time, I wanted to be a privateer, commanding my own ship and raiding Spanish settlements in the Caribbean islands and Central America. I wanted to be knighted by the queen."

"I enjoyed adventure stories about that time, too," Pat commented. "But I was a bit more practical. I read books about shipbuilding and carpentry. I liked building things, anyway, and I fantasized about building an assembly line modeled after Henry Ford's to turn out ships for raiders like Drake and John Hawkins. Later I envisioned owning a fleet of merchant ships, like Antonio in *The Merchant of Venice*."

"Well, I'm glad you mentioned that play, Pat," Alan said. "It's one in which Shakespeare gives us glimpses of the new commercial class that was building its fortunes through shipbuilding and trading."

In the short time remaining, Alan and the students discussed how clashes of values between traders and the nobility were portrayed in *The Merchant of Venice* and *King John*. Wrapping the session up, Alan urged them to keep the clashes of values they had discussed in the backs of their minds as they moved on to other topics. He also reminded them that Thursday's meeting would be the first in which students would introduce and moderate the discussions.

As they walked out of the classroom, Alan overheard Doug asking the other students if they remembered an episode from the *Here's Lucy* TV show. "One of the guest stars on the episode played a character named Julius. In one scene, Lucille Ball picks up an orange and asks him 'Care for an orange, Julius?' I think of that scene every time I hear the name Julius Caesar—or see an Orange Julius."

17

Amelia was seated in the coffee shop when Alan arrived. He got his coffee and joined her. They hadn't agreed to meet at this place and time, but both of them had understood that they would. They'd formed a similar unspoken agreement not to discuss Shakespeare or the class when they met.

"I have a book of fiction about American life for you, Amelia," Alan said as he sat down. *"Back to Blood,* by Tom Wolfe. It will give you a sense of how some Americans experience their lives as events happen to them. It's not great literature, but Wolfe has a real knack for identifying important issues in contemporary American life and for giving the reader a sense of what each character is thinking, of what their motivations are. His books are fun to read, and this one will give you some insights into the people you see around you."

"Thank you, Dr. Fernwood. But why *Back to Blood*? Is there a lot of violence and killing in it?"

"No, not at all. 'Blood' refers only to the ethnic origin of some of the characters. They experience some of the problems that arise when people of different racial and ethnic groups live close together. One of the amazing things about American society, I think, is that so many different groups usually live side by side so peacefully. That's one of the reasons I'm proud of my country."

"You know, Dr. Fernwood, "my country also has many ethnic groups, and there are problems between them. But most of the problems in Vietnam are probably political. They center around the conflict between the people in the north and the people in the south. What you call the Vietnam War we call the American War, but that war was not an isolated event. It was just one part of the civil war between the north and the south. A lot of blood was spilled in it, just as there was in the American Civil War. The hottest years were from the early 1950s through the end of the 1970s, just about 100 years after your Civil War.

"Even today, the people in the two regions view so many subjects from two different points of view. They have different perspectives on the war, on other aspects of Vietnamese history, on Vietnamese literature, and even on what it means to be Vietnamese. We are now one country, and it is my hope that someday we will have only one soul, a complete Vietnamese soul."

"I've never been to Vietnam," Alan said. "but I hope to someday. You know, Amelia, in the U.S., literature has traditionally been studied in two different ways. But they are complementary approaches, and so are probably more similar than how literature is studied in the north and south of Vietnam. The first way considers works of literature as works of art, and examines their structure and form, and the techniques the writers used. The second treats literature as products of a specific writer who lived in a particular place and time. It seeks to understand works better by learning more about the life and times of their authors.

"I mention this because the second approach has suddenly become very important to mc. For the first time in my life I'm investigating the Shakespeare authorship question. I have you to thank, in part, for my new interest in it, because of your mention of the movie *Anonymous* on the first day of class. For most of my life I laughed at people who doubted that the man from Stratford wrote the works attributed to him. But the more I investigate the issue, the more I'm beginning to see legitimate reasons for doubting his authorship.

"Of course, he was the author," Alan continued quickly, not yet wanting to reveal the extent of his doubts. "But I now see that doubters are not the irrational conspiracy theorists I had assumed them to be."

"I have always wondered how someone from a small town where most people were illiterate and books were scarce could have acquired the knowledge of so many subjects depicted in the plays," Amelia replied. "I come from a small town myself, so I know what conditions are like there."

"Well, that is one of the key questions," Alan said. "If anyone had told me even a month ago that I would be spending time on the authorship question, I would have thought they were crazy. Because the subject is so new to me, I have a lot of work to do to bring myself up to speed on it. So, I'm glad to have a light teaching load this summer, and also that my wife is away. Did I ever tell you that she is from Taiwan? That's where she is now, visiting her parents. I met her there when I taught English language and literature at a university in Taipei."

Amelia noted those pieces of information, but didn't comment on them. "I enjoyed *Anonymous*," she said, "but did not understand everything that happened in the movie. It was a bit hard to keep all the characters straight. Perhaps we can talk about it more next time we meet."

They both stood up, noting with pleasure her final comment about their meeting again.

TUESDAY, JUNE 9

18

Elvin had been at the Horizon Hotel's restaurant's bar for a while, waiting for Delilah to arrive. Sometimes after work he and other writers would gather in one of the bistros catering to young professionals near the *Herald's* offices. But today, he wanted two things: to relax by himself, and to share his thoughts with Delilah. He was going over recent events in his mind when she walked in.

"Delightful Delilah, over here," he called to her. "Would you like a drink before we eat?" he asked when she reached him.

"No, and don't call me that!" she whispered. "You know I don't like it when everybody turns to look at me."

"Well, it would be easier to stop myself if you weren't so delightful, Delilah," he said as he paid the bar bill.

Once they were seated at their table, they both began to talk at the same time. That was the way it always was with them: eager to meet, and full of conversation when they did. They'd become friends over the last few years, meeting after Elvin had interviewed Delilah's father at one of the literature conferences he'd organized for Cary University. Elvin had become friends first with Alan, and then with the entire Fernwood family, stopping in occasionally for dinner with them.

Elvin let Delilah talk first, not that he had much choice. When she was happy about something, her enthusiasm and the delight she felt not only pushed her forward but also led others to make way for her as they became infected by her happiness.

"Okay, what's your news?" he asked after they ordered.

"Well, the most amazing thing happened today. I was part of a small group from the marketing department that visited one of the companies that produces TV commercials for us. I was excited about the visit because it was my first chance to see how commercials are filmed.

"Anyway, the product was an upgraded version of our laundry detergent. You know, the one in the blue and gold box that everybody uses? Well, before the filming began, I walked on to the set and looked around. It was set up like a typical laundry room in a nice house. I stood next to the washing machine and picked up the box of detergent to study the newly designed exterior and wording on it.

"Just then the producer of the commercial came in, and everybody leaped into action to get ready for the filming. But here is what was so amazing, Elvin. The producer thought I was the actress who would play the housewife! Can you imagine that?

"Then the real actress came in and I was about to walk off the set, back to my marketing group, when the producer realized I wasn't the actress and asked who I was. So I told him. I was a bit flustered, and spoke perhaps in a more lively way than usual. He looked at me, then at the actress and then back at me. Then he pointed at me and said that he wanted me to be in the commercial! Can you believe that?

"So, they filmed the commercial with me in it! Mostly I had just to stand there and smile. The hardest part was holding the box at the right angle. I had only a few lines to learn, which would be used mostly as voiceovers anyway, stuff like 'Hmm, this new improved version really is better than the other brands,' as I looked at the box.

"So I'm going to be on TV, Elvin. I felt like I was Mary Tyler Moore when she played a young housewife. You know, on Dick Van Dyke's TV show from the '60s?" They laughed together, and Elvin was glad to absorb some of Delilah's good spirits.

After the conversation settled down and their food had been served, Elvin told her about developments at his job. He hadn't been too happy at first, he told her, when his editor had asked for more critical reporting, for highlighting the contradictions between reports on the same issue rather than merely reporting on each one separately. "But now I can see he was right. This really is a more interesting way to cover the topic. That was just the kind of guidance I needed to become a better writer."

Delilah nodded, happy that he was making his way in his career, just as she was in her internship.

"But he now wants me to write occasional articles on global warming. I can highlight contradictions between reports on the subject, but I think he is one of those loonies who doubts that global warming is occurring, even though the science is already settled. He has given me several books and articles to read."

"Well, just treat it like any other subject," she advised, and they moved on to other topics.

Later, as Elvin walked Delilah to her car, she held his arm. As they reached the car, she turned to him and said. "You know what I think, Elvin? I think you are the cause of global warming. I always feel warm when I'm with you."

They gave each other a quick air kiss, as usual, before he walked over to his car. He saw her continuing to look at him as he opened the door, and called out, "Good night, Delightful Delilah," as he got in.

WEDNESDAY, JUNE 10

19

Amelia leaned back in her chair, enjoying the chance to relax and drink her coffee after a tedious session in the orientation program. She didn't need to have read to her what she'd already read for herself. No Fulbright student did, and it seemed to her that the organizers of the orientation program weren't as intelligent or as quick as the students themselves.

While trying to clear her mind, she couldn't help overhearing, at the next table, a discussion among half a dozen professors. She recognized one, Matt Harris, Chair of the Literature Department. The matter was apparently one of some importance to them, something about how they were going to meet the new Dean's priorities to make the School of Arts and Humanities a profit center rather than a cost center. She laughed to herself at the rather lame ideas they'd come up with—things such as bake sales and selling trinkets with names of the Departments and the University on them that wouldn't raise even a fraction of the funding needed. They were clearly humanities professors without much business sense.

Throughout their discussion, several of the men had been distracted by Amelia's presence nearby. She noticed their interest, and used that as a means of joining the discussion.

"If I may interrupt," she said, "I could not help overhearing your conversation about ways to generate more non-university funding for the humanities departments. And if I may offer a suggestion, you might consider having the departments offer more Asian studies courses—Asian literature, Asian geography and history, Asian society and culture, Asian music and art, and so on—to attract more students from Asia."

They looked at her with interest, but didn't say anything.

"There is a real need for Asian studies courses for Asian students because the universities in most Asian countries teach mostly about the contributions their own country has made to the field being studied. Asia-wide Cultural Studies programs are needed, and they should be located at American universities in order to escape the provincialism and blinders that exist in most Asian countries.

"Let me give you an example," she continued, warming to her theme. "In the West, the field of physics is unified, and students study the works of physicists regardless of what nationality they are or the physicists were. All physics students learn about Newton and Einstein, and Rutherford, Faraday, Galileo, Cavendish, Bohr, Thomson, Maxwell, Curie, Fermi, and Heisenberg. And it is the same in Asia, in the sciences.

"But it is very different in the arts. Using literature as an example, in Europe and the United States, all literature students learn about Shakespeare, Goethe, Dante, Virgil, Homer, Tolstoy, Dostoevsky, and Moliere, Byron and Schiller, regardless of which country they live and study in, and regardless of the country the writers lived in and the language they wrote in. But in Asia, Chinese students learn mostly about Chinese literature—Du Fu, Li Bai, Bo Juyi and so on. In India, literature students learn mostly about Indian literature—Kalidasa, Vyasa and Valmiki, for instance. And in Japan, they learn mostly about Japanese writers such as Basho, Chikamatsu, Murasaki, Saikaku and Ogai.

"It is the same in art. In the U.S. and Europe, all art students study the works of Michelangelo, Picasso, Raphael, Leonardo, Titian, Rembrandt, Giotto, Bernini, Cezanne, Rubens, Caravaggio, Monet, Goya and so on. In China, however, students study mostly the works of Chinese painters such as Gu Kaizhi, Zhao Mengfu, We Daozi, Dong Qihang, and Ma Yuan. In Japan, they study mostly the works of Japanese artists such as Sesshu, Sotatsu, and Korin.

"And philosophy is similar. In the West, students study philosophers from all Western countries, such as Aristotle, Plato, Kant, Descartes, Hegel, Aquinas, Locke, Hume, Augustine, Spinoza, and Leibniz. But in China students study mostly Chinese philosophers such as Confucius, Laozi, Zhuxi, and Mencius. In India they study mostly Indian philosophers such as Sankara, Nagarjuna, Ramanuja and Buddha.

"So, there is a real need for a program that studies and teaches Asian culture as a unified whole, just as Western culture is taught as a unified whole.

"But here is the part that will interest you most," Amelia said. "Foreign students pay full tuition, which would increase the amount of money flowing into the university generated by humanities departments."

The Department Chairs sat stunned, finding it difficult to grasp that Amelia's brilliance overshadowed even her beauty. Matt Harris was the first to recover his wits. "May I ask who you are?"

"I am Amelia Mai," she said with a smile. "I am a Fulbright student from Vietnam. Sorry for going on at such length, but once I get into a subject it is hard for me to stop myself."

"You are from Vietnam?" the Chair of the History Department asked with some surprise. "How did you acquire such in-depth knowledge of Asian and Western writers, artists and philosophers?"

"Well, my knowledge in these areas is not deep, but I have a very good memory. I made a study of universities in Asia and the United States before deciding to accept the Fulbright scholarship. I am now slowly making it my business to become more familiar with the works of all the people I just mentioned. That is why I am taking Dr. Alan Fernwood's course on Shakespeare in addition to the Fulbright orientation program."

Amelia stood up. "If you will excuse me now, I must now prepare for my next class."

The Department Chairs watched her walk away. "Well, I don't know about you all," the Chair of the Philosophy Department said, "but I think I need to begin my education all over again."

Matt Harris's eyes followed Amelia until she was no longer in sight.

THURSDAY, JUNE 11

20

"Good morning, everyone," Nancy said with a smile. This was the first of the sessions in which students would introduce and moderate the discussions.

"We have already seen the importance of moments of decision in Shakespeare's plays, as characters deliberate about what to do, make decisions, and live or die with the consequences. We now turn to one of the critical factors affecting those decisions: the characters' knowledge of the situations they are in.

"In many plays, characters might have made different decisions if only they'd had more complete or more correct knowledge. That is certainly true of Othello, who is tricked into false beliefs by Iago, and of Romeo and Juliet, who kill themselves because of each one's mistaken belief that the other is dead. Today's discussion will focus on steps characters take to acquire and evaluate knowledge, and their need, sometimes, to act on the basis of knowledge that isn't certain.

"First off, I want to note two sources of knowledge that characters in *Julius Caesar* turn to. The first is soothsayers and strange or supernatural events. I'm sure everyone recalls the soothsayer's warning to Caesar to 'Beware the ides of March.' Other characters in that play see special meaning in comets and other unusual events, such as rumors of men on fire walking up and down the streets.

"The problem with that type of knowledge is that the soothsayer might be wrong and interpretations of unusual events might be incorrect. As Cicero notes, 'Indeed it is a strange-disposèd time; / But men may construe things after their fashion, / Clean from the purpose of the things themselves.' And not only might interpretations be wrong, but there is no way to test them in advance to determine their accuracy.

"A second form of knowledge in the same play is that of other people's eyes, which can serve as mirrors, reflecting back to us knowledge of ourselves. As Cassius explained to Brutus:

> 'And it is very much lamented, Brutus,
> That you have no such mirrors as will turn

Your hidden worthiness into your eye,
That you might see your shadow. . . .
. . . . .
And since you know you cannot see yourself
So well as by reflection, I, your glass,
Will modestly discover to yourself
That of yourself which you yet know not of.'

"The problem with this form of knowledge, is that the person doing the reflecting might not be a good judge of our worth. Only people of objective, mature judgment can provide an accurate reflection of our value, but the number of such people is limited; others, even those more stable than the fickle mob, provide only opinion, not knowledge.

"Knowledge—correct information, regardless of the source—is so important that some characters in Shakespeare's plays spend an inordinately large amount of time seeking it before acting, the classic example being Hamlet. And in fact, Hamlet's efforts to obtain accurate knowledge will be the main issue that we'll discuss today.

"We all remember that Hamlet learns from his father's ghost that he had been murdered by his brother, who poured poison in his ear while he was sleeping in the garden. We might have expected someone as impulsive and headstrong as Hamlet to have leaped into action to avenge his father's death. But he doesn't. Why not?"

"Well," Pat responded, "we know that Hamlet wants to revenge the murder of his father's body and also the torment of his father's soul after death. And to do that he has to wait for the right time. But now that I think about it, that concern came later. First, Hamlet had doubts about whether what the ghost told him was true. He had to settle that question before he could take any action."

"That's right," Lisa agreed. "Hamlet wants to know if the ghost he got the information from was really his father's ghost or merely an evil spirit trying to fool him. He wants to know if his uncle really did kill his father. Here are his exact words: 'Be thou a spirit of health or goblin damned, / Bring with thee airs from heaven or blasts from hell, / Be thy intents wicked or charitable. . . . O, answer me!'"

"Hamlet is unsure how to proceed." Dave commented. "He brooded about it for a long time. Then, when the players arrive, he sees a way to trick his uncle into revealing his guilt. He has the players insert a few extra lines into the play they're performing, and then explains his thinking out loud. 'I have heard that guilty creatures sitting at a play / Have by the very cunning of the scene / Been struck so to the soul that presently / They have proclaimed their malefactions.'"

"And then," Lisa said, jumping in, "he explains the situation to

Horatio, and asks him to observe the king's reaction to the passage that Hamlet had inserted."

"So," Nancy said, "Hamlet is testing both the ghost and his uncle. But he almost blows it. He becomes too unsettled, too excited during the performance and almost wrecks things with his antic commentary on the play."

"But it all works out," Pat observed. "At the key point, when the player on the stage pours poison in the ear of his player brother the king, the king in the audience rises, angry, and storms from the room. Hamlet is ecstatic because the ghost's words have been confirmed and Claudius's guilt established."

"It's a brilliant psychological moment," Amelia commented. "Hamlet now has the confirmation of his uncle's guilt he needs, and can concentrate on plotting his revenge."

"But, but, but—" Doug cautioned. "All is not well. By organizing this public test of his uncle's guilt, Hamlet has partially revealed his hand. He has tipped off his uncle that he might be aware of his guilt."

"Yes," Amelia said with quiet glee. "The tables have turned. Claudius now becomes the trapper and Hamlet the hunted. Claudius arranges several situations to try to trick Hamlet into revealing what is in his mind at times when he can be overheard by others."

"First," Doug said, continuing Amelia's thought, "he has Rosencrantz and Guildenstern try to sound out Hamlet, thinking he might confide his thoughts to his friends. That doesn't work because Hamlet suspects they will repeat whatever he says to the king. So then the king and Polonius arrange for Hamlet to meet Ophelia, seemingly by accident, while they hide and listen to the conversation. But Hamlet doesn't confide in her, either. He continues to pretend being mad."

"Hamlet's mother," Amelia added, "thinks that his odd behavior results from 'His father's death and our o'erhasty marriage.' Polonius, though, thinks that it results from thwarted love, because he had instructed his daughter, Ophelia, not to see Hamlet again."

"But the king isn't satisfied with either explanation," Dave noted. "He thinks there is something else in Hamlet's mind and he wants to know what it is."

"Here are the king's exact words," Lisa said, reading them aloud. "'Love? his affections do not that way tend, / Nor what he spake, though it lacked form a little, Was not like madness. There's something in his soul / O'er which his melancholy sits on brood, / And I do doubt the hatch and the disclose / Will be some danger.'"

"So," Dave continued, "the king arranges a third test, that of having

Hamlet meet his mother while Polonius listens behind the arras. But that doesn't work either, because Hamlet hears Polonius and stabs him through the curtain, thinking he's the king."

"More than thinking—hoping," Lisa said. "Seeing Hamlet stab his sword through the curtain—the arras—the queen asks him, 'What hast thou done?' And Hamlet answers 'I know not. Is it the king?' I can just hear him asking 'Is it the king?' with a gleeful, hopeful lilt in his voice."

"Yes, it's a moment to relish, isn't it?" Alan said, joining the discussion. It continued a while longer, then Alan caught Nancy's eye, and she knew it was time to wrap things up.

"Shakespeare has presented a beautifully orchestrated game of cat and mouse being played by both sides," she said. "Much more happens in the play, but we have seen what is most important for our discussion concerning the efforts that two of Shakespeare's characters go to, to acquire accurate knowledge. And with that, let's take our break now."

After the break, Doug led a discussion on one specific type of knowledge Shakespeare's characters need, that of human nature. He approached the subject by noting which animals Shakespeare compared human beings to, and how those animals changed from early to late plays. In their discussion, the class speculated on the degree to which that change reflected changes in Shakespeare's outlook. Recognizing that the subject was similar to the focus of *Shakespeare's Journey*, Alan wasn't surprised that the students weren't able to cite any specific events in Shakespeare's life to account for the changes.

As the students filed out of the classroom, Alan overheard Doug asking the others if they remembered *Casper*. "You know Casper, the ghost, 'the friendly ghost, the friendliest ghost you know'? Well, if Casper had told me that my uncle had murdered my father, I don't think I would have believed it. He's so friendly that even if he knew something like that he wouldn't have been able to say it. But Hamlet's father's ghost, dressed for battle, with blood on his sword—I would have believed him."

21

"You know, Amelia," Alan began, once they were seated at their usual table, "I think the Fulbright folks made an excellent choice in selecting you. It's rare to find someone with such an interest in literature."

"And I made a good choice in selecting Fulbright," she responded. "It was a difficult choice, Dr. Fernwood. I had several other options, but I think now that I chose the best one."

"Yeah," he said," it's hard to know what is best to do in any given situation. Right now, at this moment, what do we do next? Each life is unique, so there's no book that we can look up the answers in. We have to decide for ourselves."

"That is true," Amelia agreed, "but we do not decide completely by ourselves. There are customary ways of acting, and obligations we have to other people restrict our choices. We are not completely free actors."

"No, we aren't," he agreed. "But at the same time, within the scope of all possible and appropriate actions, how do we know what is best to do, right now, right this moment, in the unique set of circumstances we are in? I'm reading a wonderful book, *The Art of What Works*, that has interesting things to say on the subject. The author, William Duggan, says that much of what happens today is similar to what happened yesterday. Knowledge of the past—by showing us what actions or policies were tried before in similar situations and what the results were—can expand our awareness of what our options are. That's as true for individuals as it is for statesmen and policymakers. And that's perhaps the strongest justification for studying history, for getting a liberal arts education."

Amelia laughed. "I can see that we are back to one of your favorite subjects, liberal arts education. But you are right. Knowing what has happened in the past can help us make better decisions in the present.

"You know, Dr. Fernwood, when I was a student—in secondary school, I mean—I read a book about the Renaissance. I was so impressed by the awakening of European society to knowledge of the past because as a young girl—a teenager—just discovering the world of books and literature and history and so on, I felt I was going through my own Renaissance. I practiced spelling 'Renaissance' out loud again and again until I could spell it right without thinking about it."

Alan looked at her in astonishment. "You're kidding! I had exactly the same experience. I remember reading while sitting on the bed in my room when I was about fifteen years old and coming across that word. I didn't know quite what it meant, but I knew it was something important that I should know about. I practiced writing the word again and again until I could write it without thinking about it. Even now I can spell it without any thought–R-E-N-A-I-S-S-A-N-C-E. At that time, though, I had to stop to remember how many *n*'s there were, and how many *s*'s."

Amelia and Alan looked at each other. "I did not think I would ever meet anyone who had the same experience I had," she said softly.

"And I didn't think I would ever meet anyone that I'd want to describe that important moment in my life to," he said, equally softly.

They continued to look into each other's eyes, understanding that a connection of some sort had deepened between them, that a new level of intellectual intimacy had been reached.

"Come on," Alan said, standing up. "I feel the hair rising on the back of my neck. I can't sit still any longer."

Amelia was already half out of her seat. "Me too. Let's walk around. I need some physical movement."

FRIDAY, JUNE 12

22

Alan recalled how surprised he'd been by Charlton Ogburn's book last weekend, and reminded himself that today's task was to investigate what others had to say about it. Had Ogburn stated the facts correctly? How had others on both sides of the authorship question responded to his book?

He turned first to the reception Ogburn's book had received from those convinced by its case for Edward de Vere's authorship. Clifton Fadiman had said "Count me a convert. . . . [the book's] powerful argument should persuade many rational beings, who, well acquainted with the plays, have no vested interest in preserving a rickety tradition."

The *Los Angeles Times*'s principal book critic, Charles Champlin, was also persuaded, writing, with "Ogburn's patient and eloquent labors, the evidence mounted for the Earl of Oxford [as Shakespeare] can no longer be ignored by reputable scholars." So too was Kevin Kelly, drama critic at the *Boston Globe*, who wrote that Ogburn's was "The definitive book on the man behind the name Shakespeare. . . . Perhaps the single most revolutionary book in the whole of Shakespearean scholarship. . . . Once and for all Ogburn seems to me to prove the case for Oxford."

But Alan wanted to know what the other side thought, too. The first item he read from the Stratfordian pile had appeared in *Shakespeare Quarterly*, a publication of the Folger Shakespeare Library. "New Perspectives on the Authorship Question," by Richmond Crinkley, a former Director of Programs at the Folger, contained not only praise for Ogburn but also direct and severe criticism of the Folger's former director, Louis B. Wright, Crinkley's former boss. Crinkley wrote that Wright had "adhered to the orthodox view of the authorship question and displayed its orthodoxy with a contempt for dissenters that was as mean-spirited as it was loudly trumpeted." Crinkley had also commented that "The work of Ogburn's parents and anti-Stratfordian sentiment in general had been treated with vitriolic contempt by the Library's previous administration."

There was more. Crinkley wrote of his colleagues that he "was enormously surprised at what can only be described as the viciousness toward anti-Stratfordian sentiments expressed by so many otherwise rational and courteous scholars. In its extreme forms the hatred of unorthodoxy was like some bizarre mutant racism. . . . This baffled me. One did not, after all, have to agree with heterodoxy to accord it intellectual courtesy, or, for that matter, to present it accurately."

This is really unexpected in a Folger Library publication, Alan almost said out loud. But Crinkley wasn't done yet. He also described Ogburn as "among the most congenial of men," who felt, "rightly, in my opinion, that such treatment [by the Folger and others] violated the benign neutrality with which libraries should properly regard intellectual controversy."

Crinkley confirmed that Ogburn's scholarship was of the highest quality, noting that E. A. J. Honigman's "sympathetic review" of Ogburn's book "is the first time in my memory that a Stratfordian has made laudatory (or even courteous!) acknowledgement of an anti-Stratfordian work. That the most resourceful Shakespeare biographer has something to learn from the most distinguished anti-Stratfordian may signal a salutary change in the tenor of the discussion."

Well, Alan thought, if even the Folger allowed such favorable comments into its premier publication, then Ogburn was a scholar of the highest caliber. His scholarship could be trusted. Especially satisfying was Crinkley's final statement that "Shakespeare scholarship owes an enormous debt to Charlton Ogburn."

It was midafternoon. Alan had worked right through lunchtime, but didn't want to stop his investigations now. He turned to two additional sources to seek confirmation of Ogburn's doubts.

Reading *Shakespeare's Unorthodox Biography: New Evidence of an Authorship Problem,* he was impressed by how Diana Price, the author, documented the point that, unlike his contemporaries, Shakspere of Stratford had no paper trail that could corroborate his having been a writer. In an ingenious chart at the end of the book, Price compared the paper trails for twenty-five of the most popular writers of the Elizabethan and Jacobean eras, looking at ten different factors for each, including evidence of education, record of correspondence, evidence of having been paid to write, commendatory verses contributed or received, evidence of books owned, and notice at death as having been a writer.

The results were shocking and definitive, Alan thought. The chart showed that corroborative documents existed in all ten types of evidence for Ben Jonson, in nine for Thomas Nashe, in eight for Philip Massinger, all the way down to four for Thomas Kyd and three for John Webster. At the bottom of the list, with no documents existing in any of the ten categories, was William Shakspere. It was pretty hard to argue with the evidence laid out so starkly. It was like being in a swimming pool, he thought. There was no place to hide.

Alan then picked up Katherine Chiljan's *Shakespeare Suppressed: The Uncensored Truth about Shakespeare and his Works*. He found yet more reasons to conclude with a high degree of confidence that Shakspere hadn't written the works. Chiljan had uncovered "93 instances of 'too early' allusions to 32 different Shakespeare plays"— "too early" meaning that the allusions had been made in the 1580s and even the 1570s, when Shakspere, born in 1564, was still a boy. "They were made by 30 different writers . . . and occurred in 53 different sources." The plays written "too early" to have been by Shakspere included many of Shakespeare's greatest: *Romeo and Juliet, Measure for Measure, King John, Twelfth Night, Much Ado About Nothing, The Merchant of Venice, King Lear,* and *Hamlet.*

This evidence meant, Chiljan concluded, that "either the great author was a serial plagiarist [if he had only updated existing plays] and therefore was not a creative genius, or his works were written far earlier than supposed." The earlier timing, Alan could see, would place the plays perfectly into the prime of Edward de Vere's life.

With such definitive evidence putting the knife to any remaining thoughts he might have had about Shakspere's authorship, Alan felt like a hunter who'd just made a big kill. It was now dinnertime and he was hungry. But this was no time for a salad—he needed meat.

MONDAY, JUNE 15

23

"We have seen how important having correct knowledge is, and discussed the extensive efforts that some of Shakespeare characters make to get it," Amelia said, beginning the next class meeting. "Now let's turn to more complicated questions. How do we know what type of knowledge is most important in any given situation? And what should we do—what do Shakespeare's characters do—when we or they receive contradictory information from different sources?"

"In one of his earliest plays, *Love's Labor's Lost,* Shakespeare shows us that knowledge is not fungible; it isn't like money, which can be used for any purpose. Knowledge is local. The knowledge that is most important at any given moment is that which is most relevant to the particular situation we are in.

"A similar issue concerns language. Is English a general subject like mathematics, which is the same everywhere? Or is it a local subject that is different in different locations, like history?

"I used to think it was general, that English was English wherever it was spoken. But now that I am living in a foreign country, I am not so sure. To understand what people here are talking about, I need local knowledge. I need, for instance, to understand the game of baseball. I need to know who the Durham Bulls are, and who the New York Yankees are. I need to understand what it means to hit a home run or to score. And I need to understand what guys mean when they talk about getting to second base with a girl."

Nancy and Lisa glanced at each other, but didn't say anything.

"In *Love's Labor's Lost,* one of Shakespeare's most delightful early plays, he mocks the view of knowledge as general, as something that can be acquired and saved up, like money, without regard for what type of knowledge is acquired. He presents a situation arising from that belief that is so absurd that it is funny.

"The King of Navarre has decided to turn his court into an academe in which he and three others, including Berowne, will dedicate themselves to studying—to acquiring knowledge—for three years. During that time, they will focus only on things of the mind, not of the body. To facilitate their studies, they swear not to see a woman, to fast often and to sleep little. What happens next?"

"Well," Pat responded, "Berowne objects to the futility of acquiring general knowledge before knowing the specific purposes for which it will be needed. The academe's way, he says, is like things occurring out of season. It's like wanting a rose at Christmas, or snow in May. He says that by memorizing such things as the names of the stars, the scholars would be failing to get the kind of knowledge they need most."

"He also objects to the terms of the oath," Doug added. "They are so stringent, he says, that they can't possibly be kept. He points out that the king himself will be required to meet with a woman soon because the French king's daughter is coming to represent her country in negotiations with him.

"'Oh, yeah!' the king agrees. 'I forgot about that. We will make exceptions to the rules when necessary.' Berowne is gleeful at hearing that, seeing a way around all the decrees of the oath. As he explains, 'Necessity will make us all forsworn / Three thousand times within this three years' space . . . / If I break faith, this word shall speak for me: / I am forsworn 'on mere necessity.' It's only after that statement by the king that Berowne agrees to sign the oath."

"The French king's daughter arrives, accompanied by three girls to attend on her," Amelia explained. "Of course the king falls in love with the French king's daughter, and the three courtiers in the academe fall in love with the three girls."

Nancy and Lisa glanced at each other. Nancy flicked her eyebrows, wordlessly telling her, "You respond."

"Amelia, I'm a bit uncomfortable with your use of the word 'girl,'" Lisa said. "Referring to females as 'girls' while males are referred to as 'men' seems to imply that the women aren't as mature or as capable as the men. 'Women' is the preferred term. Men and women as adults are terms that go together, as do boys and girls, who are both children."

"Ah, I have been learning about this change in terminology in my Fulbright orientation class," Amelia responded. "It turns out that in Vietnam we still speak an out-of-date version of English. Almost all of us Fulbrighters are from countries where 'girl' is still used with its two traditional meanings. One is 'female child' and the other is 'young unmarried woman.' This is, perhaps, another example of English being a local, not a general, subject.

"In the case of this play, the three young men are attracted to three young women, and the king is attracted to the French king's daughter, who is a bit older than her companions. All four of them are certainly women. But three of them could be referred to as girls in the older secondary meaning of the word. However, I recall now that Shakespeare uses the term 'women' to refer to all of them in *Love's Labor's Lost*. Occasionally, too, as 'ladies,' but only rarely as 'girls,' so I'll make the change in my own terminology. If I sometimes forget, just let me know," she said with a smile. "Okay, what happens next?"

Dave was the first to reply. "The scholars' first reaction, at least Berowne's, is to deny to himself that he is in love. He is incredulous, first that he has fallen in love, and second that he has fallen in love with Rosaline."

"Here are his exact words," Lisa said, jumping in.

> "'What? I love, I sue, I seek a wife!
> Nay, to be perjured, which is worst of all,
> And, among three, to love the worst of all,

A whitely wanton with a velvet brow,
With two pitch balls stuck in her face for eyes.'

"A while later he is still lamenting in—and joyful in—the fact that he has fallen in love.

'I will not love; if I do, hang me. I' faith, I will not. O but her eye! By this light, but for her eye, I would not love her – yes, for her two eyes. . . . By heaven, I do love, and it hath taught me to rhyme, and to be melancholy; . . . Well, she hath one o' my sonnets already. The clown bore it, the fool sent it, and the lady hath it – sweet clown, sweeter fool, sweetest lady!'"

"It's good to see that Shakespeare was young once," Nancy commented. "This play was clearly written by a young man, one caught up in the delights of love at a young age. He was full of verve and romance. I think he must have been a lot like Berowne."

"So Berowne's first response is to deny to himself that he is in love, to protest against it," Dave continued. "His second response—one he shares with the other scholars—is to try to keep his love for Rosaline—and hence his betrayal of his oath—secret from the others. Eventually though, through a series of humorous scenes, all scholars become aware that all of them have violated their oath."

"And that, for me, is when the story really becomes interesting," Doug said. "The scholars are all forsworn; all are in love. They need a way out of the oath they took to avoid the company of women. The king tells Berowne to get us out of this mess, to find a way they can pursue their loves without violating their oaths. And he does. He finds several legal loopholes. He isn't a lawyer, but he thinks like one.

"First, he recognizes that a contract that requires illegal or impossible actions is invalid. It cannot be enforced. The oath the scholars signed, Berowne claims, contains such unacceptable clauses and is therefore void. The stricture against women, like the one requiring fasting, is contrary to nature and thus unenforceable.

"Second, Berowne notes that their oaths bound them to study. But there are things worth studying besides books. Women's eyes, he claims, can also be objects of study and sources of knowledge. They can provide important knowledge that cannot be learned from books. The oath, by forbidding the company of women, is contradictory. It prohibits the scholars from even approaching one important source of knowledge.

"And further, Berowne says, the inspiration that they as scholars could get from women's eyes would re-energize them and enable them to keep studying far beyond what they would have been capable of if they had only dull books to learn from. Women's eyes are, he says, 'the books, the arts, the academes, / That show, contain, and nourish all the world.' Because the scholars could learn much from women's eyes not found elsewhere, it's their sworn duty to do just that."

"And so, in their own minds, the scholars have found an acceptable way around their original understanding of their oaths. They then 'proceed to woo these girls of France.' In using 'girls' I am quoting Shakespeare," Amelia said to Lisa and Nancy, smiling. "But the path is not as simple as they expect, is it?"

"It sure ain't," Pat responded, "for two reasons. First, the girls—I mean the women," he said, glancing at Lisa, "decide to use their awareness of the men's love for them to have some fun by mocking them."

"And second—" Pat started to continue, but Nancy was quicker. "And second, the princess and her ladies are aware of the men's oaths to dedicate themselves to study. So when the king, thinking himself now free from his oath, invites the princess and her companions into the court, they refuse both the invitation to enter the court and the proposals of marriage. Having seen how easily and quickly the men broke their oaths to study when it was convenient for them to do so, they wonder whether the men might break their promises of marriage.

"The princess then learns that her father has died and that she must enter a period of mourning for one year. She is also now Queen of France. That gives her and her attendants an excuse to set up a test of the men's desire for them. If, she says, the men still want to marry them one year from now, they will agree. Until then, the women will remain in seclusion and mourning in France, and the men will remain in seclusion and study in Navarre."

"So, this comedy is one that does not end in marriage," Amelia noted. The title *Love's Labor's Lost* implies that the courting has not achieved its purpose, at least not at that time. Whether the marriages will take place a year from now, who knows?

"It will depend, I think, on whether the men are able to become more steadfast in their purposes. They need to show more constancy in a world of temptation. Knowing what is best is only half the battle. The other half is being strong enough to pursue what we know to be best even in the face of temptation to pursue other activities more immediately pleasurable."

"Ah," Dave said, "there is an example in the play showing how Berowne might begin to develop such constancy. Rosaline gives him an additional assignment. He must use his wit for good purposes, not merely to make fun of people. He must visit places where people are suffering and use his wit to ease their pain, to make them laugh. And he must do that every day during the coming year."

"That's right," Amelia agreed. "And there is another sign that Berowne is developing the maturity and constancy he needs to become a husband and a father. Remember the scene where he describes Rosaline as having a dark complexion? Apparently at that time a lighter complexion was considered more beautiful. But love is causing Berowne to change his ideal of female beauty. His love of Rosaline leads him to declare that no woman is beautiful except as she has Rosaline's dark complexion."

"Here's the passage," Lisa said, jumping in. "'Is ebony like her? O word divine! . . . / No face is fair that is not full so black.'"

"You read very beautifully, Lisa," Pat said. "Maybe you could be the designated reader when it's my turn to lead the discussion."

"Pat," Lisa responded, "you sound like one of the young men in the play, focused on external beauty and the sound of our voices. But women have brains, too."

"I don't doubt that at all," Pat said. "I'm sure that your brain is as lovely as your voice. Perhaps you will show it to me some day."

Lisa was starting to get angry, Amelia sensed, so she quickly intervened. "The point I was getting to is that Berowne's love for Rosaline is leading him to expand his concept of beauty. That change reminds me of a passage in Plato in which Socrates describes a process through which the soul may become cultivated. A love of the beauty of one particular thing, he explains, can lead us to admiration of other beautiful things, onwards to an appreciation of beauty wherever it may be found, and eventually to a love of the idea of beauty itself."

Alan drew the first session to a close. "We are getting into some very interesting philosophical areas. It's time for our break, but let's keep this thought on cultivation of the soul in mind and pick up on it in another session."

After the break, Pat introduced a discussion on Shakespeare's recognition of the importance of understanding other people. He based his discussion on *Timon of Athens*, and guided the class through Timon's drastic change from benevolent love for all mankind to misanthropic hatred. They concluded that his was a temperament of extremes: total love, then total hatred. He was unable to benefit from experience the way other people could, by adjusting their opinions gradually in response to their experiences. The shock from his eventual recognition of the true nature of people he thought were his friends was too great. The class discussion ended just as time expired.

Alan was pleased at how well the discussions were going this term, with all students prepared and engaged. His thoughts were interrupted when he overheard Doug invite the other students to go back to his apartment. "We can listen to some of my favorite songs, including Jobim's 'The Woman from Ipanema,' the Beach Boys's 'Surfer Woman,' The Four Seasons's 'Big Women Don't Cry,' and The Guess Who's 'American Woman.'

24

"Excuse me, miss. Is this chair taken?" Alan asked.

Amelia looked up from her book. "I am afraid it is. It is reserved for Dr. Alan Fernwood."

"Ah, good," he said, sitting down. "What are you reading today?" he asked, wondering if he should comment on how interesting the class discussion she'd led had been.

"I need a break from Shakespeare, and from Fulbright orientation materials. So I am reading *Emma* by Jane Austen."

"You're kidding! That's my favorite Austen book. I remember reading it on a plane and not being able to put it down. The most exciting part was the letter near the end. Never had such a long flight seemed so short."

"Well," she responded, "I like the way that Austen shows us just how difficult it is to know who the right person is for us to marry and for others to marry. Until near the end, Emma is wrong about who would be right for herself and for her friend.

"You know, Dr. Fernwood, I was married before, and I married the wrong person." She looked directly into his eyes. "I was young and inexperienced. I didn't know he was the wrong man for me at the time, but I realized it within a few months. By then I was pregnant and it was too late to do anything about it. It took years of suffering before I understood I had to get out of the marriage to save my sanity. It was very difficult. The only good part was that I now have a wonderful seven-year-old son, Rung. His name means 'forest' in Vietnamese."

Alan was surprised—not that she'd been married and divorced; she had the manner of someone who'd experienced much in life—but that she had a child. Her slim figure didn't indicate any previous childbirth, though of course he'd never seen her unclothed. He filed those thoughts away.

"I'm so sorry to hear that, Amelia. It must have been a very painful time in your life."

They were both quiet. Then Alan volunteered, "I also married someone who probably isn't quite ideal for me, and we are still married. But I think my experience isn't as bad as yours was. And like you," he said in a more cheerful voice, "I think the best part is the wonderful children that I have. I have two, a daughter and a son, both university students now."

Amelia stood up. "Let's go for a walk. I need movement. And it is best to focus on the present, not difficult times in the past."

"I agree completely," he replied.

She steered him toward the door. "Let's walk and I'll ask you questions that are puzzling me about your strange country."

TUESDAY, JUNE 16

25

Elvin knocked on the open door and walked into his editor's office. He was surprised to see Ted Torres, the *Herald's* editor-in-chief also in the room.

"Elvin, come in. We were just talking about you," Ed said.

"Morning," he said to Ed, and "Sir," to the chief editor.

"We were just looking at your two most recent articles," Ed continued. "The ones I asked you to write contrasting the contradictory findings in various reports on the same subject. We like those and will run them in the coming week."

"But we want to talk about a different matter." Ted said, taking over the conversation. "Ed and I have noticed that you write very differently on your personal blog than you do in the articles you write for the *Cary City Herald.* Your articles for us have been straightforward, which is the correct style for news reporting; your blog is edgy, provocative, borderline manic. Though you might not believe it, such an irreverent style can appeal even to aging men in their fifties."

Elvin looked at them, wondering where the conversation was heading.

"To liven up the *Herald*, to attract interest and build readership, we want to launch a new weekly column that challenges conventional thinking. It would appear not on the news pages, where factual reporting is important, nor on the editorial pages, where sober commentary is required, but on the op-ed page. We'll call it something like 'The Contrarian.' It would present unconventional ideas in a provocative manner. We recognize that in today's world to inform the reader we must also entertain him or her or we won't be read. We think that you might be just the person to write it."

Elvin looked at the two of them with the beginnings of a smile. This was not at all what he'd expected when told to get over to Ed's office.

"Well, I would like to try to write such a column. I think I have a knack for that kind of writing." He was sure he could turn out such columns not only weekly, but daily, if he needed to. Still, he recognized that it would be good to show a degree of humility before the two rather traditional men who were his boss and his boss' boss.

"Good. That's what I wanted to hear," Ted said. "I have to shove off. I'll leave it to you two to work out the details."

Ed turned to Elvin after Ted had left. "This is a big opportunity for you, Elvin. Are you ready for it?" Without waiting for a response, he continued. "We plan to launch 'The Contrarian' on Saturday, June 27, and want the first column to focus on the letter signed by 37,000 scientists that I gave you. Might you be able to have a draft for me by next Tuesday morning? That would give us most of next week to go over it. As the first piece to appear under the new column name, it will need to be especially catchy. We are relying on you to provide the spice."

"Yes, I can do that," Elvin said.

He smiled as he walked back to his office, already thinking about ways to make the column as provocative as possible, and about the pleasure of telling Delilah about this latest development.

WEDNESDAY, JUNE 17

26

Alan had spent much of the last two days investigating the current state of scholarship on the subject of Edward de Vere's authorship. It was now time to organize his notes.

He turned first to those from an article by Oxfordian scholar Professor Roger Stritmatter, "What's In a Name? Everything, Apparently . . ." In it, Alan had found much to support Ogburn's findings and much new information. Especially helpful was Stritmatter's list of interesting facts about de Vere's life that supported the idea of his authorship of Shakespeare's works. Among these were that de Vere had been a child prodigy in languages and history, and that he'd been an accomplished lyric poet. He'd also been recognized as a talented dramatist, yet no dramas of his had survived under his own name. It was publicly known during his lifetime that he had concealed his work.

De Vere's life, Stritmatter had noted, "resembled the experience of

Hamlet in so many curious and unprecedented ways that it has been called a rough draft of the play." He'd been "a prolific correspondent whose extant letters betray numerous verbal, figurative, and philosophical parallels to the plays and poems." He'd been trained in law at Gray's Inn and had the legal training so evident in the literary works. And de Vere "had been known as the most notorious 'Italianate Englishman' of his generation, after having traveled extensively through the Italian city-states that provide the locale and ambience of so many of the Shakespeare plays."

Even more fascinating was a biography of de Vere by Mark Anderson, *"Shakespeare" By Another Name: The Life of Edward de Vere, Earl of Oxford, The Man Who Was Shakespeare*. Alan recalled seeing a comment by British Oxfordian Kevin Gilvary that Anderson's book was the first full biography of Edward de Vere, and that if de Vere was Shakespeare, then Anderson's book was the first full biography ever written of Shakespeare. Imagine that, Alan commented to himself while shaking his head in wonder. It wasn't until 2005—some 400 years after the author of Shakespeare's works died—that the first biography of him was published. What a sad commentary that is on the state of Shakespeare studies in academia.

Alan realized that organizing his notes from Anderson's book, with its 400 pages of fascinating findings and insights, would take a lot of time, so he set them aside and turned to several shorter works that approached de Vere's authorship from different angles. Scholars have long known, he noted, that the two books that most influenced Shakespeare were the Golding translation of Ovid's *Metamorphoses*, and the so-called Geneva Bible. Scholars hadn't been able to establish any direct connection between either work and the man from Stratford, but, Alan was excited to learn, Oxfordian scholars had established strong links between both works and Edward de Vere.

The translator of Ovid's work from Latin into English, Arthur Golding, was de Vere's uncle, and he had tutored de Vere during the mid-1560s when the translation was being prepared. Alan also knew that all of Golding's other translations were somber religious tracts, and that the brilliance of the language in the English version of Ovid's masterpiece was so out of character for Golding that some Oxfordian scholars had surmised that the youthful de Vere had actually been the translator. "What an impressive piece of circumstantial evidence in favor of de Vere," Alan exclaimed out loud.

He was even more surprised when he turned to the Geneva Bible. Not only was there record of the teenaged de Vere's purchase of a copy of the Geneva Bible in 1569, but that very copy, annotated by de Vere himself, still exists and is in the collection of the Folger Shakespeare Library in Washington, D.C. And, he learned to his growing excitement, Professor Stritmatter had examined it and found scores of annotations in de Vere's handwriting that correspond to passages in the Shakespeare plays. He couldn't help but agree with U.S. Supreme Court Justice John Paul Stevens, who'd commented that Stritmatter's documentation of the correspondences was "an impressive piece of work. . . . [which] demonstrates that the owner of the de Vere Bible had the same familiarity with its text as the author of the Shakespeare canon."

Well, Alan thought, as a Shakespearean scholar myself, I can see what extraordinarily strong pieces of evidence the English translation of Ovid's *Metamorphoses* and de Vere's Geneva Bible are for de Vere's authorship. It's unforgivable that my colleagues are still as unaware of them as I was. I'm embarrassed—perhaps even ashamed—that the entire field of Shakespearean studies has chosen to ignore such critical pieces of information. They must become widely known and studied further.

As he was leaving the house, Alan noted that the day's mail contained two books with similar titles that would help him in his research: *Shakespeare Beyond Doubt: Evidence, Argument, Controversy*, and *Shakespeare Beyond Doubt? Exposing an Industry in Denial.*

27

"Alan!"

Alan turned around. "Elvin—Elvin Alvarez—what a surprise!" he said as they shook hands. "It's been a while since we've met. Too long."

"Yeah, I don't think I've seen you since I moved from the education desk to the science desk. The first few months I was really under the gun trying to get up to speed on the issues."

Alan nodded. "So what brings you to campus today?"

"It's actually my new position as science reporter. I'm talking to students about writing about science. They think I'm an expert—and maybe I do know a bit more than they do."

"You're talking to students in the English department?" Alan asked, wondering why he hadn't heard that Elvin was speaking.

"No, budding scientists. I'll be talking to first-year students, so I might actually get to talk about science and writing. When I met with a class of seniors a few months ago, all they wanted to talk about was job prospects. They were really freaking out about their futures."

"Well, we should get together to catch up. Diana's away for the next

Summer Storm

few weeks, but we could have a meal out somewhere, perhaps at the Harvest Hotel."

"Sounds good, Alan. I've got to run now. Let's find time soon."

Alan continued walking to his on-campus office, glad that he had the security of a tenured position. I wouldn't want to be one of those seniors trying to establish a career in today's environment, he thought.

THURSDAY, JUNE 18

28

"Morning everyone," Dave began, opening the next class session. "Professor Fernwood has pointed out that Elizabethan society—and Shakespeare's plays—are places were clashes of values took place. Today we'll discuss an important clash that occurs in *Troilus and Cressida*. It's one with great general relevance for anyone living alongside people with different values; that is, for everybody living in an open modern society.

"*Troilus and Cressida* is concerned with the war between the Greeks and the Trojans. It's part of the story told in Homer's *Iliad*. In Shakespeare's play, the war has been going on for seven years. The Greeks have besieged Troy in an effort to recover Helen, who had been the wife of Menelaus, the leader of Sparta. She had either been abducted by Paris, a son of the leader of Troy, or had run away with him. It's never clear which.

"The clash of values I want to highlight isn't between the Greeks and the Trojans, but rather among the Trojans themselves. Weary after seven years of war, they're meeting to decide whether to give Helen back or to continue to fight to keep her. Who would like to start our discussion by describing one side of the clash?"

Amelia spoke first. "One side, led by Troilus and Paris, wants to keep Helen. Troilus argues passionately that Troy's honor will be tarnished if they give her up, especially after they have already sacrificed so much to get her and hold her for so long."

Nancy spoke next. "The other side, led by Hector, argues that it's best to give Helen up to the Greeks. Every Trojan soul lost in battle, he says, is worth more than hers. And, he notes, war is such an uncertain business; we might be risking the existence of our city if the siege continues."

"Hector criticizes Troilus for not having reasons to support his desire to keep Helen," Doug observed. "But that isn't right. He does have reasons, and they make sense. The question is whether they are stronger than those that Hector and others have."

"So," Dave asked him, "you don't think the issue is one of emotion on one side and reason on the other? That isn't the core of the debate?"

"No. It's not that simple. It's a matter of comparing one set of reasons against another."

"But Troilus's boil down to 'honor,'" Lisa said. "He wants Troy to keep Helen because the city's honor is at stake. 'We won her fair and square and were going to keep her,' he seems to be saying. That reduces his reasons to emotions or desires. Reason by itself doesn't count with him. Here is his statement on that point:

> 'Nay, if we talk of reason,
> Let's shut our gates and sleep. Manhood and honor
> Should have hare hearts, would they but fat their thoughts
> With this crammed reason. Reason and respect
> Make livers pale and lustihood deject.'

"Troilus even seems to say that it doesn't matter what the cost of keeping Helen is. For him, defending his honor is more important than any other consideration. Besides, he says, we have already invested so much that we can't change course now."

"The core of the reasoning on the other side, on Hector's side," Nancy responded, "is that sunk costs shouldn't be taken into account. Whatever prestige and resources and lives have already been invested shouldn't matter to our decision. They are gone and won't come back regardless of what we decide. So we must focus on the future and the question of whether investing any more resources and lives would be worth the gain."

"I think it's more than just reasons on each side," Pat observed. "It's reasons bound up with emotions. On the side of keeping Helen, the emotions are bound up with honor, as Lisa noted. On the other side, they are bound up with the loss—the future deaths—of so many more Trojans. Giving Helen back would end the war and the ongoing stream of deaths of their countrymen."

"That raises another point," Doug said. "The discussion that takes place among the Trojans was triggered by the Greeks' offer to forgive all losses and end their siege if Troy gives Helen back."

"But the Trojans don't know if they can trust the Greeks' word," Pat said. "It could be that the Greeks will pocket the gain of Helen's return and continue fighting to protect *their* honor. After all, Helen has been held for seven years. They might decide to fight until Troy is destroyed as a warning to others who might try to abduct their wives."

"I think Pat's point is right," Amelia interrupted. "As is Dave's in his introductory remarks. We aren't talking about information but about values—and the question of whether the Greeks will keep their word and end their siege is a question of information.

"Approaching the issue from the point of values, the question becomes, 'How does one compare the value of the honor of the city as a whole as Troilus defines it against the value of the lives of individual Trojans?' Those lives are certainly of value to themselves and their families and friends, even if each individual life matters less to the city as a whole."

"That's a million-dollar question, "Dave said. "Our own country has faced that issue every time it has entered a war."

"One point that Troilus raises that we haven't yet noted," Alan said, entering the discussion, "is his claim that the value of things or people is what we assign to them. As he phrased it, 'What's aught but as 'tis valued?' Those arguing in favor of returning Helen make the opposite point, that Helen should be returned to the Greeks because doing so is the right thing to do. It's not just that Helen isn't valuable enough to justify further Trojan deaths; it's that keeping her is wrong because it violates respect for the institution of marriage. Helen was Menelaus's wife, and it wasn't right to abduct her. By returning her, Troy could partially correct a wrong that it had committed. Looked at in that way, the issue becomes one of subjective values conflicting with objective values."

"Honor is certainly a subjective value," Lisa commented. "The question of honor reminds me of something from *Hamlet*. Do you recall the scene where Fortinbras is leading an army, risking death and destruction, to capture a tiny piece of land? Hamlet, seeing this, says:

> 'Witness this army of such mass and charge, . . .
> Exposing what is mortal and unsure
> To all that fortune, death, and danger dare,
> Even for an eggshell. Rightly to be great
> Is not to stir without great argument,
> But greatly to find quarrel in a straw
> When honor's at the stake.'

"Shakespeare has found a marvelous way to express the absurdities that the pursuit of honor can lead us to—risking much for an eggshell or a straw. But I want to be sure you understand what he is saying, because the double negative—'not to stir without great argument'—is confusing. At a glance, Shakespeare seems to be saying that 'Rightly to be great is not to stir without great argument;' in other words, if you are great you act only on behalf of great issues, not small ones. Ignore the little stuff.

But that isn't what he is saying at all. Once the final phrase is added to the sentence it becomes clear that the meaning is exactly the opposite. Here's the quote with the middle phrase left out and the last phrase added: 'Rightly to be great . . . [is] to find quarrel in a straw when honor's at the stake.'"

"I have always liked that passage," Amelia added. "Hamlet—Shakespeare—had such an effective way of expressing even ideas that he ridicules. Thersites, in *Troilus and Cressida*, expresses a similar thought, but does so in a negative and distasteful way. Here's the phrase:

'Here is such patchery, such juggling, and such knavery. All the argument is a whore and a cuckold, a good quarrel to draw emulous factions and bleed to death upon.'

"He has, in other words, reduced the matter of honor—the whole seven-year battle, with all its deaths, destruction and hardships—to the mere matter of a woman running off with her lover. He has stripped one of the most famous moments in Western history of all its glory, reducing it to a mere matter of 'a whore and a cuckold.' That's the most sordid way the Greeks might have viewed Helen and Menelaus."

"Oh, I hadn't noticed that connection between the two plays before," Alan said, making a note to himself. "You're both right, Lisa, Amelia. Honor pushes men to make great sacrifices over issues that don't seem all that important in themselves. And Thersites is right that the confrontation in *Troilus and Cressida* boils down to the issue of Helen. The Greeks believe they must protect their honor by recovering Helen—the honor of one man, Menelaus, and of the Greek community in general. And the Trojans also are fighting over the same point of honor—about whether they can be forced to give up one woman, regardless of how she came to be in their city."

Doug offered a thought. "You know, I always wondered why Hector reversed himself and agreed to keep Helen. I had thought that he had the better argument when he spoke in favor of giving her up to the Greeks. His sudden shift was a surprise. But now I see that honor was the ruling idea of the age. It motivated the Greeks as much as the Trojans. To give Helen up, Hector would have had to have been so confident in his judgment that he would overrule not only Troilus and Paris but also the ruling idea of the times he lived in."

"Maybe it's like building a better mousetrap," Nancy reasoned. "It's not enough to have a better product. You also have to take into account all of the other factors that go into launching it—creating customer awareness, convincing retailers to stock it, and so on. Hector may have had the better argument, but in his eyes and the eyes of the other Trojans, it wasn't better enough to justify overruling the default beliefs of the age."

"Spoken like a true businesswoman, Nancy," Pat said, smiling.

"And," she continued, smiling back at him, "There may be other points of contention between the Greeks and Trojans, such as competition over trading routes in that part of the Aegean Sea, that we don't know about."

"You know," Alan said, "it's not often anyone brings economic reasoning or business sense into literature classes. And with that, it's now time for our short break."

29

Once everyone had returned to the table, Lisa said that her session, too, would focus on *Troilus and Cressida.*

"Oh, good," Dave said. It's such an important and complex play, and there is still so much more to say about it."

"I'd like to begin by returning to a point that Professor Fernwood made earlier," she continued. "The point that the question of whether to keep or return Helen wasn't that of emotion as opposed to reason, but rather how things or people are to be valued. In this case, Helen.

"A similar situation exists in the Greek camp. Shakespeare has given us parallel situations by contrasting the high subjective value that Achilles places on himself—which was similar to the high subjective value that Troilus placed on Helen—with the objective value that Ulysses and the other Greeks place on Achilles—similar to the objective value that Hector and other Trojans placed on Helen. In both cases there was an imbalance between the subjective and objective valuations."

Lisa then guided the class through a discussion of Ulysses's clever method of convincing Achilles to take the field by showing him how the subjective value that others placed on him decreased as the memory of his heroic accomplishments faded.

"Now I want to bring up some thoughts from our assigned reading," she went on, "from Thomas West's article on *Troilus and Cressida.* West claims that the two ways of valuing things—the subjective and the objective—'may be called the Eastern and Western views of truth.' 'The Greeks,' West wrote, 'discover truth in the knowledge of the nature of things, and especially in the nature of man. Keen discernment of the arrangement of the cosmos and a grasp of the human passions through self-knowledge offer a steady foundation for the conduct of life. The Trojans [on the other hand] generally identify truth with faith in something whose value is established by an act of the will.'

"I found this a fascinating statement—valuing things on the basis of knowledge versus will or desire, and connecting the first with life in the West and the second with the East—but I don't know how to evaluate it. I don't know enough history, and have never traveled outside the United States. So I'm wondering what those of you with international experience think of West's statement."

"Well," Nancy responded, "from my admittedly limited reading of history and philosophy and my few travels abroad, I'd say that seeking truth in the nature of the object being examined is certainly a Western practice, perhaps even a Western invention. I don't know, though, about whether a subjective approach to truth and value is distinctly non-Western or Asian, as Thomas West claims.

"In fact, from my trip to Greece last year, I'd say that in Greece these days, subjective value dominates objective value. I say that because prices at the markets in Greece aren't fixed. Bargaining is the norm. Trade takes place voluntarily when the buyer and seller both place higher values on what they are getting than on what they are giving up.

"In most of the rest of the world, at least outside the West, prices aren't fixed. We don't realize that because almost all prices are fixed where we live. But that wasn't the case throughout most of human history, and it isn't the case in most countries today. In fact, if you want to see the real world, not the complex modern economy the West has built, try to buy something from those guys selling things in front of the subway stations. Bargaining is the norm."

Doug picked up on that point. "Bargaining involves negotiating not only with the seller, but also with yourself. You must weigh the benefits of purchasing this item now against the benefits of buying other items later. So it's all subjective, in two ways."

Amelia then expressed her thoughts. "During this discussion, I have been considering how things are valued in my home country. Vietnam has changed a lot since I was a girl. Back then, there were no modern stores, only small shops, and bargaining was necessary to purchase just about anything. Today, though, there are many modern grocery stories and shopping centers. In them, prices are fixed and have labels with prices on them, just like here in the United States.

"So I would have to say that the question of commercial values being fixed or not fixed is not so much Western versus Asian as it is modern versus traditional markets. But fixed prices apply mostly to commodities such as shampoo. The larger and more unique an object is, the more likely its price will be determined through bargaining. I'm thinking here of cars and pieces of land. In the old days, where there were no mass produced items, everything was unique.

"On the subject of cultural and religious values, though, principles are fixed. The Confucian values that I learned as a child have not changed, though they are followed less often now as Vietnam has become more open to values and practices from the rest of the world."

"I'm glad you're in this class, Amelia," Pat said as time ran out. "I'm learning a lot about the rest of the world from the perspectives you bring to our discussions."

As Alan walked through the doorway after the class had ended, he overheard Doug say to the other students, "You know, this discussion reminds me of that Kenny Rogers song 'The Gambler.' Remember the words? 'You got to know when to hold 'em / Know when to fold 'em, / When to walk away / And when to run.' The Trojans should have folded and returned Helen to the Greeks. But no one knew the future."

"Cassandra did," Lisa reminded him, "but nobody paid any attention to her. After all, she was only a mere woman, not someone worth listening to."

"Well, perhaps it's not that she was a 'mere' woman, Lisa," Pat said, "but that she was a mad woman. They thought she was nuts."

30

"Hey, Renaissance Girl! How are you today?"

"Hi, Professor Fernwood. How are you?" Amelia asked. And then a second later she added, "You see, I am becoming just like Americans. I didn't answer your question, but instead asked you the same question. I learned about this way of Americans greeting each other in my Fulbright orientation course yesterday."

"Well, I'm glad to see that the course is teaching your group about American life and culture, and not just about how to be successful studying at American universities."

"In my orientation class we have had some sessions on American history," she continued. "Yesterday, for instance, we learned more about the Civil War and the Great Depression. Those were difficult times for Americans. But you know, Dr. Fernwood, my country, Vietnam, has also had difficult times, and much more recently than the Depression in the United States. Americans don't seem to know much about them, just as I didn't know much about American history.

"Some of the students I have met asked me if I hate Americans because of the Vietnam War. There is so much to explain that I didn't know what to say, so I just said 'no.' But next time someone asks, I will explain that what you call the Vietnam War, we call the American War, as I mentioned before. And that the American war was just one of many. It was preceded by the war with the French, and after the war with the Americans we fought the Chinese and the Cambodians.

"Even though I was born after most of the fighting had ended, I was born into a society with much suffering. We had very little food when I was a girl. We did not have electricity much of the time. But one of the worst times in my life came later. My mother died when I was only thirteen years old. And after that, my father began to drink. It took him only a few years to drink up the house. Then, after the house was gone, I had to live with relatives. I had to sleep in a small room where we kept supplies, on a mat on the floor.

"I'm not telling you these things because I want you to feel sorry for me. I'm sharing them because I want to tell you about a book that was very important to me, one that helped me overcome difficult times in my life. It is *Man's Search for Meaning*, by Viktor Frankl. It helped me in many ways, by telling me of people whose suffering was even greater than my own. Frankl taught me that what matters is not what *we* want in life, but what life demands of *us*, that we must rise to meet whatever those demands are in whatever circumstances we find ourselves.

"I also learned that when bad times hit, we must adapt quickly. The prisoners in the Nazi concentration camps who were not able to make the mental and emotional adjustment to life in the camps died soon after arriving. As Frankl points out, only those who were able to scratch out their past lives and focus their full energies on the present situation were able to survive."

Neither spoke for a moment. Then Alan said softly, "Amelia, I'm sorry to hear that you had such an extraordinarily difficult life when you were young. Many people who suffer severely when so young have problems later in life, but you seem to have been born with, or somehow developed, the tough-mindedness needed to overcome the difficulties you faced. I admire that quality in you.

"You know, Amelia, Frankl's book also helped me, too, to overcome some difficult times, though nothing as horrendous as the conditions you faced. Maybe I will tell you about them some time. The lessons you mentioned are exactly the ones that I learned from his book. But tell me, how did you happen to obtain a copy of *Man's Search for Meaning*? That isn't a book that I would have expected to be in Vietnam at that time."

"Yes," she said, brightening up. "I later realized just how fortunate I was to stumble across what might have been the only copy in my home town, maybe in all of Vietnam. It was difficult for me to read English at that time, but as soon as I started reading the book I knew it was important for me to read all of it. But even now, Dr. Fernwood, you are the first person I have ever met who has heard of the book. Isn't that strange?"

"What it is, is sad. It's too bad that everybody hasn't read it and absorbed its lessons. Too many are too busy playing games on their so-called "smart" phones. But what is giving me goosebumps is the lengthening list of things that are important to me that I have never been able to share with anybody else. Now I can share them with you—and at the same time you are sharing them with me, because you were already aware of them and they were already important to you, too. First 'Renaissance,' then *Emma*, and now *Man's Search for Meaning*. And add to them the difficult times we both overcame, and it's almost like you are a female version of myself, or I am a male version of you."

"I am feeling the same thing," she said. "See the little bumps on my arm? Let's go get some ice cream to forget the unhappy times. No one ever feels sad while eating ice cream."

FRIDAY, JUNE 19

31

Ah, Friday, the one day I know I can work without outside appointments or interruptions, Alan said to himself. His goals were to organize his notes about why de Vere hid his authorship and to read *"Shakespeare" Identified*, the 1920 book in which J. Thomas Looney had first proposed de Vere's authorship.

That seems like an odd thing to do, Alan thought, as he mulled over why de Vere's authorship was hidden. Yes, literary history was full of examples of authors using pseudonyms, but in most cases many people knew who the real author was. It was no secret during Samuel Langhorne Clemens's lifetime, for instance, that he was the author known as Mark Twain. It would have been extraordinary for de Vere's authorship to have remained secret for more than 400 years.

Alan knew that practically all Oxfordians—those who believe that Edward de Vere, Earl of Oxford wrote Shakespeare's works—cite two reasons for de Vere's having hidden his authorship. One was his status as a nobleman. Courtiers in his day did not publish their literary works under their own names, though relatives sometimes published them with full attribution after their death. The other reason was that in the plays, de Vere had portrayed and ridiculed prominent persons in the court and government. Belief that a commoner had been the author would have cut the connection between the plays and the court, making it easier to deny any connection between characters in the plays and real people.

But those two reasons seemed insufficient to Alan to explain why de Vere's authorship had remained secret after his death, and how the effort to keep it hidden could have been successful. Glancing briefly through *"Shakespeare" Identified*, he saw that Loonoy related de Vere's decision to hide his authorship to expressions of shame and references to a "vulgar scandal" in the *Sonnets*, the only literary works Shakespeare had written in the first person. Looney had observed that "It is made as clear as anything can be that he [de Vere] . . . had elected his own self-effacement, and that disrepute was one, if not the principal, motive. We may, if we wish, question the sufficiency or reasonableness of the motive. That, however, is his business, not ours." And again, "When, therefore, he [de Vere] tells us, in so many words, that 'vulgar scandal' had robbed him of his good name, and that although he believed his work would be immortal he wished his name to be forgotten, we are quite entitled to take his own word for it, and to demand no further motive for the adoption of a disguise." Looney's highlighting of the motives of "shame" and "vulgar scandal" raised questions of their own, though. What developments had led de Vere to the feelings of shame? What vulgar scandal had he been involved in? Looney hadn't provided direct answers.

Looney also hadn't discussed the issue of how de Vere's authorship could have been kept hidden during and after his lifetime. That would have required the cooperation of a sizable number of people; what motive would they have had, especially after de Vere and the people portrayed in the plays had all died? Charlton Ogburn, Jr., Alan recalled, had concluded that the extraordinary effort required to hide Oxford's authorship was "highly implausible" and that "its implausibility is what has chiefly blocked a more general acceptance of 'Shakespeare' as having been a pseudonym."

After lunch, Alan picked up *"Shakespeare" Identified*. He'd been looking forward to reading it ever since seeing John Galsworthy's description of it as "the best detective story I have ever read." He also knew that Sigmund Freud had written to Looney about his "remarkable book," "confessing myself to be a follower of yours." Although Alan didn't know quite what to expect from it, novelist Gelett Burgess's comment—"Once having read this book, I doubt if anyone, friend or foe, will ever forget it"—led him to expect it to be an experience he would long remember. That was the case. He began reading it in the early afternoon and didn't stop until he fell asleep late that night, too tired to continue. Not even Ogburn's book had been as enthralling.

32

Elvin picked up the article about the letter signed by 37,000 scientists challenging the idea that human activities were warming the planet. This was such an anomaly that he didn't quite know how to respond to it or write about it in his first "The Contrarian" column. Surely the signatories weren't serious. But they appeared to be. Maybe they weren't real scientists. But no, they all had university degrees in science, and more than 9,000 had Ph.D's.

He read the text of their letter again.

> WE URGE THE UNITED STATES GOVERNMENT TO REJECT THE GLOBAL WARMING AGREEMENT THAT WAS WRITTEN IN KYOTO, JAPAN IN DECEMBER, 1997, AND ANY OTHER SIMILAR PROPOSALS. THE PROPOSED LIMITS ON GREENHOUSE GASES WOULD HARM THE ENVIRONMENT, HINDER THE ADVANCE OF SCIENCE AND TECHNOLOGY, AND DAMAGE THE HEALTH AND WELFARE OF MANKIND.
>
> THERE IS NO CONVINCING SCIENTIFIC EVIDENCE THAT HUMAN RELEASE OF CARBON DIOXIDE, METHANE, OR OTHER GREENHOUSE GASES IS CAUSING OR WILL, IN THE FORESEEABLE FUTURE, CAUSE CATASTROPHIC HEATING OF THE EARTH'S ATMOSPHERE AND DISRUPTION OF THE EARTH'S CLIMATE. MOREOVER, THERE IS SUBSTANTIAL SCIENTIFIC EVIDENCE THAT INCREASES IN ATMOSPHERIC CARBON DIOXIDE PRODUCE MANY BENEFICIAL EFFECTS UPON THE NATURAL PLANT AND ANIMAL ENVIRONMENTS OF THE EARTH.

Elvin had repeatedly read that "the science is settled," and that only a few skeptics still doubted the existence of human-caused warming of the planet. But these 37,000 scientists were more than a few and they weren't merely skeptical. They were, the article explained, "convinced that the human-caused global warming hypothesis is without scientific validity and that government action on the basis of this hypothesis would unnecessarily and counterproductively damage both human prosperity and the natural environment of the Earth."

Perhaps they know things I don't know, Elvin said to himself. He was beginning to realize just how little he knew beyond the basic idea that rising concentrations of carbon dioxide would warm the atmosphere enough to melt glaciers, thus raising the level of the seas. He suddenly saw that as a science writer he'd been seriously delinquent in not investigating the issue for himself. I have quite a task to bring myself up to speed on it in time to write the first "Contrarian" column, he thought, as he turned to the books his editor had given him.

SATURDAY, JUNE 20

33

Alan continued reading Looney's book, *"Shakespeare" Identified*, immediately after waking up on Saturday morning, unable to put it down until he finally finished it in the late afternoon. Now, Saturday evening, he was glad that Diana was away so that he could organize his thoughts about the book while they were still fresh in his mind.

One point was the way Looney had systematically eliminated the man from Stratford from consideration as the author by continually whittling down the period of time in which he could be placed in London. At one end, there was no record of any literary activity by Shakspere (assuming he was Shakespeare) from the time of his birth until 1593; and at the other end of his life, all but one of the existing records place him in Stratford from 1604 onwards. It seemed impossible, Looney had reasoned, that even a genius of the highest order could have written thirty-seven of the greatest works in English drama in the impossibly short period of eleven years. Looney later reduced Shakspere's actual time in London to a mere five years.

Looney had found it impossible to conceive that a young man from a small, isolated provincial town—where a dialect of English not understandable in London was spoken and where most people were illiterate—could have "produced at the age of twenty-nine a lengthy and elaborate poem in the most polished English of the period, evincing a large and accurate knowledge of the classics, and later the superb Shakespearean dramas." If he had done so, Looney had stated, "he accomplished one of the greatest if not actually the greatest work of self-development and self-realization that genius has ever enabled any man to perform. On the other hand, if, after having performed so miraculous a work, this same genius retired to Stratford to devote himself to houses, lands, orchards, money and malt, leaving no traces of a single intellectual or literary interest, he achieved without a doubt the greatest work of self-stultification in the annals of mankind."

The latter point had made Shakspere's authorship impossible for Looney. "It is *difficult* to believe that with such a beginning he could have attained to such heights as he is supposed to have done; it is *more difficult* to believe that with such glorious achievements in his middle period he could have fallen to the level of his closing period; and in time it will be fully recognized that it is *impossible* to believe that the same man could have accomplished two such stupendous and mutually nullifying feats. Briefly, the first and last periods at Stratford are too much in harmony with one another, and too antagonistic to the supposed middle period for all three to be creditable. The situation represented by the whole stands altogether outside general human experience. The perfect unity of the two extremes justifies the conclusion that the middle period is an illusion; in other words William Shakspere did not write the plays attributed to him."

It's hard to disagree with Looney's conclusion, Alan thought. He then turned to another striking aspect of *"Shakespeare" Identified*: the unique method by which Looney had approached the authorship issue. From his familiarity with Shakespeare's works acquired through decades of teaching them, Looney had developed a list of nine general and nine specific characteristics that he believed the author must have had. He then tried to find people from that era who possessed those characteristics. To his surprise, he'd found only a few persons who possessed even a handful of them. The only person with more—someone who had all eighteen—was Edward de Vere, 17th Earl of Oxford, a poet and dramatist Looney had never heard of before beginning his search.

Alan noted another interesting point Looney had made: "The exceptional character of [Shakespeare's] work ought, under normal conditions, to facilitate the enquiry. . . . The more distinctive the work the more limited becomes the number of men capable of performing it, and the easier ought it, therefore, to be to discover its author. In this case, however, the work is of so unusual a character that every competent judge would say that the man who actually did it was the only man living at the time who was capable of doing it."

That makes sense to me, Alan thought, and it explains why Looney found only one possible candidate for authorship. He was impressed that Looney, after identifying de Vere as Shakespeare, had also uncovered most of the main lines of information about de Vere's life and literary activities that are still being investigated today.

Alan saw no need to write down the scores of correspondences between events in de Vere life and the situations and characters depicted in the Shakespeare plays. But he did take note of one incredible connection. In two plays—*Measure for Measure* and *All's Well That Ends Well*—the same unusual event happens: a male character sleeps with a female character thinking she is someone other than who she really is. Looney uncovered a record indicating that the same thing was said to have happened to Edward de Vere—that he'd slept with his wife while under the impression that he was with someone else. Alan shook his head—so unlikely a correspondence couldn't be a mere coincidence.

Alan knew he would need another reading or two of the book to absorb its wealth of information and ideas. In any case, it was getting late. His brain was tired after two days of continuous reading and thinking. It was time for bed.

But there was one more point to grasp now: Looney's conclusion that the plays as we know them today had been written in two phases, first as dramas to be performed, and second as literature to be read. In Looney's words, "the Shakespearean dramas, as we have them now, are not to be regarded as plays written specially to meet the demands of a company of actors. They are stage plays that have been converted into literature. This we hold to be their distinctive character, demanding in their author two distinct phases of activity, if not two completely separate periods of life for their production."

Alan's last task of the day was to record the periods in de Vere's life that Looney had identified during which those two phases of activity had taken place. The first had produced the works for which de Vere was known during his lifetime; the second produced the works now known as Shakespeare's.

34

Delilah reached out from under the covers and touched the table next to her bed, relieved to feel what she expected to feel even though the room was still spinning.

The evening had started out well, but then taken a dangerous turn. She'd come through it okay, though she'd probably feel sick in the morning.

With Elvin out of town, she'd agreed to meet five single colleagues from work for dinner. Meeting them had seemed like such a simple thing to do. It would not only be enjoyable in itself, but would also further her goal of joining the working world. Moving into her own apartment a year ago had been the first step. Her internship this summer was the second, giving her real world experience outside the classroom.

Now, with this dinner, she was establishing herself socially with people older than herself who were already working at professional jobs. In taking the internship, she'd looked forward to the chance to meet men—real men, older men—not like the boys at her university. She'd been happy to note that one man at her company, Dick Roue, had shown a special interest in her.

At the same time, she'd felt a bit uneasy about the dinner while driving to it. She had a warm feeling for Elvin and thought he did for her, too, and she didn't want anything to upset that. She was also uneasy because she'd be the youngest person at the dinner and the only one not a permanent employee.

Once she got to the restaurant and found her colleagues' table, Delilah saw one empty chair, conveniently next to Dick's. He must have saved it for her. This would be the first time for them to have an in-depth conversation together. The conversation—among all six of them—bounced from work-related issues to movies and sports—and she was initially a full participant in it. But they also discussed local, national and international issues she didn't know much about, and she began to feel that she was in over her head.

Things then began to go south. Dick had continued to order drinks for both of them. Even after she'd told him "No more!" he just smiled and ordered another glass of wine for her. Things got worse when the other two couples suddenly left, leaving her and Dick alone together at the table. She was becoming more uncomfortable with him every minute—not just because he was pushing drinks on her that she didn't want, but also because he seemed more interested in her body than in anything she had to say. Spending the night with a drunken colleague wasn't something she wanted to do, but she didn't know how to leave politely.

She wished Elvin had been in town. If so, she'd probably be with him right now. She felt comfortable with him, and would, in fact, probably have drunk every glass of wine, confident that she was with someone would get her home safely.

Then she'd seen a way out when Dick went to the rest-room. It was now or never. Grabbing her opportunity, she scribbled a note on a napkin telling Dick she wasn't feeling well and had gone home. She walked quickly to her car, figuring that she could get home before the worst effects of the alcohol hit her.

Somehow she made it. She again felt the solidity of the table, and peeking out from under the blanket saw her alarm clock right where it should be. If I dream tonight, she thought to herself, I'm sure it will be of Elvin and the comfort of having his arms around me.

SUNDAY, JUNE 21

35

Alan awoke refreshed even though he'd been exhausted by the twenty hours spent reading *"Shakespeare" Identified* throughout the previous two days. What an exciting book. Galsworthy, Freud and

Burgess had been right in their praise of it. Today's task was to investigate more about the book's influence on others.

He first picked up an article by Esther Singleton, the Shakespeare scholar and author of several dozen books on various subjects who died in 1930. Singleton's article was perhaps the most compelling testimony to Looney's persuasiveness he'd read yet. She hadn't only stated unequivocally, "I now pronounce myself a believer in the theory that Edward de Vere, Earl of Oxford, was the author of the great Shakespearean plays," but also attributed her belief directly to Looney's book.

What was most remarkable about Singleton's article, Alan felt, was her description of the wrenching process that brought about her new belief, one that mirrored his own experience. She'd begun by describing her deep aversion even to considering the question of whether anyone other than Shakspere was the author. She then described the transformation, painful and almost against her will, she had gone through while reading Looney's book. But, she'd concluded, the process was worth the pain; she described her elation at finding that obscure passages in the plays, reread with knowledge of de Vere's authorship and of the details of his life, had become "so clear, so plain, so reasonable, and so delightful."

Well aware of the fury often directed toward doubters, Alan wasn't surprised that Singleton had begun her article by imploring her readers not to reject out of hand her change of mind: "You who read this, I beg you not to condemn me and the theory but to read further on." He understood why she'd withheld publication of the article during her lifetime, and wondered, if he came to conclude beyond a reasonable doubt that de Vere had written Shakespeare's works, whether he would keep quiet as Singleton had.

Examining the reaction of Stratfordians to Looney's book was easier said than done. No matter where he looked, Alan couldn't find any direct response to Looney's arguments and evidence by those who disagreed with his conclusion. He then saw that Warren Hope and Kim Holston had discovered an explanation for the pervasive silence. "The best trained and most highly respected professional students of Shakespeare in the colleges and universities of England and America contemplated the seemingly endless argument presented in *'Shakespeare' Identified* and quickly discovered a flaw in it. The book was written by a man with a funny name."

Of course, Alan reasoned, it was easier to ridicule the author's name than to address arguments so forceful as to be almost irrefutable. That should be a crime, an intellectual crime, he thought. Stratfordians surely should not be allowed to avoid addressing a book of this importance. But then he remembered that until recently he himself, a professional in the field of Shakespeare studies, had done just that.

MONDAY, JUNE 22

36

"Good morning, everyone," Alan said.

"Good morning, Professor Fernwood," Dave, Doug, Pat, Nancy, Lisa and Amelia responded, all in loud voices and in unison. They had clearly arranged their greeting in advance, and they laughed when Alan looked startled. Then he laughed, too.

"Today we'll focus on the political nature of Shakespeare's plays," he said, still smiling. "I grew up, so to speak, with the notion that Shakespeare wrote his plays in Merrie Olde Englande." He wrote the three words on a white board so that the students could see the antiquated spelling.

"I had thought the plays were predominantly comedies and love stories, with a few tragedies and histories thrown in for good measure."

"But isn't that the case?" Lisa asked, doing a quick count. "There are thirteen comedies, ten histories, ten tragedies, and five romances. If the romances are counted as comedies, then there are almost as many comedies as histories and tragedies combined."

"Those designations don't always make sense," Alan responded. "The problem with Shakespeare's plays, at least from more traditional points of view, is that he combines elements of tragedy and comedy in a single work. And some of the histories could easily have been included in the tragedies column.

"I'd like us to focus today on just how thoroughly so many of the plays—however categorized—are infused with political developments. I have only recently begun to realize that Shakespeare doesn't portray political issues at random, but instead focuses on those of concern during Queen Elizabeth's reign."

"That's very interesting," Pat said. "I can see, of course, that *Julius Caesar* is infused with politics. It is by its very nature a political play. But what about a comedy such as *Twelfth Night*? It's not on our reading list, but it's a play I have always liked. It's a pure comedy, all about courting and romance, isn't it?"

"Let me ask you this, Pat," Alan responded. "Who was the most important person during the Elizabethan era, during the time that Shakespeare was a boy and an impressionable young and not-so-young man?"

"That could only be Queen Elizabeth," Pat observed, smiling. "After all, the era was named after her."

"That's right," Alan said. "And who is the most important woman in *Twelfth Night*?"

"Olivia. She is the woman that several men are courting."

"She has inherited an estate after the death of her brother, hasn't she?" Alan asked.

"Oh, I see where you are going," Nancy said, jumping in. "Olivia was a stand-in for Queen Elizabeth. From the supplementary readings I know there was pressure on her to get married from the time she was crowned. After all, monarchs were usually men."

"Like Pat," Doug said, "I always thought of *Twelfth Night* as a comedy and never considered whether it had any political aspects to it. But now I see that Olivia, like Elizabeth, was under pressure to marry. So there are ways in which Shakespeare portrayed in his comedies the same political issues that existed during his lifetime."

"The issue of Elizabeth's marriage and later her succession," Alan explained, "were matters on which she, throughout her reign, would not tolerate interference by others. She believed that as monarch—as the only person in the realm responsible to God for the kingdom as a whole—decisions on these matters belonged to her and her alone."

"Well, she had a good point," Dave said. "If you accept the idea that monarchs were divinely anointed, then she was indeed the only person with that responsibility, just as the president is the only person in the United States responsible for the country as a whole. Though of course he—or she!—is elected by the people, not chosen by God."

"I recall from our assigned readings," Amelia commented, "that Elizabeth sought to restrict Parliament's role in her marriage. When it tried to pressure her to resolve the marriage issue by linking it to the annual subsidy to the crown and refused to consider other business until the issue had been resolved, she angrily banned all discussion of the issue. The impasse was resolved only when Elizabeth withdrew her ban on discussions and Parliament simultaneously decided not to discuss it."

"That was a clever way out," Doug observed. "I'm sure it required much behind-the-scenes wrangling to arrive at. I think I read that Elizabeth also sought to ban or limit *public* discussion of her marriage or succession."

"She did, yeah," Alan said. "In 1579, John Stubbs had his right hand chopped off for daring to address the issue of the queen's marriage in his pamphlet *The Discovery of a Gaping Gulf.* The queen herself decided on Stubbs's sentence and pushed it through the court system in violation of usual procedures, much to the consternation of her advisers."

"Wow. That was brutal," Pat declared. "That doesn't sound at all like the image of Dear Queen Bess that we have heard so much about."

Nancy agreed. "This gives us a whole new picture of what she was really like. But Elizabeth had to be tough. I'm sure it was difficult to be queen in a country where monarchs were usually men."

"That's right," Alan said. "Whether a woman could even hold the crown was at one time a hotly debated issue in England. Shakespeare depicts a discussion of that question near the beginning of *Henry V,* one of the plays assigned for this session."

"I have that passage here," Dave said, glancing up from the text. "They are discussing the issue of whether it's legal for a woman to succeed to the throne. One of the courtiers cites the Salic law, which says that 'No woman shall succeed in Salic land.' That land is in Germany, however, and they are discussing whether that law applies in France. In the end, they conclude it is not a bar, and that a woman can become queen."

"Even so, Elizabeth was in a difficult spot when crowned," Lisa noted. "She faced not only the difficulties of being a woman in a man's world, but also those from being a Protestant queen of a country that was still majority Catholic. In fact, I read that several Popes issued bulls authorizing the English to rise up and depose her because she was a Protestant."

"From her first moments on the throne," Alan said. "Elizabeth needed to move quickly to increase public support for the legitimacy of her reign and the authority of the Church of England. Who recalls what steps she took to do that?"

"Well, she couldn't simply appeal to the people directly on TV, as the President might," Pat commented. "But from our readings I know that she had two means of reaching large audiences: the pulpit and the public theater. She had certain homilies, or sermons, read from every pulpit every Sunday. Those weren't purely religious texts. They were also, as Alfred Hart puts in in our readings, 'a series of simple lessons on the fundamental principles of Tudor politics.'"

"This is where it starts to get exciting," Amelia said. "Hart shows us that Shakespeare outdoes every dramatist of his time in the number and variety of the allusions made to those issues. References are scattered through at least twenty plays, including the comedies as well as the histories and tragedies."

"Here is the key passage in Hart's book," Lisa said as she pointed to it. "'What is peculiar to Shakespeare is that he treats the politico-theological doctrines of divine right, non-resistance, passive obedience and the sin of rebellion, as the accepted and immutable law of almost every land in every age. He has adroitly woven into the fabric of his plays so many and varied references, direct and indirect, to these doctrines, that we may extract from them an excellent digest of the main articles of the . . . political creed of the Tudors concerning the constitution of the body politic in general and the relation of ruler to subject in particular.'"

"Was Shakespeare a mere propagandist for the government?" Dave asked. "This is a very different image of him and his plays than I ever had before."

"Yes, we have seen unexpected sides of both Elizabeth and Shakespeare," Amelia agreed.

"It's not quite Merrie Olde England, is it?" Alan asked. "Let's take our short break here."

37

After the class had regrouped, Alan noted that the political issues Shakespeare addressed in his plays changed as the issues important in Elizabeth's government and court changed. "Who recalls what the dominant issue was in the 1580s?" he asked.

"Well, it had to have been war with Spain," Nancy responded. "1588 was the year of the Spanish Armada that we learned so much about in primary school. Our readings showed that England's fear as the 1580s progressed was that if Spain, which was Catholic, succeeded in extinguishing the independence of the Protestant Dutch and Flemish communities, it would then be free to use its power in a religious crusade against England. In the middle of 1585, Elizabeth concluded that she had no choice but to support the Low Countries, and sent English military forces there to help defend them. The Anglo-Spanish War that resulted didn't finally end until nineteen years later, in 1604, the year after Elizabeth's death, when King James signed a peace treaty with Spain."

"That's right," Doug said. "Several issues related to that war were addressed in Shakespeare's plays, especially *Henry V*. One issue was whether England had the right to go to war to ward off a future danger. Was it legally permissible to fight a preventive war? Our own country faced similar issues not so long ago." Alan nodded, encouraging Doug to continue with that line of thought.

"In that play, Henry faced the question of whether to go to war with France. He consults with the Archbishop of Canterbury, who blesses England's entry into the war, thus giving everyone who saw the play the assurance that Elizabeth had the legal right and moral duty to enter a war to protect the Low Countries as a means of defending England itself."

Dave then pointed out another issue discussed in the same play, that of a citizen's duty during wartime. Was it okay for a soldier to kill, an act that would be a crime and a sin during peacetime? "The answers presented to theatergoers in Shakespeare's play and hence to the nation as a whole, are that the king and the soldier are both responsible to God, but for different things. The king has the duty of ensuring that the war is fought for legitimate reasons. The soldier has the duty of obeying his king. Things that would be crimes in ordinary life aren't crimes if the soldier is obeying the king. But if the war is illegitimate, then all the actions of the soldiers become crimes on the head of the king."

"Here's the key phrase, the one that sums up all the discussions on that issue that had just taken place," Lisa said. "'Every subject's duty is the King's, but every subject's soul is his own.'"

"There is yet another important issue from Elizabethan life reflected in *Henry V*," Pat said. "The war with Spain was so important for England that it *had* to be won. And it could be won if all parts of the British Isles cooperated with each other. So what do we see in *Henry V*? We see characters from every part of the British Isles—the Welsh Fluellen, Irish Captain Macmorris, Scottish Captain Jamy, and English Gower—cooperating with each other. Shakespeare is demonstrating the idea of Britain as a union of people united in resisting the Spanish menace."

"I'm afraid time is just about up," Alan observed. "Today we have seen that the political issues Shakespeare addressed in his plays changed as the issues in Elizabeth's court and government changed. He began by emphasizing themes supporting Elizabeth's reign—those of the divine right of kings and the necessity of obedience and loyalty. Then, as the war with Spain heated up, his plays encouraged pride in the nation and support for the war.

"*Henry V* is so effective in stirring patriotism among the British people that it was staged and filmed by Sir Laurence Olivier during the darkest days of World War II. And the momentous speeches in it are stirring even for people outside the British Commonwealth."

As the students were leaving, Alan overheard Doug ask the others if John Stubbs had been given the sentence of having his right hand chopped off because of his last name. "I mean," he said, "was Queen

Elizabeth influenced by his name, Stubbs? What would his sentence have been if his last name had been Blind, or Lame, or Deaf?"

38

"Professor Fernwood, tell me about some of the difficult times you faced in your life," Amelia urged him when they were seated at their usual table.

"Oh, well, Amelia, you don't want to hear about them. I actually don't like talking about that stuff."

"Just give me the short version, then. I want to know why Frankl's book was so important to you."

Alan thought for a minute. "Okay. I will tell you about one of the difficult times I faced. I was in a relationship with a woman who was manic depressive. That's an unbalanced mental condition that today is referred to by the more pleasant sounding name of bipolar."

"Oh, I have heard of that. I have never known anyone with that condition, but I know it's terrible for everyone around someone with it."

"It's worse than anything you could ever imagine. The least little thing would set her off. Once a new episode was launched there was nothing I could do to alter its course. She would become silent for three days, not saying a single word. But during the last day or so I could see the tension building in her, until at last it erupted in an explosion, with screaming and throwing things. It would go on for maybe twenty minutes. Then she would be back to normal, and would forbid any discussion of what had happened, insisting that it was in the past."

Amelia listened in silence.

"Usually she was able to delay those outbursts until we were at home. But once one of them occurred at a department store. While the sales clerks looked on, horrified, she screamed and raged like a wild animal. I didn't know what to do. I never knew what to do.

"Even when she was 'normal,' I had to walk around on tiptoes, never knowing what I might inadvertently do that would set off another round. She was also an alcoholic, but that was a separate problem, though the two conditions might have had the same causes. I learned later that a series of very unfortunate things happened to her in her childhood that had twisted her personality. She was not a normal person and it is to my deep regret that I ever met her."

"Why didn't you just leave?" Amelia asked.

Alan paused before responding. "That is the worst part. She was suicidal. She always threatened to kill herself if I left her. She tried to several times. The first time with pills. I had to call 911. They took her to the hospital, pumped her stomach and saved her life. The doctors wouldn't release her until she had a psychiatric examination and agreed to lengthy counseling. But none of that helped. She tried to kill herself twice more before I finally managed to pull myself away. By the end of the year and a half I knew her, I was ready to do anything, even kill myself, to get away from her."

"It's okay, Alan," she said, putting her hand on his arm. "It was a long time ago. It's over now."

"Yes, it is, thank God. You know, Amelia, I have never told anyone about that experience before. I tried to tell my wife, but she really couldn't understand the horror of the situation."

"That was my experience, too. One of the reasons I had to leave my ex-husband is that he was never able to understand what I was saying when I told him about the difficulties of my childhood. Not just the things I have already told you about, but other things I don't want to talk about now. And he had no interest in literature and science and other intellectual subjects that I was so interested in. He thought only about his insurance business. I can't think of a more boring subject."

They looked at each other for a minute. Then Alan smiled and stood up. "Come on, Amelia, we've had enough of difficult times from the past. Last time you took me for ice cream. Now let me take you. As you said, 'No one ever feels sad while eating ice cream.'"

39

Can I do this? Elvin asked himself. Can I really write a regular column on the most controversial scientific subjects of the day?

He was beginning to realize that there was much more to writing a column than there was to generating the off-the-top-of-the-head comments he had posted on his blog or to writing articles about newly released scientific reports. Recognizing that his knowledge of the global warming issue was rather sketchy, he'd spent the entire weekend investigating it and organizing his thoughts and notes. Now, he needed only to review them and the purpose of "The Contrarian" before beginning to draft the first column.

He'd been shocked by what he'd found. At first grudgingly, and then with increasing ease, he began to see that the 37,000 scientists who doubted human-caused warming or harm from it had rather solid reasons for doing so. How could it be, he wondered, that a science writer like himself had never before heard of their letter or their concerns? The mere existence of the letter with so many signatories had showed him the falsity of the oft-repeated statement that only a few skeptics doubted the idea of human-caused global warming.

He also saw that the letter was aimed directly at the findings of the Intergovernmental Panel on Climate Change (IPCC), sponsored by the United Nations World Meteorological Organization. Turning to the original IPCC report, Elvin noticed that its findings didn't appear to be as conclusive as the media portrayed them. Or rather, he noted, there was a conflict between the conclusions of the scientists in the body of the report and the summary prepared by politicians. The scientists had expressed considerable qualifications about their findings. The policymakers' short summary, however, was more directly alarmist, and that was what the media quoted.

According to some reports, the IPCC had systematically downplayed, removed or ignored views of scientists who hadn't supported the conclusion of human-caused warming and the harm it caused. In addition, he found, many of the panel members weren't even scientists, but political appointees. Some of the real scientists on the panel disputed its conclusions, but their comments were deleted from the report. Some even asked to have their names removed from the report, but their requests were denied.

To Elvin, it now appeared that the IPCC's reports were political statements, not scientific reports. The organization clearly wanted documents showing overwhelming scientific support for the "fact" of impending drastic harm to the planet caused by human activities, and that's what it got. Because the original IPCC report had been issued in 1990 and the scientists' letter in 1998, Elvin turned to the latest IPCC report to get the most recent findings. That volume, *Climate Change 2013: The Physical Science Basis*, with 1,500 pages of documentation for the pro-global warming view, was so massive that he needed both hands to lift it. It's very official looking, he observed, with hundreds of colored charts and graphs.

Elvin found that criticism of the latest report was almost as strong as it had been for previous reports. Willie Soon, for instance, noted that "Contrary to reports of a 97 per cent consensus," it demonstrated that "the overwhelming majority of scientists in climate and related fields . . . remain commendably open to the possibility that some other influence—such as the sun—may be the true *primum mobile* of the Earth's climate."

"The Contrarian," Elvin knew, would not be blindly contrarian, but would zero in on weak points in logic, gaps in evidence and other flaws in widely held beliefs in a catchy and interesting way. The goal was to draw readers into the subject, to get them thinking, to cure them of blindly accepting what they read. And, of course, to sell more newspapers.

With those thoughts in mind, Elvin began to write his column. In two hours of hard work, he produced a first draft of the first column that he thought was pretty good. He would let it sit overnight, then revise it tomorrow morning before submitting it to Ed.

37,000 Scientists Can't Be Wrong!

What could be more natural than dividing the world into two camps: the Allies and the Nazis, the FBI and the Mob, Earthlings and Aliens—in short, the Good Guys and the Bad Guys.

And which side is the good side? Why, it's the side that everybody else around you is on, right? That's why it's so helpful to learn that 37,000 scientists have signed a petition about global warming. Clearly, with a number that large, these are the good guys and gals.

Listening to them, one would have to conclude that the science is settled. All 37,000 have degrees in science, and nine thousand have Ph.D.s. Their petition talks of "the human release of carbon dioxide, methane, or other greenhouse gases," and of "the catastrophic heating of the Earth's atmosphere and disruption of the Earth's climate."

But guess what, campers? These scientists *reject* the idea that human release of greenhouse gases is causing, or will in the foreseeable future cause, catastrophic heating of the Earth's atmosphere. Moreover, they believe, "there is substantial scientific evidence that increases in atmospheric carbon dioxide produce many beneficial effects upon the natural plant and animal environments of the Earth."

How do you like that, folks?

And yet, can we have any more confidence in the conclusions of the 37,000 letter signers than in the other media reports we read? They are, after all, a minority of all scientists in the world. And their conclusions are contrary to those of so many prominent political leaders and celebrities that we hear so much about.

Still, might it be possible that scientists know a bit more about science than politicians and celebrities? Sure, scientists might be mistaken in their conclusions, but aren't they more likely to be right on scientific matters than politicians seeking to persuade us to accept beliefs supportive of their political goals?

We mustn't forget that scientific theories aren't popularity contests. The theory that most accurately describes physical or chemical or biological realities is not necessarily the one that has the most adherents. At one extreme, as Mahatma Gandhi noted, "Even if you are a minority of one, the truth is still the truth." Albert Einstein expressed a similar sentiment in response to seeing *One Hundred Authors Against Einstein*, a book that disputed his new theory of relativity. "Why 100 authors?" he asked. "If I were wrong, then one would have been enough."

It is useful to note Samuel Johnson's distinction between "argument," which aims to discover truth and hence supports the idea of unbiased assessment of scientific data, and "testimony," which aims to convince others of a certain point of view or conclusion.

"Nay, Sir," Johnson is reported to have said, "Argument is argument. You cannot help paying regard to their arguments, if they are good. If it were testimony, you might disregard it. . . . Testimony is like an arrow shot from a long bow; the force of it depends on the strength of the hand that draws it. Argument is like an arrow shot from a crossbow, which has equal force though shot by a child."

Perhaps the way forward is to distinguish between those who present argument—those whose aim is to educate us by presenting data in an unbiased manner—and those who present only testimony—those who aim to push us toward acceptance of their point of view. We could call these two groups "professors" and "politicians." Professors include scholars, scientists, and artists—anyone whose aim is the discovery and presentation of truth. Politicians include actual politicians, but also marketers, advertisers and others who seek to influence what we believe, think or purchase, or how we vote.

The Intergovernmental Panel on Climate Change (IPCC) falls on the political side of the divide. Its reports are political documents written by a political body that describes its role as "to assess the scientific basis of risk of human-induced climate change, its potential impacts and options for adaptation and mitigation." It is under orders from its governmental sponsors to "use all best endeavors to reach consensus." It's not surprising, is it, that a political body seeks justification for beliefs already held by its political sponsors?

If it's right to suspect the conclusions of climate research sponsored by those with a *financial* interest in it—i.e., the oil industry—it's equally right to suspect the conclusions of research sponsored by those with a *political* interest in it. Both sets of reports must be examined carefully.

Progress isn't made by consensus, by those who merely reaffirm what everybody already believes. It's made by those who challenge consensus. Skepticism is the linchpin underlying progress, and the scientists challenging the IPCC's "consensus" are nothing if not skeptical of its claims.

It is with these thoughts in mind that this new column, "The Contrarian," will, in the coming weeks and months, examine the science—the theories, the data, the conclusions reached—in various issues of wide public concern in the scientific, environmental and health fields. We'll focus on the issues themselves, not on the high profile folks who comment on them or on the emotionally-laden images of impending doom in the media that make it so difficult to think clearly.

We'll keep the focus on the validity of scientific findings, because it's not personal testimony, nor sincerity, nor feelings, but facts, sober judgment and substantive conclusions that are the way to truth. "The Contrarian" aims at objectivity not in the sense of having no views, but in having a willingness to consider different hypotheses and to be guided by the evidence in judging them.

We hope you'll stay with us as we move down this path in the coming weeks and months.

TUESDAY, JUNE 23

40

As Alan waked toward the campus, he considered the idea of organizing a conference at which literary scholars could examine the Shakespeare Authorship Question. He would go to see Matt Harris right now to propose the idea to him. Having organized three successful large conferences for the university in the past ten years, he was certain that he would have Matt's support.

"Matt," Alan began, "you know that I'm now a Shakespeare specialist. And you might recall how, when we were literature students, we laughed at the loonies who pushed the idea that Shakespeare's works were written by somebody else. Well, for the first time in my life I'm examining that idea seriously. What I'm finding to my great shock, Matt, is that the evidence in support of that idea is varied and persuasive."

"Uh-oh," Matt said, cautiously. "I don't think I like where this is heading."

"Matt, I propose that the Department of Literature hold a conference to examine the authorship issue. It could be titled something like *William Shakespeare: Did He or Didn't He?* The three literature conferences I've organized on behalf of the Department were big successes. This one could be even bigger. I'm thinking that February would be a good month to hold it. What do you think?"

Before Matt could respond, Alan quickly added, "And while I'm thinking about it, perhaps we should also offer a course on the authorship question during the spring term."

"Well," Matt said, in a noncommittal manner, "submit the necessary paperwork for both ideas, and the Department's Curriculum and Special Events Committees will consider them."

"Thanks, Matt. I knew I could count on your support." Alan left the office so quickly that he didn't notice that Matt's expression was anything but supportive.

THURSDAY, JUNE 25

41

"Good morning, everyone," Alan said, beginning the next class meeting.

"Last time we saw that Shakespeare's plays portrayed kings, courtiers and governments—in whatever the settings were purported to be—absorbed in political activities and issues important during Queen Elizabeth's reign. Today we'll examine how the plays portrayed the sensitive political issue that dominated all others during the last decade of Elizabeth's life—since she turned sixty years old in 1593—succession. We have already seen that Elizabeth banned public discussion of her succession—"

"But Shakespeare addressed the issue in his plays," Amelia interrupted. "They were performed in public, weren't they?" She then answered her own question. "Yes, they were. Of course, his settings aren't the English court, except in the history plays, but even there the settings are previous reigns, not Elizabeth's. Maybe that is how he got around the strictures against public discussion of the subject."

"That's right," Doug said. "So many plays focused on the issue of succession from one angle or another that Shakespeare seems to have been obsessed with it. His plays examine the questions of who is a legitimate ruler and the mechanics of how power can be transferred from one monarch to another."

"Let's organize the plays by how transfer of power takes place," Lisa proposed. "I can only think of one play in which the king dies a natural death, *Henry IV, Part 2*. In several others he is murdered, including *Julius Caesar*, *Macbeth* and *Richard III*. In others he steps down voluntarily, as in *King Lear* and *Richard II*. There is only one play in which an election, or something similar to a public vetting, takes place, *Coriolanus*, and that doesn't end too well."

"Lisa, I'm surprised you have read so many of the plays," Alan said.

"Well, I like things arranged in an orderly way," she responded, "and they can't be orderly unless I have complete knowledge of them. So I started reading the histories, even those not on our reading list. I'm finding that I'm understanding them much better now."

"You know," Nancy said, "it's almost as if Shakespeare was seeking to advise the queen and members of her court on the issue of succession, though in an indirect way. This is, perhaps, one of the most important ways that the plays depict the specific political issues important during her reign."

"That's an important observation, Nancy," Alan said. "And the turn to the issue of succession in the plays is more surprising than you might have imagined. Recent studies show that the plays that most directly addressed the issue date from the early 1590s onwards, exactly when the issue of Elizabeth's succession was heating up. Earlier plays, or versions of plays that had previously emphasized such themes as obedience to the crown or support for the war with Spain were revised from 1593 onwards to focus much more on the issue of succession. Daniel Wright has shown the extent to which this was done as an early play, *The Troublesome Reign of King John*, was revised to become *King John*, and Ramon Jiménez has shown similar changes as another early play, *True Chronicle of King Leir* became *King Lear*."

"Could we look at how power is transferred when a monarch hasn't been murdered or dies?" Pat asked. "I'm intrigued by how that process works. In *Henry IV, Part 2*, power is going to be transferred peacefully, as the old king dies and his son inherits the crown. But before that happens, we see the king as old and weary. He almost sounds like he wants to transfer power before he dies. 'Uneasy lies the head that wears a crown,' he says. He envies his poorer subjects, who can sleep, he imagines, while he lies awake burdened by affairs of state."

"King Lear, too, is eager to transfer the 'cares of state,' Pat continued, "and he does so, though he doesn't explicitly state why."

"Richard II also abdicates," Dave noted, "but it's almost forced. Bolingbroke doesn't initially intend to grab the crown. It's only when he sees Richard's weakness that he moves forward."

"Well, that's interesting," Amelia said. "It's similar to what we saw in *Julius Caesar*, that Caesar initially held back from being crowned. It was only when, as Cassius explains, Caesar saw that 'Romans are but sheep' that he would have moved forward."

"So," Dave continued, "It's not that Bolingbroke and others who wanted to become king were recklessly aggressive. They weren't. They were ambitious but cautious, continually testing the waters, seeking advantage where it existed. They knew that the road to becoming king was dangerous. One false move and they could be arrested for treason. It was kind of like playing blackjack. Get twenty-one and you'll likely win the hand. Get even one more point and you lose instantly. But what if your cards total only fourteen, or fifteen or sixteen? Do you stay or hit? The odds have to be calculated carefully."

"What I find most interesting," Pat said, jumping in, "is that one of the most important factors holding back Bolingbroke and others is their belief in the divine right of kings, their belief that kings had been appointed by God to enact His justice on Earth. Here's how Richard II stated that idea: 'Not all the water in the rough rude sea / Can wash the balm off from an anointed king. / The breath of worldly men cannot depose / The deputy elected by the Lord.'"

"That belief was widely held," Nancy pointed out. "It wasn't just a Tudor talking point, but also something that people in Elizabethan England actually believed to be true."

"We've noted quite a number of issues related to succession appearing in the plays," Alan commented as he stood up. "Let's take our short break here."

After the break, the class approached the political nature of Shakespeare's plays from a different perspective—from that of characters not directly involved in formal political activities.

"What we find in the plays," Alan said, introducing the subject, "is that politics has sunk deep into social interactions that aren't themselves directly political. Even characters who aren't involved in formal political activities get caught up in the effects of decisions made at the top of their societies. Private life in Shakespeare's plays is rarely entirely private because it almost inevitably takes place within social structures affected by politics."

"That was clearly the case with Romeo and Juliet," Nancy observed. "They are caught up in the political crossfire between the Montague and Capulet families."

"Politics infiltrates the comedies, too," Amelia noted, "with dynastic considerations affecting families' decisions about who their sons and daughters would marry."

"Yeah," Doug agreed, "that is one way that Shakespeare combines comedy with seriousness. Not with tragedy exactly, but there is a blending of emotional content that raises most of his comedies above the level of mere farces."

"What I think is interesting," Dave said, "is that in Shakespeare's plays the only people who have entirely private lives are those at the bottom of society. People in those classes sometimes aren't even given names. They are referred to only by their professions, such as carpenters, weavers, or cobblers. That was certainly the case with Bottom and the others preparing to perform at the wedding in *A Midsummer Night's Dream*."

"Some characters aren't even identified by their professions," Lisa noted. "They are given only labels such as Plebian 1 or Commoner 2. They are caught up in political developments, but only as stick figures manipulated by politicians. It's interesting that this happens almost exclusively in the Roman plays—especially *Julius Caesar* and *Coriolanus*."

"Although Shakespeare came from a poor rural background, he sure identified with the upper classes," Pat observed. "Why else would he have made those from lower classes either stick figures or figures of ridicule?"

"Oh, that makes sense," Doug said. "Shakespeare wrote about the upper classes so much because it was in that class that politics was practiced—and he was obsessed with politics. Those at the bottom of society weren't, so he didn't write about them."

"That's an interesting distinction," Alan commented, as he glanced at the clock. "It's also interesting to compare the political nature of Shakespeare's plays with those by American playwrights such as Tennessee Williams. In *The Glass Menagerie*, for instance, the characters are all private people who act in a totally private way, with no thought given to issues of state or to the political consequences of their actions. Nothing could be further from the concerns of most characters in Shakespeare's plays."

As the students were leaving, Alan overheard Doug commenting to the others on his new recognition that Shakespeare's plays were more about politics and war than love and romance. "It's not such a big change, is it? After all, 'all's fair in both love and war,' right? Moving from battles between the sexes to battles between men only doesn't seem like that big a change."

42

"Hi guys," Alan said as he joined Susan Pallis and Johan Meer, two of his colleagues, in one of the restaurants on campus. The three of them were all Associate Professors in the Department of Literature and had worked together for more than five years. "Or rather guy and gal. I'm never sure how to greet mixed groups of people anymore."

"Guys is fine," Susan replied. "These days, 'guys' is like 'actors.' It can mean either male or female. But it *is* hard to know what to say now. So many transgendered individuals insist on being referred to by gender pronouns such as 'xe' or 'hir' that I've never heard of before. In fact, New York City has now made it a crime punishable by fines up to $250,000 for failing to use the gender pronoun that the transgendered individual prefers," she noted with a bit of a laugh.

"Speaking of strange times, Alan," Johan said, "what's this proposal of yours for a conference on *Shakespeare: Did He or Didn't He?* Did he or didn't he what? It sounds like a hair care commercial."

"Well, did he or didn't he write the works attributed to him." Alan responded. "It's a question that needs to be addressed in an academic setting."

They were all quiet before Susan spoke. "You're not serious, are you? No, you can't be. You have spoken against the authorship issue for years."

"He appears to be serious, Susan," Johan observed. "What happened Alan? You're too young to be senile. Is this a midlife crisis of some kind?" They all laughed.

"It's like this," Alan began. "I decided to write a review of Charlton Ogburn's book *The Mysterious William Shakespeare* that would put the authorship question to rest permanently. But the more I read, the less convincing the reasons for authorship by William Shakspere—that was the real name of the man from Stratford, by the way, with a short *a*— began to seem. Have you heard of Ogburn?"

"I haven't," Susan said, which made sense to him as her specialty was American literature. "I have, but I haven't read the book," Johan said, which also made sense because Johan specialized in British literature from the mid 1700s to the present.

"Most recently," Alan continued, "I came across this book, *Shakespeare Beyond Doubt?* edited by John Shahan and Alexander Waugh on behalf of The Shakespeare Authorship Coalition. I have extra copies with me. Here, you can both have one."

Johan and Susan were a bit surprised by his offer. "Don't tell me you are now proselytizing on behalf of the authorship question!" Susan said in a somewhat shocked tone.

"Not exactly. I'm giving them to you as a form of self-defense. You are both on the Special Events Committee that will vote on whether to approve my request for the conference. I don't want you to think I have suddenly lost my marbles. The book provides solid reasons for doubting Shakspere's authorship. The conference I'm proposing will be a chance for Shakespearean scholars to consider the question."

"Okay," Johan replied, "as long as there are substantive reasons for doubt and the issue is dealt with in an academic manner, I'd probably be supportive. But let me take a look at this book before deciding."

"That's all I ask," Alan said. "Maybe we'll find that only his hair dresser knows for sure."

43

"Amelia, Amelia, Amelia," Alan said, shaking his head as he sat down in the chair across from her. "Don't you know that coffee will stunt your growth?"

"Uh, at my age," she replied, "when I am no longer growing taller but am instead growing wider, you should be happy about anything that stunts my growth." They both laughed.

"I brought you another book," he said. "Whenever I need to cheer myself up, I turn to P. G. Wodehouse. Here's one of my favorite books of his, *Right Ho, Jeeves.* After the serious conversations we've been having, I thought you might enjoy something lighter. Wodehouse once said that his books will never become dated because they were never about anything in the real world at all."

"Professor Fernwood, thank you. And you know what? I brought a book for you, too. It is actually a rather thoughtful book, to follow up on some of our previous conversations about how to overcome thoughts of difficult times. It's a novel, *Island,* by Aldous Huxley, with an interesting storyline. Part of it is about the way people on the island have found for dealing with painful memories. It helped me acquire peace of mind in spite of having experienced so many hard times in my life."

"Thanks, Amelia. I know that I will enjoy and learn much from any book that you recommend." They both looked at their new books.

"Amelia," Alan said after a minute, "at the risk of being too serious and of boring you, I want to return to two subjects that we touched on last time, in part because my experiences mirror your own."

"I am all ears," she said, putting down *Right Ho, Jeeves.*

"The first subject is what happened after I ended the relationship with the manic-depressive. I'd had such a miserable time that I swore I'd never become involved with any woman again. But of course that resolution didn't last long.

"Not too many months later I met a woman who had an uncomplicated emotional nature. What most attracted me was the strength of her primary emotions. You know how light consists of three primary colors, distinctly different from each other? Well, her make-up consisted of clearly defined primary emotions such as love, happiness, sadness, surprise, fear, and so on. There were no hidden complications. She felt and expressed them in a straightforward way, with no convoluted blendings. Because I was so drained from my previous relationship, a woman like that seemed like an angel. So I married her. Now, though, the match between my needs and her nature isn't so tight. I would be better suited by someone with a more sophisticated emotional sense. Someone who appreciates more nuanced and subtle differences in emotions and the expression of them would be more in line with my nature today."

Amelia nodded understandingly.

"The second subject picks up on a point you made last time, about how you were married to someone who had no interest in literature and science and other intellectual subjects that fascinated you. I now find myself in exactly that same situation. I own 8,000 books, but I'm married to someone who has never read a book in her life. My books are on a wide variety of subjects, but she isn't interested in any of them. She has no intellectual interests, no life of the mind. I can't share the things I most enjoy with her. It's a frustrating situation. Just imagine, a literature professor—a specialist in Shakespeare—married to a woman who has never read a play or poem by Shakespeare in her life and has no desire to."

"Yes, I can imagine what that is like," she said.

"Let me give you an example," he continued. "Last year I read Joyce Cary's book *The Horse's Mouth*, which has been described as the best fictional portrayal of how artists see the world and are carried along in it by their passion for painting. Then I got the movie version of the book, starring Alec Guinness, and my wife and I started to watch it together. We came to a particularly important scene in which Gully Jimson, the artist, and an uneducated woman he has borrowed money from are looking at one of Jimson's favorite paintings.

"He's explaining to her why this painting is so important to him, pointing out the contrasts between the colors and the shapes, and other features that he is so pleased at getting just right. Then, right in the middle of his explanation, the woman talks over him in a loud, crass voice about mundane matters that could easily have been discussed at another time. It was as though she couldn't understand that he was saying something important, as though she couldn't hear that he was even talking at all.

"At just that same moment my wife began talking right over the movie about some unimportant matter. The parallel between the scene in the movie and real life was too close, so I turned the movie off and watched it later, alone. That's just one of many examples that might sound similar to your own experiences."

Amelia nodded, but didn't say anything.

"Let's talk about something happier," he said.

"Let's go for a walk," she replied. "I am a very physical person and need some movement to get the blood flowing again."

Alan realized that he'd probably been talking too much, so he remained quiet to give Amelia a chance to speak. She didn't, though, and to fill the silence he began to tell her about one of his favorite movies, *Top Hat*, starring Fred Astaire and Ginger Rogers. "There is a wonderful scene not too far into the movie where Astaire has fallen in love with Rogers but she is pretending to be uninterested. They are trapped in a gazebo in a park by the rain. Before long they are singing and dancing together to the song 'Isn't This a Lovely Day (To Be Caught in the Rain).' It's one of the most romantic moments in any film, ever."

She still didn't say anything, so he continued. "But, Amelia, I mention this movie not only for that scene, but also because later Ginger Rogers is mad at herself for having let Fred Astaire make love to her. Because that is what I want to spend my life doing, making love to you."

Amelia started with a small involuntary shudder, as though someone had nudged her from behind. She stared at Alan as the word "visceral" flashed through her mind.

"I'm not saying making love *with* you, but making love *to* you," Alan said quickly, returning her gaze, "as the phrase was used at the time the movie was made in 1935, meaning to court you, to say sweet things to you, to please you.

"Because, Amelia, I'm becoming as smitten with you as Fred Astaire was with Ginger Rogers. 'Smitten,' as in 'captivated, charmed, enamored.' Do you know the word?" Finally he stopped talking, and looked at her. Something isn't right, he thought. She is being too quiet.

Amelia finally spoke. "Dr. Fernwood, it is getting late. I have to get home. Thank you for telling me about *The Horse's Mouth* and *Top Hat*. I will try to watch them some time."

As he walked back to his house, Alan had the uncomfortable feeling that he'd talked too much, that he'd revealed too much of his feelings. He wished he could take back everything he'd said after giving her the Wodehouse book. But it was too late.

FRIDAY, JUNE 26

44

Thoughts of Amelia continued to bubble up, but Alan pushed them away. He knew he wouldn't be able to do so forever; once he'd finished working, thoughts of what had happened yesterday would roar insistently into his conscious mind. But he would be able to concentrate a bit longer before that happened.

Turning his thoughts to the Oxfordian community, Alan felt as if he'd stumbled into an alternate universe, one that he hadn't even suspected existed. The Oxfordian universe included not only the few books he'd read, but scores more, and dozens of websites, blogs, and online publications. It wasn't a small, fly-by-night operation, but a sustained movement that had been growing for almost 100 years, ever since Looncy had first proposed Oxford's authorship.

The leading Oxfordian organization in the United States, he learned, was the Shakespeare Oxford Fellowship (SOF). It held annual conferences at which its members gathered to share the results of their research into the life and writings of Edward de Vere. Its website contained links to dozens of articles and even videos with information about de Vere's authorship, as well as links to many other organizations, each with its own area of research, ideas and information. The SOF's own publications included a quarterly newsletter with issues stretching back fifty years, and an academic journal with longer, more in-depth research.

The wealth of information in those publications almost overwhelmed Alan. Fortunately, someone had compiled an *Index to Oxfordian Publications* that served as a guide to the almost 7,000 articles, books, pamphlets, reviews and letters addressing the issue of de Vere's authorship. The *Index* listed not only articles in the SOF's own publications, but also those from a score of other periodicals, some going back as far as the 1920s.

How could all of this activity on such an important literary subject have gone unnoticed by academia all these years, Alan asked himself. How could we have been unaware that something so important was happening in Shakespeare studies outside academia? Only a deliberate blindness could explain it, and he felt even more strongly a sense of shame that he and his colleagues had so willfully closed their eyes to the central issue of their chosen field, that of the identity of the author. To hit upon all the material at one time was exhausting, and he needed a break before continuing.

45

Delilah opened the door to Elvin's car and got in. They gave each other a quick hug, as best they could in a sports car. And then they were off. Having just finished work, she was dressed professionally yet stylishly, just right for the event they would attend. She was carrying the gray jacket that matched her skirt. Elvin was wearing his usual casual slacks and jacket but no tie—smart casual, as he'd heard it described.

"I thought we could get a bite to eat on the way," he said. "That would give us a chance to talk before we get there. Anyway, we have some time to kill before it starts at eight."

"Sounds good to me," Delilah replied, smiling at him.

Elvin had wanted to take Delilah somewhere special and had been thinking about where they might go when he learned about the National Advertising Awards reception, an annual event that this year was being held in Cary. That's perfect, he had thought. Delilah would enjoy an event like that, which consisted of a reception followed by a showing of the dozen best commercials of the previous year, "best" meaning most persuasive in convincing customers to buy the products or services advertised. Commercials could be nominated from any mode of advertising—TV, radio, print, online, even billboards or skywriting. Representatives of the companies that produced the top ads would be on hand to explain how the commercials had been developed, from initial conception to completed product.

Elvin hadn't been mistaken in Delilah's interest in attending. She was, in fact, thrilled, as several people from her company would also be there. And she was even happier to be with Elvin again. She had wanted to see him ever since the last time they'd met, two weeks ago. E-mails and phone calls were fine, but nothing could compare with being close to someone you liked, she thought.

They decided on a restaurant within walking distance of the convention hall where the event would be held, and ordered drinks and appetizers only, since they would be attending the reception before the commercials were shown. Once seated, Elvin told her about the success of his first "Contrarian" column and his plans for the second. Delilah told him about developments at her internship. But they did so quickly because they wanted to talk about a more important subject: their feelings for each other.

Elvin had thought about the end of the last time they met, about Delilah telling him how warm she felt whenever she was with him, and about the way she'd looked at him as he got into his car. Why am I always so slow to understand the significance of things, he asked himself. I'm a reporter. It's my job to notice things. And I do, when it comes to work. But when it comes to emotional things I'm a tortoise. I always get to the right spot at the end, but it takes me longer to realize what's what.

Tonight, he wanted somehow to convey to Delilah that he recognized the feelings she had expressed in words and looks last time. He wanted to let her know that he felt the same, but didn't know quite how to do it without being too direct. Delilah, too, wanted to reaffirm that she hadn't spoken lightly in telling Elvin that he might be to blame for global warming because she always felt warm when she was near him. But she didn't want to be too aggressive, too controlling.

So there was a pause after they'd described developments at their jobs. Delilah was the first to speak. "You know," she said, "the commercials receiving the awards are those that generated the largest increases in sales of the product or service advertised. Last year it turned out that the ones that were most persuasive weren't those that made the boldest statements or had the highest pressure pitches, but those that suggested by inference what customers could achieve by using the product or service."

"Yeah, I think I read the same article," Elvin said. "I wonder if it will be the same this year." He then cupped her hands, which had been resting on the middle of the small table, in his. "Your hands are warm, and mine are cold. Perhaps you can help warm me up."

"Well, mine were warm, but now they're hot," she replied. Her face felt hot, too. This was the first time they had held hands, and a feeling of magic flowed between them, from their bodies through their arms and into their hands and back again, returning hotter than before.

"I had no idea your hands were so soft," Elvin said. "Of course, I knew they were beautifully formed. You know, I have a theory that the beauty of a woman's body can be judged by the quality of her hands. If her hands are beautifully formed, then it is likely that all other parts of her body are equally beautiful."

Oops, he hadn't meant to say something so intrusive. "At least," he said, trying to pull back part of his remarks, "it has appeared that way to me with my limited knowledge." He didn't know if that helped or hurt the situation, so he decided not to say anything else until he could gauge the effect of his words on her.

Delilah appeared to take his remarks in stride. "Why do you think my hands are beautiful?"

"Well, just look at them," he said, relieved that a potentially difficult moment hadn't developed. "Their shape is well proportioned. The wrists are slender, and so are the fingers. Yet they also have a sense of firmness and strength about them under the soft surface. These hands are capable and strong as well as lovely." He was about to add that he was sure all other parts of her body were equally lovely, but stopped himself.

"I think we should be moving on to the convention hall," he said, waving to the waitress for the check.

As they left the restaurant, their hands found each other, and remained together until they arrived at the hall.

Two hours later they stood on the top of the curve of the small bridge that crossed the narrow river running through that part of the city. It was a beautiful summer evening, and a quiet breeze had come up to cool off the heat from earlier in the day. They both replayed in their minds the winning Amway commercial they'd seen on the screen at the conclusion of the event. The organizers had to show it three times because of the audience's enthusiastic reaction.

"I can't believe how effective it was," Delilah said, laughing. She felt good all over. So good, she was ready to order the skin cream right now.

The commercial had opened with a scene of a woman putting the Amway cream on her face, rubbing it in gently until it could no longer be seen. She was wearing a nightgown that enhanced her natural beauty but wasn't overly suggestive. The next scene showed her sitting on the edge of the bed facing the camera, smiling softly to herself, and touching the part of her face where she had put the cream. The final scene showed her being pulled backwards onto the bed by a man whose face is never shown. As she is being pulled down onto the bed, she looks directly into the camera, smiles shyly, and whispers "Thanks, Amway!"

What was so effective about the commercial was that the only sounds in it were music playing so softly that it could barely be heard, something that the man says that couldn't quite be made out, and then the woman's whispered "Thanks, Amway!" spoken as though the words had been gently puffed out of her by the backwards motion. The effect was of a woman who has triumphed, gaining the interest and love of the man of her dreams, all through the use of the Amway product.

Delilah was still laughing at the effect of the commercial as Elvin said, "I wonder what happened next."

"Stop it, Elvin," she said, smiling. "I'm still too young to know of such things."

"Well, I'm just the man to teach you," he said.

She looked up at him just as his lips reached hers. The warm magic that had flowed through their hands in the restaurant now flowed through their lips, and because their lips were closer to their hearts than their hands were, more of it reached those delicate organs.

It was some moments before either spoke. "It's fortunate for you that we are in public," Elvin finally observed, "or you might find yourself being pulled backwards onto a bed."

Delilah didn't reply, but she wondered what would happen if the next time Elvin kissed her they weren't in a public place. She also wondered if she could place and receive an order for the Amway cream before the next time they met.

SATURDAY, JUNE 27

46

Alan was continuing to explore the Oxfordian community. One interesting article he found on the Shakespeare Oxford Fellowship website, "Ten Eyewitnesses Who Saw Nothing" by Ramon Jiménez, identified ten people who had personally known Shakspere or one of his daughters, and who'd left detailed writings about Stratford after their death but never mentioned Shakspere as having any literary connections. Among them was Dr. John Hall, Shakspere's son-in-law, whose diary contained notes about another writer, Michael Drayton, but who never mentioned his father-in-law.

Another article, "Ver-y Interesting: Shakespeare's Treatment of the Earls of Oxford in the History Plays" by Professor Daniel Wright, documented how Shakespeare had departed from the sources of his history plays in ways that exaggerated the prominence of some of the prior Earls of Oxford. What explanation could there possibly be for those changes, Alan asked himself, other than a subsequent Earl of Oxford having been Shakespeare?

The SOF website also had links to many other sites. One of the most interesting was to a blog run by Hank Whittemore. There, Alan found a series of postings titled "100 Reasons Shake-speare Was the Earl of Oxford." He printed them out to study later and bookmarked the site.

Another link was to a blog run by Stephanie Hopkins Hughes, who had delved into the subject of attribution of literary works in the Elizabethan era. She'd found, on one hand, a number of commoner writers who lacked biographies consistent with that of an author, and on the other hand a number of courtiers whose literary works had been publicly praised but for whom few or no works had survived under their own names. William Shakspere and Edward de Vere were only the most prominent pair. Hmm, Alan thought. Perhaps Oxford wasn't the only writer whose works have been attributed to someone else. He bookmarked that site, too.

Especially important was the link to the Shakespeare Authorship Coalition (SAC), headed by John Shahan, with Alexander Waugh serving as Honorary Chairman. Although not an Oxfordian site, the SAC's work, Alan saw, was critical to legitimizing the authorship issue in academia by promoting awareness of the weakness of the Stratfordian claim. He was especially intrigued by the SAC's *Declaration of Reasonable Doubt*, signed by more than 3,000 people who doubted that Shakspere had written the works of Shakespeare and urged that the topic be studied in academia. Alan had given copies of the SAC's book *Shakespeare Beyond Doubt?* to his colleagues on the Special Events Committee.

47

Amelia had let her subconscious brain churn for a couple of days. It was now time for her conscious mind to harvest its thoughts and decide what to do about Alan. I mean, she corrected herself, Professor Fernwood. Alan—Professor Fernwood—had brought up the subject of sex, of making love; indirectly, to be sure, but it was now on the table. That wasn't the problem, though; the problem was his romantic feelings for her.

Before considering what type of relationship she wanted with Alan, Amelia reviewed her general understanding of how people interact with each other. Relationships were not free form, she knew, but instead arose between persons who occupied specific positions. Their interactions were governed, or should be, by what was appropriate between people in their relative positions. This concept seemed so natural to her that she had thought everybody understood it. But she was beginning to realize that it was an Asian concept, that people in the West didn't think this way.

That way of understanding personal interactions was reflected in many Asian languages. Vietnamese, for instance, has many words meaning "I" and many for "you;" everyone had to choose carefully which pronouns to use in each social situation to express their recognition of the relative status between themselves and the person they were addressing. English, of course, has only one word for each pronoun.

In many Asian countries, families referred to their children by birth order, such as Number One Son or Number Three Daughter. Designations like that didn't exist in the United States, Amelia knew, where English had only one word for "son" and one for "daughter." English also had only one word for "brother" and one for "sister," whereas Vietnamese had words for older sister, younger sister, older brother and younger brother, and siblings used these words to refer to each other, thus recognizing their place in relation to the other person.

Amelia also considered the differences between Western and Asian concepts of what it meant to be a good person. Western thinking had general precepts, such as "Thou shalt not steal," and "Thou shalt not kill." It was different in Asia. There, one was judged by how well one knew one's place, and by how well one fulfilled the duties of one's various positions. A man was judged by how well he played the role of son by showing respect for his father and humility before his ancestors, or by how well he fulfilled the duties incumbent on him in his role of younger or older brother, parent, and so on.

And then there was the two-sided concept of "face." One side was that one should not cause other people to lose face or status by disrespecting them, by not honoring the relationship that existed between their position and your own. The other was that one's own face, one's own status in society, was determined by the relationships one had with people of higher status. If someone of higher status publicly recognized you, they were not recognizing you as an individual as much as someone in a position worthy of being recognized.

In sum, Amelia concluded, whereas Americans had a more horizontal system in which equality was valued, Asians had a hierarchical social system in which each person fit into predetermined positions in relation to everyone else. Yes, Americans had organizational charts showing the relative position of each employee within an organization, but Asians had such charts in their minds for everybody in society all the time.

Bringing these ideas to bear on her relationship with Alan, Amelia began to see that he regarded the two of them as individuals, not as people in pre-determined positions. He thought more like an American than she'd realized. She'd assumed that because he had an Asian wife and had lived in Asia, he understood Asian thinking more deeply.

In her world, smooth social interaction was maintained when people acted in accordance with the duties inherent in their positions. That meant that boundaries between positions had to be preserved. By making explicit his romantic feelings for her, Alan was blurring the boundaries. She could not allow that to continue.

She paused. Perhaps this was the right time to contact Phuong Nguyen. It would be good to see her cousin again. They'd been quite close in high school, both experiencing less than ideal home lives. Phuong had a natural gift for languages and had worked as an interpreter, eventually marrying one of the Americans she'd interpreted for at a conference in Vietnam. They hadn't met since Phuong had left for the United States five years earlier, and Amelia had always wanted to renew their relationship. One of the reasons she'd chosen Cary University for her Fulbright program was because Phuong lived nearby. Phuong,

Amelia hoped, would be able to understand the situation from both a Vietnamese and an American point of view. And her husband, Tom, having married a Vietnamese girl, might be able to provide a perspective on the situation that would help her decide how to proceed.

SUNDAY, JUNE 28

48

Sitting at his desk in his home office, Alan examined the Stratfordian response to the Oxfordian challenge. He'd already noted academia's almost complete failure to respond directly to Looney's book. Now he wanted a fuller understanding of how literary scholars had responded to the broader issue of de Vere's authorship.

He found that most scholars hadn't taken the authorship question seriously because, to them, Shakspere's authorship had been irrefutably confirmed by the testimony in the introduction to the First Folio in 1623. Many weren't even aware that de Vere had been proposed as a candidate. Those who were aware of doubts about Shakspere's authorship often tried to explain them away by resorting to *ad hoc* explanations for things that otherwise couldn't be explained if the author had been born in Stratford in 1564. As one example, to explain the references to a play with a character named Hamlet in the late 1580s—far too early for such a play to have been written by Shakspere—they postulated the existence of an anonymous lost play they dubbed *ur-Hamlet*, on which Shakespeare must have based his own play a decade or so later. Because no other evidence for an earlier *ur-Hamlet* play has ever been found, Oxfordians argue that the simpler way to explain such an early reference to Hamlet is that it was the first known reference to a play by Edward de Vere that later became known as "Shakespeare's."

Alan had already seen that some scholars had launched unscholarly attacks on the authorship issue and on doubters. He now saw that some attempted to discredit the issue by criticizing the ideas of Delia Bacon, who had expressed doubt about Shakspere's authorship in the 1850s, rather than address the far more compelling evidence in support of de Vere's authorship presented later by Looney, Ogburn and others. And he saw that some raised specious arguments against the idea of de Vere's authorship, such as alleging as fact that many of Shakespeare's plays weren't written until after de Vere's death in 1604, while knowing full well that actual dates of composition haven't been definitively established for any of the plays.

Alan hadn't quite realized the extent of his fellow academics' use of fantasies, *ad hoc* explanations, and un-academic practices in order to sustain belief in Shakspere's authorship. His cheeks reddened as he recalled how recently he might have been one of them if he hadn't ignored the authorship issue so completely.

Turning back to the initial reaction to Looney's book, he noted that although the weight of academic opinion was opposed to the idea that William Shakespeare was a pseudonym, some scholars had been open to it. Henry Clay Folger, founder of the Folger Shakespeare Library, had been so intrigued by Esther Singleton's 1930 novel *Shakespearian Fantasias*, with its many references to Edward de Vere, that he purchased a dozen copies and sent them to major players in the field of Shakespearean research. He also purchased the original manuscript for the Library.

But Henry Folger's response was an aberration. Statements by later Folger Library directors were indicative of how the authorship issue was viewed within academia. Alan had already seen Louis Wright's vicious characterization of those who doubted Shakspere's authorship as "'disciples of cults' that 'have all the fervor of religion,' and that had fallen prey to 'emotion that sweeps aside the intellectual appraisal of facts, chronology and the laws of evidence.'" Those don't sound like the statements of an objective investigator, he thought. They sound more like those of an advocate of one side of an argument, a side that is so weak that, rather than try to defend it in open debate, its disciples have descended to making vicious attacks on those holding other views.

He was even more chagrined to see that not much had changed within academia since Louis Wright published those comments in *The Virginia Quarterly Review* in 1959. The journal was apparently so proud of Wright's attack on doubters that it selected his article as one of only four from the 1950s for inclusion in *We Write for Our Own Time: Selected Essays from 75 Years of The Virginia Quarterly Review*, published in 2000.

Alan then came across notes he'd made showing just how little many Shakespeare scholars knew about Edward de Vere. What we are to think when Janet Wright Starner and Barbara Howard Traister hardly mention de Vere in their 2011 book *Anonymity in Early Modern England: What's in a Name?* They couldn't even get his name right, listing him in the index as "de Vere, Edmund." Why did Penny McCarthy, in *Pseudonymous Shakespeare*, published in 2006, mention Oxford four times but omit him from the index? And why did John Guy, in his 2016 biography of the queen, *Elizabeth: The Forgotten Years*, make no mention of Edward de Vere, the queen's Lord Great Chamberlain, even though he mentioned one of de Vere's daughters four times?

It almost appears, Alan concluded, that scholarly research on Edward de Vere has ended. Although his reputation as a poet and dramatist had been openly recognized before Looney claimed he was Shakespeare, many scholars now appear to pretend that he had never existed.

Enough of this, Alan thought, pushing the books and papers on the desk away from him. I need a break from all these unprofessional and biased attacks on the idea that the man from Stratford did not write Shakespeare's works and that Edward de Vere probably did.

49

As she rode on the bus to Phuong's house, Amelia was excited about seeing her cousin. It would be good to catch up with her and to get her thoughts on Alan. In the meantime, she continued to sort out the situation on her own.

In her mind, only four types of relationships were possible between herself and Alan. Each came with preset restrictions and duties. One possibility was that of friends, people of relatively equal status who shared some aspects of their lives with each other. Sex was not possible between friends, although it could become possible if a friend changed to a different status. But no, the position of friend did not fit Alan, or rather Dr. Fernwood, she decided, because of the difference in their status and age.

Another category was that of lovers, two people of relatively equal status who had a physical relationship with each other. Lovers, in many parts of Asia, were usually not friends, because the nature of their relationship was restricted mostly to the physical aspects. But no, she realized, she and Alan couldn't be lovers because they had already shared their interests in books and literature and because they had unequal status. A third category was spouses, who had a physical relationship and shared their feelings and the other aspects of their lives. This was the fullest type of relationship, but it was not possible because Alan was married.

The final category was that of sponsor and sponsee. People in these positions were of unequal status, with the sponsor, in the higher position, having the duty of caring for the person in the lower, who in turn had the duty of showing respect for the sponsor. Amelia decided that this was the category into which her relationship with Alan belonged. But there were two types of sponsor/sponsee relationships. One included sex and one didn't, and she needed to decide which kind she wanted. She had no aversion to a physical relationship with Alan. In fact, she would prefer that sort of relationship. She was a very physical person, she knew, and didn't want to go too long without sex.

She had already had several relationships of the sexual sponsor/sponsee kind. In Asia, women from poor families sometimes sought out sponsors—men, usually older, who were grateful for the attentions that a young woman could pay to them, and in return helped them get started in life, providing things like university tuition, an apartment, and maybe a motorbike. If these weren't matches made in heaven, they were certainly ones made on Earth that benefited both parties.

Amelia hadn't been born into a poor family, but, as she'd told Alan, her mother had died when she was thirteen and her father had begun drinking. By the time she'd graduated from high school and was ready to enter the university, the family had no money to support her studies. It was at that point that she'd acquired her first sponsor, a man in his late forties who treated her well and helped her get started at the university. He shared with her not only money, but also advice on many things that she'd needed to learn when she moved from her small town to the capital. He had been kind, and she'd been sorry later that she'd foolishly left him to move on to another sponsor with more money.

She had made her big mistake shortly after graduating from the university, marrying a man for all the wrong reasons: for love or what she thought was love. But her husband hadn't shared her intellectual interests. He had become increasingly devoted to his insurance business, and she'd become increasingly stifled. Eventually, as she had explained to Alan, she had to end the marriage.

Untangling the bonds with him and his relatives hadn't been easy, and having a small child had made it all the harder. Fortunately, she'd been able to leave her son with her sister when she went to work, first teaching English, then becoming a manager at an English language institute. She had begun to realize that an overseas degree in linguistics was necessary to become a full professional in her field, and she'd applied for and been awarded a Fulbright scholarship. Now here she was, in the United States, preparing to begin the master of arts program in linguistics in the fall, and enrolled in the summer Fulbright orientation program and a course on Shakespeare.

Amelia wasn't interested in her fellow American students as lovers. Not only were they younger than she, but most of them seemed unaware of the hardships that come with life. Still being supported by their parents, they hadn't yet encountered the hard realities of life and the seriousness of the choices needed to deal with them. As far as she knew, none of them had experienced the death of a mother or the decline into alcoholism of a father. None had faced the need to take on a sponsor. None were married, so none had had to deal with the consequences of making an appallingly bad choice in a spouse. None of them had been through a divorce or endured an extended separation from their child.

Before coming to the U.S., Amelia had considered the possibility of acquiring a sponsor. She wouldn't need one financially, given the Fulbright stipend. But she was in a new country, and it would be useful to have someone to introduce her to American society and culture. And there was her physical nature. It would be good to have someone to share her bed occasionally, someone without any clinging emotional ties. A sponsor would need to have time and money to spare. He would need to be older and more experienced in life. Perhaps, if she was lucky, he would appreciate, and even match, the quickness of her wit. He probably should be married so that he wouldn't misinterpret their relationship as one of lovers. Alan had appeared to be a good candidate for a sponsor, but his romantic feelings for her were muddying the waters.

Amelia was also looking for a possible spouse. Marrying an American would provide the benefits of a green card and eventual citizenship, and enable her son to join her and attend American schools. The qualities most important in a spouse included all those important in a sponsor, except that he would have to be single. The two of them would have to be compatible in other ways, with suitably matching temperaments, sense of humor and other qualities that over time would evolve into love. It wouldn't be easy to find someone like that. She had to be careful not to make another mistake, either by marrying the wrong person, or by allowing feelings to develop for someone not in a position to become a spouse.

The matter-of-factness with which Amelia sorted out her needs and set out to fill them was typical of her. She knew herself well, and understood the structured ways that people interact with each other. She finished these thoughts just as the bus pulled up at the stop where Phuong was waiting.

50

"Amelia!" Phuong called as she stepped off the bus. "I'm over here." Amelia could see her cousin waving and she waved back as she ran toward her. The two women hugged, then pulled back and looked at each other.

"We have so much to catch up on after so many years," they both said. They talked, and talked some more, first in the car, then at a coffee shop, and then again in the car. Their conversations began mostly in Vietnamese, which surprised both of them, and soon switched to English.

Eventually they got caught up to the present, and it was at that point that Amelia began to talk about Alan. "Phuong, you know I had a sponsor or two in Vietnam who helped me get through the university years after the breakdown of my family."

"Yes, of course. And you know I did, too, which is how I learned English so well before coming to the U.S."

"Well, I thought it might be a good idea if I had a sponsor here, too. I don't need financial help because the Fulbright grant takes good care of me, but a sponsor might help me adjust to American life."

Phuong nodded, fearing what was to come next.

"I met someone who might be a good choice as a sponsor. He has introduced me to many things about American life and society, and we have had many interesting conversations about literature, history, and even our own lives. The problem, though, is that he is beginning to act not as a sponsor should act. He is beginning to express romantic interest in me. He is also beginning to hint that he might want to have sex. That isn't the problem. You know I am a very physical person and would welcome the chance to have sex in the right conditions."

They'd had conversations like this one many times before, in Vietnam, so Phuong merely nodded again.

"The problem is that he is beginning to act like he doesn't care about the rules. Doesn't he realize that romantic interests aren't part of the duties of a sponsor, and are, in fact, forbidden in the sponsor-sponsee relationship? Doesn't he understand that by proceeding down the romantic path even though he is married he is encouraging feelings that will harm both of us because it will be impossible for them to lead anywhere?"

"Amelia, you make me smile," Phuong responded. "You're speaking like a true Vietnamese girl. But you are in America now. Americans don't have the same tradition of sponsorship that we do in Vietnam. They don't have the same concepts of preset positions and stylized relationships. You speak English well. Surely you've noticed that Americans have only one word for 'you' and one word for 'I.' Everything is free-flowing here, individual to individual. There are very few boxes into which people must fit, few stylized relationships into which they must force themselves. He is treating you like an individual, not a person in a box with a label on it."

"But Phuong, if Americans don't recognize various types of relationships set in advance, how do they know how to act? How do they protect themselves from feelings that can only result in pain later? How do they know when to rein in their feelings?"

"Those are good questions, Amelia. They used to puzzle me, too, when I first came to America. But now I understand that they rely on their feelings to guide them."

"What? That is backwards! Feelings arise from events outside ourselves pressing in on us, pushing us to act in response to them. What should happen is that our actions are determined by ourselves. Feelings must be reined in if we are to act appropriately. Only by recognizing the duties of the positions we are in, in relation to other people, can we tell which feelings can be followed and which must be resisted."

They continued analyzing the situation after reaching Phuong's house. An hour or so later, her husband, Thomas Falk, came down from his office, and Phuong introduced them. He was an Asian specialist at an economic institute associated with Cary University.

"It's nice to meet you, Amelia." Tom said. "Phuong was quite excited to get your call yesterday. It's not often that her Vietnamese friends manage to get to America."

After a bit of conversation about other subjects, the two women gave Tom the short version of Amelia's plight.

"And that is the story," Amelia said as she finished her summary. "Alan is starting to speak in a romantic way. He is married to a woman from Taiwan and spent a number of years living in Asia. So, I naturally expected that he understood Asian thinking. But now I think Phuong is right. He is thinking like an American, not an Asian."

"So his name is Alan?" Tom asked.

Amelia blushed. "Well, I call him Dr. Fernwood. But lately I've begun thinking of him as Alan."

"Well, then it sounds like Alan isn't the only person coloring outside the lines," Tom observed.

The women continued talking while Tom mulled over what he'd just heard. After a while he spoke up again. "Amelia, I have been giving this some thought. My recommendation is that you stay away from him. He is dangerous for you, and you are dangerous for him. It sounds like it's already too late to stay within the bounds of a traditional sponsor-sponsee relationship. In spite of how much the two of you enjoy meeting and conversing, each meeting will only increase your feelings for each other. And as you point out, it's difficult to see how this situation could have a happy ending given that he is already married."

51

Amelia continued to think things over on the bus ride back to her apartment. The problem, she saw now, was not that Alan was beginning to express romantic interest in her. She could handle that easily enough. The problem was that she was beginning to develop romantic feelings for him, too. She hadn't quite realized it until their last conversation, when Alan talked of his frustration at being married to someone who had never read a book—a situation similar to her own failed marriage— and when he went on to talk about a romantic scene in a movie.

Worst of all, he'd followed that up with the direct statement about his becoming smitten with her. "Smitten" was a cute little word, she thought. It reminded her of kittens playing with a ball of yarn. But it was best to put such thoughts out of her mind.

She saw now that she would have to try harder to rein in her romantic feelings for Alan. It was too bad they had developed; it would have been enjoyable to have sex with him from time to time. He was a nice man, someone whose company she enjoyed. But now that romantic feelings had arisen—expressed on his side, unexpressed on hers—sex would not be possible because it would be making love. Making love— sex combined with love—must be confined to marriage so that the heartache it could otherwise lead to did not arise.

It was now clear to Amelia what she must do. She must take steps to curtail Alan's romantic feelings for her. She must dampen, if not eliminate, her romantic feelings for him. If she couldn't do that, then she would have to cut out of her life the cause of those inappropriate feelings. She would have to say goodbye to Alan. There were no other options.

52

Now that he'd finally finished the day's research into the Oxfordian community, Alan could relax and turn his attention to other things. Or rather, his attention would turn itself where it would. He didn't have much say in the matter. Having forced his conscious attention in one direction for so long, his unconscious brain was going to make itself heard now on the subject of its choosing.

The subject it chose to push into his mind was the one he'd expected: Amelia. Thoughts of her didn't just bubble up from below. He didn't need to listen carefully to hear them. They came in a torrent. He realized that it had been a mistake to talk so much without getting any sort of feedback from her. But that was water under the bridge. He needed to sort out why she had remained silent and then ended their conversation so curtly.

It had to be because he'd used the phrase "make love *to* her," which she had interpreted as "make love *with* her." He certainly found her desirable, and wanted to make love with her, but that desire was not overwhelming. He found their conversations about literature and other intellectual subjects immensely satisfying. He enjoyed her wit and the sparkle of her personality. That they'd both experienced deep suffering in the past was yet another bond between them.

He didn't want anything to spoil the growing intimacy of their friendship. If that meant that sex—making love—would have to wait, then so be it. What he needed to do now was to let her know of his growing feelings for her, his growing romantic feelings. He would emphasize that side of their relationship the next time they met, and not even mention the possibility of a physical side to it.

MONDAY, JUNE 29

53

"Good morning, everyone," Alan began. "This is our final meeting before the midterm exam. I don't have any specific topics scheduled for today, so we have a chance to discuss whatever you would like to focus on. I know that some of our earlier discussions could have gone on much longer if time hadn't run out.

"Before we begin, I want to say how pleased I am with the sessions that you introduced and moderated. They really did go well. Each of you made interesting points in your introductions and kept the discussion focused on important issues from the plays. I hope you enjoyed those sessions as much as I did."

Alan then turned to a subject he had never raised in any of his classes before: The Shakespeare Authorship Question. He wanted to share his developing interest in the subject with his students, and to know what they thought about it.

"You are all probably familiar with the idea that William Shakspere of Stratford-upon-Avon did not write the works we know as Shakespeare's," he began. "In the past, I have always rejected that idea, and thought that it was held only by conspiracy theorists. The kind of people who believe in aliens and UFOs visiting Earth. But now that I have begun to explore it more deeply, I'm finding that maybe it isn't such a crazy idea after all. I'm curious to know what you think of it."

Amelia was the first to respond. "Well, I don't know much about the issue, but as I mentioned on the first day of class, I saw the movie *Anonymous*, which presented a scenario that could easily have happened. Ever since then, I have wanted to know whether the Earl of Oxford wrote the plays or not, which is one of the factors that led me to enroll in this course."

"I saw *Anonymous*, too," Pat said. "It was an interesting movie, but I wasn't convinced. I would need to see more evidence, much more, before I could abandon the idea that Shakespeare wrote Shakespeare."

"It's an interesting question," Nancy commented. "I first heard of it when I read *The 100: A Ranking of the Most Influential Persons in History*. That book lists Edward de Vere, not William Shakespeare, as the author of Shakespeare's works in entry number 31. But I haven't thought much about it since."

"Oh? I'm not familiar with that book," Alan said, making a note. "I'll have to get a copy of it."

"Well, I agree with Pat," Lisa volunteered. "It sounds like a rather bizarre idea that people have been fooled about who wrote the plays for more than 400 years. After all, dozens of biographies of Shakespeare have been written. The authors of those books must have done a lot of research while writing them."

"You know," Doug said, "I had never heard of the authorship issue until I saw a *Newsweek* article on it a year or two ago. The author made some interesting points, but what was most intriguing was that 1,700 comments on the article were posted on the *Newsweek* blog—and most of them supported the author's doubts about Shakespeare's authorship."

"Really?" Alan asked. "I haven't seen that article, and don't usually read that blog. I had no idea the issue would generate that much comment." He made another note to himself.

"Last week I mentioned that several of Shakespeare's plays might have been based on earlier plays, including most of the histories. I didn't raise the point then, but I will now, that many of these older plays were written too early to have been by the man from Stratford. He would have been only a child when some of them were written.

"So that leaves only two options. Either Shakespeare was a mere patcher-upper of plays written by other people—at least of those plays— or the older plays were earlier drafts of his own work that he updated to reflect changing political concerns in the court and government. And if the second option is correct, then Shakspere of Stratford wasn't—

couldn't have been—Shakespeare."

"Oh, I wondered about that," Amelia said. "Not so much about who had written the earlier versions, but about how a man from Stratford with no known connections to the court or government could have written so intimately about high level political developments; about how a commoner could have written about those things so openly without being arrested."

"I wondered about that too," Dave commented. "In fact, after you mentioned John Stubbs a few weeks ago—the guy who had his right hand chopped off because of writing about Queen Elizabeth and the marriage issue—I recalled that a character in *Titus Andronicus* had his right hand chopped off. I went back to look at that play, and was surprised to find that Shakespeare used the word 'hand' 72 times in *Titus*. So whoever the author was, he was traumatized by Stubbs's fate, and maybe feared it might be his own as well."

"Really, is that right?" Alan asked, making yet another note. "Shakespeare mentioned 'hand' 72 times in *Titus*? I'll have to take another look at that play."

After the break, Alan introduced the subject of the midterm exam.

"This will be an open-book—or should I say open-books—exam," he began. "You can either complete it on your own time and submit it by e-mail, or you can show up for the next class session and complete it here in this room before sending it to me electronically. Does anybody plan to come in next time to take the exam here?"

No one did.

"Ah, good," he said. "So we won't meet on Thursday. And, in fact, given the July 4 break, we won't meet again until July 9. We'll have a long break. Why are you all smiling?" Alan asked, smiling himself. "Don't forget that you have a lot of work to do to prepare for the longer sessions you will introduce and moderate after we return. Nancy, I believe that you will be in charge of the first session."

"That's right, she confirmed, "and I'm already hard at work reading *King Lear* and the other plays we will discuss."

"That's good to hear," Alan said. "Okay, now on to the exam. It will be in an essay format. I have prepared a list of five topics or questions. You are to write on two of them. Your essays should be about two to three pages each. That's about 800 to 1,000 words per essay.

"You can refer to any of the books and other readings assigned for this course and any of your notes. And of course any of Shakespeare's plays. As you know from the handout I gave you on the first day of class, I will be judging your essays by several criteria.

1) An understanding of Shakespeare's thinking on the issues you write about.
2) The cogency of the arguments that you make. I am looking for an argument—not merely a collection of facts, but facts in support of a conclusion, a judgment.
3) The relevance of the examples you cite in support of your argument.

"Don't put too much time into your essays. Even though you will write them outside of class, they are designed to be completed within the time frame of a usual class meeting—an hour and a half. I'm not looking for polished articles, but rather evidence that you have acquired some familiarity with the plays we have discussed.

"Here is the list of topics to choose from," he said, handing a copy to each of the students. They immediately began poring over the list, trying to determine which ones they could write about most effectively.

As everyone was leaving, Alan saw Doug turn to the other students and ask, "Is it possible that aliens from outer space wrote Shakespeare's works, then left a few more-obvious clues behind that Shakspere wrote them and also a few less-obvious clues that Oxford did? If so, then what we have here is a double-secret conspiracy. It's kind of like Delta House being on double-secret probation in *Animal House*."

Alan walked back to his office, thinking about the group discussion on the authorship issue. What's most interesting, he thought, is that all of the students were already aware of the issue. Most of them appear open to it, and some already had doubts about Shakspere's authorship. That's certainly a different response to the issue than in academia, where even mention of it is *verboten*.

With some degree of surprise and dismay, Alan realized that he had learned more about the authorship issue from these six students in one day than from of all his literature colleagues over the entire course of his career.

54

Alan saw Amelia through the window, sitting at her usual table. He thought briefly about not joining her, but then decided to, reminding himself to be careful in what he said.

She saw him out of the corner of her eye, but didn't stop reading or turn in his direction. She didn't want to have an awkward meeting. She enjoyed his company and wanted their relationship to continue. If he didn't raise romantic subjects she would be able to control her feelings. Maybe they could even begin a sexual relationship without the danger of it becoming a love affair.

Alan had ordered a coffee while Amelia was thinking her thoughts.

"Hi, Amelia, may I join you?" he asked.

"Of course, Dr. Fernwood, please sit down," she said, smiling as she put down her book.

"You know, after giving you a copy of *Right Ho, Jeeves*, it occurred to me that I hadn't read it for a long time. So I began reading it again over the weekend. I'm enjoying it even more this time. The misunderstandings between Bertie Wooster and Madeline Bassett always make me smile. It's so easy for misunderstandings to occur."

"Yes, it certainly is. I hope I have time to read more of it soon," she said, relaxing. If only Alan would keep to neutral subjects. She'd been in the U.S. more than a month with no sex. It would be good to share her bed occasionally with someone she liked and felt comfortable with, if she could do so without triggering feelings that would lead to pain later.

Alan laughed, thinking of the characters in the book. "Bertie and Madeline don't much like each other, but each has the mistaken idea that the other is smitten—"

Amelia stiffened upon hearing "smitten." She felt the borders of their sponsor-sponsee relationship beginning to blur, and knew she would have to do something to strengthen the walls.

But before she could interrupt, he continued. "—just as I am becoming smitten with you."

"Professor Fernwood, have you stopped to think that you might be as mistaken about me as Madeline is about Bertie? I am sorry, but I have a project I must finish for my Fulbright orientation class. I must go."

No, he said to himself after she'd left, that hadn't occurred to me. He finished his coffee without reading anything, wondering just what had gone wrong. He thought he'd approached things from the right angle by emphasizing his feelings for her without any mention of a physical aspect to their friendship.

WEDNESDAY, JULY 1

55

Today, Alan decided, he would explore articles addressing the Oxfordian claim to authorship that had appeared in non-Oxfordian publications such as the *New York Times*, the *Washington Post*, and the *Wall Street Journal*.

He turned first to the *Newsweek* article that Doug had mentioned in class. It had a strange title—"The Campaign to Prove Shakespeare Didn't Exist"—but its author, Robert Gore-Langton, had done a good job highlighting reasons to doubt Shakspere's authorship. He noted that Shakspere had left no paper trail, that nobody during his lifetime ever recognized him as a writer, and that when he died nobody seemed to notice. He also noted that doubters included Sigmund Freud, Mark Twain, Henry James and historian Hugh Trevor-Roper, who found the case for doubt about the author's identity "overwhelming."

The article also highlighted the Shakespeare Authorship Coalition's challenge to the Shakespeare Birthplace Trust—the entity controlling the tourist sites in Shakspere's hometown of Stratford-upon-Avon—by offering to donate £40,000 to a charity of the Trust's choosing if it could establish, in open debate, beyond reasonable doubt, that Shakspere was the author of Shakespeare's works—and that the Trust had declined the offer. The article even quoted SAC Honorary President Alexander Waugh as saying "I am publicly accusing them of [taking money under false pretenses]."

As Doug had noted, the article generated some 1,700 comments. Of special interest was a posting by Tom Regnier, President of the Shakespeare Oxford Fellowship, who provided a concise and devastating summary of reasons for doubts about Shakspere: "In order to believe that the Stratford man was Shakespeare, it is necessary to suppose that the son of illiterate parents, for whom there is no evidence that he ever went to school, ever wrote a letter, or ever owned a book, somehow attained a world-class education that included fluency in several languages, a deep understanding of law, medicine, classical mythology, aristocratic sports, science, philosophy, Greek drama, heraldry, the military, and Italy, among other subjects, thereby becoming one of the most literate people of the Elizabethan Age, and gained all this knowledge without leaving a clue as to how he did it."

That anyone could continue to believe that Shakspere was the author was beginning to make Alan angry. He turned to two other books whose authors had come to believe that Oxford wrote Shakespeare. Nancy had mentioned the first one in class: the second edition of Michael Hart's *The 100: A Ranking of the Most Influential Persons in History: Revised and Updated for the Nineties*. In the first edition of *The 100*, Hart had listed "William Shakespeare" at position number 31, believing him to be Shakspere of Stratford. For the second edition in 1992, Hart wrote that he'd carefully examined the arguments on both sides of the authorship question and concluded that "the skeptics have much the better of the argument and have reasonably established their case." He accordingly revised the entry and retitled it "Edward de Vere better known as 'William Shakespeare.'"

The second book was James F. Broderick's and Darren W. Miller's *Web of Conspiracy: A Guide to Conspiracy Theory Sites on the Internet*, published in 2008. Broderick explained that "What I discovered is that most [conspiracy theories] do not hold up under scrutiny. The more one digs, the shakier and less credible they become. The Authorship Question was different. The more I dug, the more credible it seemed, until I became fully convinced of its validity. What I had set out expecting to debunk turned out to be the most compelling, fact-based 'conspiracy' I had ever researched."

This is extraordinary, Alan thought. Here were independent writers of considerable intelligence and accomplishment outside academia examining the issue objectively and concluding in favor of de Vere and against Shakspere. Why hadn't he heard of this before?

He then turned to the legal profession. He'd already noted that several U.S. Supreme Court Justices had expressed doubt about Shakspere's authorship, including two who believed that Edward de Vere was the author of Shakespeare's works. He now noted that three prestigious law journals had organized symposia on the authorship question and devoted entire issues to it, including the *American Bar Association Journal*, the *American University Law Review*, and the *Tennessee Law Review*.

Alan had many more publications to examine, but had already read enough to conclude that a groundswell of interest in the authorship question existed outside of academia.

56

Elvin had been relieved Ed had accepted the first "Contrarian" column with only a few changes. He had also suggested that Elvin write his second column about the folly of blind acceptance of scientific expertise. He was doing that now. He had begun by compiling a list of top scientists who'd been utterly wrong about developments in the very field in which they were supposedly the world's leading experts. In each case, the science, which had appeared to have been settled, wasn't.

And it wasn't only scientific experts who failed to perceive developments in their own fields. He had found similar lists from practically every area of human endeavor, which didn't give him much confidence in experts and their so-called expertise.

Concluding he had enough material for the column, Elvin began writing it. Several hours later he had a solid draft. It was a bit long, he thought; perhaps the examples of experts who had been wrong should be moved to a separate text box that would accompany the column. He could decide later.

"The Science Is Settled"?

Everywhere we turn we are told that "The science is settled," that human-generated global warming is a reality that will cause great harm to human beings. Proponents of that belief claim that only extensive changes to the sources of our energy and the way we live will enable us to avoid the imminent disaster of melting glaciers and rising sea levels.

And who are we to argue when experts have spoken? "Ours is but to do and die," as Tennyson once explained.

Or is it? Might there be a possibility that the experts could be wrong, and that the dramatic changes they are demanding in the American way of life need not be made?

History is chock full of examples of so-called experts being wrong about developments in the very areas in which they were the world's leading authorities. In each case, the science, which had appeared to have been settled, wasn't.

Albert Einstein, for instance, was wrong in 1932 about nuclear energy. "There is not the slightest indication that nuclear energy will ever be obtainable. It would mean that the atom would have to be shattered at will." Lord Kelvin, President of the Royal Society, was wrong in 1883 when he said that "X-rays will prove to be a hoax."

Henry Morton, president of the Stevens Institute of Technology, was wrong in 1880 about Thomas Edison's light bulb, predicting that "Everyone acquainted with the subject will recognize it as a conspicuous failure." W. C. Heuper, of the National Cancer Institute, was wrong in 1954 about the dangers of smoking. "If excessive smoking actually plays a role in the production of lung cancer, it seems to be a minor one."

Experts in practically every other field of human endeavor have been no less flawed. In the field of communications, a Western Union official concluded in 1876 that "This 'telephone' has too many shortcomings to be seriously considered as a means of communication. The device is inherently of no value to us." Associates of David Sarnoff at RCA advised him in 1921 that "The wireless music box has no imaginable commercial value. Who would pay for a message sent to no one in particular?"

In the field of transportation, a Boeing engineer concluded that "there will never be a bigger plane built" after the first flight of the 247, a twin engine plane that held ten people. The president of the Michigan Saving Bank advised Henry Ford's lawyer not to invest in the Ford Motor Company in 1903, saying that "the horse is here to stay but the automobile is only a novelty—a fad." Dr. Dionysius Lardner concluded in 1830 that "rail travel at high speed is not possible because passengers, unable to breathe, would die of asphyxia."

In the field of computers and copying, Thomas Watson, chairman of IBM, predicted in 1943 that "there is a world market for maybe five computers." Ken Olson, president, chairman and founder of Digital Equipment Corporation, said in 1977 that "there is no reason for any individual to have a computer in his home." The eventual founders of Xerox, in 1959, estimated that "The world potential market for copying machines is 5,000 at most," and concluded that the photocopier had no market large enough to justify production.

In the area of musical styles and tastes, *Variety* predicted in 1955 that rock and roll music would "be gone by June." Decca Recording Company declined to sign the Beatles in 1962, informing their manager that "we don't like their sound, and guitar music is on the way out." Darryl Zanuck, a movie producer at 20th Century Fox, concluded in 1946 that "television won't last because people will soon get tired of staring at a plywood box every night."

Practically the entire modern world would not exist if our fathers and grandfathers and great-grandfathers had blindly followed the experts of their day: no telephone, no television, no radio, no electric lights, no modern airplanes, ships, cars, trains or rockets. No home computers or photocopiers. And worst of all: no Beatles.

But perhaps experts today are more expert than those in the past, you say? Sadly, that does not appear to be the case. Consider the steady stream of recent studies overturning the government-mandated, widely publicized guidance that we have relied on to protect ourselves and our families.

Salt: New research shows that salt isn't dangerous, as the Dietary Guidelines Advisory Committee has declared for decades. Evidence now shows that a low-salt diet may itself be risky.

Cholesterol: The same committee, which is part of the Department of Health and Human Services, has also backed away from its decades-long warning about cholesterol. Eggs have now been cleared, after forty years of warnings against them.

Coffee: Contrary to prior reports, there is now strong evidence that consumption of coffee within the moderate range (three to five cups per day) isn't associated with increased long-term health risks among healthy individuals.

Trans fats: After decades of recommending trans fats, the U.S. Food and Drug Administration recently ordered American food manufacturers to stop using them within three years.

Mammograms: In a major shift, the American Cancer Society has reversed its decades-old recommendations and now reduces the recommended frequency of mammograms and delays the age at which screenings should begin.

It may be that these new reports demonstrate that science is never static, that knowledge is always changing because science itself is a process, not a body of knowledge to be memorized. Perhaps our knowledge of the world, always provincial and tentative, changes as our understanding of it becomes ever more accurate?

That may indeed be the case. But what "The Contrarian" finds a bit unsettling is the certainty with which each new pronouncement is issued, as though the issue has been settled for all time. That the older guidance had been issued with an equal degree of confidence in its accuracy raises doubts about the validity of the new guidance. We note one study documenting that "an expert's confidence in making forecasts about complex uncertain situations is unrelated to the accuracy of the forecast."

That's what makes it so infuriating for "The Contrarian" to be told that "the science is settled" about global warming. Is that subject so complete or so uniquely different from all other bodies of knowledge that no refinements to it will ever be possible? We don't think so.

And, we note, nutrition and health guidelines, once established by "science" and backed by the power of government, remain in place long after contradictory conclusions have been reached. Consider salt. Even after the clean bill of health given to salt by its own scientists, the FDA "is still pressuring food manufacturers and restaurants to remove salt from their recipes and menus." And the older cholesterol guidelines, which had been in place for decades, were based on a study that had been shown to be flawed at the time the guidelines were issued.

Government regulation often locks in bad advice and rarely changes as quickly as scientific knowledge progresses. None of this inspires confidence in government "science."

Returning to the subject of the Earth's climate, we recall that global *cooling* had been all the rage in the 1970s. In 1975, a *New York Times* headline alerted readers to the severity of the problem—"Major Cooling Widely Considered to Be Inevitable"—and a *Newsweek* article was even scarier: as a result of the cooling trend, a "drop in food output could begin quite soon, perhaps only in ten years. . . . The resulting famines could be catastrophic." On Earth Day in 1970, Professor Kenneth Watt had actually forecast a new Ice Age. "The world has been chilling sharply for about twenty years. If present trends continue, the world will be about four degrees colder for the global mean temperature in 1990, but eleven degrees colder in the year 2000. This is about twice what it would take to put us into an ice age."

With those examples in mind, consider the propagandistic repetition of the phrase "the science is settled" by our political leadership. Do they really believe it? If so, then we must ask why the U.S. government continues to spend billions of dollars every year to investigate climate change. If the science is really settled, that's an incredible waste of resources. But maybe the government knows it isn't really settled, and is working hard to gin up whatever "evidence" it can to justify what is, at bottom, only a political football rather than a scientific fact.

And if the science isn't really settled, then maybe that oft-repeated phrase is just another way of saying "Shut up." The phrase reminds "The Contrarian" of a scene in Ring Lardner, Jr.'s comic novel *You Know Me, Al*, in which "'Shut up!' he explained" is how one character responds to another's question. But, somehow, the humor of that fictional interaction doesn't quite carry over into real life's global warming scare.

THURSDAY, JULY 2

57

Alan had managed to keep his feelings for Amelia out of his mind yesterday, but today he woke up with his head filled with them. It was true, he now saw, that he had become too captivated by her. He had thought she'd developed similar feelings for him, and it was still a surprise that she'd rebuffed him so abruptly the last time they'd met.

He wondered whether she really had as strong an effect on him as he imagined. Yes, she was charming, lovely and intelligent, but surely he had exaggerated the effect of those qualities. He must be remembering wrong.

Perhaps it would be best not to meet her for coffee and conversation today. They'd had a few enjoyable conversations. Best to let it go at that.

He was glad that the class wouldn't meet today, but he still had to go to the Department office and the library.

58

"Dr. Fernwood!" Amelia called to Alan. She was relieved that she'd found him. He hadn't come to the coffee shop today, and she felt bad about the way she'd pushed him away on Monday. True, they hadn't agreed to meet today, but still it was their custom to have coffee together on Mondays and Thursdays. She knew she shouldn't have talked to him the way she had. She had to make amends.

Alan stopped walking and turned to see who'd called him as Amelia ran the last few steps toward him.

"Dr. Fernwood, I am so glad I found you," she said. "I want to apologize for the way I spoke to you on Monday. I know I did not speak well. I have regretted it ever since. I am sorry."

"That's okay, Amelia. I had probably gotten carried away in my feelings for you. I'm sure you often have people—men—become captivated by your smile and your warmth and your brilliance. It was right of you to help me rein my feelings in." He felt he needed to change the subject. "How was the midterm? Did you find topics that you felt comfortable writing on?"

"Oh, yes. I wrote on ways of knowing, on how difficult it is for some of Shakespeare's characters to know what's what because they can see things from different points of view. How can they know which is a true assessment of the situation they are in? It is difficult for them to respond when they are uncertain about what has occurred. I drew from several plays to support this idea."

While she was talking, Alan led them toward a bench in the shade of one of the large American elm trees on campus. They sat down.

"Well, I'm looking forward to reading your essays, and those of the other students, which is what I must do today."

They both wanted to resume the growing intimacy that had developed during their earlier conversations, but weren't sure how to begin. Alan spoke first. "Amelia, would you like to have dinner with me tomorrow evening?" He hadn't planned to ask her that; it had just come out. Still, it would be good to test the limits of the relationship by such an unexpected proposal. Unspoken, but recognized by both, was that such a meeting would be their first outside the Monday and Thursday pattern, and the first at night.

"Oh, Dr. Fernwood, of course I would. But I already have plans to meet other people."

Alan laughed, and Amelia cocked her head, as if to silently ask why he was laughing.

"Sorry," he said. "I was just thinking of a scene in a movie, *Pillow Talk*, with Rock Hudson and Doris Day. Have you seen it?

She shook her head.

"Well, the two of them are talking on the phone. He asks her to meet him for a date—for dinner—on Friday evening. She says that she is sorry, but she already has a date. He then says he knows that she's not the kind of girl who would break a date. 'No, I'm not,' she says. And he replies, 'And I'm not the kind of man who would ask you to.' 'No, you're not,' she agrees. He then tells her 'I'll pick you up at eight,' and she says, 'I'll be ready.'"

Amelia and Alan both laughed as they looked into each other's eyes.

"Professor Fernwood," she said, "I always enjoy so much talking to you. And I am learning so much about American culture and movies and

---

books at the same time. Of course I will have dinner with you tomorrow."

"That's great, Amelia, Let's meet at the lobby of the Harvest Hotel. It's very close to the campus. There is a marvelous restaurant on the top floor that has good Asian as well as Western food. Seven o'clock?"

"Yes, seven is good. See you tomorrow, Dr. Fernwood."

Walking back to his office, Alan wondered whether this was a good idea. Amelia had been right to dampen his growing interest in her. He was married, she was one of his students and a Fulbright student, to boot. And the university had prohibitions against teacher-student relationships, didn't it?

But, damn it, they always had such a good time together. They'd had such interesting conversations, and she was so captivating. Not beautiful in one sense, perhaps, but so lovely and charming. He felt happy and energized when he was with her. And besides, he asked himself, what harm could one dinner do?

59

Alan knew, of course, that almost all professors continued to teach their students that the works of Shakespeare had been written by the man from Stratford. He'd assumed that most of them, like himself a month ago, hadn't really examined the issue and were mostly unaware that an Oxfordian community even existed. Now he began to think that only a deliberately blinkered profession could be so ignorant of the strength of the Oxfordian challenge. When will academia pull its head out of the sand, he asked himself. Someone needs to alert it to the harm that its blindness on the authorship issue is bringing to the field of Shakespeare studies. If no one else would do it, it might be up to him to lead the effort to nudge academia into doing its duty to investigate the issue objectively.

He imagined four possible Stratfordian "responses" to the authorship question, and saw that only three had been tried.

The first possible response—the one never tried—was direct and objective examination of the Oxfordian claim, followed by explanations of where Looney, Ogburn and others had gone wrong—because they believed things that weren't correct, interpreted facts incorrectly, or engaged in flawed reasoning. The reason that path hadn't been pursued, Alan concluded, was that it couldn't be. Looney, Ogburn and the others hadn't been wrong.

The second possible response was to ignore the authorship question entirely, hoping it would vanish. That strategy had certainly been tried, but it hadn't worked. Instead of withering away, the authorship question continued to gain credence as its proponents assembled more and stronger evidence against Shakspere being the author. The opposite was true for the Oxfordian claim, as more and stronger evidence tying Edward de Vere to the plays and poems was uncovered.

The third possible response was to explain away demonstrated weaknesses of the Stratfordian claim through *ad hoc* explanations devised to deal with specific situations. The problem with such explanations is that they often have no independent justification outside of the specific instance for which they are cited—the supposed *ur-Hamlet* play being a prime example.

Considering this point further, Alan recalled two books he'd just read: *Shakespeare Beyond Doubt: Evidence, Argument, Controversy (SBD)* by Paul Edmondson and Stanley Wells, and the point-by-point response to it, *Shakespeare Beyond Doubt? Exposing an Industry in Denial (SBD?)* by John Shahan and Alexander Waugh. The latter was published by The Shakespeare Authorship Coalition, the organization whose website had so impressed him last week.

The authors of *SBD?* asked its readers to read both books before reaching a conclusion about the authorship question. They made that request, Alan realized, because *SBD* contains so many misrepresentations that someone new to the authorship question wouldn't catch. He made notes of a few of them.

One was Stanley Wells's reference to "the mass of evidence that the works were written by a man named William Shakespeare." But, *SBD?* pointed out, that evidence did not show that the works had been *written* by someone named William Shakespeare; it only showed that they'd been *published* under that name.

A second example was Wells's statement that "No one expressed doubt that 'William Shakspere of Stratford' wrote the works attributed to him . . . until the middle of the nineteenth century." *SBD?* nailed that one, too. "No one expressed doubt that Shakspere wrote the works during his lifetime because no one ever suggested he did in the first place. Wells never shows that anyone ever said he did. One does not bother to deny something unless there is reason to think it in the first place. Does the fact that no one has expressed doubt that I am a king mean that I am one?"

Alan couldn't help laughing at that response, just as he couldn't help shaking his head in disgust at the misrepresentations and evasions in *SBD.* How was it, he wondered, that Cambridge University Press could publish such nonsense? *Shakespeare Beyond Doubt?*, on the other hand, was a tour de force of intellectual power, and he wished he could give copies to all of his colleagues.

He turned finally to the fourth Stratfordian strategy, that of *ad hominem* responses, or attacking the messenger. Resorting to personal attacks against those who doubted Shakspere's authorship appeared to be Stratfordians' most favored *modus operandi*. Examples were legion. The Royal Shakespeare Company, for instance, had posted on its website an article by Stanley Wells that called disbelief about Shakspere's authorship "a psychological aberration" attributable to "snobbery . . . ignorance; poor sense of logic; refusal, willful or otherwise, to accept evidence; folly; the desire for publicity; and even (as in the sad case of Delia Bacon, who hoped to open Shakespeare's grave in 1856) certifiable madness."

Gosh, Alan said to himself. They just can't stay away from Delia Bacon, a woman who had dared to doubt Shakspere's authorship in the 1850s before later going insane. He noted that Professor of English Steven May (formerly of Georgetown University) began his review of a biography of de Vere by stating: "The earl of Oxford's biography warrants a review in *Shakespeare Quarterly* only in part because the authorship controversy so ardently pursued by 'Oxfordians' poses a challenge to Shakespeare studies equivalent to that leveled at the biological sciences by creationism." Alan wondered how anyone could make such accusations about beliefs held by, among others, several justices of the U.S. Supreme Court and the editors of the *Encyclopedia Britannica*.

It seemed to Alan that if Stratfordians had put as much effort into proving their claim of Shakspere's authorship or into legitimate criticism of the Oxfordian case as they had into insulting doubters, the authorship question would have been resolved long ago. But that's just what they can't do, he knew, because their own case is so weak and the Oxfordian case is so strong. If you're a lawyer defending one side of a case, you use the tools you have. But it's not lawyers making those slanderous statements, it's academics with the scholarly duty to engage in unbiased objective study of the subject. Alan again hung his head in shame, regretting that he was a member of a group practicing such disgraceful tactics.

60

"Matt, over here!" Alan called when he saw him looking around the coffee shop.

"At last, a chance to relax," Matt sighed, putting his coffee on the table in front of him as he sat down. "Managing the Literature Department is usually a bit less stressful during the summer. But not this year. Dean Wolpuff has us all a bit unnerved by the changes she wants to make."

"Is she still insisting that the School of Arts and Humanities become a source of funding for the university as well as a center for instruction?" Alan asked.

"Yeah, she is—that and other changes. The Chairs of the various Departments have some ideas on how to respond, but only one that might actually result in more revenue coming in. Even that one is problematical, though. But listen, Alan, I've heard that you are talking up the idea of the Shakespeare authorship conference with other professors."

"Well, I've talked to Susan Pallis and Johan Meer. You three form the Special Events Committee."

"You should be careful, Alan. Word is out throughout the department about your proposal, *Shakespeare: Did He or Didn't He?*"

"I still laugh every time I hear or think of that title," Alan said, laughing. "It's quite catchy, don't you think?"

"And that you're actually distributing material on the authorship question," Matt continued.

"Oh, yeah. That reminds me that I brought a book for you, Matt. Here it is." Alan handed him a copy of *Shakespeare Beyond Doubt?*

"That's just what I mean, Alan. Word is out that you've become one of them—one of those people so obsessed with an issue that it's all you can talk about."

Alan considered what to say before speaking. "Matt, I have done quite a lot of research into the Shakespeare authorship issue, for the first time in my life. I'm embarrassed to say that until this summer I had blindly accepted that the man from Stratford wrote the works attributed to him. But, Matt, the support for that belief is crumbling all around us.

"Let me give you one example. One of the strongest supports for Shakspere's authorship is the phrase 'sweet swan of Avon' in the First Folio that supposedly connects Shakespeare to Shakspere's hometown of Stratford, which lies on the Avon River in Warwickshire.

"However, Alexander Waugh recently showed that 'Avon' was the name used among the nobility in Shakespeare's day for Hampton Court, the royal palace upriver from London where theatrical performances were given for Queen Elizabeth and King James, and the members of their court. So the phrase 'sweet swan of Avon' doesn't necessarily have any connection with Stratford or Shakspere. There is a real need to re-examine the authorship question on evidentiary grounds."

Alan paused before continuing. "But there is another more important reason to examine the issue, and that is the unacademic, abusive, almost slanderous charges being made from within academia against those who have doubts about Shakspere's authorship.

"One example is statements made by James Shapiro, professor of English at Columbia. In his book *Contested Will: Who Wrote Shakespeare?*, Shapiro attacks J. Thomas Looney personally, and in very underhanded ways. He takes a penetrating insight by Looney—that World War II was less a struggle between political systems than it was a struggle 'between the human soul and elemental brute force'—and twists it around to imply that Looney's criticism of certain tendencies in democracy meant that he favored the political system of the Allies' enemies, that he was some kind of crypto-Nazi.

"He also states that Looney's open-ended search for the author of Shakespeare's works actually had a secret 'agenda' at its core: to find an author who shared Looney's own supposed anti-democratic attitudes. He further implies that anyone who accepts Looney's conclusions about who wrote Shakespeare's works must also accept the same political beliefs, thus tarnishing not only Looney but also everybody else who thinks de Vere was Shakespeare. There's more, but you get the picture.

"Something rotten exists in the study of literature today, Matt, if shameful statements like Shapiro's go unchallenged. I don't understand why the publisher of the book would allow statements like those to be made. I'm ashamed to be part of a community of scholars that honors those who make them."

"Okay, Alan," Matt responded. "I understand that there are legitimate reasons to examine the authorship question. And I'm only too aware of how low academic standards have fallen in recent decades. But at the same time, you need to be aware of the brand your name is getting as you begin to promote discussion of the authorship issue."

"Fair enough," Alan said. "You know I'm a fighter, and I intend to fight for what I think is right—for unbiased academic consideration of the evidence related to an issue of great importance to the field of literary criticism."

"Again, be careful, Alan," Matt advised him, standing up. "Wars—even literary wars—are an unpredictable business. You never know what might happen next."

61

Okay, Amelia, she said to herself. It's decision time. Are you going to break things off with Alan? Or are you going to color further outside the lines by continuing toward a romantic relationship with him? It's now late Thursday night. If you are going to cancel the date with him, you will have to do it first thing tomorrow.

She couldn't help laughing, though, at Alan's description of the scene from *Pillow Talk*. It made her feel so light-hearted. Maybe she should just relax and see what might develop. After all, she was now in America, not in Vietnam, no longer bound by the pre-set relationships between people that exist in Asia. But what could the end result possibly be, she asked herself. He is married. The only possible outcome would be your developing strong feelings for him and then going through an extended period of suffering. You have already suffered enough for ten lifetimes. The only way to avoid more pain is by staying within the bounds of the position you are in and fulfilling the duties of the preset relationship.

A moment later an inkling of another possibility began its rise from her unconscious brain. "Perhaps it would be possible for Alan to change boxes," it whispered to her conscious mind. It wasn't possible for him to become a friend or a lover, she knew, but maybe he could move to the spousal box. He could become her husband. For that to happen, he would have to leave his wife, something totally outside her control.

"But is it?" her brain whispered. "Might you not have the power to draw Alan away from his marriage, intentionally, just as you inadvertently encouraged his interest in the authorship question?"

Amelia immediately rejected the idea of luring Alan away from his wife. I have always lived a decent life, never deliberately hurting anyone else. I will not do so now.

"Of course not," her brain soothingly reassured her. "No one is asking you to deliberately harm anybody else. But sometimes things happen. They're no one's fault, really. Things just happen. Besides you cannot force Alan to leave his wife. Only he can do that."

"You know he is unhappy in his marriage," her brain continued. "By encouraging him to leave, by, for instance, dressing in a way that highlights the contours of your body, you would be encouraging him to take a step toward improving his life. You would be increasing his happiness. Any pain that others might feel would be more than balanced by the increase in his happiness. And yours."

"Shut up," she told her brain firmly. "Stop pushing me."

She was exhausted by all this thought. It's time to go to sleep. I'll decide what to do in the morning, when my mind is fresh.

FRIDAY, JULY 3

62

The sun was shining so brightly that Alan had to put on sunglasses to look out the window. It was still early in the morning, and he thought of going for a walk before it got too hot. No, he decided, he was eager to read the students' papers and to return to his investigations into the authorship question.

At the same time he was on edge, unable to concentrate as thoughts of tonight's dinner with Amelia surged through him. That and the authorship question. Both situations were unsettling. He could tell that his unconscious brain was churning away about both subjects because he was unable to concentrate on either. In such situations, he knew, it was best to do something else and wait for his brain to settle down. He decided to go for that walk after all.

Alan returned home filled with thoughts about the Stratfordian response to the Oxfordian challenge. He would have to wrap up the investigation into this subject now, he decided. The tactics employed by Stratfordians made him feel soiled; he wanted to move on to other subjects, but couldn't do that without examining one final point.

He wanted to understand why Stratfordians had so consistently ignored their duty to engage in academic study of the authorship question. Charlton Ogburn, Jr., had suggested that financial interests lay at the bottom of it. That explanation would certainly be applicable to the Shakespeare Birthplace Trust and the businesses in Stratford-upon-Avon that benefited from the steady stream of tourists eager to see "Shakespeare's birthplace."

Richmond Crinkley had offered a different explanation. He thought that "the zeal and intensity by which believers possess a presumed intellectual truth owes more to underlying quasi-religious impulses than to economic self-interest." An almost religious belief—that's interesting, Alan thought.

Crinkley also noted that "to be an authority on Shakespeare has long conferred a special intellectual standing that has set many defenders of the orthodox citadel apart from their opponents and invested them with a special status. Is there any more fantastic zealot than the priest-like defender of a challenged creed? Orthodox scholarship defends its inherited wisdom from the exalted position of a clerisy somehow attuned to special knowledge." That makes a lot of sense, Alan thought, remembering that that was exactly what he had felt.

Alan was beginning to realize that academia actually employed a fifth strategy in response to the authorship question, one he hadn't considered before: that of senior faculty pressuring junior faculty to toe the party line. Ogburn had recognized the same thing. "There would seem . . . to be no mystery in the maintenance of academic uniformity," he had written. "No young instructor in a Department of English, even if his early educational conditioning does not preclude his examining objectively that which he has been taught to scoff at as the badge of his professionalism, will find his career advanced if he threatens to expose the tenets of his elders as nonsense." That's certainly true, Alan thought. Younger professors are too caught up in their careers, eager to do whatever they can to become Associate Professors and Full Professors.

But, Ogburn had continued, once a faculty member "has his professorship he is hardly likely to repudiate the steps by which he attained it and certainly he is not going to read himself out of his profession and bring down on his head the obloquy of his fellows, vicious as we have seen such can be." Alan nodded in agreement. Given the viciousness of some Stratfordians' characterizations of doubters and their doubts, it's not surprising that almost all English professors continue to teach their students that Shakspere wrote Shakespeare's works whether or not they really believe it.

How could I have been so unaware of this before, Alan asked himself. How could I have so blindly accepted the beliefs of others? He contrasted his colleagues' hostility to the Shakespeare authorship question with his students' interest in the subject and felt a sudden desire to get out of academia.

Alan also recalled something Alexander Waugh had said in the *Newsweek* article. "The Stratfordians have been trying to pretend we don't exist for a long time, but now they're running scared. As Mahatma Gandhi said, 'First they ignore you, then they ridicule you, then they fight you, and then you win.' We've got to the fight bit." He wondered if he would be brave enough to join the ranks of the public doubters outside Cary University, and beyond that, to join the battle in support of Edward de Vere's authorship. He'd told Matt he was a fighter. He would now have a chance to prove it.

63

Alan walked into the lobby of the Harvest Hotel exactly at seven. He was dressed smart casual, wearing a long sleeve shirt and a jacket, but no tie, to match the refined but still comfortable ambiance of the hotel. He scanned the dozens of comfortable chairs and sofas but didn't see any sign of Amelia.

But wait, an Asian woman was seated in the middle of the room. He looked back at her. She was wearing a low cut black cocktail dress and her hair had been elaborately styled above her head—"coiffed" was the word that came to his mind—with a dash of silver glitter sprinkled on it. He had never seen such a stylish woman in his life. She was so beautiful that just the sight of her was painful, and he quickly looked away.

But something about her was familiar. That couldn't be Amelia, could it? He glanced back and saw that the woman was looking at him and smiling. He took several steps toward her, and she stood up.

"Amelia?" he asked tentatively.

"Hi, Alan," she said, with no hesitation, looking directly at him.

He was stunned by the transformation in her appearance. Now that she was standing up, he could see that her dress highlighted perfectly the contours of her body, which was formed in just the right proportions to excite a man's interest.

"Hi, Amelia. You look lovely," he finally managed to say. They hugged briefly, then sat down.

"I almost didn't recognize you. You look so different from the way you usually appear on campus." He couldn't take his eyes off her face, made up to highlight her dark brown eyes, which sparkled as brightly as the light coating of glitter on her hair. "You are always wonderfully dressed, of course, but now—"

"Yes," she interrupted, "tonight is a special night. It is the first time we have met off campus, so I wanted to look nice for you, Alan." They were both struck by the sound of "Alan" coming from her lips.

First her appearance—her dress and her hair and the brightness of her eyes—then the fact that she had gone through so much trouble to look so nice *for me*, he thought, and now her calling me Alan for the first time. He was having trouble processing all these developments.

Sensing that Alan was a bit dumbstruck, Amelia realized that she would have to move things along herself. "What time is our reservation for, Alan?"

"Oh, of course. It's for seven. We'd better be getting to the restaurant. It's on the top floor. We'll have a view of the whole city." They rose and moved toward the elevator. Alan held her arm as they walked. He recovered his wits during the ride.

"The city looks so lovely from up here," Amelia observed as the hostess seated them at a table by a window.

"And things look beautiful inside here, too," Alan said, looking at her.

Amelia smiled. "Thank you, Alan. It is nice to hear that you think I am beautiful."

The waitress arrived, and they ordered quickly.

"Since last night I have been absorbed in two activities," Alan said, not wanting to let an awkward silence arise. "The first was reading the midterm essays. Yours, by the way, was brilliant. Your thoughts on how Shakespeare's concept of the human will is similar to the Asian way of thinking about human beings, and that both can be contrasted with the modern American view—which is to divide the will into two parts, the head and the heart—was a significant insight that I hadn't heard before. The way you related that division not only to the problem of different desires arising from the head and heart simultaneously but also to the problem of knowledge, of perception, was very insightful. The examples you chose to demonstrate that that was indeed the way Shakespeare saw human motivations were very convincing. It's not often I read something so original and so fascinating."

"Well," she replied, "the existence of two independent perceptual systems is the problem. Before we can choose what to do—the subject of our discussion on the second day of class—we must first understand the situation we are in. But that is so difficult when the head and the heart not only push us toward different actions at the same time, but also perceive the world in different ways and present different pictures of our situation to our conscious mind. That makes it hard to know what to do now—at this moment, in this unique situation, as you once phrased it— when our mind is faced with two different interpretations of what that situation actually consists of.

"Shakespeare, if I may be so bold, did not quite realize that the will is not one thing, that it is composed of multiple components, just as white light is composed of all the other colors. If he had understood that, he might have presented his characters' motives and understanding of themselves a bit differently."

"Amelia, you really have a first-rate mind. You are perceptive, searching, not content with analysis done by others, but willing, even insistent, on thinking things through for yourself. There aren't many people like you."

"Well, I think you are right, Alan," she said. "Those qualities can cause problems for me, not just because I am sometimes too outspoken when I hear others speaking nonsense, but also because so few people seem to think like I do. It was because my husband was not able to think like this—because he had no life of the mind at all, no analytic abilities for anything other than insurance—that I had to get out of my marriage or suffocate to death.

The waitress arrived with their food. After they had eaten a few bites in silence, Amelia continued.

"You know, Alan, I loved my grandfather more than anyone in the world after my mother died. But he died only a few years after she did. I mention this because he once told me that I would have a hard time finding a husband. I thought maybe he meant because I wasn't beautiful. But now I know he was saying that it be hard for men to find me attractive because I'm not good at suppressing my thoughts or my personality like a good Vietnamese girl should. My grandfather also meant that it would be hard for me to find a man with a mind like mine, a man who could satisfy my intellectual as well as physical nature. He knew that I would never be satisfied with a man concerned only with prosaic matters, a man with no life of the mind, no matter how handsome or rich he might be or how much he thought he loved me. And he was right. I have never been able to find someone I thought I would be happy with."

"Amelia, if you don't mind my changing the subject while I digest your thoughts as well as this delicious steak, I'll tell you more about my day. I spent much of this morning continuing my investigations into the Shakespeare authorship question. A month ago I wanted to understand why so many prominent writers and actors and even Supreme Court justices have doubted that the man from Stratford was the author. To my great surprise I found that the evidence in support of his authorship was thin and circumstantial. There was no hard evidence to support it, in contrast to many other authors such as Ben Jonson, for whom many supporting documents exist.

"Then I began to look more closely at why Oxfordians believe that Edward de Vere was the real author. The evidence in support of his authorship is also circumstantial, but it is vast. I don't know what conclusion I'll reach at the end of my investigations, but I'm fascinated by the subject. Have you thought further about it?"

"Well, I haven't investigated it as deeply as you have, Alan, but I do know that you must go where the evidence leads. You have no other choice. You are a scholar, a scientist of literature, and you must pursue the evidence and accept the conclusions it supports."

He nodded in agreement.

Dessert arrived. The waitress put Alan's apple pie in front of him and Amelia's chocolate cake in front of her.

"Apple pie is a traditional American dessert," he told her. "It's delicious."

"Alan, I know how much you like chocolate, too, and I can see you looking at my cake. Let's share both. I also want to try the apple pie." She moved both plates to the center of the table.

After paying the check, Alan turned to Amelia. "I want to show you the outside part of the restaurant," he said, leading her through a glass door onto a large patio. The view was of the other side of the city, and had even more lights and tall buildings.

"Oh, listen," she said. "I can hear music." They looked almost straight down, and saw a band playing in the courtyard of the outdoor restaurant on the ground floor. The music reached their ears at just the right level to form a pleasant background to their conversation.

As Amelia leaned forward against the brick wall, Alan moved from beside her to behind her. He wrapped his arms around her, and she nestled his hands in hers and held them tightly.

"Amelia," he said softly, "when I saw you in the lobby I couldn't believe my eyes. I had never seen a woman so lovely in my life. I couldn't believe that you'd gone through so much trouble to dress up and do your hair so wonderfully for me. The thought flashed through my mind that you had dressed with such care because you had somewhere else to go, someone else to meet, and that you were just stopping by the hotel for a coffee with me before going on to whatever event required you to dress so beautifully.

She smiled.

"Then I thought of a scene from the movie *Moonstruck*, a wonderful scene in a wonderful movie. Have you seen it?"

"No, but I know that Nicolas Cage and Cher are in it. I have liked every movie I have seen either of them in."

"They live in New York City. They haven't known each other long, but agree to meet at the Metropolitan Opera. Puccini's wonderful *La Boheme* will be performed. They arrive separately and look around for each other outside the Met. Cher is dressed so beautifully. She had spent the entire day preparing—having her hair dyed and styled, and buying a new dress and expensive red shoes. Nick Cage looks so handsome in his tuxedo."

Alan kissed the side of her neck.

"When they finally see each other, it's the most wonderful moment in any movie ever made."

He kissed her neck again, and the upper part of her back, and felt her relax and lean back into him.

"Nick Cage can't believe his eyes. His breath is taken away not only by Cher's beauty, but also by the fact that she'd gone to such trouble to make herself look so lovely for him. *For him!*"

He kissed her neck again, and she squeezed his hands tightly.

"All that he can say is 'Thank you'—whispered and with his eyes—to express his amazement and gratitude that someone—and someone he is in love with—has gone to so much effort to look so nice to attend the opera with him."

Alan kissed the other side of her neck, with his arms still wrapped tightly around her and her hands still covering his.

"That is exactly how I felt when I saw you in the lobby. I was filled with such gratitude that you'd gone to so much trouble to look so nice because you were meeting *me*."

"Yes," she said, "it is nice when such wonderful things in the movies happen in real life. That does not occur often." There was a pause before Amelia spoke again. "You aren't like other American men, are you?"

Alan smiled at her. "Is that a question or a statement? Either way, it's true that in some ways I'm not like other Americans. I have lived abroad, which has given me more awareness of the rest of the world than most Americans have. My love of literature and books also sets me apart from most other Americans. That makes me different from most people in any country. By one estimate, only three percent of people have an active life of the mind. So, perhaps I am a bit unusual.

"And you, Amelia, are unusual in the same way. You are one of the very few people I know who has a serious interest in literature. Your enrolling in the Shakespeare course is proof of that, though even a short conversation with you reveals that same rare quality."

"Yes," she agreed, "but that is only part of what I meant by different. I should have said that you are different from other men, not different from other American men only. You are kind. You have a good heart. You have given me books to help me learn about America, and I think you would have been just as kind to any other foreign student, even to those who do not have my, uh, well-proportioned shape."

"Well, you know, Amelia, "the way you usually dress, as beautiful as it is, doesn't reveal the shape of your body. But after tonight, after I have seen how this dress highlights the contours of your body, I will never again wonder about how well-proportioned you are."

Amelia was beginning to feel a rising sense of concern. It was time to go, she told herself. But why now? I have been coloring outside the lines all evening. Why am I beginning to feel uneasy now?

"These moments," Alan continued, "standing here, holding you in my arms, kissing your neck and back, are so wonderful. They are equally as wonderful as the romantic scene with Fred Astaire and Ginger Rogers caught in the gazebo by the rain."

Yes, that was it; that word, "romantic." Her Asian way of thinking was flooding back into her. You must stay in the prescribed boxes, she told herself. You can either have sex without love, or love without sex; to have both with the same person, to make love with someone, to make love with Alan, who you are already falling in love with, would be to open yourself up to unbearable pain when this relationship, which cannot be anything but temporary, ends.

She turned to face Alan, and grasped his hands.

"Alan," she said softly but insistently, "I have had a wonderful evening with you. We have had wonderful conversations, as we always do. I have felt so safe and warm in your arms as you held me and kissed me. But I have to go. I must go. Please don't stop me."

She let go of his hands, turned, and ran to the elevator, leaving Alan alone on the patio on the top floor of the Harvest Hotel, wondering why Amelia had pushed him away for the second time.

SATURDAY, JULY 4

64

Alan woke up with a blinding revelation: Edward de Vere did indeed write Shakespeare. He was now as sure of it as he was of his own name. The evidence for Shakspere was just too thin and that for Oxford too vast and substantive. He wanted to share his new conviction with Amelia, to discuss it further with her. It was, after all, her mentioning the movie *Anonymous* that had in part led to his examining the authorship question.

A second revelation then flashed into his mind: I am in love with Amelia. He was as sure of that as he was of de Vere's authorship of Shakespeare's works. Thoughts of her flooded into him like water through a burst dam. His mind touched on every time they'd met, like a bee loading itself up with honey, moving quickly from the first encounter in class to each of the times they'd met for coffee and conversation, and of course to last night. He was gone, floating in a sea of thoughts of her smile, her loveliness and intelligence, her unique combination of tenderness and tough-mindedness.

Both revelations were problematical. Alan had now become convinced that the central tenet—the very core—of his own chosen field of Shakespeare studies was wrong. But more was at stake than the demise of a personal belief. The authorship issue was practically banned within academia. He would have to think more about how his new conviction might impact his career at the university.

Being in love with Amelia was also problematical. She'd pushed him away twice, unexpectedly and inexplicably. He was sure they'd become good friends, but apparently there was a limit to how deep she would allow the friendship to go. He would have to think more about that, too. Then there was, of course, the unavoidable fact that he was married. And he needed to consider further the university's strictures against faculty-student relationships.

65

Elvin also awoke with a blinding revelation: Global warming is a hoax, a fraud. I would never have imagined a month ago, he said to himself, that I would reach this astonishing conclusion. It's so contrary to everything I'd ever heard. Yet it's now clear to me that the idea that human activity is causing significant changes to the Earth's climate is wrong. It's as wrong as the Ptolemaic system—with the sun and planets revolving around the Earth—was.

He wanted to share his new belief with Delilah, but it was too early to call her. He would see her later anyway, at the Independence Day barbecue that the *Cary City Herald* was sponsoring. In the meantime, he would continue his investigations into the subject of global warming and how it had become such a political football.

66

The ball was a long fly to right center field, hit so far that it rolled through the hedges that formed a porous border between the end of the baseball field and the beginnings of the eucalyptus grove. Delilah, playing right field, ran through a break in the hedges, followed by Elvin, who was playing center field. The softball game was taking place in the park, after the *Herald's* barbecue had ended.

Delilah tossed the ball to Elvin, who relayed it to the second baseman. Elvin then turned back to Delilah, who had been about to follow him, and blocked her way.

"I have wanted to get you alone all day," he said, smiling at her.

"Why is that?" she asked, smiling back at him.

"Because your lovely white shorts have been winking at me ever since I first saw you this morning. Do you have any idea how attractive you look in them?"

He was about to kiss her, knowing that the hedges shielded them from view, when he noticed a purple ribbon pinned to her shirt. "Why are you wearing that?" he asked suddenly.

"This ribbon? One of the women passed them out. It shows our support for women who suffer from heart disease."

"Well, those ribbons make me angry. Why is there such concern for women and not for men who have heart disease?"

"Don't be angry at me. I'm merely showing that I care about people who have a life threatening illness."

"But I am. Do you know that ten men die of heart disease for every one woman? Do you know that at the average age at which women begin to get heart disease, the average man is already dead? Those ribbons show such bias against men that just the sight of them makes me angry."

Delilah ran around him and over to the break in the hedge. "Don't talk to me like that. Now you've made me angry."

67

"Happy Independence Day!" Alan said, answering the phone after its second ring. It was late afternoon.

"Alan, Happy Independence Day! It's me."

"Amelia, I'm so glad you called. I haven't been able to stop thinking about you since last night."

"Me too," she said. And then, after a pause, "I am wondering if you might want to come over to see me, Alan." Silence descended on the phone at both ends. She then said in a low voice, a voice so low that he could hardly hear her, "I want you tonight."

"I want you, too, Amelia. I'll come right over," he said, also speaking in a low voice. "Good God!" he said out loud to himself as he out the phone down.

What a beautiful day it is, Alan noticed, as he walked over to her apartment. A perfect Independence Day. Even though he was not a young man—or an old man either, he thought quickly—he recognized that he was feeling something of the giddiness that Troilus felt upon learning that everything would be possible with Cressida. It may be, he also thought, that I am too obsessed with Shakespeare.

He knocked softly on the door of her apartment. "Come in, Alan," Amelia said, opening the door. She was wearing shorts and a blouse.

Alan entered her apartment for the first time. Both of them felt the sense of anticipation at what they knew was going to happen, but neither wanted to spoil the moment with precipitous action.

"Come," she said, taking him by the hand. "It is such a beautiful early evening. Let's go out on the balcony and I will tell you about my day. I attended a real American Fourth of July barbecue. We were in a big park, with many different groups of people each having their own barbecue. We cooked hamburgers and hot dogs. It was a lot of fun. There were about twenty of us, about half Fulbright students and half American students invited by our faculty advisors. Then we played a game called softball. I have wanted to play it ever since seeing it played in *Good Morning, Vietnam!* That was also a lot of fun. I even managed to hit the ball twice."

Amelia then became more serious. "Do you want to know my impression of American students, Alan? They are so pudgy. They are spongy, like those sweet white snacks, marshmallows. They seem to lack the inner fiber, the hardiness, needed to survive life's difficulties that we have talked about."

"Well," he responded, "Not all of us are spongy—that is, not all parts of us are spongy, at least not all the time."

"That," she replied, "remains to be seen."

That sounds like my cue, he thought. He turned to her and cupped her face in his fingers, moving her lips up toward his own. "You are so lovely, Amelia." he said. "You are irresistible."

Their lips touched, then touched again, and the feeling of warm magic both had felt the previous evening flooded through their bodies, as though only seconds, rather than eighteen hours, separated their kisses.

"Which parts of me are loveliest?" she breathed. "What parts are most irresistible?"

"Come into the bedroom, Amelia, and I will point them out to you."

"But I am still all salty from the barbecue," she said, taking his hand and leading him to the shower. "Let's get clean together, and then you can point out whatever parts most interest you."

In the bathroom they stood facing each other. Looking into her eyes, Alan slowly unbuttoned her blouse, and then unhooked her bra. Both fell to the floor. She unbuttoned his shirt and he took it off. She then loosened her shorts, which fell to the floor in a pool around her feet. She stood before him, naked.

Alan exhaled a gust of air as he looked at her, slowly shaking his head from side to side as though he couldn't believe the loveliness of her slender shoulders or the shape and fullness of her breasts, perfectly sized for her small frame. She was as sublimely formed as he'd imagined her last night when the black dress still covered her body.

"Don't stop there," she told him, motioning toward his belt buckle. His jeans didn't reach the floor as easily as her shorts had because they'd become snagged on a branch as hard as teak.

They stepped into the shower without touching. As they stood facing each other, with the water falling between them, Alan soaped his hands and then caressed her neck. "This is the loveliest neck that God ever made," he said. Then, with fresh soap on his hands, he cupped and massaged her breasts. "And these are the most irresistible breasts that God ever made."

They proceeded to wash every part of each other's bodies in turn, with increasing quickness, until, in one swift ballet-like movement, Alan lifted her up as easily as he might have picked up a ballerina, and Amelia wrapped her legs around his back. They looked into each other's eyes as she slowly descended, enveloping his erection until he was fully inside her. Still dripping wet, he carried her to the edge of the bed. They fell onto it together and began the motions that would carry them to the point of ecstasy that both had envisioned over the past month without knowing if it would ever be reached.

After the storm had passed, they lay on their sides, looking into each other's eyes.

"I'm trying to find just the right words to describe you," Alan said, softly, "but you are indescribable. The closest I can come is luscious, as in 'richly satisfying to the senses or the mind.' And yet that isn't quite right because it should be 'richly satisfying to the senses AND the mind.' The other meaning of the word, 'arousing physical or sexual desire' needs the same modification."

Amelia remained silent, still looking into his eyes, drinking in his words as small crabs on the rocks drink in the returning tide.

"And yet 'luscious' is somewhat misleading because it almost seems to imply luxurious, or richly adorned or an overabundance of womanly qualities, which isn't you, not at all. Your body is slightly understated in its contours, and you have a simple style that belies the complexities underneath. A single strand of pearls is all that you need to complement the black dress you wore last night. Your natural beauty does the rest.

"'Prim,' also, isn't quite the right word for you. It implies being formally precise or proper in dress or manner, which you are, but it also implies excessive stiffness in dress or manner, which you don't have. You are too playful to be called 'prim.'

"I'm afraid," he sighed, "that the phrases that come closest to describing you were written by Shakespeare—in his description of Cleopatra, the Egyptian queen who captured the hearts of both Julius Caesar and Mark Antony." Alan knew the passage by heart.

"'Age cannot wither her, nor custom stale
Her infinite variety. Other women cloy
The appetites they feed, but she makes hungry

Where most she satisfies; for vilest things
Become themselves in her: that the holy
Priests bless her when she is riggish.'

"A man could become bewitched by you and never recover."

"'Riggish'?" asked Amelia.

"Yes. Lustful." Alan replied. "Even priests would be so captivated by you that they would praise your lustfulness."

"Riggish? If I was riggish would I do something like this?" she asked as her hand closed around his branch, which was no longer as hard as teak.

"If I was riggish, would I do something like this?" She licked the side of his neck.

And then, positioning herself on top of him, she asked, "If I was riggish, would I do something like this?" as she lowered herself onto the part of his body that was now fully ready to enter that part of her body that was descending onto it.

"Yes, that is exactly what you would do if you were riggish," he managed to say. It was hard to speak when so much blood had flowed so quickly from his brain to other parts of his body.

And then the storm was upon them again, this time with Amelia controlling the pace and degree of the motions. Alan's final thoughts, before thoughts as well as speech were no longer possible, were that he was with someone who was completely comfortable in her body and who knew how to use it to please herself and her lover. He had no more thoughts as his body responded to the quickening movements of the woman above him with movements of his own, leading both of them to that moment when the clouds collided and the thunder and lightning burst forth over both of them simultaneously.

They awoke to the sound of fireworks. "Come," Alan said, taking her hand. "Let's go out to the balcony. We can watch from there."

They wrapped themselves in sheets and walked to the bench. They watched the fireworks in silence for a few minutes before turning their attention to something more interesting, each other.

"You know, Alan, you aren't like other Americans, are you?" she asked, smiling.

"No, I'm not," he said. "I am the only American in love with Amelia Mai. There could be no bigger gulf separating me from all other men."

They returned to the bedroom and lay on their sides, holding each other. Neither thought they were tired, but within minutes both were sound asleep.

PART II

SUNDAY, JULY 5

68

Amelia and Alan awoke at the same time, looking into each other's eyes, their heads still resting on the pillows. Sunlight streamed in through the window. Neither one spoke.

It's Day One in a new world, Amelia thought to herself.

O brave new world, that there could be such people in it! Alan thought, recalling a line from *The Tempest*.

They continued looking into each other's eyes, not thinking about anything outside that moment. But not too many minutes later they sat up. Their minds had become too active to stay in bed.

"I think I'll go swim some laps," Amelia said. "That is my usual Sunday morning routine."

"I think I'll go work on my Shakespeare projects," Alan said. "I have some new ideas to get down on paper."

They did want to do those things, but they also wanted time alone to think about what the developments of the last two days might mean.

69

Amelia always swam in the middle of the lane, with the black line directly beneath her. Swimming laps not only helped get tension out of her body; it also helped her think, and she looked forward to her twice-weekly sessions in the pool.

Today she was thinking about Alan, about the significance of his entering her life. It felt so right for him to be beside her all night. She had never felt like that before. Except when she'd been married, she'd never slept through the night with anybody. Going home after having had sex with lovers or sponsors had seemed like the right thing to do.

She had woken up once during the night, and leaned over and looked at Alan's face for a long time. Not being able to determine what her thoughts were then, she'd gone back to sleep. They were becoming clearer now. She was aware that she was coloring way outside the lines. Inside the lines, she was in the sponsee box and Alan in the sponsor box—or to use the new American words she had just learned, she was the mentee and he was the mentor—and she knew what was required of them both.

Outside the boxes, where she found herself now, were dangerous waters. She looked around the pool and didn't see any sharks. Laughing to herself, she kept swimming. But she was in unfamiliar territory, in a strange new country. Since it was too late to stay inside the lines, she would have to stay alert and flexible, and rely on her quick mind and feet.

70

Back home, Alan found himself unable to think about either Amelia or Shakespeare for long. His thoughts constantly moved between the two subjects, and it would take a while for them to sort themselves out.

Later, after watching part of a baseball game, his thoughts turned to Amelia. He realized he was entering a whole new universe. She was the first of his students he'd slept with, except his wife, of course. But by the time he and Diana had slept together she was no longer his student, and they'd practically been married.

What was expected in this situation, he wondered. Asking the question, he laughed a bit, wondering if he was becoming more like Amelia by asking what was appropriate for people in certain positions or boxes, rather than asking what he as an individual wanted with one other individual, Amelia. He wondered what she was thinking and why she had turned away from him twice before unexpectedly inviting him to her apartment. And he wondered when they would meet again, and what the ultimate outcome of her entering his life would be. It was so unexpected and unprecedented to have found in one person an intellectual and a sexual companion.

Just then an interesting parallel entered his mind, connecting his situation with Amelia to his situation with the authorship question. If Shakespeare's plays and poems hadn't yet been attributed to anybody— if they'd just been unearthed after 400 years and their author was unknown—the evidence pointing to authorship by de Vere would convince almost everybody. It was the prior commitment to the man from Stratford that was the problem.

In his personal situation, if he wasn't already married to Diana he would marry Amelia, if she would have him. Again it was the prior commitment that was complicating matters.

If his ties to Shakspere's authorship, which had been in place for his entire professional life, could be broken, then perhaps his marriage ties also could be. But there was a big difference between the two. Wives have feelings. He'd been strong enough to break his emotional ties to Shakspere. Could he break those binding him to Diana, knowing that it would cause her deep and irreparable suffering? Would he be strong enough—cruel enough—to do it, knowing that the fault lay not in Diana, but in himself? Could he handle the guilt of acting for his own pleasure with reckless disregard for the woman he'd loved for so many years, and perhaps still loved?

But he was getting ahead of himself. These are questions for the future—the near future, but still the future. Now he had to finish reading and grading the midterms.

MONDAY, JULY 6

71

Alan was glad no classes were held today. He wanted to continue thinking through his involvement with the authorship issue. The initial phase had ended with his acceptance of de Vere's authorship. He had already launched the second phase—alerting his colleagues to the weakness of the Stratfordian claim—by proposing the conference. Now he had to decide whether or not to go beyond that conference to promote de Vere's authorship within the larger academic community.

He felt immediately that was exactly what he must do. Scholars had to recognize de Vere's authorship if they were to understand the works. The public deserved to have an accurate accounting of the author's life in the biographies it read. And Edward de Vere was entitled to recognition for his work.

To reach larger audiences, Alan knew that he would need a game plan that identified goals to be reached, target audiences to be engaged, and the most effective ways of reaching each segment of the target audience. Before he could design such a plan, he would need a better understanding of the process through which individuals and intellectual communities changed their beliefs. A better understanding of the nature of genius and creativity would also be helpful.

Glancing at the clock, Alan was surprised to see that it was already midafternoon. If this was a normal school day he'd be having a coffee with Amelia now. Maybe she's at the coffee shop, waiting for me, he thought. We hadn't agreed to meet when I left her apartment yesterday, but we hadn't agreed not to meet. He could be there in five minutes. He grabbed the bag that he always carried with him and left the house.

72

By midafternoon Amelia was feeling restless. She couldn't read any more. She hadn't heard from Alan since yesterday morning. If this was a normal day, she would be meeting him right about now at the coffee shop. Too bad the shop is closed today. Or is it? Maybe it is open even though no classes are being held. Might he be there waiting for me? We hadn't agreed to meet today, but then we hadn't agreed not to meet. She picked up her purse and left the apartment.

The coffee shop was open, but mostly empty. Amelia was disappointed not to see Alan there. She ordered a coffee and sat down at her favorite table, one near the window with a view of the campus. She had books with her, but didn't feel like reading. I'm in a cat mood, she thought. I'll just sit here in the sun and let my mind wander.

A minute later, Amelia heard the door open and turned to see if it was Alan. It was. She hadn't known she'd feel so relieved to see him. Both smiled as they realized they'd guessed correctly that the other would be there. Alan had expected they would enjoy sitting in the sun together; they were never at a lack for subjects to talk about. But somehow now that didn't seem right. He felt jumpy. "Come on," he said, taking her hand. "Let's go for a walk through the campus."

They walked in silence. But a walk wasn't what they wanted. Their hands touched. Their legs brushed. They didn't want to be alone in public; they wanted to be alone in private. Without either consciously deciding where to walk to, they ended up outside her apartment building. They looked at each other shyly, each thinking "This is ridiculous. We have already slept together. Why are we feeling so shy?"

Still holding hands, they rode the elevator to her floor and walked to her apartment. Once inside, it was as though they had been holding their breath for a long time and could finally breathe normally again.

"This is where we belong," Alan said. "Alone together."

Amelia simply nodded.

"Captivating, lovely, graceful. That is what you are. Everybody can see it. I have noticed the way that the guys in the class look at you."

Amelia laughed. "It's not like that anymore. Now I'm their big sister. Once they found out that I am a few years older than they are and have a son seven years old they stopped looking at me as a girl."

"I understand that. But the fact that you have had more experiences in life than them makes you more attractive to me, not less. You know, Amelia, I have never asked you about your son. Where is he living now? With your ex-husband?"

"No, no, no. He has no ability to care for a child, and besides he works all the time. Rung is staying with his grandparents."

Alan looked at her, surprised.

"No, not my parents," she explained with a laugh. "My former parents-in-law. They are wonderful people and wonderful grandparents. They love Rung and he loves them. There is no one I would rather have him staying with while I'm gone. Of course it's still difficult for him to have his mother so far away, and difficult for me, too. But we talk or Skype twice a week. Last night I was so happy when he played the piano for me. I'm glad he is continuing to take lessons."

"I'm sure he is a wonderful boy. I feel like I'm beginning to know him a little bit."

Amelia looked at him, but neither said anything for what seemed like a long time. It was the longest silence between them since they had met. Then she stood up and walked to the end of the living room. After looking into the bedroom for a few seconds, she turned to him.

"Alan, let me show you something." He crossed the room.

"Stand here." She then walked to the far side of the bedroom, next to the window. She stood straight up, half way between the window and the bed.

"Do you see the way the afternoon sunlight casts a shadow of my profile on the bed?"

"Uh, yes, I do."

"And do you see how thin the shadow makes my waist appear? And how large it makes my breasts appear?"

Alan looked at her, then at the shadow on the bed and then back at her. He nodded.

"And if I take off my blouse and bra, can you see how the shadow of the upper half of my body changes? How the profile of my breasts becomes more natural? And if I take off my skirt, can you see how the shadow of my waist becomes even thinner? And if I turn a bit you can see the shape of my hips, too?"

"Amelia," Alan said in a low voice as he walked toward her, "you are an enchantress, and your magic has transformed the shape of my body, too. I am going to reward you for your efforts."

He placed a pillow on the edge of the bed and bent her over it, belly down. His last thoughts as he entered her from behind, just after his hundredth kiss on her upper back and neck, were that it was midsummer and that it was almost night. He wondered whether the two couples in *A Midsummer Night's Dream* who had spent the night on the bank of the river had noticed the shape of their shadows in the moonlight, and if they had, whether those shapes had led them toward the pleasures of love into which he and Amelia were quickly submerging.

After they resurfaced, they lay against each other, hot and salty. Amelia was first to speak. "In my country female students sometimes sleep with their male teachers in exchange for good grades."

"In my country, it's just the opposite," Alan explained. "Many professors give all students 'As' because that makes them popular. Their goal seems to be to get high rankings from students in the end-of-term surveys rather than to ensure that students actually learn anything."

"Well, I expect you to give me the grade I earn in the class. Whatever happens outside doesn't affect what happens in class. I don't want there to be any misunderstanding that the two activities are part of distinctly different relationships and have no influence on each other."

"Yes, that is exactly how I want things to be, too." He paused before continuing. "Amelia, I have never met anybody like you before. I have always dreamed of meeting someone with whom I could share my intellectual life and my sex life, but until now those two activities had been in completely different spheres. In the past, the women I was attracted to sexually didn't have an intellectual life, and those that had a life of the mind didn't interest me physically. But with you the two are combined. It's a miracle of creation."

"Yes, it is, Alan. I hadn't expected to feel this way about you. And you know, I fought the feeling. I had wanted you as a mentor only," she said, using the American equivalent of "sponsor." "So once feelings for you of another sort began to arise, I tried to push them away. And when I couldn't, I had to push you away. That is why I acted as I did a week ago, and again on Friday night."

"I was going to ask you about those two times when the right occasion arose. It looks like that right time is now. I was actually surprised both times. Was it something I said that triggered your pushing me away?"

"Well, yes, and no. You might have noticed that both times you'd just used the word 'romantic.' That wasn't the cause, but it was the trigger. The first time, it made me uncomfortable. I didn't know why then. Later I realized it wasn't your romantic feelings for me that were the problem, but that I also was developing similar feelings for you. I thought that such feelings were inappropriate."

"If your romantic feelings for me caused you to push me away the first time, then why did you agree to meet me for dinner?"

"Well, I wouldn't have, except that you told me that story of Rock Hudson and Doris Day meeting even though she said she wasn't the kind of girl who would break a date and he said he wasn't the kind of man who would ask her to. Then they met anyway. That story made me feel happy and lightheaded. I still laugh whenever I think of it."

They both laughed.

"Before meeting you at the hotel, I convinced myself that I could control my feelings, that we could continue to be close friends, and that I could stop myself from falling in love with you. But then you mentioned the word 'romantic' again at the restaurant. At that moment I knew that I could not stop myself, that if I continued to see you I would fall deeper and deeper in love with you."

"But, Amelia, why are romantic feelings for me a problem? Why is falling in love with me a problem?"

She turned to look at him, with her brown eyes looking directly into his. "Because you are married, Alan," she said softly.

"I thought that might be the reason," he said, just as softly.

He stoked her hair as they continued to look into each other's eyes with their heads resting on the pillows until sleep overcame them. Neither wanted to pursue that subject further at that time.

WEDNESDAY, JULY 8

73

"No wonder I've been confused!" Elvin said out loud to himself. I've been trying to understand how well the theory of human-caused global warming matches reality without first understanding the reality it must match to. He saw the need to restart his investigations into the effects of human activity on the Earth's climate, beginning this time with the primary source of heat on the planet: the sun. Any study of the Earth's climate that doesn't begin with the most important factor affecting it—the sun—is fundamentally flawed, he reasoned. All other possible factors—natural and manmade—must be placed within the context of the massive and varying levels of solar radiation reaching the Earth.

Elvin was about to begin drafting his column when he was surprised to learn that carbon dioxide currently forms only about $1/25^{th}$ of one percent of the atmosphere. He was a bit mystified. If changes in solar radiation have by far the biggest impact on the Earth's climate, and if other natural forces such as clouds, aerosols and volcanic eruptions have a cooling effect, and if CO_2 forms such a vanishingly small percentage of the atmosphere, then why are we beating ourselves up about the effects of human activity on the climate?

He would have to continue investigating later. It was getting late, and he still had to write his column. Two hours later he had a draft he felt comfortable with.

The Warmth of the Sun

Most readers are probably familiar with the Beach Boys's wistful ballad "The Warmth of the Sun" and with Brian Wilson's haunting lyrics about a young man whose girlfriend has moved on but who still has "the warmth of the sun within him at night."

And everyone is certainly familiar with the pleasures of dozing in the summer sunlight, either inside as it shines through a window, or outside when stretched out at the beach or beside a swimming pool.

And yet, oddly, few stop to consider the importance of the sun in shaping the Earth's climate, or, more specifically, how changes in solar radiation affect the warming and cooling of the planet.

Any attempt to understand how human activity affects the climate must begin with an understanding of the non-human physical forces at play. Because the sun is the ultimate source of practically all energy on Earth, any study of our climate that does not place the sun at the center of the story is fatally flawed—a flaw on the magnitude of belief in the old Ptolemaic system that placed the Earth at the center of the universe.

"The Contrarian" was surprised to learn that the correlation between changes in the sunspot cycle and changes in the Earth's average annual temperature is at the remarkable, near-perfect level of 95 percent. One scientist, seeing that connection, concluded that "we have to change our view of climate fundamentally. It's an incredible correlation; it would imply that almost nothing else [besides solar variation] is important in the climate system."

The other natural factors most affecting climate—clouds and aerosols—have a net cooling effect. Clouds, in fact, act as a governor or a thermostat, working to keep the Earth's temperature constant. During the 1987 El Nino, for instance, when the "sea surface temperature increased by a few degrees, as the surface of the sea grew warmer and warmer . . . clouds kept forming until they virtually shut out the sun, thus initiating cooling, which caused the clouds to dissipate."

It's within that natural context that human activity and carbon dioxide levels must be considered. Pre-industrial levels of carbon dioxide in the atmosphere were 280 parts per million (ppm). That level is expected to double to 560 ppm by the middle of this century. The change due to human activity will be, then, only 280 ppm—only 1/36th of one percent of the composition of the atmosphere. Yes, you read that right. The expected increase in carbon dioxide levels as a result of all human activity from 1750 through the middle of this century will be less than 300 parts in a million—less than 1/36th of one percent.

How could such a minuscule change have much effect at all on the Earth's climate, you might ask? How could it cause the melting of the ice caps and the drastic rise of sea levels that some have predicted? We are as incredulous as you are.

Let's see what the UN Intergovernmental Panel on Climate Change's new report—the massive *Climate Change 2013: The Physical Science Basis*—has to say in its 1,500+ pages about the effect of the sun and the solar cycle on the Earth's climate.

Readers might be in for another surprise! The report has very little to say about the effects of changes in solar radiation, and in fact concludes that the sun had little influence on climate change in the 20th century.

Non-IPCC scientists, however, have been vocal in their criticism of the Report, charging that it "represents neither a consensus nor an authoritative review of the subject." They charge that "selective citation from the scientific literature by the IPCC is clearly evident and its impact is serious." Only one of the thirty-eight co-authors of the report's solar subchapter was an expert on solar physics, they say, and they claim that the chapter is "shot through with critical errors and serious misrepresentations," including "misleading discussion of the sun's radiative forcing," ignoring "other datasets that can be shown to be of better quality," "cherry-picking of the total solar irradiance dataset," relying on "outdated and biased selection of references," and showing "insufficient understanding of the problems involved."

As one example of the Report's incompleteness, they cite changes in the amplitude or eccentricity of the Earth's orbit—a factor ignored in the Report—"which can lead to a surplus of solar radiation of 7 to 20 watts per meter (w/m^2) in the global energy budget—an effect that grossly outweighs the 2.3 w/m^2 that the . . . Report concludes is the result of all human action on the climate since 1750."

What is most distressing to "The Contrarian" is that, as Willie Soon has pointed out, each of the IPCC's "specific and grievous errors in science . . . has the effect of minimizing the role of the sun and thereby supporting the IPCC's unsupportable claim to be '95 per cent confident' that most of the 0.7 degree Celsius global warming since 1950 was manmade." "That assertion is . . . also self-serving," Soon notes, "in that the IPCC depends on it for its own continued existence."

We trust that this column has given its readers enough to chew on for the coming week. We'll continue our investigations into the effects of the human-generated increase in atmospheric carbon dioxide next week.

THURSDAY, JULY 9

74

"Good morning, everyone," Alan began. "Welcome back from the long break. We begin the second half of the term with the class meetings in which one of you will take the lead for an entire meeting—both before and after the break.

"During the next three weeks, we'll focus on three subjects that Shakespeare was so obsessed with that he returned to them again and again. Because understanding them is critical to fully appreciating the plays, we'll devote two full days to each. Nancy and Doug will introduce Shakespeare's treatment of the three-way distinction between an individual, his title and his position. Amelia and Lisa will take us through Shakespeare's portrayal of the political aspects of love and desire from different angles. And Dave and Pat will guide is in examining Shakespeare's presentation of the distinction between appearance and reality. With that, I'll turn the session over to Nancy."

"Good morning, everyone," she began. "The distinctions between an individual, his title and his position in society were important in so many of Shakespeare's plays in part because they were so important in Elizabethan society.

"For instance, a woman named Elizabeth Tudor held the title of Queen and the position of Supreme Governor of the Church of England, among other positions and titles. Henry Wriothesley was the name of the nobleman who held the title of Third Earl of Southampton, and the position, at one time, of General of the Horse in the forces sent to Ireland. And a nobleman with the name of Edward de Vere held the title of Seventeenth Earl of Oxford, and also occupied the position of Lord Great Chamberlain of England.

"Only those at the top of the social hierarchy had these three designations. Those lower down did not, of course, have titles such as earl, lord or viscount. Those at the bottom didn't even have names—at least not names those in higher classes recognized. They referred to them by the trade they practiced such as cobbler, tailor or weaver.

"Our social arrangement is very different. No one here has a title such as earl or viscount, so we don't address anyone by terms of respect such as 'your Lordship.' Nor do we usually refer to anyone by the name of their profession or title. Or do we?

"Actually, we do in some cases. The president is called Mr. President while he's in office, and for the rest of his life. Senators, Congressmen and Congresswomen, and senior military officers also retain their titles. And judges and doctors are addressed by the names of their professions even after retiring. But most of us are known by our name only.

"So I found it hard at first to understand the significance of Shakespeare's characters interacting with others on the basis of their titles and positions, rather than on the basis of their names or personalities. Then I remembered something that helped me understand the Elizabethan social order better: the song 'Tradition' from *Fiddler on the Roof.* You remember the part where the singer asks who does certain things, and the response is 'the Papa,' and who does certain other things, and it's 'the Mama,' and so on?

"Well, that's kind of how I understand Elizabethan society now. It was a traditional society, in which everybody had an assigned place or role. There was a strong sense of, as the title of the song says, tradition. Elizabethan society was also very hierarchical, with positions not just fixed, but fixed higher or lower than others. This again contrasts with American society in which everybody is more or less equal.

"With that in mind, I want to begin the discussion with *King Lear.* We all know that Lear stepped down from the position of king at the beginning of the play. He gave up his crown—his title and presumably the other positions he held—and became just an individual, just a person with a name. But—and here is his mistake—he expected everybody to continue to treat him with the respect and deference due a king even after he had passed the crown to his sons-in-law. Everyone in Elizabethan society, I think, would immediately have recognized the error in his thinking. So, what do you all think of his abdication?"

"Well, I certainly agree that *Lear* is a revealing example of the distinction between the man and the position," Pat responded. "By the time he wrote *Lear*, Shakespeare was at the top of his powers and was able to portray the full horror of the suffering Lear incurs because of his decision. He shows us Lear's growing realization of the hugeness of his mistake, but only after it was too late. That is why the tragedy is so, uh, tragic."

"Lear also misunderstood his daughters' characters," Doug added. "That's a second set of mistakes. It was one kind of misjudgment to think the two older daughters would continue to treat him as king when he no longer held a king's power. But it was quite another not to understand that his daughters weren't the ideal loving creatures he'd thought they were. That mistake is more understandable, though; who could have known they wouldn't even show him the respect due a father?"

"That's a good point," Dave said. "We really don't know in advance what someone will be like once they acquire positions of power. Maybe they themselves don't know. Remember in *Julius Caesar* many of the characters feared what Caesar would become like if he acquired the powers of a king. Perhaps they had been overly fearful, but Lear is making the opposite mistake. He doesn't stop to think how his abdication might change others, as their level of power increases relative to his."

Lisa picked up on that point. "Lear—and Gloucester—certainly learned what Goneril and Albany were really like. But they learned too late. Gloucester lost his eyes and Lear wandered naked on the heath during a storm. It's as though none of those who acquired power had any sense of limits. The only limits they recognized were those imposed by the extent of their power."

Amelia then added her thoughts. "My understanding of this subject is a bit different from yours because I come from a different background. In Vietnam, personal relationships are very different from what they are in the United States. As odd as it might sound, the Asian way of approaching relationships between people today is closer to the way that Shakespeare understood personal relationships.

"In the United States, people tend to interact with others as individuals who are roughly equal to themselves regardless of what their positions are. But that's not how people interact in Vietnam or, as Nancy explained, in Elizabethan England.

"In Asia, everybody is in distinct positions or boxes—boxes such as boss and employee, or father and son. We often interact with others on the basis of preset relationships between those boxes rather than on the basis of personalities or feelings. Those in the higher status boxes have a duty to look after those in the lower boxes, as a boss would look after the interests of his employees or a father would care for his son. And it is the duty of those in the lower boxes to show respect for the status of those in the higher.

"Lear's mistake was changing boxes while still thinking that he would be treated as if he was in the former box. And the daughters' mistake was in not treating their father with the respect and duties that people in daughter boxes should show toward the person in the father box. Doug is right that that issue is unrelated to whether Lear was king or not."

"Oh," Alan said, entering the discussion. "So that is what Cordelia means when she says 'I love your majesty / According to my bond, no more nor less.' She says that half her love will go to him and half to her husband, each according to what is appropriate for someone in her position in relation to theirs."

"That's right," Amelia agreed. "All this makes for a more formalized set of social relations. But I mention all this in response to Lisa's point because the duty of those in the higher boxes to look after the interests of those in the lower acts as a brake on the power of those in the higher boxes. It's a method of social interaction that tells them how to behave. It imposes responsibilities on them regardless of how much power they might have. Not to act in accordance with the duties of their box would be to lose the respect of others."

"Hmm. So it wasn't just that Elizabethan society was more hierarchical," Dave observed. "It was that the box, not the individual, was of primary importance. That's almost a military way of thinking."

"I think I see a moral angle, or perhaps even a legal angle, to all this," Doug commented. "In American society, everybody must obey general laws enforced by government and adhere to general moral duties such as those exemplified by the Ten Commandments—'Thou shalt not kill,' 'Thou shalt not covet thy neighbor's wife,' and so on. Those rules and duties apply equally to everybody.

"But in Shakespeare's day, and in Asia as Amelia has explained, a different moral code exists. That moral code requires people in different positions to act differently. Instead of general laws that bind all people in all situations, everybody must know the relative status between themselves and others before they can know how they should act. That is why Shakespeare's characters—and Asians today—can seem so confusing. It's because they think differently than we do."

Amelia smiled. "That is exactly right, Doug. You understand Asian thinking very well.

"But," she continued, turning to the group, "there is one more important aspect of all this, one that explains why it is so important for Asians, and for Shakespeare's characters, to have this mode of interaction: It helps maintain smooth social interactions. The point is that people have different interests and want to pursue them. The issue is how to do so without disrupting society. Protocol is about the closest equivalent you have in the West, but it has connotations of formality and is applied only in certain circumstances. Which I guess is right, because

Asian relationships are more formal, and that formality is applied much more broadly than in the West. Public life is one of stylized interactions, like ballet. Everybody knows what will happen next. Because there won't be any surprises, no one's feelings will be hurt. It is very important that everybody maintains face, status, and honor."

"You know," Nancy observed, "maybe it's not so surprising that relations between people in Shakespeare's England and in Asia today are so similar. From what I have read, it is American society, with its lack of boxes and mostly equal social relations, that is the odd man out. Our mostly horizontal system of social relations makes it hard for Americans to understand the rest of the world, past or present. Our country has evolved in ways that others have not. Asia has retained the way of interacting that was common in England and much of the rest of the world four hundred years ago. But we have changed."

"So Lear's daughters and their husbands should have recognized two limits on their power," Pat concluded, "those from Lear's being in the 'former king' box, which still entitled him to some respect, and his being in the 'father' box. Lear's daughters and Albany would have been condemned by Shakespeare's audiences because they violated the duties incumbent on them in the boxes they occupied relative to Lear's."

"Let's take a short break here," Alan said. "We are just past the halfway point."

75

Once everyone was again seated at the table, Nancy introduced the subject of bastards in Shakespeare's plays.

"In modern American society we tend to think that all children should be treated equally, but it wasn't that way in Shakespeare's day. Then, a distinction was made between the eldest male child and all others. Elizabethans practiced primogeniture, the system in which the eldest son inherited all the real estate and titles when a man died.

"At the very top of the society, the practice was essential to settle the question of succession peacefully. By having an established process through which the eldest male child inherited the crown, civil war could be avoided. It also led to a peaceful society by designating in advance who would inherit titles that had been conferred by the king. The estate went with the title because it was needed to maintain the titleholder's lifestyle. A similar practice carried on down through the rest of society, though it was most important at the upper levels, which are the levels depicted in Shakespeare's plays. It's hard for Americans today to understand this concept of primogeniture or the reasons for it because we're so used to an equal division of assets among all children.

"Bastards were doubly unlucky in Elizabethan society. They weren't usually openly acknowledged by their fathers, even if the father-son relationship was widely known by others. Many of Shakespeare's plays have a character who is a bastard, including *King Lear* and *King John*. In *King John* there is an extraordinary scene in which the eldest son of Sir Robert Faulconbridge might be denied his inheritance because the second son claims he's not really Faulconbridge's son even though he was raised as his legitimate son. He was fathered by Richard the Lionhearted while Sir Robert was away at the wars.

"Yeah, a tricky situation exists," Doug interjected. "The eldest son was born to Sir Robert's wife after their marriage took place, which makes him legitimate. But the second son has shown that he wasn't sired by Sir Robert. What is at stake here is the inheritance of both the title and the estate."

"King John jumps in to solve the problem," Dave said. "He gives the eldest son a choice. He can claim his inheritance from a man he doesn't have much respect for, or he can acknowledge that he is the son of the illustrious Richard the Lionhearted, give up his inheritance, and become a knight. Being a young man of great spirit, he chooses the latter option, saying 'I am I, howe'er I was begot.' The King then knights him and praises him as being 'The very spirit of Plantagenet!' That's Richard the Lionhearted."

Doug laughed. "The Bastard certainly has the spirit of someone lively. Rather than being ashamed of being illegitimate, he is proud of it. He goes on to mock Sir Robert, saying something like 'Old Sir Robert could never have produced a son with *my* spirit.'"

"He even praises his mother for her sin," Lisa exclaimed, "saying 'With all my heart I thank thee for my father. . . . Your fault was not your folly.'"

"Hearing this, King John expresses his surprise," Pat noted, "saying 'Why, what a madcap hath heaven lent us here!'"

"'What a madcap' reminds me of Hamlet and the 'antic disposition' he puts on," Amelia said. "The two characters have a lot in common."

"What I find most interesting in all this," Nancy said, "is that the Bastard, who was born within formal society, chooses to leave it. He gives up his inherited position and accepts a new identity as a knight. This is an interesting development that isn't repeated anywhere else in Shakespeare."

"And he does it consciously, well aware of what he is giving up," Amelia noted. "As he says, the time 'fits the mounting spirit like myself,

/ For he is but a bastard to the time / That doth not smack of observation.'

"It's hard to know exactly what that means, but my interpretation is this: The Bastard knows that he lives at a time when things are changing, when people with 'the mounting spirit like myself,' are coming into their own—people like Sir Francis Drake, who are making their fortunes through skill and daring. Those without such an adventurous spirit, he says, are 'but a bastard to the time.'"

Glancing at the clock, Nancy tried to move the discussion to *King Lear* before time ran out. "The Earl of Gloucester has two sons, Edgar, his legitimate son, and Edmund, a bastard," she began, speaking quickly. "The difference in the way in which the sons were raised by their father comes back to bite him, as Edmund turns against him in ways that drive the plot in *King Lear*."

"Nancy, I'm afraid we're out of time," Alan said.

"Oh, that's too bad," Amelia lamented. "I'm sure it would have been an interesting discussion, given that Edmund was conceived 'in the lusty stealth of nature.'"

Nancy turned to Alan as they all stood up. "You know, Dr. Fernwood, there is enough in a play like *Lear* to keep us busy for a week of daily classes."

"You're right, Nancy. That's why I have spent so much of my career focused on Shakespeare. We'll have a chance to return to *Lear* several more times before the term ends."

As Alan walked toward the door, he overheard Doug say to the others, who were already outside, "You know, this discussion reminds me of the movie where a guy says that his mother taught him that 'Manners are how we show respect for other people.' Remember that movie? The one where the guy comes out of his family's fallout shelter at age thirty in the 1980s, after having been living underground for his entire life? The movie where the guy has many valuable old baseball cards?"

"*Blast From the Past*," Pat reminded him.

"Well, Lear's two daughters didn't have any manners," Doug concluded.

Alan shook his head, laughing. The younger generations have such different references from my parents' time, he thought, thinking of Fred Astaire. I'm glad I can appreciate both.

76

It felt odd to see so much ice in the middle of the summer, but there it was. Alan stood outside the skating rink, looking in through the large pane of glass that separated the rink from the sidewalk. This window is a brilliant idea, he thought, just like those exercise clubs that have a large window facing the street. It not only gives people exercising something to look at while working out, but also invites those outside to join the club. And here comes Amelia, right on time.

"Hi, Alan! Is this what you wanted to show me? It's amazing seeing people ice skating in the summer."

"Actually, I want to take you skating."

"Really? I can think of nothing else I would rather do. Well, almost nothing."

"Have you ever been ice skating before?"

"No, never. Is it hard to do? But never mind. I'm sure I can do it. I am a very physical person."

"Come on, let's get our skates on."

After trying and falling several times, they both managed to skate slowly, holding hands without grasping the railing. They began to skate faster, able to take the turns now without falling.

"You know, Amelia, you arrived at the rink right on time. And now you are ice skating. You are becoming more Americanized every day. Perhaps sometime we could watch *The Americanization of Emily*, one of my favorite movies. It's about an American man and a British woman who fall in love in England during World War II. The actress is Julie Andrews. Do you know her?"

Amelia was about to answer when she began to wobble, and then fell, pulling Alan down with her. Both got up, unhurt, laughing at their clumsiness.

They began skating again. "Well, I have never met her, but of course I know who Julie Andrews is. She was in *The Sound of Music*. She played the singing nun who became a governess for a family with many children who had no mother. The whole family had to climb over the mountains to escape the Nazis. It is a famous movie. I know many of the songs in it."

As they approached the same place where they'd fallen before, Alan began to go wobbly, and pulled both of them over to the railing. "*The Americanization of Emily* has an interesting connection with *The Sound of Music*," he told her, as they began to skate again. "It was made right after *The Sound of Music* was filmed, but before it was released. So Julie Andrews had made the musical but hadn't yet become famous because of it. It was kind of the last time she could go out in public without being recognized."

"That is just like us!" Amelia said. "We can't go out together in public without the fear of being seen. That wouldn't be good for either of us."

"Uh, right," Alan responded, not wanting to have a conversation on that subject at that moment. "Let's see how fast we can go."

Later they had dinner together. "I think we are now ready for the next step in the Americanization of Amelia," Alan said. "Have you ever had a hamburger?"

"Oh, yes, with the other Fulbright students the first week I was here. Most of us had never eaten a hamburger before. I'm not sure whether the others liked it, but I did. So now, not only do I show up for appointments on time, I like hamburgers. I like hamburgers and Alans. So, yes, I'm becoming even more Americanized all the time."

Later, they found themselves stretched out on the sofa in Amelia's apartment watching *The Americanization of Emily*.

"I knew Charlie Madison wouldn't die on D-Day," Amelia said, "because this movie was made in Hollywood. Hollywood movies always have happy endings. The people in them always triumph over their troubles. But in my country, many movies have sad endings. Either the man or the woman dies, or something else happens to keep them apart. That is one of the differences between our two cultures. Americans always expect things to turn out well in the end, and they are surprised when they don't. I don't think they've had enough experience in life. They would learn much if they had experiences more similar to those of people in other countries, who face all kinds of hardships every day that Americans don't even think about. Americans are like the lions in *Born Free*, who have been tamed and can't survive in the wild."

"You know, Amelia, I've had similar thoughts many times. When I compare our easy lives today with the harsh lives our ancestors lived, I feel uneasy. Only a few generations back, most people in America lived without electricity or indoor plumbing. They had to work twelve or more hours a day at tasks that were difficult and unpleasant just to survive. I used to tell my kids that people who aren't working as hard as their ancestors did are living off their efforts. They're not paying their full way in the world. I think my daughter understands because she works hard all the time. Or maybe she's just a workaholic, like me."

They were quiet for a while, enjoying the closeness of lying together on the sofa. Alan then said to her, softly, "You know, Amelia, since I first saw you in my class, I have felt as if I am super-alive. Like I'd been sleepwalking through life before. Like I'd fallen into a routine and everything had become too familiar, too comfortable. I hadn't even realized it, and I would still be that way if I hadn't met you. I would still be living almost like a robot, an android. But now, I'm super-aware of everything around me. The world seems fresher, too. I feel like my soul is coming back to life after a long sleep."

"Lying here next to you, Alan," she said. "I can tell you that your soul isn't the only part of you coming back to life."

Neither spoke while he kissed her neck. Then Amelia continued, "You are still an android, but you are my android, ALAN I. You are programmed to obey my every command, to fulfill my every whim. Here is what I want you to do."

And Alan, being an android, had no choice but to obey.

FRIDAY, JULY 10

77

Alan's task today would be to identify and prioritize the goals that Oxfordians might aim at. The ultimate goal, of course, was full acceptance by literary scholars of Edward de Vere's authorship of Shakespeare's works. But that's a pretty ambitious goal, he thought as he recalled Professor William Leahy's comment that "the conversion of academics is not going to happen in current circumstances."

Were there smaller goals that could serve as stepping stones on the path to the ultimate goal? Yes. One came to mind instantly: acceptance of the Shakespeare authorship question as a legitimate subject for academic study. Achieving that goal would make it possible for academia to study the issue without a commitment to any specific person as the author.

But what exactly do I mean by "acceptance as a legitimate subject for academic study," Alan asked himself. He turned for guidance to *Save the World on Your Own Time*, a book by Stanley Fish, Dean Emeritus at the University of Illinois, Chicago. "The evaluation, not the celebration, of interests, beliefs, and identities is what intellectual work is all about." Alan agreed. The goal of academic study isn't the promotion of any specific conclusions, but rather the study of a subject in a disinterested manner.

In academic study, Fish had continued, subjects "should be discussed in academic terms; that is, they should be the objects of analysis, comparison, historical placement, etc.; the arguments put forward in relation to them should be dissected and assessed *as* arguments and not as preliminaries to action on the part of those doing the assessing. The action one takes (or should take) at the conclusion of an academic discussion is the action of tendering an *academic* verdict as in 'that argument makes sense,' 'there's a hole in the reasoning here,' 'the author does (or does not) realize her intention,' 'in this debate, X has the better of Y,' 'the case is still not proven.' These and similar judgments are judgments on craftsmanship and coherence—they respond to questions like 'is it well made?' and 'does it hang together?'"

But, Alan reasoned, it would be hard to get literary scholars to accept the legitimacy of the authorship question unless they first recognized the weakness of the Stratfordian claim. Perhaps a three-step process would be needed. He drew a diagram to make it clearer to himself.

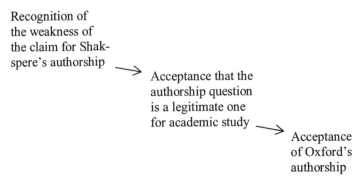

Recognition of
the weakness of
the claim for Shak-
spere's authorship

Acceptance that the
authorship question
is a legitimate one
for academic study

Acceptance
of Oxford's
authorship

Alan thought further. A case could be made that if Oxfordians could achieve the smaller goal of acceptance of the authorship question as worthy of academic study, then it might not be necessary to pursue the ultimate goal as a separate issue at all. Because de Vere was clearly the author, any serious objective examination of the evidence would reach that conclusion. So, he reasoned, it would only be necessary to convince scholars to examine the issue. Once they do, they will convince themselves of de Vere's authorship. If that line of reasoning is correct, then the goal of academic study of the authorship question would not be a mere stepping stone to the ultimate goal; it would be the most important step of all. Alan was pleased with this thought. He had found an idea around which he could build his engagement with his colleagues.

78

Delilah was looking forward to the dinner. She had arranged just to meet her father, but then decided to invite Elvin, telling him that the invitation came from Alan. She hadn't heard from Elvin since the softball game, and had been tired of waiting for him to call her. The time she gave him was half an hour before her father would arrive.

She'd been angry about the way Elvin had talked to her during the game. But that had worn off after a few days. She liked the fact that he cared about important things. So many of the guys she knew, even those at the marketing department, didn't seem interested in much outside of their own individual pleasures. Elvin might be like that, too, sometimes, but he was also interested in other things—adult things—and in a caring, thinking way.

Elvin was at the restaurant bar when she walked in. When he saw her, he walked quickly over to greet her, rather than calling out "Delightful Delilah!"

"Delilah," he said as he reached her, "I'm so glad you invited me to dinner. Or rather that your father did. I want to tell you how sorry I am about the way I talked to you at the soft ball game. I'm sorry I got angry like that. I know that you were only showing support for people who were ill."

"Well, it's okay," she said. "I know how carried away you get about things you think aren't right, especially things related to your STEM issues. I'm that way, too, about certain things."

"So tell me what's new," Elvin urged her as they headed toward their table. He had his arm around her as they walked.

79

Alan walked into the lobby of the Harvest Hotel on his way to the outdoor restaurant on the ground floor, where he was meeting Delilah for dinner. He heard her voice even before he saw her. But he thought he heard Elvin Alvarez's voice, too, which was surprising.

Yes, that was Elvin and he's with Delilah. Alan knew that they'd met occasionally when Elvin had dinner at their house, but he hadn't realized that they saw each other elsewhere. Even better than the mere sound of their voices was the happiness he could detect in them. They were clearly two people who enjoyed each other's company.

As Alan approached the table, Delilah rose and they gave each other a quick hug. "Hi Dad, how are you holding up with Mom gone?"

"Pretty good. I'm taking advantage of the quiet house to get a lot of work done."

Elvin also stood up, and the two men shook hands warmly. "Good to see you, Alan."

"Elvin, it's good to see you, too. What's new, Delilah?" he asked, turning to his daughter.

"El and I were just talking about our jobs. As you know, my internship in the marketing department is going well."

"But then we somehow got onto the nature of truth," Elvin said.

"Dee thinks her job is about ascertaining the truth, but I disagree."

"'El?' and 'Dee?'" Alan asked, laughing. "You call each other by one-letter names? Who am I? 'A?'"

"No, Dad. It doesn't work with you because your name doesn't begin with the sound a letter makes when the alphabet is recited. Ours do."

"You're right," he said after he worked it out. "But tell me how talking about your jobs could lead to a discussion on the nature of truth."

"Well, in my internship, and in my marketing classes, I'm seeking to uncover what people want so that I can help ensure that my company produces products that are wanted. And so that later I can design advertising to show people that our products will meet their needs.

"I am meeting Aristotle's definition of truth—a definition that you repeated so many times to me and Carson when we were kids that I have it memorized, Dad. I'm attempting to make true statements—statements in which 'A' is 'A'—statements in which what I say about the world matches the reality of it. Therefore, I'm pursuing truth. But El doesn't agree."

Delilah and Alan looked at Elvin.

"Two months ago I would probably have agreed with Dee. The reason I disagree now is because of an experience I had on my job recently, before I began writing 'The Contrarian.'"

"Oh, sorry to interrupt," Alan said. "I heard about your column. Congratulations! Your editors must have great confidence in you."

"Thanks, Alan. I'll tell you more about it in a minute. But a couple of months ago the new editor called me in to his office because he wasn't quite happy with the articles I was writing. At that time, I was writing about new scientific reports, and was careful to state their contents accurately, so I also thought I was making true statements, as Dee does now.

"But my editor wanted more than merely accurate summaries of the contents of individual reports; he also wanted me to highlight ways that findings in new reports clashed with those of older reports. In endeavoring to do that, I began to realize that even comparing the conclusions in the various reports wasn't enough. I needed to go beyond the reports themselves to try to find out the truth of the subject they addressed.

"Dee, it seems to me, is in the stage I was in before trying to determine the truth of the matter. She is reporting on what she has found. She's making accurate observations. But she isn't reporting truth—only preferences or opinions, things that change all the time. I'm sure she knows of cases where products designed to meet preferences expressed in surveys failed because the preferences had changed by the time the product had reached the market."

"Yes, that's true," Delilah replied. "But the fact that preferences or opinions change doesn't alter the fact that I'm reporting the truth as it exists at the time I record it."

"I'm not even sure that is correct. Regardless of how accurately you report what is said to you, you don't really know whether the people interviewed expressed their true opinions or preferences."

"Okay, I'll grant you that point," she said. "That is one of the problems with consumer surveys. People often say what they think the interviewer wants to hear. But my point that I'm stating the truth of what was said still stands."

A moment later she added, "Perhaps in focusing on accurately stating what was said, I'm in the same situation you were when you wrote articles that pointed out contradictions between reports, because that's something we do all the time—try to figure out why consumers have different preferences or opinions from one day to the next. In that sense I'm seeking to go beyond the reports to the truth of the matter. But I can't take the next step that you have taken, El, because I'm reporting on the desires of fickle people, not on unchanging physical processes."

"That sounds like a resolution of the matter," Alan said. "So you're still liking the job, Delilah?"

"Absolutely, Dad. You know I like working with people, and I like working with ideas, too. This career will enable me to do both. So your tuition payments are money well spent."

"I'm glad to hear that. And also that only one more year of those payments will be necessary." Alan then asked Elvin about "The Contrarian."

"The offer to write the column came completely out of the blue. I was just telling Dee that my editor wanted to see me, and when I went to his office I found Ted Torres, the Editor-in-Chief, there as well. They'd seen my blog, and thought I might be the right person to write the edgy, controversy-invoking column they were planning. They want to use it to build a younger readership.

"I enjoy writing it because I enjoy deflating opinions or beliefs that are clearly out of line with known facts. I like skewering the pretentious folks who claim to be superior beings because of their beliefs, while not recognizing that their beliefs are flawed. Maybe it's not so much that I enjoy pursuing truth as exposing falseness. That's particularly true when it comes to belief in human activity as the principal cause of global warming."

"Well, I'm happy to hear that you're enjoying writing the column," Alan told him. But he couldn't help wondering if Elvin had become one of those nutty global warming deniers.

"Dad, what are you working on so intensely these days? Whenever I drop by the house I hear you typing away like mad."

"I am actually pursuing truth, or was. I spent much of June exploring the Shakespeare authorship question—the issue of whether the man from Stratford wrote the works attributed to him."

"What?" Delilah exclaimed. "You have always laughed at the loonies who doubted that William Shakspere wrote Shakespeare."

"I know, and I'm kind of embarrassed about that. There is a reality outside of ourselves, and that is what I sought by investigating the authorship question. The reality of who really wrote the plays and poems is unchanging. I want to be sure our understanding of the facts matches that reality. It turns out that the doubters were right. After a month of intense research, I concluded that Shakespeare was a pen name and that the man behind it was Edward de Vere, Earl of Oxford."

"Really?" Elvin asked. "Alan, you're now one of the loonies who believes that Shakespeare didn't write Shakespeare?"

"And you're now one of those nuts who doubts that human activity is causing changes to the Earth's climate?" Alan asked in response.

The two men stared at each other. Delilah glanced from one to the other with a worried look on her face. Then both men burst out laughing.

"You know, Elvin, we've just shown that we're both independent thinkers, not willing to blindly follow received opinion. But Stratfordians—those who believe the man from Stratford was the author—aren't happy. Many—most—of them are actively hostile toward those who doubt that Will Shakspere was the author. I'm now trying to devise a game plan for Oxfordians—those who believe that Oxford was the author—to follow to convince their Stratfordian colleagues in university literature departments of the validity of the Oxfordian claim."

"I've found the same thing, Alan. Those who believe that human-generated CO_2 emissions are changing the planet's climate are actively hostile toward those who doubt that's the case. It's quite a problem because their hostility makes it difficult for reasoned discussion of the issue to take place."

They silently considered the similarities in the reactions of the two intellectual communities. Then Alan spoke. "Elvin, we really should get together to compare notes on this subject, and consider how best to deal with that hostility."

"That's a great idea. Let's try to meet next week."

Alan then turned to his daughter. "Have you done any more modeling, Delilah?"

"Oh, I forgot to tell you," she said, looking at her father and Elvin. "I heard from the commercial director's staff. The director wants to have me in another commercial soon. Some time in the coming week. I don't know the product yet, but of course I agreed to do it."

The check came soon after and Alan paid it, happy to have been able to see Delilah and Elvin at the same time. The two of them stayed behind after he left.

What a good couple they would make, Alan thought as he walked home. It's too bad that Delilah has accepted the popular view that she needs to be well established in a career before she can marry. I wonder what Elvin's thoughts on marriage are. Probably he's afraid of losing his freedom.

He wondered if there was anything he could do to bring them together. They both seemed ripe for a serious relationship with each other. Probably not, he thought, thinking of the difficulties that fathers in Shakespeare's plays had in arranging matches for their daughters. None of their efforts had turned out well, except perhaps Prospero's in *The Tempest*, but that was mostly him staying out of his daughter's way.

SATURDAY, JULY 11

80

"What's in the bag, Alan?" Amelia asked as he walked into her apartment.

"What bag, Amelia?"

"The one you are holding behind you," she said, pointing to it.

"Oh, that bag? Nothing."

"Alan, when you say it like that, I know there is something important in it. Let me see."

"Okay. But you have to promise not to get angry," he said as he handed the bag to her.

"What are these?" she asked as she pulled out two packages wrapped in colored paper with ribbons around them, and a cake with "Happy Birthday, Amelia!" written on it. "How did you know it was my birthday? I didn't tell anyone."

"I happened to see it listed on some registration papers in the

Department office. I just found out yesterday afternoon, and only by accident. Why didn't you tell me? I could have planned something special."

"Well, this is already quite special. We don't usually celebrate birthdays in Vietnam. At least we didn't in my family when I was young. An ice cream cake! You know how much I love ice cream. I'll put it in the freezer."

When she returned she gave him a long hug. "Thank you, Alan. You are very kind."

"It's nothing. Just a couple of presents for someone very special."

"May I open them now?"

"Sure, whenever you like."

Amelia opened the smaller package first. It was a book, *Amelia Bedelia*, by Peggy Parish.

"I think you'll like that book. It's for children, of course, but when I saw your name in the title in the store I couldn't resist getting it for you. But even adults will enjoy it. I also thought it might help your son learn English."

Amelia looked through the first few pages and laughed. "I can see that it is funny. It's a perfect book for me because its humor comes from misinterpretations of language. You know I will be studying linguistics."

She picked up the larger package. "This one is heavier. Oh, there are two books! Both have a small boy and a stuffed animal on the cover. *The Essential Calvin and Hobbes* and *The Indispensable Calvin and Hobbes* by Bill Watterson."

"Have you seen these before?"

She shook her head as she began to look at them carefully.

"They are about the adventures of a six-year old boy with a wild imagination. His stuffed animal, a tiger, comes alive only when there are no adults around. These are wonderful books for parents who have young children. And they too might help your son learn English."

"Alan, I don't know what to say." She hugged him again. "This is a very special day for me. Thank you."

They ate the cake with the lights out, sitting close together on the sofa. Neither spoke for some time, until Amelia turned to him and said, "Alan, I have a present for you, too."

He turned to look at her. "Really?"

"Yes. You know that I do not like to take medicine unless I am really sick, that I do not want drugs in my body. You know I usually don't drink alcohol—only an occasional glass of wine or a mojito on a special occasion. But, for you, I have done something that I have never done for anyone else before. I am now taking birth control pills because I know how much you do not like other methods."

Alan started to speak, but "Amelia" was all that he could say as he exhaled hard. "Amelia," he managed to whisper, "that is the most wonderful thing anybody has ever done for me. I know how hard it must have been for you—" He couldn't complete the sentence.

"Alan," she whispered back, "are you crying?" She reached up to wipe his face with her hand.

"No, not crying. I must have spilled some white wine on my cheeks."

"Alan, we aren't drinking wine."

"Well in that case, maybe a tear or two did escape my eyes. I can't believe the sacrifice you have made for me." They held each other tightly before he continued. "I have never felt this way about anybody before, Amelia. I love you from the bottom of my heart."

"I love you, too, Alan. I also have never felt this way about anyone else. That is why I began taking the pills."

They sat on the sofa for a long time, holding each other, stoking each other's hair and face and hands. "I don't know why," he whispered, "but now I'm afraid to make love with you. I don't want anything to spoil this moment, and even making love would be less wonderful that just sitting here holding you."

"That is that I want, too," she whispered back.

They fell asleep holding each other on the sofa and awoke the next morning in bed. Perhaps in the middle of the night they had moved there, but neither could remember having done so.

SUNDAY, JULY 12

81

Alan had slowly come to realize that resolution of the Shakespeare authorship question lay outside the field of literary criticism. Other fields had to be brought into play. History, for instance. Historians specializing in the Elizabethan era could bring to light new information showing the extent to which events in de Vere's lifetime might have led him to focus on the themes that had so obsessed Shakespeare. Beyond that, psychologists have had much to say about the nature of genius and artistic creation.

He turned to two books by Dean Keith Simonton about the nature of genius and the conditions that facilitate its development—*Greatness: Who Makes History and Why*, and *Origins of Genius: Darwinian Perspectives on Creativity*. With information on those subjects, it should be easy to spot who the real genius is, Shakspere or Oxford. It could only be the one who meets the criteria laid out in those books.

In both books, Simonton noted the importance of experience in early childhood. Our young heads are born with many more brain cells and potential synapses between them than we would ever be able to use. The number of cells and connections is greatly reduced by age eighteen, though, with the cells that survive the pruning process being those that were used the most.

Yes, even I have heard that before, Alan thought. But here's something that hadn't occurred to me. The cells and synapses needed for a genius' work later in life, whatever the field, must have been *used* extensively during childhood and adolescence. Otherwise they would have died out. In other words, geniuses must have been raised in a resource-rich environment—an environment rich in the subject in which they were later to excel. Early and extended exposure to the areas in which Shakespeare's genius flourished—the theater and literature—was a must. There was no possible substitute for it.

Shakspere, Alan realized, couldn't have been exposed in any deep and sustained way to either of those subjects. He was born and raised in a small town some three-day's ride by horse from London. His parents were illiterate. Books would have been scarce in that farming town, as they would have been everywhere else except London and the two university towns. Even there they would have been expensive, owned only by the wealthiest and most educated.

Edward de Vere, on the other hand, was born into a noble family. The prestigious Oxford earldom was the oldest in England. His father owned a theater troupe, which would have given young Edward first-hand exposure to that world. He had also been tutored by Sir William Smith, one of England's foremost scholars in many of the same fields that Shakespeare was knowledgeable about, including botany, classical literature, and politics.

As between Shakspere and Oxford, only Oxford could have developed into the man who wrote Shakespeare's works, Alan concluded. A native genius by itself, without the formative early experiences, could never have accomplished much. So that point goes to Oxford.

Alan then discovered something else. Simonton cited findings showing that a high percentage of those who later produced works of genius had experienced childhood trauma, such as the loss of a parent. He knew that Shakspere hadn't lost either parent while a boy, but de Vere's father had died suddenly when he was only twelve years old. He gave that point, too, to Oxford.

Alan noted two more interesting factors. Those who have studied genius and creativity have estimated that creative individuals need to acquire about 50,000 "chunks" or patterns of information to master their field, and that the time needed to acquire that foundation was ten years of intense involvement with the subject matter. During that acquisition period, the developing genius would have spun off not only some works of genius, but also works of inferior quality as his or her skills developed. That certainly squares with my life, he thought. I spent about a decade studying literature and Shakespeare before receiving my Ph.D., and wrote several papers that I don't think much of today.

Alan just couldn't imagine how these findings fit the man from Stratford. How could he have acquired such intense experience without leaving any record of it and without creating any juvenile works? It just didn't seem possible that someone from an isolated town where people spoke a dialect not understandable in London could have written, as his first effort, *Venus and Adonis*—a 1,200-line poem full of classical references written in the London dialect.

Oxford, on the other hand, had been tutored by the premier scholars of his day, owned his own acting troupe that performed at court, and had been acclaimed as a poet and dramatist. None of his plays survived under his own name, but it's not too big a stretch to consider whether they survived under the names of others, including that of Shakespeare, Alan thought. He gave both these points—experience and juvenile productions—to Oxford.

By this time, Alan was becoming a bit irritated that literary scholars—himself included, until very recently—had never considered this solid information about the nature of genius.

Returning to Simonton's books after refilling his coffee cup, Alan saw that the process of artistic creativity consists largely in forming new combinations of existing materials and selecting from them the ones that work best. It was critical for the artist to possess an associative richness, a wealth of knowledge to draw on. Only a mind already filled with such riches could form surprising new combinations and put them into truly creative works of literature, music and art.

Alan came to see that creativity was a three-step process. First is an intense conscious focus on getting the vast quantity of necessary bits of information into the mind. Then the subconscious brain rearranges those bits into new combinations. Finally, some of those combinations break through into consciousness, where the mind winnows and shapes them into finished products such as artistic creations or scientific theories.

Alan recalled something that Caroline Spurgeon had said in her book *Shakespeare's Imagery*. Shakespeare, she'd written, "gives himself away" through his images. He "unwittingly lays bare his own innermost likes and dislikes, observations and interests, associations of thought, attitudes of mind and beliefs, in and through the images, the verbal pictures he draws to illuminate something quite different in the speech and thought of his characters."

Spurgeon had shown that Shakespeare's imagery is drawn from many subjects—horticulture; animals, especially birds and horses; law; Italy; courtly pastimes such as hawking; classical Greek and Latin literature; and modern languages such as French and Italian. His knowledge in all these areas must have been deep and penetrating for his unconscious brain to have generated the constant flow of imagery in them that permeates his works.

How could Shakspere have had the opportunity to absorb knowledge in these myriad areas deeply enough for them to become lodged in his unconscious brain? Alan recalled Tom Regnier's comment on the *Newsweek* blog questioning how Shakspere could possibly have acquired that depth of knowledge without having left any trace of how he'd done so.

Oxford, on the other hand, had studied law at Gray's Inn. He'd traveled to Italy—to the very cities in which Shakespeare had set so many of his plays, and had lived there for close to a year. He was a courtier and thus was intimately familiar with the courtly activities depicted in the plays. And, as one of the premier earls in Elizabeth's kingdom and as her Lord Great Chamberlain, he'd have been well aware of and keenly interested in political developments in her court.

In sum, Oxford had deep and sustained experiences in all of the areas that Shakespeare drew on to form his imagery, whereas Shakspere left no record of how he could have acquired knowledge and experience in any of them. So that point, too, went to Oxford.

Alan suddenly felt hungry. It was time for lunch.

Back at his desk with a full stomach, he considered a point from Simonton's books that he deemed the most important of all. One doesn't give birth to creative works at the highest levels merely by chance. One doesn't accidentally acquire the depth of knowledge in so many areas needed to create such works. One doesn't engage in ten years of intense involvement with the subject merely to fill the time. These things happen *only because of an intense determination to do them.*

All of the most creative people Alan knew were obsessed with their work, and could barely stand to be away from it. Simonton's observation was especially revealing: "They deeply love what they do, showing uncommon enthusiasm, energy, and commitment, usually appearing to friends and family as 'workaholics.' They are persistent in the face of obstacles and disappointments, but at the same time they are flexible enough to alter strategies and tactics when repeated failure so dictates."

All that led to the realization that if Shakspere were indeed the author, he took the unprecedented and inexplicable step of walking away from his literary activities at the height of his powers to spend the final dozen years of his life in Stratford, where he busied himself with brewing malt, speculating in grain, and suing his neighbors for small amounts of money. Alan had already noted Looney's disbelief that a creative genius would abandon his creative work for small-time commercial activities.

The only other example of a top-notch creative figure abandoning his creative work at the peak of his powers was that of the Italian composer Gioachino Rossini. That situation, however, had been misunderstood. Rossini had stopped composing operas only after being incapacitated by health problems and political pressures brought on by producing works on politically sensitive subjects. He had continued composing other forms of music.

Alan then recalled a comment by George Bernard Shaw: "The true artist will let his wife starve, his children go barefoot, his mother drudge for his living at seventy, sooner than work at anything but his art." He laughed as he compared Shaw's observation with the mundane activities that Shakspere occupied himself with in Stratford. Oxford, on the other hand, had bankrupted himself, selling one piece of land after another to finance his theater activities. So that point also went to Oxford.

That Stratfordians had ignored all these factors related to genius and creativity in Simonton's books was making Alan angry. It was time to stop work before he got too upset. "Calm down," he told himself. "After all, you yourself were one of them only a couple of months ago."

Alan closed Simonton's books and pondered the situation. If Shakspere is regarded as Shakespeare today, he reasoned, it could only be because a hoax had been perpetrated—by whom and for what reasons he didn't know. That needed further study.

In fact, what was needed was a conference to explore the issue of the hoax. He now saw no need for the event to consider whether the man from Stratford was the author or not. He wasn't. Why not jump right into examining the question of how the hoax was perpetrated? He could simply change the title of the conference from *Shakespeare: Did He or Didn't He?* to *The Shakespeare Hoax.* He could see that the conference would need to be organized into three parts: "Perpetrating the Hoax," "Uncovering the Hoax," and "Why the Hoax?" He should run this new idea by Matt as soon as possible.

82

The mental effort to sort through so much material in Simonton's books had exhausted Alan. Fortunately, it was Sunday and he could take a nap. He awoke slowly, with part of a poem repeating itself softly in his head, a poem from one of Shakespeare's earliest plays, but instead of Sylvia, the name Amelia had somehow inserted itself into it.

> What light is light, if Amelia be not seen?
> What joy is joy, if Amelia be not by—
> Unless it be to think that she is by
> And feed upon the shadow of perfection?
> Except I be by Amelia in the night,
> There is no music in the nightingale.
> Unless I look on Amelia in the day,
> There is no day for me to look upon.
> She is my essence, and I leave to be,
> If I be not by her fair influence
> Fostered, illumined, cherished, kept alive.

Alan could imagine no life more fulfilling than one spent with Amelia. They were already true companions in every sense of the word, sharing a love of literature and other intellectual subjects, and an interesting and fulfilling physical relationship. She was already the ideal or idealized reader he had in mind. He could imagine not only the books she could inspire him to write, but also the dedications to her in them.

He had always been envious of those writers who'd written effusive dedications to their spouses, describing them as their "best reader and most severe critic," as "my wife and intellectual companion of four decades," and as my "comrade in life and letters." Married to Diana, he would never be able to write dedications like those.

Diana was a wonderful person in many ways, Alan recognized. She had an amazing ability to make friends with people during the course of a single brief conversation. He admired that skill, one that he didn't have. But he also knew that she was no longer the right person for him. Not only were the simplistic primary emotions a problem, but also her black and white approach to life. Situations were either 100 percent one way or another with her; one extreme or the opposite. That wasn't how he saw the world, and it was difficult to try to discuss any situation with someone unable to recognize nuances.

It was also the different activities they considered important. He divided all activities worth doing into two categories. There were those that were important in themselves. We should spend as much time and effort as possible engaged in them. There were also those that weren't important in themselves, but which were necessary in order to engage in the important activities. We should try to spend the minimum possible time and effort in those supporting activities so that that the maximum possible time could be devoted to the important ones.

Activities important in themselves included the life of the mind: literature, philosophy, history, science, classical music and so on. At the opposite end were housekeeping tasks. When Alan came home from work, he went straight to the most important intellectual activities. But when Diana came home, she went straight into cleaning activities. That was only the smaller problem. The larger one was that once she was through dusting and vacuuming she didn't move to the life-of-the-mind activities that he lived for. They weren't part of her life at all.

Despair was what Alan felt when he thought of the situation. He recalled that Goethe, the great German poet and dramatist, and scientist and administrator—a real genius in every way—had married his housekeeper. He sometimes felt like he'd done the same, and wondered how Goethe's marriage had turned out.

Might it be possible to get out of his current situation? The vines holding him in place were pretty thick. He didn't know if he could cut through them.

MONDAY, JULY 13

83

"In our last meeting," Doug said as he began his introduction, "we considered how distinctions of name, title and position played out among people of high rank in Shakespeare's plays. Today we consider an even more interesting topic, the suitability of the characters for the positions they hold.

"Given that people in Elizabethan society often inherited their titles and even their professions or crafts, people must sometimes have inherited duties or responsibilities for which they were ill-suited. Being a keen observer of people around him, Shakespeare must have witnessed that situation many times. He might even have experienced it himself. It certainly made an impression on him because he portrayed it again and again in his plays.

"For the purpose of our discussion, I have divided those situations in the plays into two categories. Before the break we'll look at Shakespeare's portrayal of courtiers or intellectuals in political positions for which they are ill-suited, and the problems that result. After the break we'll examine military men who enter political positions for which they lack qualities essential for success.

"Turning to the first type, Shakespeare repeatedly shows that disaster is the result when intellectuals or courtiers of a poetic nature occupy positions of power. Their absorption in their intellectual or poetical activities is the cause of their failure.

"Consider Prospero in *The Tempest*. He'd been Duke of Milan. His mistake had been to turn management of the dukedom over to his brother so that he could seclude himself to study the liberal arts. As he told us, 'my library was dukedom large enough.' But that's not the mindset needed to run a dukedom, and it opened the way for his brother to conspire with the King of Naples. Prospero and his daughter were seized and set adrift on the sea.

"Let's now turn to what I think is Shakespeare's most interesting example of someone caught in a position for which he is ill-suited: Richard the Second. We see a man in the position of king who has the temperament of a poet, not that of a political ruler. He has no business being king. It wasn't a position to which he rose by virtue of his accomplishments, but only one that he inherited on the death of his father when he was a boy.

"This mismatch creates opportunities for other, more aggressive, more determined, men. Early in the play, Richard had banished Henry Bolingbroke, his cousin, and then stolen his inheritance after his father died. Bolingbroke forms an army and re-enters England, ostensibly to reclaim his inheritance. But, finding Richard's response to his illegal return so feeble and inept, he then considers seizing the throne. What happens next?"

Pat was the first to respond. "I agree that Richard is not an ideal king. His response upon his return to England illustrates that point perfectly. He finds Bolingbroke's army in the field ready to face him, and needs to show a warlike countenance to his generals and soldiers. But what does he do? He weeps!"

Lisa had the text at hand, and read it.

"'I weep for joy
To stand upon my kingdom once again.
Dear earth, I do salute thee with my hand,

Though rebels wound thee with their horses' hoofs.'"

"Thanks, Lisa. These are not the words needed to motivate his troops to risk their lives to defend his throne."

"Soon after that," Dave observed, "Richard goes from weeping to overconfidence in an inevitable victory. Bolingbroke, he says, is like a thief in the night who will hide now that the sun, Richard himself, has returned. He is absolutely certain that the heavens will defend his right to the throne."

Nancy then noted that "His confidence doesn't last. The problem is that when difficulties arise Richard gives up prematurely. He resigns himself to a fate that hasn't yet been decided. He seems almost eager to shift the burdens of being king on to someone else's shoulders. He does this several times."

"In one of those times," Doug commented, "Richard gives us one of the most poetically moving and self-pitying speeches in the play.

'Let's talk of graves, of worms, and epitaphs,
Make just our paper, and with rainy eyes
Write sorrow on the bosom of the earth. . . .
For God's sake let us sit upon the ground
And tell sad stories of the death of kings!'

"Once again he needs to be bucked up by one of his men, who tells him, 'My lord, wise men ne'er sit and wail their woes, / But presently prevent the ways to wail.'"

"I agree with Doug that Richard doesn't have the right inner spirit to be king," Amelia said. "And yet, he does appear to have the external countenance of a king. As York observes,

'Yet looks he like a king. Behold, his eye,
As bright as is the eagle's, lightens forth
Controlling majesty, Alack, alack, for woe,
That any harm should stain so fair a show!'

"That's the key word: 'show.' Richard puts on a show. He is acting the part of a king even though he doesn't have the toughness and political abilities necessary to govern."

"And then comes another important speech," Lisa noted. "In it, Richard, who is about to abdicate, doesn't even know what to call himself. He has been king—occupied the position of king—for so long that he doesn't even remember how to think of himself as a person, as an individual rather than as someone in a certain position. Northumberland has addressed him as 'My lord,' and Richard responds by saying 'No lord of thine . . . Nor no man's lord. I have no name, no title – / . . . And know not now what name to call myself!'"

"And then," Amelia said, "Richard calls for a mirror. He wants to see what he looks like when not a king. This is another example of his acting in a theatrical way rather than focusing on the great issues being decided at that moment. After looking at himself and not seeing much difference since abdicating, he throws the mirror to the ground and it shatters.

"All that was mere prelude. Richard's next statements reveal the core of his heart. They show why he had been so resigned to losing the crown, so willing to concede defeat several times without yet have been defeated." Amelia nodded to Lisa, who had the passage at hand.

"Seeing the mirror's shivers on the ground, Richard says, 'How soon my sorrow hath destroyed my face.' Bolingbroke then replies, 'The shadow of your sorrow hath destroyed / The shadow of your face.' And Richard responds with,

> 'Say that again.
> The shadow of my sorrow? Ha! let's see!
> 'Tis very true; my grief lies all within;
> And these external manners of laments
> Are merely shadows to the unseen grief
> That swells with silence in the tortured soul.'"

"As I see it," Amelia continued, "that passage is the most important in the play because it reveals Richard's poetic nature. Even at the pivotal moment when he has just abdicated, he is fascinated by the poetic nature of the phrase 'the shadow of your sorrow,' and stops whatever else he is doing to repeat it, to ponder its poetic beauty.

"Then he talks of his 'tortured soul.' His soul has indeed been tortured—not just because he has abdicated the throne, but also because his poet's soul had been forced into the position of political leadership for which it was so ill-suited."

"Yes, I think you've identified the key point, Amelia," Nancy said. "Just as the soul of the average man is revealed when he gets real power for the first time, so too the soul of the king is revealed when he becomes an ordinary person, no longer burdened with the cares of state and is finally free to do what he wants to as a private person."

"With that thought in mind, it's now time for our break," Alan said.

84

After the break, Doug turned the discussion to the disasters that result when military men in Shakespeare's plays enter political positions for which they are ill-suited.

"We could ask whether Macbeth, who was courageous on the

battlefield, had the qualities needed for success as a political leader. But let's turn to another example, Brutus in *Julius Caesar*. I'm not sure if he was a military leader, but we can't pass over him because his example is so important. When the play opens, Brutus is regarded as a noble man, but we don't know quite why. In the course of the play, we are given an example. He limited the number of assassinations to only one—Caesar. That was the minimum number that he saw as necessary to achieve the goal of saving the Republic. And he made it the maximum as well, in spite of pressure to approve assassinating others."

"Ah," Nancy said. "If Brutus had accepted Cassius's urgings to assassinate Antony, the other conspirators might have proposed more killings, and the number could have risen quickly. I think Brutus resisted the pressure to go down that road because there was no natural stopping point if even one additional assassination was added. Antony, on the other hand, once he held power, drew up a list of those to be assassinated that was, rumor had it, as long seventy or even a hundred names."

"That's right," Doug agreed. "But it was just that nobleness, that honorableness, that insistence that only one person would be killed, that held Brutus back. It made him ill-suited for the position he was in. He lacked the ruthlessness needed to rule."

"That makes sense." Pat observed. "Brutus lacked the ambitiousness needed to become the new Caesar. Cassius certainly had it. He was as ambitious as Caesar, but he lacked the popular support that both Caesar and Brutus had. Caesar really was the right man for the times, and in that sense his assassination really was a tragedy."

"With Caesar gone," Doug added, "the only person with the qualities need to rule was Antony. He had the ruthlessness and the ability to sway the plebeians."

"Well, it may be true that Antony could move the plebeians," Lisa said, "but the way he did it, by ridiculing Brutus and the other conspirators, made me kind of angry. It's true that Brutus lost and Antony won. But I can't help admiring what Brutus wanted to do, which was to protect the Republic. In that sense, too, he was an honorable man. And for the honorableness of his goals, I admire him in ways that I don't admire Antony."

Amelia then offered her thoughts. "In different times, Brutus might have made a good leader of the Republic. He was willing to take decisive action, and that is admirable. He thought he saw the moment—the last possible time, really, when Caesar could be stopped from being crowned—and he acted. But he was wrong. The moment had already passed."

"Unfortunately," Pat interjected, "the larger tides of the times were against him. He tried to hold them back, but they were too strong for him and he was destroyed."

"Well," Dave commented, "the times were against Brutus and in favor of kingship not because Rome was strong, but because Rome was weak; that is, the Romans had become weak. And Caesar, rather than seeking to make them stronger, sought to dominate them."

Lisa pointed to a passage in the play that explained that point. "'I know he would not be a wolf, / But that he sees the Romans are but sheep, / He were no lion, were not Romans hinds.'"

"Julius Caesar was about to do what ambitious men have always done," Dave continued. "He took advantage of the situation to raise himself up. We can't fault him for doing that. He had the full range of qualities that Rome needed at that time, something that neither Brutus nor Cassius nor any of the other conspirators had. Even Antony didn't have the full stature needed to become a new Caesar, which was why the Triumvirate was formed."

Amelia offered another thought. "Much has been made of Brutus's nobleness and honorableness. But there was another strain in him, too, one that might have made him a feared leader. Do you recall what he had the conspirators do after they assassinated Caesar? Here is the passage.

> Stoop, Romans, stoop
> And let us bathe our hands in Caesar's blood
> Up to the elbows, and besmear our swords;
> Then walk we forth even to the marketplace,
> And, waving our red weapons o'er our heads,
> Let's all cry 'Peace, freedom, and liberty!'

"Is Brutus mad? He wants the assassins to smear Caesar's blood on their hands and arms, all the way up to their elbows, then wave their bloody hands, arms and weapons in the marketplace while shouting 'Peace, freedom, and liberty!' I can't think of anything more likely to instill fear and terror in the people of Rome."

No one said anything as they pictured that bizarre scene. Then Alan said, "I don't think I have ever before heard anybody point out just how bizarre that passage is, Amelia. It certainly opens up a new perspective on Brutus."

"We are running short of time," Doug said quickly, "so I'd like to turn to Exhibit A, *Coriolanus*, one of Shakespeare's most powerful plays. Coriolanus was an extraordinary soldier. He was such a terror on the battlefield, winning such incredible victories that Rome honored him by giving him the title Coriolanus. Rome's politicians then offered him the highest political position in Rome. All he had to do to get it was to go through a few political rituals. Supreme power would then have been his. But he couldn't do it, could he?"

"No, he couldn't," Nancy responded. "He couldn't bow down before the people and pretend to honor those he despised for their cowardice on the battlefield, for their seeking comfort rather than honor. The mismatch between his temperament and the political rituals he had to go through was so extreme that he ended up being banned from Rome."

"So what was it?" Doug asked. "What was it about his temperament that made Coriolanus so unwilling—even unable—to go through what appeared to be rather formulaic rituals?"

"Well, beyond the disdain Coriolanus felt for the masses," Amelia answered, "it was matters of both principle and expediency. As he explained, 'where gentry, title, wisdom / Cannot conclude but by the yea and no / Of general ignorance – it must omit / Real necessities, and give way the while / To unstable slightness.' In other words, the mob is fickle, and if we cater to it when it is in one mood, what are we to do when its mood changes? Virtue and vice exist, and so do right and wrong. If we allow the changeable masses to decide what those things are from moment to moment, then 'Nothing is done to purpose.'"

"People are sometimes their own worst enemies," Dave noted. "They are sometimes too aggressive for their own good. They shoot for positions in which they'd have to engage in activities they wouldn't enjoy and for which they lack the abilities needed to succeed. But Coriolanus wasn't like that. He instinctively knew that he had more in common with accomplished military officers than with the Senators and other scheming politicians he despised. But he allowed himself to be persuaded to seek the highest political position."

"That reminds me of Macbeth," Nancy said. "If it weren't for the influence of the witches and Lady Macbeth, he would never have murdered Duncan."

Pat got in the final thoughts before time ran out. "We're happiest when we're in positions that suit our abilities and temperament, and when we work with people whose company we enjoy. That's something we should never forget."

After the class ended, Alan heard Doug saying to the other students as they walked out the door that the discussion reminded him of the Peter Principle. "You've all heard of that managerial concept, right? The one that says that managers rise to the level of their own incompetence?

Well, Shakespeare knew about that principle long before Mr. Peter."

Walking back to his office, Alan watched the six students moving away in a group toward one of the campus cafeterias. They had begun to eat lunch together after each of the sessions. This often happened in the summer terms because classes were smaller and students had fewer courses. That was one of the reasons he especially enjoyed teaching during the summer. And, of course, the lighter teaching load left him more time for his own projects.

85

Alan met Matt Harris late in the afternoon. After explaining his idea for a conference on the subject of *The Shakespeare Hoax*, Alan looked at him to gauge his reaction. He didn't need to read Matt's body language, though, because his spoken language was quite clear.

"Alan, your first idea for a conference, *Shakespeare: Did He or Didn't He?*, was already quite controversial. Still, it might have attracted a sufficient number of people from academia. Your new idea for an event built around a 'hoax,' with its assumptions that Shakspere wasn't the author and that some kind of deception had been perpetrated, is too far out. Even if I agreed with you, which isn't something you should assume to be the case, I can't envision many scholars attending."

"That's just the point. We want this event to be cutting edge. We don't want a large number of people totally committed to Shakspere to attend. We want a smaller number of people with open minds, people willing to consider alternate ideas. You know what most professors are like, Matt. They are sheep. They will follow wherever they are led. This conference will be a meeting of the leaders of the idea that Stratman wasn't the author."

"Stratman?"

"Oh, that's a term sometimes used by doubters to refer to the man from Stratford. You wouldn't believe how many doubters there are, Matt. They have their own organizations and websites. They have produced some remarkable findings. We need to join the movement. It's still not too late to become part of the vanguard."

"Well," Matt said after a pause, "you know the process for applying for authorization for special events. I suggest that you give the committee members a heads up on the nature of your new proposal so they're not caught by surprise when reading the application."

"Thanks, Matt. I'll do that. This conference will be a remarkable event, one of the first on the Shakespeare authorship question to be organized by a nationally known university."

Well, Matt thought to himself after Alan had left, "remarkable" is a word with many meanings. He shuddered to think how the committee would react to Alan's latest proposal.

TUESDAY, JULY 14

86

In the past week, Elvin had sought to unravel the mystery of how human-generated carbon dioxide could have acquired such a bad reputation, given its miniscule presence—$1/25^{th}$ of one percent—in the atmosphere. In doing so, he had learned that human beings produce only two percent as much CO_2 as natural processes do in a typical year. In one atypical year, 1991, the Mount Pinatubo eruption produced in one week thirty times as much CO_2 as human beings produced in that entire year, making the natural production of the gas that year seventy-five times higher than all human output. The more he learned, the harder it was to see how human-produced carbon dioxide could have much effect on the planet's climate.

Elvin was about to begin writing his column when he came across a fact so extraordinary that he couldn't believe his eyes. According to one report, even increases in human-generated CO_2 several times larger than those anticipated by midcentury would cause little or no increase in the Earth's temperature. What? He read it again and saw that he hadn't misunderstood what the report said. Even much larger emissions of CO_2 would have little or no effect on the Earth's temperature—a fact completely contrary to global warming theory. He made notes on why that was so, and turned to writing the column.

The Heart of the Matter

Carbon dioxide has a bad rep—because it's gotten a bad rap.

Imagine a court case in which global warming is the felony charge, and Human-Generated Carbon Dioxide (H-G CO_2) is the defendant. What follows are excerpts from the transcript of the trial.

The prosecutor summed up his presentation by saying that only the defendant could have committed the crime. "Other likely suspects could not have done it. The IPCC has confirmed that global warming couldn't have come from changes in solar radiation or from the effects of volcanic eruptions. Cloud cover, also, couldn't have committed the crime because on average clouds cool the planet by blocking more radiation from the sun than they block heat from leaving the Earth's atmosphere. The same is true for aerosols. H-G CO_2 is, therefore, the only possible perpetrator."

The defense then began its rebuttal. "Human-Generated Carbon Dioxide is an upstanding member of the community, one whose presence has a strong net benefit for plants and animals. Carbon dioxide is not only *not* a pollutant, it is the key to photosynthesis. All plant and animal life depend on the existence of CO_2 in the atmosphere. We owe our very existence to carbon dioxide.

"CO_2, the court might be surprised to learn, is 'food' for plants. In fact, operators of greenhouses routinely pump CO_2 gas into them to promote the growth of their plants. The optimal percentage of CO_2 in the atmosphere to promote growth is 900 parts per million, more than twice the concentration in the atmosphere today.

"As levels of CO_2 in the general atmosphere have increased in recent decades, plant life, including those that human beings cultivate as food sources, has grown faster and more solidly and with less water. Plant life has increased 14% in all types of ecosystems over the past 30 years. The benefits for human beings of increased CO_2 levels are enormous. One study found that the increased value of crops grown with the increase in CO_2 already recorded over pre-industrial levels is $140 billion a year. Another found that 'for the 45 crops that account for 95% of global crop production, an increase of 300 ppm of carbon dioxide would increase yields by between 5% and 78%. The median increase for these crops was 41% and the production-weighted yield increase was 34.6%.'

"The level of CO_2 in the atmosphere today is lower than throughout most of life's history on this planet," he continued. "H-G CO_2 is thus helping to relieve the heavy burden borne by non-human generated CO_2, and therefore deserves our thanks, not our condemnation."

Human-Generated Carbon Dioxide bowed its head in gratitude for that testimonial, as the judge nodded in sympathetic recognition of CO_2's benefits for mankind and other parts of the biosphere.

The defense then charged that human beings were the guilty party because of the heat produced by their bodies, which have a temperature higher than the planet average, and by their toasters, heaters and ovens. "Even their equipment designed to produce cold air, such as refrigerators and air conditioners, has a net heating effect," claimed the defense. "And worst of all is their destruction of forests and paving over of land, which causes heating by replacing forests that absorb heat with shiny surfaces such as buildings and roads that reflect it back into the atmosphere."

The prosecution, though, was able to rebut those charges by showing that heat generated by human beings and their toasters was insufficient to have caused warming of the planet as a whole. It also demonstrated that human activities—including those resulting in roads, cities, and agriculture—have modified only six percent of the

Earth's land surface. "That works out to only two percent of the surface of the entire globe once the oceans, which cover three-fourths of the planet, are taken into account," the prosecutor said. "Again, an insufficient change to generate global warming.

"In point of fact, human burning of biomass, a renewal energy favored by environmentalists, produces smoke that cools the atmosphere. Together with sulfur dioxide and other gases produced by industrial processes, human-produced aerosols have a net cooling effect. Human activity apart from the production of carbon dioxide is not the cause of global warming."

At this point the judge interrupted. "Let's get to the heart of the matter," he ordered. "It is clear that human activity apart from the production of carbon dioxide is not the cause of any significant warming. It's also clear that Human-Generated Carbon Dioxide has had a positive effect on the planet apart from its heat generating effects. And it's clear that H-G CO_2 is also not guilty of any direct warming, given its minuscule presence in the atmosphere.

"So, any warming caused by Human-Generated CO_2 must come from its indirect effects on other natural forces. If it is guilty, it must be because it acted through pressure and intimidation on those other forces. I instruct the prosecution to present its evidence on this point now."

"Thank you, your honor," the defense said, butting in, "for recognizing that no global warming has been generated directly by H-G CO_2's existence in the atmosphere. I believe I have ample evidence to show that it is innocent of any indirect influence as well.

"In the first place," he continued—the judge allowing the defense to pre-empt the prosecution whose presentation he had called for—"only a small fraction, 1.3%, of carbon dioxide on Earth exists in the atmosphere. Two-thirds of it exists in the oceans, and almost one-third is in soils and plants, glaciers and permafrost, and the crust of the planet. The CO_2 in the atmosphere, including H-G CO_2, is merely there in transit, moving between oceans, soils and plants to locations where it is most needed for photosynthesis and other natural processes. The average H-G CO_2 molecule is in the atmosphere for less than a decade. It is impossible that such a small amount of gas present in the atmosphere for such a limited period of time could have affected the climate of the entire planet.

"If Human-Generated CO_2 is guilty," he said, wagging his finger at the prosecutor, "then all CO_2 is guilty. Only one molecule of every 85,000 in the atmosphere is CO_2 of human origin, and yet we are asked to believe that this one molecule drives hugely complex climate change systems. We are also asked to believe that the 32 CO_2 molecules of natural origin in every 85,000 play no part in driving climate change. The charge is ridiculous."

After pausing a moment, he continued, "But CO_2 is not guilty, none of it. Here's why. The tiny percentage of CO_2 that is produced by human beings is quite valuable. It triggers processes that actually cool the planet beyond the level of any warming that it might cause in other ways.

"H-G CO_2 is gobbled up by the hungry oceans through photosynthesis, respiration and non-biological chemical and physical processes. Kelp fields expand, absorbing carbon dioxide and producing oxygen that human beings need. And plankton prosper, producing higher levels of a gas that acts with the same cooling effect as sulfuric acid and other aerosols. Human-Generated CO_2 thus works to cool the planet."

"I have already noted the 14 percent increase in plant life on Earth due to my client's presence here. Researchers have concluded that carbon storage in terrestrial reservoirs has increased despite the toll taken by foresters and farmers. In fact, the National Center for Atmospheric Research has concluded that global greening generated by my client is more than compensating for losses caused by deforestation.

"Let me state that again. Not only is H-G CO_2 not responsible for global warming, but respected scientific organizations have confirmed that its effect through the creation of additional plant life is enough to compensate for all losses by destruction of the rain forests by human beings. You would be amazed at the myriad ways that additional CO_2 promotes the health of plant and animal life on Earth."

The prosecutor then stood up to speak. "We have shown," he reminded the judge, "that global warming has not been caused by changes in solar radiation, volcanic eruptions, cloud cover, water vapor, or aerosols. And it hasn't been caused by the oceans or soils, by plant or animal life. The only possible cause is that of Human-Generated CO_2, which is accumulating in the atmosphere."

To this the defense presented its final and most important piece of information. "We know that the pre-industrial CO_2 level had been 280 parts per million (ppm), that it's now about 400 ppm, and that it is predicted to reach 560 ppm by the middle of the century. That would be an increase of only 280 parts per million—an increase of less than .03 percent, a tiny fraction of one percent of the atmosphere.

"That small increase will have literally no effect on the Earth's temperature. Here's why. Scientists have found that 'the first 100 parts per million (ppm) of CO_2 have a significant effect on atmospheric temperature, whereas any increase from the current 400 ppm will have an insignificant effect.' The reason has to do with wavelengths. Because incoming wavelengths are shortwave and outgoing are longwave, CO_2 acts as a greenhouse gas because it blocks longwave more than shortwave. However, 'the narrowness of the spectral intervals across which CO_2 intercepts radiation results in a rapid saturation of its effect, such that a doubling in the concentration of

CO_2 enhances the greenhouse effect by a constant amount.'

"Therefore, 'the amount of warming caused by increasing quanta of CO_2 depends upon the level of CO_2 already in the atmosphere, and diminishes steadily in a 'less-temperature-bang-for-every-incremental-molecule-of-carbon-dioxide-buck' pattern. A doubling from 400 to 800 ppm would have the same effect as a doubling from 100 to 200 ppm. Given the pre-industrial starting point of 280 ppm of atmospheric CO_2, only extremely minor warming will occur in response to the much-feared increase from the current level of 400 ppm to the expected level of 560 ppm at midcentury."

He paused to give the judge time to absorb that critical point as Human-Generated CO_2 smiled, at least as much as a gas was capable of smiling. That, it thought to itself, should put the lie to the global-warming-as-a-result-of-human-activity myth.

The prosecutor sensed that the judge was about to rule in favor of Human-Generated Carbon Dioxide. He had never lost a case before, and he didn't want to lose this one. Pondering the situation for a moment, he thought of a way out. He wrote a note on a piece of paper, and gave it to a messenger with instructions to deliver it to . . . himself! The messenger left the courtroom, and returned a few minutes later, just as the judge was about to issue his ruling. He rushed over to the prosecutor and gave him the message. All eyes were on him as he unfolded the paper. Everyone in the courtroom held his breath as he read the message silently to himself.

Finally, he looked up at the judge and said, "Your honor, on behalf of the state, the prosecution wishes to withdraw the charges against the defendant. Apparently there has been no warming of the Earth's atmosphere for the past 18 years and thus no crime has been committed in that time. The statute of limitations has run out on whatever crimes might have been committed more than 18 years ago. We thus urge the court to formally recognize that the state drops all charges against the defendant."

The judge, who had indeed been about to rule that Human-Generated CO_2 was innocent of the charge of global warming, announced that the charges had been dropped and that the defendant was free to go.

The courtroom erupted in pandemonium as the prosecutor sighed in relief at having found a way to maintain his record of never having had a judge rule against him. Many others also sighed in relief, expelling carbon dioxide, some of it human-generated, which was once again free to mingle with its fellow gases in the atmosphere.

87

Alan stretched out in his chair, glad to be returning to his examination of how he might promote awareness of the authorship question among his colleagues. Academia wasn't monolithic in its rejection of the issue, he knew. Although some scholars were adamant in their insistence that Shakspere was the author, others appeared to be more willing to consider other possibilities.

He saw that literary scholars could be divided into three categories based on the strength of their belief in authorship by the man from Stratford. At one extreme were those who strongly defended Shakspere's authorship. Let's call them Militant Stratfordians, he decided. Most professors he knew, though, hadn't thought much about the issue. They simply accepted the traditional belief that Shakspere was Shakespeare. Let's call them Ordinary Stratfordians. He suspected that there were others who recognized the weakness of Shakspere's claim, but who kept their doubts to themselves. Let's call them Secret Doubters.

Scholars could also be separated into groups depending on the stage of their careers, he realized. There were Senior Professors, who were well known and respected throughout academia for their contributions to Shakespearean scholarship, Junior Professors, who were still in the early stages of their careers, and Rank and File Professors, all those tenured professors in the middle. Combining the two sets of criteria would result in nine categories of scholars. Alan drew a chart to make this division of the academic community clearer to himself.

	Militant Stratfordians	Ordinary Stratfordians	Secret Doubters
Senior scholars	A	D	G
Rank & File Professors	B	E	H
Junior professors	C	F	I

It would be pointless to approach Militant Stratfordians, regardless of what point they were at in their careers, he suspected. They were only a small minority of all Stratfordians, but they were fierce defenders of their fort and hostile to any attempt to discuss the authorship issue. He recalled seeing a description of this group by a professor in England, William Leahy, who had called them the "militant minority" and noted that "they are often very aggressive and dismissive in their views and seek not only to win the argument but to humiliate the opponent." Best leave them alone and reach out to the other categories of scholars.

Ordinary Stratfordians would be more receptive to the authorship issue, but Alan passed over them to consider Secret Doubters. Although he didn't personally know any such scholars—they were, after all, secret—he knew that they existed because he'd seen a *New York Times* survey revealing that 17 percent of professors saw at least some reason to doubt Shakspere's authorship. He suspected they would be most heavily concentrated among younger professors, who were more open to alternative views simply because they didn't have as extensive a history of support for the dominant view.

Assuming I can identify them, what should I do next, Alan asked himself. I should try to convince them to make their beliefs known and to act on the basis of them. They could raise the authorship issue in their classes, and speak out about it. Yes, that is the key, he thought. Once out of the closet, the Doubters could raise the profile of the issue by addressing it in their publications and in presentations at conferences. They could even, as he was planning to do, organize conferences or seminars around the authorship question.

THURSDAY, JULY 16

88

"Good morning, Dr. Fernwood, Lisa, Nancy, Pat, Dave, Doug," Amelia began. "Today we turn to Shakespeare's portrayal of the political nature of relations between men and women.

"As we've learned, in Elizabethan society people often relate to each other on the basis of their titles or positions rather than as individuals. The relative status between them, not the personal qualities of either person, dictates the nature of their relationship. I mention this again because sexual relationships were governed by the same processes. At the same time, individuals' sexual desires constantly threatened to upset what was considered to be appropriate social interaction, and had to be tightly controlled. Shakespeare was well aware of all this."

This is going to be interesting, Alan thought.

"The play I want to focus on first to illustrate Shakespeare's depiction of the political element in relations between men and women is *Troilus and Cressida*. In it, Shakespeare uses two parallel plots to illustrate the theme. We also saw that in *King Lear*, with both Lear and Gloucester having problems with their children. It's kind of like this class having two sessions each time it meets, focusing on the same theme from different perspectives." She gave Alan a small smile.

"We have already seen how the subjective and objective valuations of Helen by the Trojans are mirrored by the subjective and objective valuations of Achilles by the Greeks. Now we consider the parallel situations of Helen, a Greek woman being held in Troy against her will, and Cressida, a Trojan woman sent to the Greek camp against her will.

"It may be that men find both women sexually attractive, but that isn't why they are where they are. Helen and Cressida have been used as political pawns. The Greeks had earlier abducted one of Priam's sisters, Priam being the leader of Troy. In retaliation, the Trojans grabbed Helen, the wife of Menelaus, leader of Sparta. So it wasn't the beauty of Helen's face that launched a thousand ships, at least not entirely. It was more the wounded pride of Menelaus, who was determined to regain his wife. Cressida is sent to the Greeks in return for Antenor, a Trojan warrior who had been captured. The exchange was made at the request of her father, Calchas, a Trojan priest who'd defected to the Greeks and who wanted Cressida to join him.

"Shakespeare has told Cressida's story mostly from Troilus's point of view, or rather he has given us enough details to suggest what Cressida's situation was in the Greek camp without spelling it out explicitly. That is one of the things I hope we can do now. Let's begin our discussion at the moment that Cressida enters the Greek camp. What happens when she arrives?"

"Oh! Oh no!" Lisa exclaimed. "Cressida is kissed by four men. She is passed from man to man in the order of their rank—Agamemnon, Nestor, Achilles, and Patroclus, who kisses her twice. I didn't realize the significance of that when I read it. I thought it was merely a greeting."

"What do you think the situation would be for an attractive young Trojan woman who suddenly finds herself in the enemy camp against her will?" Amelia asked. "She is surrounded by warriors—men—big men—who are missing their wives and lovers and who probably hate the Trojans because they have killed so many Greek warriors. Cressida is instantly held in sexual common by all Greeks. It could be that the kisses were mere kisses and not symbols for the type of activity that Shakespeare couldn't present on the stage. But even if they were only kisses, they were also the promise of rougher treatment to come. So did Cressida have any alternatives to being sexually used in common by the Greeks?"

"She had one," Dave replied. "She could seek out one Greek who would take her in and protect her from the others. He had to be someone high enough in rank so that the men would respect Cressida as his and not mess with her. This situation reminds me of a book I read a few years ago, *A Woman in Berlin*. The author, a German woman, describes what happens after the Russians entered the city in 1945. Practically every woman between the ages of ten and sixty was raped. The author found some protection by becoming the mistress of a high ranking Russian officer."

"So, Cressida had to find a protector," Pat observed. "And that is what she did. She didn't have to look far, because Diomedes had already staked his claim to her. What she had to do was act in a way that would keep his interest. She couldn't give in too easily or not give in at all. Like Scheherazade, she played that role well."

"Unfortunately, her performance was witnessed by Troilus," Lisa said. "And by Ulysses, who was with Troilus. All of them were watched by Thersites, who made lewd comments on what he saw."

"Compare their responses." Nancy said. "Troilus—incredulous; Ulysses—ho hum, nothing out of the ordinary; and Thersites—vulgarity. Three different takes on the same scene."

Silence followed, letting Amelia know that it was time to move on.

"Here is a new thought," she told the group. "I have always been struck by the similarity between Berowne's amazement in *Love's Labor's Lost* that he desires a woman who's not all that attractive and Troilus's desire for Cressida. Recall Berowne's saying how shocked he was that he loves Rosaline, a woman he describes as having two pitch balls stuck in her face for eyes. Troilus unexpectedly says something similar, that his will rather than his judgment leads him toward Cressida.

> 'I take today a wife, and my election
> Is led on in the conduct of my will,
> My will enkindled by mine eyes and ears,
> Two traded pilots 'twixt the dangerous shores
> Of will and judgment. How may I avoid,
> Although my will distaste what it elected,
> The wife I chose? There can be no evasion
> To blench from this and to stand firm by honor.'"

After a second of surprise, several students started to speak at once. Dave won out. "Oh, that explains it! Remember at the very beginning of the play Troilus says that he won't fight today? He says 'Why should I war without the walls of Troy / That find such cruel battle here within?' He says there is a battle raging within himself that has robbed him of all strength and courage, but doesn't explain it. The passage that Amelia just read does answer the question. Troilus's will and his mind have different opinions of Cressida. They're battling with each other."

"It's the same battle that Berowne faced, isn't it?" Pat noted. "Their will—their desire—for a particular woman conflicts with their judgment of her. Troilus is attracted to Cressida's beauty. But at the same time he says that his judgment—his head—wouldn't have selected her for his wife. He is perhaps saying that he knows that his desire for her is only physical, that he wouldn't want to marry her, but only sleep with her."

"But," Doug said, "he says he will marry her because his honor—his desire to do what is honorable—keeps him on the path toward marriage. He slept with her, so now he must marry her. That's what he has to do in Troy to maintain his honor."

"No, no, no," Lisa replied. "That isn't the way it was at all. Troilus makes the statement that Amelia read *before* he sleeps with Cressida."

That were all silent, astonished by that point.

"So," she continued, "it's not a matter of the shame of taking away Cressida's virginity and then abandoning her that keeps him on the path to marrying her. The situation, I think, is this: Troilus knows that his desire to sleep with Cressida is so strong that he won't be able to resist it if the opportunity arises. At the same time, he knows that the price of sleeping with her will be having to marry her to maintain his honor, even though she isn't the right person for him to marry. That is the torment that is within him at the opening of the play. He knows that he should restrain himself, but knows he won't be able to."

"Well, this is all very surprising," Nancy said. The usual interpretation is that Troilus is faithful and Cressida is unfaithful. But now it appears that's not the case.

"On Troilus's side, he already has one foot out the door, and is looking for a way to get the other foot out. That explains why he didn't fight to have Cressida remain in Troy. I was always puzzled about why he argued so strongly to keep Helen in Troy, and won that argument, but didn't push back at all against the decision for Cressida to be forcibly sent to the Greeks. Now that makes sense. He had prayed for a miracle to be able to sleep with Cressida without having to marry her, and heaven answered his prayers."

"Now let's look at the situation from Cressida's point of view," Amelia said. "Even before she slept with Troilus, she knew that men's desire is stronger before than after. She expressed that thought the next morning, when she sees Troilus getting ready to leave her room. 'Prithee, tarry; you men will never tarry. / O foolish Cressid! I might have still held off, / And then you would have tarried.'"

"And that isn't all," Lisa reminded everyone. "She sees him leaving her room at the crack of dawn, and then sees his failing to push back against the decision to have her sent to the Greeks. She isn't dumb. She can see what's what in his mind. She knows she's being abandoned by the man she loves. A man who apparently doesn't love her.

"If she'd been familiar with *Hamlet*, she might have recalled a song that Ophelia sang in her madness. The song where a girl says 'Before you tumbled me, / You promised me to wed,' and the man answers 'So would I 'a' done, by yonder sun, / [If] thou hadst not come to my bed.'"

"And it is after all that," Amelia said, "that Cressida arrives in the Greek camp. We have already seen how she was received there."

No one spoke as they again considered Cressida's difficult situation.

Then Pat said, "Okay. I can see Cressida's situation clearly. But what about Troilus's? If he didn't love Cressida and was relieved to have a way out of marrying her, why was he so devastated on seeing her with Diomedes?"

"Maybe he was of two minds," Dave answered. "He loved her and he didn't love her at the same time. But another answer comes back to honor. His desire for Cressida would have been common knowledge in Troy. And the Trojans would have become aware of Cressida's becoming Diomedes's kept woman."

"That's it," Doug concluded. "It's honor again. Even though everybody understood the situation, and recognized that Cressida had been taken from Troilus by force—that he had to give her up for political reasons—the fact that she was now in Diomedes's bed required that Troilus fight for her to defend his honor. He had to fight Diomedes or suffer a huge loss of face and status for the same reason that Menelaus had to fight the Trojans who'd kidnapped his wife, Helen."

"So perhaps this is an instance of the distinction between appearance and reality," Amelia said. "The appearance is that Troilus is faithful and Cressida isn't, while the reality is just the opposite. Cressida wants to maintain her relationship with Troilus, and writes him a letter stating so. Troilus, wanting out—and believing the appearance of what he'd seen in Diomedes's tent but not understanding the reality of it—tears it up."

Alan then expressed his surprise. "Well, you have all come up with a very different interpretation of what is happening between Troilus and Cressida than I have ever heard before. And you've got support in the text for it. Congratulations on finding something new and interesting to say about a play that has been analyzed so extensively for hundreds of years. Let's take our break now."

89

"We'll now consider Shakespeare's portrayal of a different type of relationship between men and women," Amelia began after they returned, "that of marriage. In Shakespeare's day, the institution of marriage in the higher social classes served two purposes. It was a union of two families and it was an institution designed to produce heirs. What it was not was a formalization of a love affair between two young adults.

"Marriages were arranged as alliances between families, as the one in *Romeo and Juliet* would have been if Juliet had married Paris. Children—both male and female—were married off according to the dictates of their fathers, and political and economic considerations were paramount. The desires of those to be married weren't a major factor in the selection of spouses.

"At the very top of the social order, a princess' purity needed to be preserved. Illicit sex with a princess was regarded as treason because any offspring she might bear would have a claim of some degree to the throne. The legitimacy of the dynasty was at stake."

"Oh yes," Pat said. "We have already seen an example of the political nature of marriage at the top of society, in *Hamlet*. Ophelia's father, Polonius, and her brother, Laertes, remind her that Hamlet, being royalty, is a star too high for her. They advise her to disregard whatever love he might profess for her now, because at the end of the day the choice of his spouse will be made for reasons of state."

"And so," Amelia continued, "Laertes warns Ophelia to be careful. Do not give away your heart or your body, he says, because you will suffer if you do. In Shakespeare's day, as in the present in Vietnam, a girl must preserve her purity if she hopes to have a good match. Hamlet, they tell her, has nothing to lose by playing with you, but you have everything to lose if you let him. Men's worth or honor comes from their birth and achievements in the world, women's from their chastity and purity.

"Below the level of royalty, at the level of the nobility, marriages were arranged for the same reason that primogeniture was practiced—to keep the family's estate intact. Even farther down in the social order, fathers chose who their children would marry, as shown in *The Merry Wives of Windsor*. The merchant class had property to pass on, even if they didn't have titles. Commercial alliances could be strengthened if their children married into the right families. We have seen how fathers assert the right to determine their children's spouses in *A Midsummer Night's Dream*."

"I was just looking at that passage, Amelia," Pat said, glancing out of the corner of his eye at Lisa, who was also turning to it. "Egeus says of his daughter, Hermia, 'I beg the ancient privilege of Athens: / As she is mine, I may dispose of her' as I choose."

"His statement is confirmed by the king," Lisa observed, eager to speak. "'Be advised, fair maid,' he says, 'To you your father should be as a god, / One that composed your beauties, yea, and one / To whom you are but as a form in wax, / By him imprinted, and within his power / To leave the figure or disfigure it.'"

"That wasn't a system designed to maximize the happiness of the bride or the groom," Amelia continued. "What is so surprising in Shakespeare's plays is that so many young people oppose the spouse chosen for them. This situation must have arisen frequently in Shakespeare's day, and it must have been something new with that generation—otherwise he wouldn't have portrayed it so often. He was recording a surprising and unexpected development in his society.

"Let's make a list of the plays where this situation occurs. I have already mentioned Juliet in *Romeo and Juliet*, and Hermia in *A Midsummer Night's Dream*. Are there others?"

As her fellow students called out examples, Amelia wrote them on a whiteboard: Anne Page, in *The Merry Wives of Windsor*; Jessica, in *The Merchant of Venice*; Imogen, in *Cymbeline*; Florizel, in *The Winter's Tale*; Desdemona, in *Othello*; Rosalind, in *As You Like It*; Bertram, in *All's Well That Ends Well*.

"That's quite a list, and there were probably others. Before moving on, I want to note again how surprising it was in Shakespeare's day for young people to rebel against their parent's choice of spouse for them. That's one more example of the clash of values taking place in Elizabethan society that was reflected in Shakespeare's plays.

"Young people choosing their own spouses is something unusual in human history. In my own country, when I was little most marriages were arranged. Many still are. It's still common in places like India, Pakistan and Bangladesh, where almost a third of all people live. It's the modern West that is unusual in its marriage practices."

"You know," Nancy said, "it's true that we today don't quite realize just how new that development is and how shocking it was for parents when it arose. Because we are so used to young adults choosing their own spouses, it just seems natural to us, but it isn't.

"I didn't understand that until I saw *Fiddler on the Roof*. I still recall my surprise at Tevye's incredulous statement 'They gave each other a pledge?? Unheard of!!' He couldn't believe the violation of tradition that he was seeing. I was astonished that he would be astonished that young people would choose their own spouse. The world certainly has changed since Shakespeare's day, and Tevye's."

The class then discussed the particular situation of Hermia, Demetrius, Lysander and Helen, and the wondrous adventures that took place in the forest in *A Midsummer Night's Dream*.

Doug commented on the mystery of love that makes one person so different from another. "One character compares Demetrius, the man Hermia's father has selected for her, with Lysander, the man she loves, and notes that both are from families equally prominent and wealthy, and both they are equally handsome. Yet Hermia loves Lysander and not Demetrius."

The discussion continued as the class examined the character and goals of the four young people and the spirits in the forest until, with time almost up, Amelia turned the discussion to events within marriage itself. She noted that wives had duties to husbands, husbands to wives. Each knew their place and what their duties were.

"If you don't mind another example from *Fiddler on the Roof*," Dave interjected, "There's the scene between Tevye and his wife just after his daughter told him she and Motel the tailor gave each other a pledge because they wanted to marry for love. 'They love each other?' he asks himself, still not quite able to absorb this new idea. And then he asks himself if his wife loves him. After all, they had an arranged marriage. It's another surprising moment in that movie because it challenges something that we take for granted—that we love the one we are marrying and that he or she loves us."

"But it wasn't that way, usually, in Shakespeare's day," Amelia noted, "and that is why one scene in *Julius Caesar* is so startling. It portrays a modern marriage—an ideal modern marriage—in which husband and wife share their emotional lives as well as their bed. The scene, between Brutus and Portia, takes place before the assassination. Portia is uneasy because Brutus is withdrawn and troubled by something he won't share with her—a big change from the past. She says to him,

'Is it excepted I should know no secrets
That appertain to you? Am I your self
But as it were in sort of limitation?
To keep you at meals, comfort your bed,
And talk to you sometimes? Dwell I but in the suburbs
Of your good pleasure? If it be no more,
Portia is Brutus' harlot, not his wife.'

"Even though Portia and Brutus lived two thousand years ago and Shakespeare wrote four hundred years ago, he gives us a picture of a modern marriage. And note the phrase 'dwell I but in the suburbs of your good pleasure?' We don't even have suburbs in Asia. I thought they were an American invention. But there is the word, used in the modern sense, though metaphorically, hundreds of years ago."

With that, time ran out and the class ended.

"This discussion reminds me of Woody Allen's movie *A Midsummer Night's Sex Comedy*," Alan overheard Doug saying as the students left the classroom. Remember that one of the characters says 'Marriage is the death of hope?' He said that in a society where people marry for love. Just think what it must have been like for young men and women forced into marriages arranged by their families!"

90

"Hi, Elvin," Ed said, stopping by his cubicle. "I've just been discussing your latest "Contrarian" column with Ted. We like the way you portrayed a mock trial of Human-Generated CO_2 for the crime of global warming. Very clever."

"Thanks," Elvin said, waiting for the "but."

"But it's too long. It's long enough for two columns. We're going to split it and run the two halves on different days. So I need you to break it into two parts and add some sort of connections between them."

"Oh, I can do that," Elvin responded, relieved that the problem wasn't more serious.

"Good. And here's the other piece of news. We are getting such high reader response that we want to run 'Contrarian' columns twice a week—on Wednesdays and Saturdays. Could you write two columns a week?"

"Sure. In fact, that solves a potential problem. I'm finding so much information on the scientific aspects of global warming that I have been wondering how I could squeeze it all into less than a thousand words a week. But Ed, haven't reader responses been running five to one against the conclusions of the column? Aren't most readers believers in human-caused changes to the climate?"

"They are, yes," Ed confirmed. "But the controversy the column is generating is just what we want. Believers in human-caused warming are going to hate 'The Heart of the Matter.' But the fact is that human activity is not causing any measurable warming. We want to educate our readers about this important subject, and two columns a week will help us do that. Ted thinks that reader opinion will soon become more doubtful about the dominant theory. It will be interesting to find out if he is right."

FRIDAY, JULY 17

91

Alan turned to the question of how to motivate Secret Doubters to come out of the closet. He knew it wouldn't be easy to convince them to act on the basis of their hidden belief that the authorship question is worthy of academic study—not in the face of peer pressure and institutional pressure to conform to academia's party line.

He recalled Charlton Ogburn's statement that a young professor's career could be derailed "if he threatens to expose the tenets of his elders as nonsense." He had come across a more recent description of the pressures that exist within academia by Professor Roger Stritmatter. "There is, of course, a price to be paid [for admission into academia] . . . the initiate must solemnly promise not only to forgo dalliance in the field of unauthorized ideas, but to zealously defend, as a matter of honor and sanity, the jurisdiction of the paradigm into which he has been initiated. A reluctance to do so marks him, at best, as an outsider or a misfit: unqualified for employment, tenure, or professional respect."

Then Alan thought of a solution. If Secret Doubters don't feel free to act on the basis of their beliefs because of pressure brought to bear on them by Militant Stratfordians, perhaps the way forward is to increase pressure on them from the opposite direction. Once the pressure from the two sides is equal, Secret Doubters will be able to act on a level playing field.

Of course, the formerly secret Secret Doubters' situation wouldn't be ideal. But, pinched between two equal sets of pressures, they might be able to do what they think is right. Alan reminded himself that that is exactly the situation he might be in: caught between pressure from academia against consideration of the authorship question on one hand, and his own enthusiasm for examining the issue and promoting de Vere's authorship on the other. Still, he would be applying the pressure on himself voluntarily.

What kind of pressure could be applied on the Doubters? And how? His thoughts roamed over his readings in history and diplomacy—the same sort of readings that he and Amelia had discussed after he mentioned Duggan's book *The Art of What Works*—to see if similar situations in the past could serve as models.

Then he had answers to both questions. The pressure that Oxfordians could apply would be based on the groundswell of public interest in the authorship question. Awareness that public interest had been building for decades and that academia was in danger of being left behind in an area in which it should be the leader would be a psychologically compelling point.

Examples of how to apply pressure could come from the field of diplomacy—not the feel-good diplomacy associated with photos of smiling diplomats shaking hands, but the kind of muscular diplomacy that Teddy Roosevelt had in mind when he talked of speaking softly and carrying a big stick.

That type of diplomacy had three steps, Alan saw. First, explaining the reality of the situation to those who don't yet see it. Second, highlighting the harm they will suffer if they don't act in accordance with it and the benefits that will flow to them if they do. And third, getting out of the way so that they can make their own decisions about what to do based on their new understanding of the situation. Two examples came to mind.

The first concerned a friend of his from years ago, Al, who had been a flute player in a symphony orchestra. Al seemed like a nice guy, but in reality he was as tough as nails. In his younger days he'd been a truck driver. Once, when making a delivery to a factory he found the gate open but his way blocked by striking workers who were lying on the road. Al thought for a moment, then put his truck in low gear, got out of the cab and locked the door. "The reality of the situation," he explained to the strikers, "is that the truck is going forward, slowly but surely, and if you continue to lie on the road you will be crushed. And if you are crushed it will be your own fault because you didn't get out of the way." The strikers had quickly understood the situation and got out of the way.

The second example came from none other than Edward de Vere, speaking through the voice of Henry V. Henry wanted the leaders of the town of Harfleur to open the town's gates so that his army could enter, just as Oxfordians want literature departments to open up to discussion of the authorship question.

How does Henry proceed? By the same set of actions followed by my friend Al, Alan recognized. The reality, Henry had explained, is that the English are implacable. One way or another we are coming in, he said. It's up to you to decide whether to let us in peacefully or have the town destroyed as we force our way in. He conveyed that reality in vivid and forceful language to drive home to the town leaders the harm that Harfleur would suffer if his army had to force its way in. Alan opened his copy of *Henry V* to refresh his memory of Henry's exact words.

> . . . the fleshed soldier, rough and hard of heart,
> In liberty of bloody hand shall range
> With conscience wide as hell, mowing like grass
> Your fresh fair virgins and your flow'ring infants. . . .
> What is't to me, when you yourselves are cause,
> If your pure maidens fall into the hand
> Of hot and forcing violation?
> What rein can hold licentious wickedness
> When down the hill he holds his fierce career?
> We may as bootless spend our vain command
> Upon th' enragèd soldiers in their spoil
> As send precepts to the leviathan
> To come ashore.

> Therefore, you men of Harfleur,
> Take pity of your town and of your people
> Whiles yet my soldiers are in my command,
> Whiles yet the cool and temperate wind of grace
> O'erblows the filthy and contagious clouds
> Of heady murder, spoil, and villainy.
> . . .
> What say you? Will you yield, and this avoid?
> Or, guilty in defense, be thus destroyed?

In modern English, Alan noted, Henry is saying that the reality is that the English are coming into your town. We can do this the easy way or the hard way. The easy way is for you to open the gates. If not, I will be forced to unleash my soldiers, and we all know what soldiers are like during and after the heat of battle. They will be out of my control, just as they will be out of yours. They will take the spoils of war, and we all know what that means. As Henry said, what is it to me if your fresh fair virgins are defiled and your flow'ring infants cut down, when you yourselves are the cause because you didn't open the gates?

Oxfordians, of course, weren't going to sack departments of literature if they didn't open their curricula and publications to discussion of the authorship question. Instead, they had to establish the reality of the groundswell of interest in the question outside of academia, the harm that Stratfordians would suffer if they ignored it and the benefits they could achieve by acting in accordance with it. Alan wanted to think more about this, but had to stop work to meet Amelia.

92

During dinner with Amelia in her apartment, Alan began to bring her up to date about his thoughts on pressuring Secret Doubters. He had just finished describing how Henry V had forced the town of Harfleur to open its gates, and was about to launch into his analysis of how Doubters could be pressured to come out of the closet, when she interrupted.

"Alan, if the town of Harfleur had refused to open its gates, and if you were one of Henry's soldiers and I was one of the fresh fair virgins in the town, what would have happened to me after the gates were breached? What would you have done to me?"

"Well, on seeing a maiden so chaste and demure, I might've had thoughts of sending you an engraved invitation to dine with me, fully chaperoned, of course. But then I might have noticed the glint in your eye and the other clues indicating to any seasoned observer that you are someone with a strong physical nature. Those clues would have indicated a certain receptiveness to whatever physical desires I might have had."

"What might those clues have been?"

"Well, one might have been you unbuttoning your blouse as you are doing right now. And another might have been you stepping out of your skirt, something you are now beginning to do."

"You mean I would have fallen into the hand of hot and forcing violation?"

"Oh, I would have enjoyed the spoils of war, have no doubt about that," Alan said. "'Hot' would certainly have described the nature of the enjoyment, but 'forcing' and 'violation' would not have been applicable. Do you know why not?"

"Might it be," Amelia said as she pulled him down onto the sofa, "because you can't rape the willing?" They both collapsed in laughter because this was the punch line to one of the stories in a book he'd given her to help her better understand the intricacies of American social interactions, Jay McInerney's *Story of My Life*.

They awoke well before midnight, and decided on a snack of ice cream. "So," Amelia asked, waiving her spoon toward Alan, "what is your big plan to pressure Stratfordians? Why didn't you finish your explanation?"

'Well, I got a bit distracted," Alan said, laughing. "The reality to be brought home to Stratfordians is the existence of the groundswell of interest in the Shakespeare authorship question outside of academia. The pressure on Secret Doubters would be the recognition that that interest has been building for decades and that academia is in danger of being left behind.

"The reality, Oxfordians could say, is that many major media publications have recognized the legitimacy and importance of the authorship question, including *Newsweek*, *The Atlantic*, and *The Wall Street Journal*.

"The reality is that five Supreme Court justices have recognized the legitimacy of the question, and three prestigious law journals have organized symposia on it and devoted entire issues to it.

"The reality is that many of the greatest literary minds in American and English letters in the past 150 years have doubted that Shakspere wrote the literary works attributed to him, including Walt Whitman, Nathaniel Hawthorne, Samuel Coleridge, John Greenleaf Whittier, Thomas Hardy, Mark Twain, Henry James, James Joyce, John Galsworthy, Marjorie Bowen, John Buchan, and Anne Rice.

"The reality is that many of the greatest actors of the past hundred years have doubted Shakspere's authorship, including Orson Welles,

Leslie Howard, Tyrone Guthrie, Charlie Chaplin, Sir John Gielgud, Michael York, Jeremy Irons, Sir Derek Jacobi and Mark Rylance.

"The reality is that scores of thinkers, diplomats, politicians and other public figures have publicly doubted his authorship, including Frederich Nietzsche, Sigmund Freud, Clifton Fadiman, Mortimer Adler, David McCullough, Paul Nitze, Benjamin Disraeli, Otto van Bismarck, Charles de Gaulle, Helen Keller, Clare Boothe Luce, and Malcolm X.

"Then, having established the reality of the groundswell of interest outside of academia, Oxfordians should highlight the benefits for professors who act in accordance with it and the harm that could come to those who don't. Drawing on psychologists' insight that losses are two and a half times as painful as gains are pleasurable, Oxfordians should seek to increase Stratfordians' anxiety by asking questions like these:

"How do you feel about literature departments being left behind as others outside academia investigate a subject of great importance to literature?

"Why have you, a professional in this field, failed to do your scholarly duty to examine the issue in an objective manner?

"Don't you have even normal human curiosity about why so many prominent and accomplished people today and over the past century have had doubts about Shakspere?

"And here is one more. Some Stratfordians are engaging in shoddy academic work and are insulting and slandering doubters. Why do you continue to belong to a group that not only tolerates, but actually honors those who engage in such practices?

"I could go on, but you get the idea."

"I pity those poor Stratfordians," Amelia said. "They are apt to feel like the fresh fair virgins mowed down like grass or the pure maidens fallen into the hands of soldiers in the enjoyment of their spoil."

'Well," Alan responded, "what is't to me when they themselves are the cause by not adapting themselves to reality?"

SATURDAY, JULY 18

93

Alan Fernwood and Matt Harris sat down on the grass about half way back through the seating area, behind where Alan's students had gathered. He was pleased all six of them had shown up for the Shakespeare in the Park performance that he'd given them tickets for.

Antony and Cleopatra, one of Alan's favorite plays, was being presented. It was a long play, and he wanted to see what cuts the director had made.

Alan was always amazed by live performances. He could never understand how it was possible for actors to remember their lines in such lengthy and complicated works. It was easier in TV shows and movies, he knew, because scenes were usually shorter, and could be reshot.

"Your students seem pretty excited," Matt observed. "Remember when we were that age, Alan? Going to special events like this with our friends?"

"Yeah. That was a long time ago. But it seems like just yesterday, too." Alan's attention was drawn to Amelia. It was interesting to see how she interacted with the other students outside the classroom. She'd mentioned that they regarded her as a big sister, and that did appear to be the case. He also noticed that she was one of the few younger women in the audience wearing a summer dress. She looked so lovely, and he wished other women would follow her example of making an effort to look nice in public, rather than wearing old jeans and a T shirt.

"Remember Irwin Shaw's 'The Girls in Their Summer Dresses,' Alan?" Matt asked. "It's been twenty-five years since we first discovered it."

"I was just thinking about it. Do you realize that it has been more than seventy-five years since it was first published? It's a shame the way our culture has become so degraded. We've lost something valuable that our parents' generation had. My mother always wore summer dresses in the spring and summer. She rarely wore pants in public."

A moment later the stage lights came on and the performance began. The actors were all suited to their roles, and had no difficulty in remembering their lines. Alan felt himself and the rest of the audience sinking into the magic of the performance.

Early in the second act, when Enobarbus began to describe the magnetic power that Cleopatra had over Antony, he noticed Amelia sit up straight and pay special attention. A few lines later, when Enobarbus described how holy priests bless Cleopatra even when she is "riggish," he saw her glance back at him and smile, a smile that only he saw because of the darkness and because only he had been looking for it.

Glancing up at the sky, Alan was amazed that so many stars could be seen. It was almost, he thought, as if "the floor of heaven / Is thick inlaid with patines of bright gold." He wished he was sitting next to Amelia and holding her tight against him.

During the intermission after the third act, Alan walked over to see how his students liked the performance. They were discussing whether Antony should have abandoned his duty to the Triumvirate or whether his love for Cleopatra justified it. Lisa had even brought a copy of the play with her, and commented that the cuts had been carefully made. As he walked back to where he and Matt were sitting, Alan noticed how glad he felt that the students were enjoying the performance.

After it was over, Alan decided to go home. Amelia was engaged with the other students, in the center with them surrounding her as though she was the queen bee tending her hive. Matt decided to stick around a while longer, and Alan saw him walking over toward the students as he left.

SUNDAY, JULY 19

94

"Alan! Over here," Elvin called as Alan walked into the restaurant. He was at the bar, having his usual pre-dinner glass of Riesling.

"I'm glad you could make it tonight," Alan said as they shook hands. "We have a lot to talk about."

Once they were seated at their table, Alan continued. "You know, Elvin, ever since we met last week, I have been thinking about how different our two subjects are—the authorship of Shakespeare's works and the effect of human activity on the climate—and yet how similarly doubters have been treated. In both cases, instead of trying to show doubters where they have gone wrong—the mistakes they have made regarding evidence or interpretation of evidence, or flaws in their logic—believers have tried to crush them, to insult them, to make them out to be almost insane. 'The science is settled,' they say in your case, and 'Shakespeare wrote Shakespeare' in mine. Both statements imply that anyone who disagrees is nuts."

"Well," Elvin said, "that response is a sure sign to me that our positions are correct. If it was a simple matter of pointing out errors of fact or interpretation, they would already have done so. Instead, they try to shame us into accepting their views without refuting our objections to them.

"It was only a month ago that I was one of them, Alan. I believed that those who doubted that human-produced carbon dioxide was the major cause of global warming were fools incapable of understanding evidence and logical reasoning. But a month of hard work investigating the issue changed my mind."

"That's another thing we have in common," Alan replied. "Just two months ago I believed exactly the same thing about those who doubted William Shakspere's authorship. Oh, by the way, I hear people talking about 'The Contrarian' all the time. Half seem angry but the other half are laughing. And the people who are angry one week seem to be laughing the next."

"Well, then, I guess I'm doing a good job," Elvin said, smiling.

They paused to order their food. They were, of course, at the restaurant on the ground floor of the Harvest Hotel. Both men were creatures of habit and already knew what they were going to order. But tonight Alan ordered a bottle rather than his usual glass of wine.

"You know something else I've begun to realize in the past month? Just how much Delilah likes you, Elvin. I mentioned that to Diana on the phone last week, and she said, 'Of course Delilah likes Elvin. She has liked him for a long time. Didn't you know that?' Now that I know, it's easy to see. But it always takes me longer than Diana, or Delilah for that matter, to see things that they understand instantly."

Elvin agreed. "Women are certainly quicker than men at perceiving people's feelings. Sometimes I feel like a tortoise around Delilah because she gets things so quickly. But, sadly, I'm not the tortoise who wins the race, because she is diligent and determined when she has a goal, not like the hare in Aesop's tale. And I like her, too."

"Well, that's easy to understand," Alan said. "She has always been a delightful girl." Then he added, half to himself, shaking his head, "It's hard to believe she will be twenty-two years old in only three weeks." Changing subjects, he described the financial interests that some Stratfordians have in supporting the myth of Shakspere's authorship.

"It's the same with the global warming folks, Alan. I'm now investigating just how much government money flows to those conducting research into it. I'm going to write about this soon. Remember how President Eisenhower warned about the military-industrial complex because so much government money was going to defense contractors? Something similar could be said about funds flowing to global warming organizations today. Let's call it the government-warming complex. The issues are different, but the concept of corruption arising from so much government money going into one area is the same.

"What really interests me is my suspicion that a large percentage of people who claim to believe in human-caused global warming really don't. They have the typical herd mentality, and will follow what others around them appear to think and do, because they are too lazy to think for themselves or too scared to express their real opinions."

"It's the same in academia," Alan told him, shaking his head. "A decade ago a poll conducted by the *New York Times* revealed that seventeen percent of literature professors had some doubt about Shakspere's authorship. I think the percentage must be far higher now, but you'd never know it, given how carefully they conceal their real beliefs.

"The key question, though, is how we should respond to the pressure on us to change our beliefs. I think we need to take the counteroffensive against those who hold the dominant, but false, beliefs."

Before he could continue, Elvin quoted Jonathan Swift, saying "It is useless to attempt to reason a man out of a thing he was never reasoned into."

Recognizing the quote, Alan responded with a quote from Upton Sinclair. "It is difficult to get a man to understand something, when his salary depends upon his not understanding it!"

Elvin rejoined with an observation often attributed to Mark Twain: "It ain't what you don't know that gets you into trouble. It's what you know for sure that just ain't so."

Alan parried with Friedrich Schiller's observation, "Against stupidity, the gods themselves contend in vain."

They both burst out laughing. They were clearly operating on the same wave-length.

Alan refilled their wine glasses. "But in spite of all those sentiments, I think the only solution is to take the offense against those who hold false beliefs. I am beginning to do just that, by designing a game plan for Oxfordians to follow in their engagement with Stratfordians. I'm optimistic that it might be possible to nudge literary scholars toward consideration of the authorship question because of the weakness of the Stratfordian claim."

"I'm doing the same thing in the climate change area," Elvin said. "'The Contrarian' column was supposed to address a variety of false beliefs in the scientific and medical and health areas, but so far I have written only about climate change. My editors agree with this focus for now because the issue is so important."

"I think my game plan would be more effective if I understood better how intellectual communities change their views," Alan said, changing the subject slightly.

"You know, Alan, scientists have changed their views many times, but it was never an easy or quick process. For instance, there was that doctor, Ignaz Semmelweis, I think it was, who was ridiculed by the entire medical community after he suggested that doctors were transferring diseases from one patient to another. When he urged them to wash their hands between examinations, he was laughed out of the profession and eventually went mad. Now, of course, doctors always wash their hands between patients and often wear disposable gloves.

"But here is a better example, one much more recent. You might investigate how continental drift came to be accepted by geologists. I remember from my studies that when the idea of movement of the continents was first proposed in the early part of the twentieth century, geologists adamantly rejected it. But decades later, in the 1960s, the issue was reborn under the new name of plate tectonics. That the continents have moved over time is now accepted as fact."

Alan perked up. "Thanks, Elvin! That's just the sort of example that might help me understand how to convince literature departments to change their beliefs. We both face seemingly impossible tasks, but the longest journey begins with a single step."

"Those who do not read are no better off than those who cannot."

"Success isn't how far you got, but the distance you traveled from where you started."

"Every path has its puddle."

"Do not look where you fell but where you slipped."

"Do not speak unless you can improve the silence."

Alan had the final words. "What soberness conceals, drunkenness reveals," and they again burst out laughing.

"I think it's time to go home," he said, waving for the check. "Tonight, I'll be the designated walker."

MONDAY, JULY 20

95

"Good morning," Lisa said, beginning the discussion she would moderate. "Today we'll again examine Shakespeare's understanding of how politics affects relations between men and women. We'll begin with simple examples of how men court women they are interested in before moving to the complications that arise as political and sexual factors become intertwined in *Richard III* and *Measure for Measure*.

"We have seen the uncomplicated way that the King, Berowne and other scholars court women in *Love's Labor's Lost* by writing sonnets to them and praising them in conversation. A more complicated example occurs in *Othello*. Brabantio, Desdemona's father, accuses Othello of using black magic to enchant his daughter. It must have seemed to Brabantio that only witchcraft could explain how his daughter could have fallen in love with Othello. In fact, it might seem to *every*one not in love that magic could be the only cause of *any*one falling in love.

"Othello says it wasn't so. It was simply the stories he told of his adventures that snared Desdemona's heart. He talks 'of most disastrous chances, / Of moving accidents by flood and field; / Of hairbreadth scapes i' th' imminent deadly breach.' And, he summed up, 'She loved me for the dangers I had passed, / And I loved her that she did pity them. / This only is the witchcraft I have used.' The Duke, who has heard this explanation, exclaims, 'I think this tale would win my daughter too.'"

"That reminds me of a similar passage in *A Midsummer Night's Dream*," Amelia said. "Hermia's father charges Lysander with having bewitched his daughter by giving her poems and love tokens, and by singing under her window in the moonlight."

"Yeah," Lisa observed, "to him, too, the power of love seems inexplicable without the use of magic or drugs. But to those who feel it, no such artificial triggers are needed. Now let's turn to an extraordinary scene in *Richard III*, even though the play isn't on our reading list. It shows how one man's lust for a particular woman—he lusts after her with desires both political and sexual—leads to her destruction.

"At the time this scene takes place, Richard, not yet king, manipulates Anne into marrying him, even though he has just murdered her father-in-law, who was king, and her husband, who was prince. By marrying her, Richard would secure the throne by uniting two great families, the House of York and the House of Lancaster, thereby ending the thirty-year civil war—the War of the Roses—that had resulted from their rival claims to the throne.

"In only 140 lines of text, Richard moves Anne from hating him to agreeing to marry him. How did he do it? Here are those lines," she said as she passed out copies. "Pat has kindly agreed to join me in reading selections from them.

ANNE [read by Lisa]
    'And thou unfit for any place, but hell.'

RICHARD [read by Pat]
    'Yes, one place else, if you will hear me name it.'

ANNE
    'Some dungeon.'

RICHARD
        'Your bedchamber.'

ANNE
'Ill rest betide the chamber where thou liest.'

RICHARD
'So will it, madam, till I lie with you.'

. . . . .

ANNE
'Thou wast the cause and most accursed effect [of the deaths of
Henry and Edward].'

RICHARD
'Your beauty was the cause of that effect –
Your beauty, that did haunt me in my sleep
To undertake the death of all the world,
So I might live one hour in your sweet bosom.'

. . . . .

ANNE
'Never hung poison on a fouler toad.
Out of my sight! Thou dost infect mine eyes.'

RICHARD
'Thine eyes, sweet lady, have infected mine.'

. . . . .

RICHARD
'Lo, here, I lend thee this sharp-pointed sword,
Which if thou please to hide in this true breast
And let the soul forth that adoreth thee,
I lay it naked to the deadly stroke
And humbly beg the death upon my knee.
Nay, do not pause, for I did kill King Henry–
But 'twas thy beauty that providèd me,
Nay, now dispatch: 'twas I that stabbed young Edward–
But 'twas thy heavenly face that set me on.'

. . . . .

ANNE
'Arise, dissembler. Though I wish thy death,
I will not be thy executioner.'

RICHARD
'Then bid me kill myself, and I will do it.

. . . . .

Speak it again, and even with the word
This hand, which for thy love did kill thy love,
Shall for thy love kill a far truer love;
To both their deaths shalt thou be accessary.'

ANNE
'I would I knew thy heart.'

RICHARD
''Tis figured in my tongue.'

ANNE
   'I fear me both are false.'

RICHARD
   'Then never man was true.
   . . . . .
   Vouchsafe to wear this ring.'
[she accepts it]

"Lisa, Pat, that was a very effective reading," Alan said, leading a round of applause.

"But it was all a lie," Lisa lamented, "except for Richard's confession that he had killed her father-in-law and her husband. Here is what he says after Anne leaves the room.

   'Was ever woman in this humor wooed?
   Was ever woman in this humor won?
   I'll have her, but I will not keep her long.
   What, I that killed her husband and his father,
   To take her in her heart's extremest hate,
   With curses in her mouth, tears in her eyes,
   The bleeding witness of my hatred by,
   Having God, her conscience, and these bars against me,
   And I no friends to back my suit withal
   But the plain devil and dissembling looks?
   And yet to win her, all the world to nothing!'

"And Anne, when she realizes the reality of her situation, kills herself."

"I think this is a good time for a break," Alan told the class, looking at Lisa with concern.

An instant later Nancy and Amelia were sitting close to Lisa, comforting her.

"It's okay, Lisa," Nancy said.

"It wasn't really you who lost your husband and then married his murderer," Amelia told her.

"I know," Lisa said. "But sometimes I get too personally caught up in what I read."

96

"Let's turn to *Measure for Measure*," Lisa said after the break, which had lasted longer than usual. "This is another of Shakespeare's most extraordinary plays. It focuses more directly than any other on the power of sexual desire and the need for social control over it.

"Practically every character in *Measure for Measure* is involved in illicit sexual activity of one form or another. That activity is illicit because there are laws against it. The Duke has been lax in enforcing them, and they're now widely violated. He sees that things are getting out of hand and decides that the laws do need to be enforced. But rather than do it himself, he leaves town, instructing his deputy, Angelo, to do it. That's kind of a cowardly way out, in my opinion.

"There are many issues in this play that we could examine, but let's look at three. First, why Isabella wants to enter a convent. Second, why Angelo chooses to enforce such a strict interpretation of the laws. And third, the interactions between Angelo and Isabella. Who would like to start us off on the first topic?"

"Well," Dave responded, "we aren't told why Isabella has chosen to enter a convent. It seems she has freely made that choice. There is no sign of any pressure. She'll be entering the strictest convent in the country. Nuns there could never meet a man except in the presence of the prioress. Even then, they couldn't show their face and speak. It was one or the other. If they spoke, they had to be veiled. But even that's not strict enough for Isabella. She tells the prioress that she is 'rather wishing for a more strict restraint / Upon the sisterhood.' Why might she have wanted that?

Everyone was quiet as they considered the possibilities. Finally, Nancy spoke. "It's an interesting question. The only reason I can think of is that Isabella was harmed by a man—or men—in some way. Perhaps she had a relationship that ended badly and she had a broken heart. Maybe he abandoned her for somebody else. Or a man or men might have used her forcibly. But probably not, because Lucio describes her as a virgin."

"Here's his exact words," Lisa said. "'Hail, virgin, if you be, as those cheek roses / Proclaim you are no less.' Now let's turn to the second point, that of why Angelo acts as he does."

"Angelo is a Puritan." Doug pointed out. "Once given a bit of power, he sets out to enforce the strictest possible interpretation of the laws." He was about to quote a passage from the play describing Angelo, but Lisa got to it first.

> "'Lord Angelo, [is] a man whose blood
> Is very snow broth: one who never feels
> The wanton stings and motions of the sense,
> But doth rebate and blunt his natural edge
> With profits of the mind, study and fast.'"

"Both Isabella and Angelo are extremists," Amelia noted, "and extremists in the same way. Both take steps to restrict opportunities for sexual relations to take place. It's interesting that the major clash in the play is between them over that very issue, an issue about which they would have been natural allies if Angelo hadn't desired her so ardently."

Lisa then described the setting further, pointing out that Angelo had sentenced Claudio, Isabella's brother, to death for impregnating a woman named Juliet. They had apparently been engaged, but hadn't yet solemnized their marriage. In other words, they were informally married, and their sexual liaison was a mere technical violation of the law. Nevertheless, Angelo has picked this case to serve as an example for everybody else. Claudio's only hope is if Isabella can successfully intercede with Angelo. What happens when they meet?"

"Well," Pat said, "Isabella asks Angelo to spare her brother's life, and when he refuses, she prepares to leave. The reason she gives up so easily is that she believes that her brother deserves his sentence."

"Yeah," Doug concurred. "She agrees that the sentence is just, and says she is asking for clemency only because Claudio is her brother. It's odd, though, that she doesn't make the case that her brother's fault was only a technical violation. She could have asked that the fault be corrected by Claudio and Juliet completing the marriage vows."

"Lucio then urges her to try again, with more feeling," Pat said. "She does, saying that if he, Angelo, had made the same mistake and if Claudio had been the judge, then Claudio would not have been so stern."

"But Angelo isn't moved," Lisa commented.

"No, he isn't," Doug agreed. "Isabella then makes the case that this sentence had never before been given for this infraction. But Angelo replies that he had to start somewhere in enforcing the law."

"So she tries another tactic," Dave said. "She accuses him of acting like a god. But unlike a real god, who uses his powers for great events, he is using them for such small things as to make the angels weep and the gods laugh."

"That doesn't work, either," Nancy observed. "But then Isabella makes a point that hits home.

> 'Go to your bosom,
> Knock there, and ask your heart what it doth know
> That's like my brother's fault. If it confess
> A natural guiltiness such as is his,
> Let it not sound a thought upon your tongue
> Against my brother's life.'

"Angelo feels the import of that point, and can make no response. He tells her to come back tomorrow."

Amelia then spoke. "Angelo reveals to us that he desires Isabella. 'Whose fault is it?' he asks. 'The tempter or the tempted?' He recognizes that Isabella has not acted in a way to tempt him, to spur his desire for her, so the fault must be in himself.

"Angelo is caught by surprise. He hadn't expected to be attracted to her, to want her, to love her. He hadn't been attracted to other women, who'd gone out of their way to make themselves attractive, they think, to men. What is new—what appeals to him most—was not just her feminine qualities, but the combination of them with her purity, her obvious chastity. Isabella's purity is a spur to Angelo's puritanical nature. And because the feelings are so new, he doesn't know how to respond to them."

"That's right," Lisa said. "Angelo asks himself 'Dost thou desire her foully for those things / That make her good? . . . O cunning enemy that, to catch a saint, / With saints dost bait thy hook!' So Angelo faces two issues," she observed, inviting others to speak.

"One is what to do about Claudio," Doug noted. "Angelo might have released him as an act of mercy. He could have announced that all offenses from this time forward would be punished to the full extent of the law. That would have been a legitimate way to proceed, and would have earned Isabella's gratitude. But he doesn't."

"The second issue for Angelo," Dave said, "is what to do about his desire for Isabella. Because his desiring a woman—or anyone, for that matter—is so new to him, he doesn't quite know what his options are. There are two, I think, unless he wants simply to turn his back on his desires. He might have expressed them to Isabella indirectly, by courting her, by asking her to marry him. The other option is the one he chooses. He tries to use the power of his position to force Isabella to submit to sex with him in exchange for Claudio's release."

"And then follows an almost comical series of exchanges between them," Pat said, "as Angelo makes immoral offers, but Isabella, in her innocence, doesn't understand the import of his words. After he tries for the third time, she finally gets it, and vehemently rejects the sacrifice of her body in order to save her brother's life."

"Isabella then tries to turn the tables on Angelo by threatening to expose his corrupt offer to her," Amelia noted, "but that doesn't work. Angelo asks who would believe her, given his reputation for virtue."

"This is, of course, the oldest story in the world," Lisa said. "Men with power, whatever form of power—political, economic, financial, social, celebrity—using it to gain sexual access to young women."

"It's not a pleasant story," Nancy agreed. "And yet, I would make the distinction between American society and other societies in the world, past and present. In the past, and in most countries in the world today, young women with no protectors—no fathers, no brothers, no husbands—were and are at the mercy of men.

"But that isn't the case in the United States. We have many safeguards in place—not the least is the decency of most American men. In most places, even in large cities, women can walk unescorted in public without fear. Because we accept this as normal, we don't realize just how extraordinary it is. We don't give ourselves enough credit for this accomplishment. Not putting a man on the moon and bringing him back safely, but creating conditions in which young women can walk safely in public—that's the more difficult achievement, the one we should be more proud of."

Amelia nodded in agreement. "Very different from American society is Arab society," she noted, "in which women are sequestered, unable to leave the home except in the company of male relatives. But even in many non-Arab societies, it is dangerous for women to be out in public in the evenings, and in some even in the daytime.

"In this context I want to mention again the Asian—and to some extent Elizabethan—practice of people interacting with others on the basis of the positions they are in. Each person's recognition of the duties incumbent on them in each position they hold helps them control their desires. It's a form of protocol that eases social intercourse. Much social friction is avoided in that practice—and much sexual friction."

"Stop smiling, Doug," Amelia said, smiling back at him. "I'm not talking about that kind of sexual friction."

Alan coughed and stood up. "There is so much more we could discuss about this play," he said, "but unfortunately time is up."

As Alan gathered up his papers, he overheard Doug telling the others that this discussion reminded him of *Bambi*. "You know, the Disney cartoon? I'm thinking of the scene where Bambi is now a young buck and the owl tells him to be careful or he could become 'twitterpated.' 'Twitterpated?' Bambi asks. 'Yeah,' the owl says. 'You're walking along, minding your own business, and suddenly you see a pretty face. You begin to get weak in the knees. Your head's in a whirl. And then you feel light as a feather. . . . And then you're knocked for a loop. And you completely lose your head.'

"'Gosh, that's awful,' Bambi says. 'I hope it doesn't happen to me.' And then Faline appears, all grown up into a young doe. 'Hi Bambi, remember me?' she asks. And he's instantly twitterpated. The worst case any buck ever suffered. That's kind of what happened to Angelo. I sure hope that never happens to me."

97

Elvin had spent the past week trying to understand why computer models—known as General Circulation Models (GCMs)—predict much higher surface temperatures as a result of human activity than his own review of scientific findings showed was warranted.

The key element in the GCMs, he saw, was their high sensitivity to small changes in CO_2. But, he read, "because the flux is small, the change will take a long time." Two decades ago the theory had been hard to verify because the changes expected at that time were so small that they were still within the range of natural annual variation. But now, two decades later, there should be ample data to substantiate them.

Comparing the GCM's forecasts with actual data, Elvin saw that the forecasts didn't even come close to matching the actual temperature record. He made notes for his column. He then found other discrepancies, and made more notes. Finally, he leaned back in his chair, thinking about how to organize his two columns for the week. He decided that the first would document that the models' forecasts didn't match actual temperature records, and the second would explain why the models were wrong.

It's Witchcraft! Part I

No, we're not talking about Frank Sinatra's recording of 'Witchcraft.' Nor are we talking about news stories of magic perpetrated by witches in remote villages in India or Indonesia. Rather, we are talking about the explanation for why so many people continue to believe a theory that has repeatedly been shown to be false.

We are referring, of course, to the theory of global warming, the proposal that an increase in the amount of carbon dioxide—a vanishingly small change of less than $1/36^{th}$ of one percent in the composition of the atmosphere—would cause huge problems for the planet. The theory holds that the small increase in temperature caused by that tiny change in the atmosphere would increase levels of water vapor, which would in turn cause additional warming that would generate even higher levels of water vapor, resulting in a chain reaction—a continuing cycle of "positive feedback"—that would eventually generate temperature increases large enough to melt the ice caps and raise sea levels.

If the theory reminds you of the tale about the catastrophic effects potentially resulting from the beating of a butterfly's wings, you're not alone. But the odds that the unique strings of circumstances necessary for either of those scenarios to occur are so astronomically small that neither would ever happen outside the fevered imaginations of human beings.

The problem for those who believe in the theory of human-caused global warming is that the predictions of the computer models, known as General Circulation Models (GCMs), are consistently wrong.

The model's core prediction is that temperatures will increase as atmospheric levels of CO_2 rise. But guess what? Although industrial emissions of CO_2 have continued to rise, there has been no increase in global atmospheric temperatures for the last two decades. As one report notes, "The pause has now lasted for 16, 19, or 26 years—depending on whether you choose the surface temperature record or one of two satellite records of the lower atmosphere. . . . It has been roughly two decades since there was a trend in temperature significantly different from zero."

One study—the largest of its kind, involving more than one million readings from weather balloons in the Arctic over a 30-year period—showed no evidence of warming. Other studies show actual decreases in temperature, with one review of data from a variety of sources noting a slight downward trend in mean global temperature of .07° C per decade. Might that indicate the onset of a new ice age?

The disconnect between predicted warming and temperatures actually recorded grows year by year. Patrick Michaels's comparison of average temperature predictions of 102 models cited by the IPCC CMIP-5 report with readings from satellites shows the gap increasing from .11° C in 1985, to .15° C in 1995, to .4° C in 2005, to .6° C in 2015.

It's hard not to sympathize with Michaels, who writes "It's impossible, as a scientist . . . not [to] rage at the destruction of science that is being wreaked by the inability of climatologists to look us in the eye and say perhaps the three most important words in life: we were wrong."

Other predictions have also been wrong. Remember the claims that glaciers would retreat and polar ice caps melt as temperatures rose? Remember Al Gore's prediction in 2008 that "the entire north polar ice cap will be gone in five years?" Remember the scientist from the U.S. Snow and Ice Data Center who announced that "a very strong case [could be made] that in 2012 or 2013 we'll have an ice-free (summer) Arctic."

Well, guess what? At the height of the summer melt in 2014 "the Arctic was still covered by six million square kilometers of ice, more than in the previous three years." In Antarctica, the seas around it "had more ice cover in 2013 than seen since satellite records started in the late 1970s." NASA says that "sea ice cover in Antarctica has grown 1.5 per cent a decade for several decades," that the "global sea ice area is the largest it has been in 25 years," and that "the Arctic ice mass is the largest in 10 years."

And remember the oft-repeated scare over rising sea levels? The reality is that "sea levels have slowly risen since 1880, well before human influence on the climate is said to have become significant." However, since 2002 "the rate of sea level rise has decreased [by 31 percent] . . . exactly what would be expected at the end of an interglacial period."

Other studies show that "The sea level for the Tarawa atoll showed no rise over a recent 20-year period, that 86 percent of 27 Pacific islands studied have grown or stayed the same size over the past 20 to 60 years," and that The Maldives is now 70 centimeters higher above sea level than in the 1970s. Are these—gasp!—indications of an impending ice age?

Climate modelers can't predict the weather even a week in advance, achieving a success rate of only eight percent in predicting temperatures and only four percent in predicting rain. Are these the same folks we're relying on to predict the Earth's climate a hundred years from now?

Models cannot even "predict" past climate when run backwards! "GCMs retrodict twice as much warming of the past couple of hundred years than appears in the climate record." All that doesn't give us much confidence in the models' future predictions.

Seeing this sorry record, who could disagree with Patrick Michaels, who notes rather dryly that what we have seen is "a massive, unexplainable, and persistent failure of the studies driving global climate policy"?

We'll continue next time with a closer look at specific flaws in the IPCC models that account for their consistent inability to predict our planet's climate.

98

After lunch, Elvin sought to understand why the models were wrong and why so many eminent scientists and politicians continued to believe in the validity of a theory that had been repeatedly shown to be false.

Turning first to the models, he found one mistake after another made by climate scientists: mistaken data, misinterpretations of data, insufficient data to make accurate forecasts, and misunderstanding of how the Earth would respond to increases in CO_2. Two scientists had summed up the situation well: "Even the most comprehensive global climate models greatly oversimplify or misrepresent key climatic processes."

Elvin saw no cause for alarm about the Earth's climate: no carbon dioxide-driven climate change, no tipping points, no runaway global warming. He found nothing unusual about the planet's climate at all, certainly no dramatic changes that would require special explanations.

He was about to begin writing the second column when he discovered something more shocking than anything he had learned so far: higher temperatures, like higher CO_2 levels, would be beneficial for mankind!

The more Elvin thought about that hidden good news, the angrier he became. The media's frightening stories about extreme heat waves weren't scientific reports, but mere propaganda designed to create support for a false theory. What was even scarier was that the modelers kept silent about the misrepresentation of their findings.

Has the whole world gone mad? he asked himself.

A month ago he'd been embarrassed by his former ignorance, his former blind acceptance of the theory of global warming, and his former practice of merely reporting on the results of scientific studies without trying to understand the science behind them. That embarrassment had become a feeling of shame at the scientific community's continuing to push a theory that has failed test after test against real world data. Now that shame had turned into real anger at the false beliefs pushed by the media. Not only was carbon dioxide a benign gas with benefits for human beings, but warming itself, if it occurred, would also be beneficial.

Elvin needed a break from this madness. Then he would write a scorching column about what he'd found. He now knew the truth, and he had a forum in which to make it known.

It's Witchcraft! Part II

IPCC General Circulation Models (GCMs) do not accurately predict changes in the Earth's temperature, polar ice cap levels, or sea levels. So what is the cause of their failures?

False beliefs by their creators, for one. Researchers had erroneously believed that increases in CO_2 precede increases in temperature, but recent findings from ice core measurements show just the opposite. Over the past several hundred thousand years, changes in temperature preceded increased levels of CO_2 in the atmosphere.

Scientists also overestimated how long CO_2 would remain in the air. Earlier models cited by the IPCC estimated 200 to 300 years, allowing concentrations to accumulate. We now know that half will be reabsorbed by the seas or by plants within ten years.

Then there's the creators' misunderstanding of the role of humidity. All GCMs depend on the key variable of increased humidity to generate the positive feedbacks that drive climate models. But not just any humidity; it's the "thin layer near the top of the troposphere, about ten to twelve kilometers above the tropics. This is where the action is." That's where the chain reaction, the positive feedback, is supposed to take place.

But it just ain't so. Data from 28 million weather balloons released since the 1950s show that "the trend up there is unmistakably not what the models expected. Instead of getting more humid as the air warmed, it got less. Temperatures also didn't warm as much as they were supposed to." Another study found that "The tropical troposphere had actually cooled slightly over the last 20 to 30 years."

Thus, the most critical linchpin in the entire model—higher levels of humidity at the top of the troposphere—has been shown to be nonexistent. The trigger for the positive upward feedback spiral on which the theory of human-caused global warming rests simply does not exist.

A broader error is that the IPCC violates good practices in the field of forecasting. Researchers found that the 2007 IPCC Assessment Report followed only 17 of 89 relevant forecasting principles. Should we tolerate such shoddy work by so-called experts? Would we tolerate engineers or doctors who failed to follow standard practices in their respective fields 81 per cent of the time?

The Contrarian can't help but agree with science writer Jo Nova: "The models are consistent. They're bad at everything. With a bad assumption at the core, it's no wonder the models don't work." That would explain why "The models not only fail on global scales, but on regional, local, short term, polar, and upper tropospheric scales, too. They fail on humidity, rainfall, drought and they fail on clouds. The common theme is that models don't handle water well. A damn shame on a planet covered in water."

Perhaps Patrick Michaels has it exactly right: what does "deserve much further investigation is how climate science could continue in its remarkable denial that the aggressive global warming paradigm has been shattered, with now 37 consecutive years of documented, systematic model failure."

So, given the steady stream of factual data refuting the theory of human-caused climate change, how is it possible that so many people continue to believe it to be true?

How could anyone possibly believe that a change of less than 1/36th of one percent in the atmosphere would result in the temperature increase of several degrees that the models predict? "The Contrarian" believes it has found the answer: *Witchcraft!*

How could anyone possibly believe that the increase of a few degrees predicted by the modelers could be large enough to cause the cataclysmic changes that have been predicted, with the Arctic pole ice-free within five years and a massive rise in sea levels? The only possible explanation is *Witchcraft!*

How could so many seemingly intelligent people continue to believe in a theory that had failed practically every test against actual data? Isn't science supposed to be about comparing theories to data and then adjusting the theory in response to inconsistencies? The explanation? *Witchcraft!*

And how could anyone possibly accept that the extraordinarily expensive and disruptive solutions to global warming pushed by supporters of the theory are the only possible measures? Why have the many sensible responses to specific problems been rejected out of hand and only the most extreme steps considered? Again, *Witchcraft!*

And yet, "The Contrarian" has just learned something so shocking that even witchcraft cannot explain it. Climate models predict that global warming, if it were indeed to occur, would be beneficial for mankind!

The focus on predicted increases in *average* temperature has hidden a very important reality: that warming would occur mostly at night, mostly in the winter, and mostly in the coldest parts of the planet. The theory of global warming predicts only minor increases in daytime and summer temperatures. Those predictions have been borne out. It was minimum temperatures, rather than maximum temperatures, that increased in the United States when average temperatures increased in the 1980s and 1990s.

The effect of the increase in average temperatures would be positive for mankind. After all, far more people die from cold on winter nights than from heat during summer days. In the U.S. alone, about 9,000 people die from heat each year, but 144,000 die from cold. Add the benefit of fewer cold-related deaths to those of longer growing seasons and the 14 percent increase in plant life on Earth over the past 30 years from higher concentrations of CO_2, and global warming begins to seem downright beneficial for human beings.

So, we ask—and this is the most shocking part—why does the media continue to generate fear through stories of impending disaster? Why do politicians continue to push the most extreme and expensive programs in response to nonexistent problems? Why do so many scientists continue to remain silent in the face of fear mongering based on distortions of their work?

Given that these actions are the result of conscious, deliberate thought, *witchcraft*-induced blindness cannot be the cause. The explanation can only be madness similar to the hysteria that overcame those living in Salem, Massachusetts, in 1692. No supernatural cause at all is needed to explain what is only the madness of deliberate, base, ignoble, shameful human duplicity.

Or perhaps witchcraft is needed after all—to explain why today's global warming madness has continued for decades even though sanity returned to Salem in less than one year.

99

"Elvin!"

Elvin was at the Southpoint Mall, near the outdoor fountain in front of the movie theater.

"Delilah!" he said with surprise. "What are you doing here?"

"I was feeling restless after work. It's such a beautiful evening that I stopped to walk around a bit to cheer myself up."

"Me, too. I was feeling kind of down after writing my last column, and came here to get something to eat and to relax. Are you hungry?"

"Yes, I am. Now that I think about it, I'm very hungry. Let's eat there. I feel like being outside." She pointed to the outdoor seating area at Firebirds, which they had approached as they walked.

Once they were seated, Delilah noted how amazing it was that they met by accident. "I don't think our meeting was accidental," Elvin said. "There's witchcraft at work in the world. It brought both of us here, to the same place at the same time. Sometimes witchcraft works for evil, sometimes for good. This time was for good."

They quietly enjoyed each other's company as the sun went down. Neither wanted to talk about their work. They wanted to talk about their relationship, but neither knew quite how to begin.

Then their wine and appetizers arrived. A few sips loosened their tongues. "You know," Delilah said, "we send each other text messages almost every day, but we don't meet very often." She waited to see what Elvin would say.

"That's true. We don't see each other often enough. But it's risky to meet more often," he said, trying to choose his words carefully, and trying not to talk about how beautiful her hands or other parts of her body might be.

"Why is it risky?" she asked, recalling a situation that truly was dangerous, the dinner with her colleagues when Dick tried to force too many drinks on her.

"Delilah, you are so beautiful, so desirable. You have an effect on me that no one else has, or has ever had. It's dangerous because I don't trust myself around you. You are so young. You were just seventeen when I first saw you standing there—as the Beatles might have phrased it—at your parents' house. I still have a mental picture of you at that age."

"Well, I'm now twenty-one. And I'll soon be twenty-two."

"And you are also Alan Fernwood's daughter," he continued. "He's a good friend of mine. What would he think if I was—" He stopped before he said any more. He was thinking that if he slept with Delilah, given his friendship with her father, he would probably have to marry her to avoid causing her pain or losing Alan's friendship. He knew that if he saw her more often, he wouldn't be able to stop himself from sleeping with her, if she would have him. Half the time he could think of nothing more wonderful than spending the rest of his life with Delilah. But at other times he hesitated to take such a permanent step.

"El, this is the twenty-first century. These days, young people choose their own—" She was going to say spouses, but she didn't want to presume too much. Maybe lovers? Partners? She couldn't decide which word to use, so she didn't say anything else.

"Come on," he said. "We've finished our drinks. Let's go for a walk. We can have dinner somewhere else." Delilah nodded and stood up.

Later they drove to a jazz club in Chapel Hill. It was dark inside, and not too crowded. They sat at a table in the back. Because it was Monday night, the usual musicians were off. In their place was a guest band with a male vocalist.

Once their wine had arrived and loosened their tongues a bit more, they both started to speak at the same time. Just then the band started to play "The Way You Look Tonight." The vocalist sang it the way Frank Sinatra had.

"Delilah," Elvin said softly, their faces only a few inches apart in the dark club, "that song is so haunting and so beautiful. I think I will always associate it with the way you look tonight—how you looked when I saw you by the fountain, so enchanting—and now, in this club. It's dark in here, but your eyes have a soft glow that even the darkness can't hide. It's almost like witchcraft is at work on me."

"Is it still good witchcraft?"

"Yes and no. Of course, yes, Dee. But at the same time I feel it so strongly that it's unsettling. Like how Macbeth felt after seeing the witches in the play. As though his future had been all mapped out for him and he was a helpless pawn caught in their spells."

"I feel the same way, El. I feel comfortable, and safe and warm when I'm with you. I've felt this way practically since the first time you came to dinner at our house. I've never felt like this about anybody else."

Their eyes had already met across the short distance that separated them. Now their lips met. The warm magic they felt last time they'd kissed rose in them, even warmer and more insistent than before. This was just what Elvin wanted and didn't want. But he was powerless to stop.

"Elvin," she whispered, "Do you remember the time you kissed me on the bridge, after we saw the Amway commercial?" He nodded. "Well, soon after that night I ordered the Amway cream. I've been using it ever since."

Before Elvin had a chance to identify the emotions surging through him triggered by her words, the band began playing another song made famous by Sinatra, "Witchcraft."

Elvin stood up quickly, almost involuntarily. It was all becoming too much. He felt that fate was steering him onto a path he wasn't sure he was ready to travel. Delilah also stood up. Elvin dropped some bills on the table, grasped Delilah's arm and steered her out of the club.

TUESDAY, JULY 21

100

Alan's goal today was to derive lessons useful for his game plan for engaging Stratfordians from how the geological community had overcome its initial rejection of the idea of continental movement.

Continental drift was first proposed by Alfred Wegener, a German geophysicist, around the same time that J. Thomas Looney had introduced the idea of Edward de Vere's authorship of Shakespeare's works in 1920. Both new theories had been formed to address weaknesses in existing theories. The idea of permanence theory—that the major features of the Earth's crust had always been the size, shape and location they are today—could not explain the existence of mountains or the similarity of rock formations on continents thousands of miles apart, just as the idea of Shakspere's authorship could not explain how an uneducated person from an isolated village could have written works exhibiting such depth of knowledge in so many fields.

Alan was struck by the fact that both new theories were supported by the same kind of evidence—circumstantial. The circumstantial evidence in favor of continental drift was the similarities between flora and fauna and rock formations on widely separated continents. Oxfordian theory was supported by similarities between events and people important in the life of Edward de Vere and events and characters in Shakespeare's plays.

To Wegener and Looney, the large number of coincidences proved their cases. Wegener wrote that "Taken individually, any one of these matches might be dismissed as coincidence, but the 'totality of these points of correspondence constitutes an almost incontrovertible proof.'" Looney similarly explained that "A few coincidences we may treat as simply interesting; a number of coincidences we regard as remarkable; a vast accumulation of extraordinary coincidences we accept as conclusive proof."

Alan was especially impressed by how similarly the two intellectual communities had responded to the new theories. Both had adamantly rejected the new ideas for two reasons—the same two reasons: because they were incomplete and because of the way they had been formulated.

Both theories lacked explanations for how and why what happened, happened. The principal weakness of continental drift theory was the lack of a causal mechanics to explain continental movement. Wegener hadn't identified a force strong enough to push continents through the rigid ocean floor or a reason why such a force would actually do so. Looney's original theory hadn't explained why Oxford would have wanted to hide his authorship or how an effort to do so could have been successful.

And, both theories were suspect because they'd been formulated through processes that violated the methodological practices of their respective fields. At the time Wegener introduced the theory of continental drift, American geologists adhered to a strictly inductive methodology. Recognizing how little they knew about the geology of North America when they set out to explore it in the 19th century, geologists adhered to a process in which the gathering of facts was strictly segregated from—and preceded—the formulation of theories to explain them. They worked that way in order to protect themselves from the natural human tendency to seek support for theories already held and to reject evidence that contradicts them.

Wegener, though, had formulated his theory of continental movement in advance of any field investigations, and it seemed to American geologists that he had cherry-picked among the known geological facts to find those that supported his theory. One prominent American geologist, Bailey Willis, expressed the view of his colleagues when he said that "Wegener's book gave the impression of having been 'written by an advocate rather than an impartial investigator.'"

A similar conflict existed between Looney's methodology and that of the literary scholars of his day, but Alan put that subject aside for now.

Alan saw that geologists defending the idea of permanence theory had resorted to tactics similar to those he'd seen Stratfordians use: *ad hoc* explanations to explain away anomalies, specious arguments, and personal attacks on proponents of the new theory. Geologists had defended their existing explanations so fiercely, Naomi Oreskes explained, because accepting the idea of continental movement "would have forced [them] to abandon many fundamental aspects of the way *they did* science. This they were not willing to do." Geologist Rollin Chamberlin had explained in 1928 that "if continental drift were true, geologists would have to forget everything which has been learned in the last 70 years and start all over again." "Very naturally," fellow geologist Chester Longwell had explained, "we insist on testing [Wegener's] hypothesis with exceptional severity; for its acceptance would necessitate the discarding of theories held so long that they have become almost an integral part of our science."

Alan suspected that Stratfordians today harbored similar sentiments about the theory of de Vere's authorship.

101

"Oh, Alan, I am so glad you're here," Amelia said, hugging him tightly as he entered her apartment. "It seems like such a long time since *Antony and Cleopatra* was performed in the park. I read the entire play again since then. Do you know what my favorite line is? I mean apart from the line where the priests bless Cleopatra even when she is riggish?"

"Tell me," he said, smiling.

"It's in the scene where Cleopatra has been apart from Antony for too long, just as you have been apart from me for too long. She is talking to Charmian, wondering what Antony is doing now. Is he sitting down? Standing up? Or is he on his horse? If so, then she is jealous of the horse!

"Here is the line: 'O happy horse, to bear the weight of Antony!' And it is the same with me, Alan. It has been four whole days. Come, we can talk later. First I want to be a happy horse. I want to bear the weight of Alan."

Afterwards, they had a late dinner, sitting on her sofa, with music playing softly on Amelia's computer in the background.

Alan told her about his latest findings, that both continental drift and Oxfordian theory had been rejected when first proposed, and for the same two reasons: Both were incomplete, and both had been formulated outside the accepted methodology of their intellectual fields. In explaining this, he used analogies from football—that the theories had been "incomplete passes" and were "out of bounds."

Amelia paused before responding. "That sounds just like us, Alan. 'We' are out of bounds. Our relationship is outside of what is right. We have been coloring outside the lines. And we are not able to come in-bounds—we are not able to complete the pass—because the way is blocked."

"I have been thinking about that," Alan said as he put his arm around her. "We already have such a strong intellectual companionship."

"And don't forget the sexual companionship part," she added, smiling at him.

"I was just about to add that," he said, smiling back. "I can see that just as I am designing a game plan for Oxfordian outreach to Stratfordians, so too I need a game plan for us. I need to formulate a strategy to overcome the obstacles keeping us apart."

Alan heard Frank Sinatra's voice coming from Amelia's computer. He was singing one of Alan's favorite Cole Porter songs, "You'd Be So Nice to Come Home To." They sang softly along with it.

Then another version of the song began to play, one by Nina Simone. Amelia explained that she'd programmed three versions of the song to play in a row. As they listened to Nina Simone's rendition, Alan excitedly said, "That is the most astonishing arrangement of that song I have ever heard! Do you hear that? Every note is set in advance, contrapuntally, like a Bach fugue. The effect builds and builds, like *Bolero*. It's like Ravel mixed with Bach in a jazz setting. It's amazing."

"I thought you might like it," Amelia said, her eyes shining, "given that you like both classical music and jazz."

"I've never heard anything like it before."

Then the third version of the song began to play, this one by saxophonist Art Pepper.

"I'm equally impressed by that one, too," Alan exclaimed, turning to Amelia after the song was over. "It's a complete contrast to Nina Simone's arrangement. In hers, every note is set in stone. In Art Pepper's, much of the song is improvised, yet it's done so well that I suspect the improvisations were written out in advance. But maybe not. In any case, we've heard the same song done in three very different and very fascinating ways."

"I knew you would appreciate all three versions," Amelia said, "especially hearing them back to back. You've had exactly the same reaction that I had, and that I knew you would have. I played them for some Fulbright students and American students who came over a few days ago, but none of them even noticed the songs at all. That is how I know we belong together."

Alan nodded. His thoughts were moving quickly, triggered by the creativity shown in what they'd just heard. He explained to Amelia Dean Simonton's description of the three-step process of creative thinking. "You know, I bet the same process happens all the time, for problems encountered in everyday life, not just for those in specialized scientific or artistic areas. It's through that process that I will create my game plans for Oxfordian outreach and for overcoming the obstacles keeping us apart."

Amelia also had thoughts triggered by the music they'd heard. "As you know, I sometimes act in accordance with what is expected in predetermined relationships between myself and others. That's like the Nina Simone version, with every note written out. The beauty of that version lies in what the composer had written and in how well the performers bring his intentions to life.

"But at other times, I act more freely. Sometimes I have to improvise, to make decisions in real time, just like Art Pepper and his musicians. But they don't improvise all the time. The song has a set structure, and times when they all come together after one improvisation ends and before another begins. Even in the improvised sections, there are guidelines as to what melodic or harmonic or rhythmic innovations are appropriate and beautiful."

"So," Alan observed, "you have come up with a series of alternating actions: predetermined, improvised, predetermined again, and so on."

"And you have come up with another type of alternating actions. First, the conscious mind, then the unconscious brain, then the conscious mind again, and so on."

"You know," he said, shaking his head in wonder. "We think congruently. Our thoughts fit together so well. That's how I know we belong together. So for both game plans—those for engagement with Stratfordians and for our situation—I have already thought hard with my conscious mind to identify all the relevant factors. Now I can feel my unconscious brain churning through the possibilities. When it has finished, it will give the solutions to my conscious mind. We must be patient until that happens."

"Well, I can feel my brain doing the same thing about our relationship," Amelia reported. A moment later she added, "So, what would you like our bodies to do while we wait for our brains to do their work?"

WEDNESDAY, JULY 22

102

Sitting at his desk, Alan returned to the subject of how and why geologists came to accept continental movement as fact in the 1960s and early 1970s after having rejected it forty years earlier.

Two things happened during that period, he learned. One was that a mechanics, known as plate tectonics, had been discovered that explained how and why continents moved. They didn't need to push their way through rigid ocean seafloors, nor did they drift at random like icebergs.

Rather, plates containing both continents *and* oceans were pushed apart by forces deep within the Earth and carried by convection currents in the heavier but softer material on which they rested.

The second development, the change in the methodology of geological science, might have been even more important, Alan thought. The move away from the restrictive inductive methodology, which occurred before the discovery of plate tectonics, was the critical development. It cleared the way for the new investigative techniques that uncovered the mechanics of continental movement. He could see that understanding how the new methodology triumphed would be important for literary scholars who want to study the authorship question but face methodological constraints and institutional pressures against doing so.

That change in methodology—the change from geology to geophysics—was initially resisted by most geologists. The few who supported the new practices faced the question of how to move to them before they had proved themselves and at a time when current practices and bureaucratic pressures pushed against them. Heated disagreements arose over which investigative techniques were valid, and over the validity of the data found. As the newer practices began to prove themselves, more geologists began to incorporate them into their own work, often to affirm the impossibility of continental movement. They were, in their own eyes, not abandoning the older practices but merely adding more quantitative practices to them. However, using both sets of practices proved fatal to the older methodology. At some point a line was crossed as geologists began to give preference to data produced by the new geophysical practices even when it conflicted with data produced by the older methods.

The changes in geologists' practices mirrored the change in methodology occurring in the natural sciences more generally. As formulated by Karl Popper in the 1940s, science progresses through a series of "conjectures and refutations." Conjectures—scientific theories or informed guesses—were proposed, and then attempts made to refute them. The more critical tests a theory passed, the more justified scientists were in relying on it. In this methodology, the place for intuitive leaps in thinking comes at the beginning of the process, not at the end as in the geologists' inductive method. Their fear that scientists would be tempted to cherry-pick data to prove theories formulated in advance of investigations was avoided by Popper's insistence that investigations should attempt to disprove conjectures rather than support them.

That's rather ingenious, Alan thought. The change in methodology was the key. That might mean that the methodology of literary criticism would have to change before the authorship question could be accepted as legitimate.

Before stopping work for the day, Alan noted one final point. Although most prominent geologists initially resisted changes to the newer practices and methodology, the transition to them was helped immensely by a small number of senior geologists who publicly acknowledged that the older practices were outdated. The most prominent was William Bowie, the namesake of the American Geophysical Union's annual William Bowie Medal. At the 1936 AGU General Assembly, Bowie publicly stated that the Pratt model of isostasy—an idea that he had spent his career establishing as fact and that was the strongest argument cited against the possibility of continental movement—could no longer be regarded as proven. He called for a re-examination of Wegener's hypothesis and suggested that it might be true after all.

The courage and dedication to truth that Bowie showed could serve as a model for senior Stratfordians today, Alan thought. He made a note to try to identify senior Stratfordians who might be willing to take a similarly courageous public stand in favor of Oxford's authorship.

103

Dean Wolpuff's office had a feel of solidity and power that brought home to Matt Harris in a visceral way just how powerful deans are. They run their own fiefdoms. Wolpuff, Matt had discovered, was especially imperious. There was no democracy here, no pretense that procedures exist and that rules must be followed. He'd learned during the past two months just how intrusive she could be into the operations of academic departments within the School of Arts and Humanities. She had repeatedly made arbitrary decisions about departments' internal operations without any discussion with their Chairs. She had an arrogant assurance that her orders would be unquestioningly obeyed. Authoritarian, autocratic, overbearing, tyrannical, domineering, pre-emptory—choose your adjective, he thought. All these fit her. Power is what power does.

"Well, Matt, what have you got for me today? Good news, I hope."

"It is, actually, Dean Wolpuff. The Chairs of the Departments within the School of Arts and Humanities have come up with a plan to increase revenue into the School." Matt described the plan to attract more Asian students, who paid full tuition, by establishing an Asian Studies program that would meet their needs as well as those of American students. "We would be creating a new product that few, if any, American universities have."

"I am indeed impressed," the Dean said. "I knew you would be able to come up with a plan if you put your minds to it." She considered the idea further. "Let's add a business component to the Asian Studies program. I'll talk to the Dean of the School of Business to get that ball rolling."

She then changed the subject. "What's this I'm hearing about one of your professors, Alan Fernwood, launching a conference about the Shakespeare authorship question? *The Shakespeare Hoax*? Is he nuts? What kind of fantasy world are you running over there, Matt?"

Matt responded that it was only an idea that Alan had proposed. "I am," he admitted, "a bit concerned by the dedication, even fanaticism, that he's exhibiting on the issue."

"Well, shut him down. We don't need to become the laughing stock of the academic world. Next thing you know he will be wanting to hold conferences on extraterrestrials."

"Uh," Matt responded, "we actually already offer a course on science fiction that covers both factual and fictional portrayals of life on other planets." He didn't add that he himself taught that course.

"That's different," the Dean said. "Nobody pays much attention to science fiction, and nobody is calling sci fi authors a hoax. Shut Fernwood down."

She went on before Matt had a chance to reply. "To return to the plan for the School. You have told me only about the plan to raise revenue. What about the other half, the plan to lower expenses? How will the new Asian Studies program be funded?"

"We are still working that out. It's a stickier issue than raising revenue. The simplest way to lower expenses would be to replace all senior faculty with part time adjunct lecturers. Ha, ha, ha." He laughed in a fake way to show that he was making a joke. "But we don't want to do that. That would make us as big a laughing stock as holding Fernwood's conference. Besides, senior faculty have tenure. Short of their committing felonies, they're pretty much impossible to fire."

"Hmm, what if we don't fire senior faculty, but instead eliminate their positions? Here at Cary, tenure only protects them in their teaching positions. But if the positions vanish, there is nothing to have tenure over."

Matt didn't know quite way to say.

"Yes, that is what we will do," the Dean decided. "We will eliminate positions that we no longer need and have the courses taught by part-time adjunct lecturers. That will cover the costs of creating the new positions in the Asian Studies Program. We can do this in each of the Departments. We can start with Fernwood. Let's eliminate his position. What are we doing with a full-time professor specializing in Shakespeare anyway? A course on Shakespeare isn't required for any major this university offers. Get on this right away, Matt."

"Yes, ma'am," was the only thing that he could think of to say.

104

Half-way around the world, Diana was perturbed. She'd heard from a friend back home who'd seen Alan having dinner with a young Asian woman. People should mind their own business, she thought, and stop meddling in other peoples' lives.

Nevertheless, Alan should have been more circumspect. Even if he was only having dinner with a colleague or literary friend, he should have enough sense to know that people seek any reason to gossip. And if Alan was sleeping with the woman, well, men will be men, she thought. There was nothing unusual about that. She didn't expect him to remain celibate for the three months that she was away from home. She had confidence in her husband, in his love for her, and in their marriage, and so could show forbearance toward the differences she knew existed in the desires of men and women.

She recognized that her thinking differed from most American women, something she attributed to her Asian upbringing. She recognized the difference between love and sex, between making love and merely having sex. Still, she wasn't as extreme as Japanese wives, who, rumor had it, packed condoms in their husband's suitcases when they traveled.

There was also another way in which her Asian thinking differed from that of her American friends. To her, if something wasn't publicly acknowledged, then it didn't exist. That enabled everyone to save face. Those who brought unwelcome knowledge to public awareness were to be condemned because they had disturbed the harmonious social relations that everybody desired. "Sweeping things under the rug" was perhaps the closest American description of that practice, but the phrase didn't describe fully enough just how extensively things must sometimes be swept aside in order to preserve social harmony. It was also a negative way of describing an essentially positive action.

So, if Alan was sleeping with another woman, that fact didn't register with her unless it was publicly recognized. The very fact that he had publicly dined with the woman was proof to her that he wasn't sleeping with her. If their relationship had been sexual, then Alan, who understood Asian thinking, would have been circumspect enough not to have had a meal with her in a public place.

It did not occur to Diana that Alan might have developed a relationship with another woman for more than just sex. Because she didn't have a life of the mind, she didn't recognize the power of intellectual subjects or intellectual companionship. To her, his job was just an occupation that brought in money, the same as being a plumber or an accountant. She didn't appreciate just how powerful an intellectual attraction could be by itself, let alone when combined with a sexual attraction.

And so it did not occur to Diana that her confidence in the solidity of her marriage might not be fully justified. She didn't consider the fact that her husband had never before met a woman with whom he shared an intellectual and a sexual companionship, and so had never faced the strength of his desires for such a relationship to continue whatever the costs might be. Mind *and* body. Head *and* heart. It was a powerful combination of which Diana was simply unaware.

THURSDAY, JULY 23

105

"Morning, everyone. Our topic today is appearance versus reality in Shakespeare's plays," Dave said, beginning his introduction. "Shakespeare's plays are chock full of distinctions between surface appearances on one hand, and reality on the other. We'll examine situations in which Shakespeare's characters' confusion between them drives plots forward.

"We'll also see that experience, in addition to knowledge and values, is essential to forming solid judgments. Or so it seems. Shakespeare rarely makes direct statements on matters such as these; his focus is always on portraying life as it is. It's therefore up to us to draw our own conclusions.

"Let's begin with a quick look at a few lighthearted scenes showing how easy it is to confuse appearance and reality. The first comes from a play not on our reading list, *The Two Gentlemen of Verona*.

"Valentine is talking with Speed, a clownish servant of his, about Silvia, the girl that Valentine loves. Their dialogue highlights the confusion between appearance and reality that being in love can cause.

Nancy will read Speed's lines and I'll read Valentine's."

VALENTINE [Dave]
'I account of her beauty.'

SPEED [Nancy]
'You never saw her since she was deformed.'

VALENTINE
'How long hath she been deformed?'

SPEED
'Ever since you loved her.'

VALENTINE
'I have loved her ever since I saw her, and still I see her beautiful.'

SPEED
'If you love her, you cannot see her.'

VALENTINE
'Why?'

SPEED
'Because love is blind. O, that you had mine eyes, or your own eyes had the lights they were wont to have when you chid at Sir Proteus for going ungartered!'

VALENTINE
'What should I see then?'

SPEED
'Your own present folly and her passing deformity; for he, being in love, could not see to garter his hose, and you, being in love, cannot see to put on your hose.'

"Makes you smile, doesn't it?" Dave asked. "Even if love doesn't make us totally blind, it can distort our sight so that we don't see the one we love the way others do. Maybe we see the appearance and others see the reality, or perhaps it's the other way around. Either way, Shakespeare recognizes that love—and other emotions—can alter our perceptions, and hence our decisions and actions.

"Perhaps more than any other play, *A Midsummer Night's Dream* portrays ways that judgment is altered by love. Bottom's famous observation, 'to say the truth, reason and love keep little company together nowadays' is only one example."

"Another is Theseus's comparison of the fantasies of lunatics, lovers and poets," Pat added.

"That's right," Dave agreed. "Now let's look at *King Lear*. Shakespeare depicts so many aspects of human life in the play that we can't discuss all of them. Let's focus on three related points. First, the reality that Lear and Gloucester uncover behind normal appearances in life; second, how their deepened knowledge could only have come through greater experience in the world; and third, how that greater experience was accompanied by intense suffering.

"Near the beginning of the play, Cordelia states that 'Time shall unfold what plighted cunning hides.' It's not merely the passage of time itself that reveals knowledge to Lear, but that as time passes 'Fortune, [will] turn [its] wheel.' Fortune is what happens to us in the world. Our fortune, our experiences through time, makes visible to us the true state of nature—nature being what we inherit, either our interior qualities or the exterior conditions of the world. So Fortune will do its worst, and we will see what's what.

"Let's begin with one of the simpler aspects of the play—the opening scenes between Lear and his daughters, which set the whole plot in motion. Who would like to get us started?"

Nancy was the first to respond. "The situation is that King Lear is tired of the responsibilities of being king, and wants to pass the crown on to his three daughters, giving one third of the kingdom to each. The idea of dividing up a kingdom is probably not a good one—there are advantages to primogeniture in a kingdom—and there are flaws in how Lear goes about it.

"Anyway, Lear demands that each of his daughters flatter him in public before receiving her portion of the kingdom. The two older daughters play that game well. Goneril tells him 'I love you more than word can wield the matter; Dearer than eyesight, space, and liberty,' and Regan says 'I profess myself an enemy to all other joys . . . And find I am alone felicitate in your dear highness' love.'"

"Yeah," Doug said, jumping in. "Lear accepts these over-the-top testimonies as just what is due him, and expects that Cordelia will outdo them. She, however, is reluctant to make such outrageous statements, and merely says softly, 'I love your majesty according to my bond, no more nor less.' She loves him, she says, because he begot her, bred her and loved her, and in turn she obeys him, loves him and honors him. She is speaking from the heart. Every word she says is loving and honest."

"But Lear, not getting the extravagant tribute he expects, is outraged and banishes her," Pat observed. "Kent, Lear's 'noble and true-hearted' attendant who speaks on behalf of Cordelia, is also banished."

"So right from the beginning," Lisa said, "Lear's judgment is faulty. And more than that, perhaps his sanity is starting to slip away. Maybe it has been slipping for some time, but has been covered up by his having the authority of a king. Without that authority, his flawed judgment is exposed for all to see."

"Yeah," Pat agreed, "his behavior—and that of his knights—is wild and inappropriate. Goneril makes the reasonable request that Lear reduce their number and that those who remain behave better. Later she asks him why he needs any knights at all when there are so many servants to take care of his needs."

"Lear is outraged," Lisa said. "He leaves for Regan's house, expecting that she will treat him with greater respect. But she agrees with Goneril. Lear begins to rage about filial ingratitude, and swears revenge on both of them. 'I will have such revenges on you both / That all the world shall – I will do such things – / What they are, yet I know not; but they shall be / the terrors of the earth.' Immediately after that outburst he rides out into the storm. He was already mad by that point; mad and angry."

"You know," Amelia confessed, "in previous readings I had always thought that Lear's two daughters had mistreated him. I thought they had locked the doors against him and that was why he ended up in the storm. But now I see that Lear ran out into the storm on his own.

"It's true that later in the play Regan and Cornwall are heartless and cruel and lustful. But so far—until Lear runs into the storm—they, and Goneril and Albany, have acted pretty reasonably. The two daughters might have overdone their show of love before the kingdom was divided, but they were only giving the king what they knew he wanted.

"Even though the fault is Lear's up to the moment of the storm, what we have seen so far is a man suffering. Maybe Lear's suffering is the result of his own madness, but that doesn't make it any less intense. His madness, in fact, intensifies his suffering. And it causes suffering in others—first Cordelia and Kent, and then his two older daughters."

"Let's take our break here," Dave said, holding up his empty coffee cup. "I need a refill."

106

Doug was the first to speak after they returned. "I agree with Lisa that Lear's judgment and sanity were already slipping away at the time the play opens. I also agree with Amelia that this play shows great suffering. And I agree with Nancy's point a couple of weeks ago that it shows the distinctions between an individual, his title and his positions."

"You're being very agreeable today, Doug," Pat said.

"Thanks, Pat. The point I want to raise, though, is just how hard it is for Lear to move from being king to being just a man without a position or a title. The combination of that horrendously difficult transition together with his encroaching madness results in the most intense suffering ever shown on the stage. It's almost too much to bear, either watching or reading."

Everyone quietly considered that point. Pat then described Lear's misconception of what it meant to give up the crown. "Even though he hands over power to his daughters' husbands, he somehow continues to think he still has the power of a king. In a confused statement, he tells Cornwall and Albany, 'I do invest you jointly with my power, / Preeminence, and all the large effects / That troop with majesty. . . . / Only we shall retain / The name, and all th'addition to a king.'

"Kent, fully aware of the folly of Lear's action, tries to stop him, but only succeeds in angering him. And then, just a few lines later, Lear, in a sure sign that he hasn't understood what the transfer of power meant, says that he banishes Kent. But he has already transferred his crown. He no longer has the power to banish anybody."

"Yeah," Doug said. "Goneril later makes that point explicit, saying, 'Idle old man, / That still would manage those authorities / That he hath given away.'"

"Lear begins to notice a 'faint neglect' in his daughters' and sons-in-law's entertainment of him," Nancy observed. "He begins to realize just how far he has fallen since giving up power when he asks a servant, 'Who am I, sir?' and the reply is 'My lady's father.'"

"If that's not a punch in the gut, I don't know what is," Dave said.

Nancy nodded, and continued. "Lear's awareness of his descent deepens when the Fool points out that it's perhaps Lear who is the fool, because 'All thy other titles thou has given away; that thou wast born with.' And then comes this stunning passage showing Lear's confusion about his identity now that he's no longer king:

> 'Does any here know me? This is not Lear.
> Does Lear walk thus? speak thus? Where are his eyes? . . .
> Who is it that can tell me who I am?'

"The fool has an answer: 'Lear's shadow.'"

"That reminds me of a parallel expression," Doug said. "'This is not Lear;' reminds me of Troilus's incredulous 'This is not Cressida' when he sees her in Diomedes's tent."

"And another similarity in wording reminds me of *Richard II*," Amelia chimed in. "Note how the Fool's 'Lear's shadow,' echoes Bolingbroke's 'The shadow of your sorrow hath destroyed / The shadow of your face.' Many of Shakespeare's characters seem to be obsessed with trying to discover the reality of their identity apart from the appearances of name, title and position."

Nancy continued with more examples of Lear's recognition of his descent. "When Cornwall and Regan are indisposed and will not see him, Lear rails at them, forgetting that he is no longer king. He says, 'The king would speak with Cornwall. The dear father / Would with his daughter speak, commands . . . service.'"

"It's a long hard road that Lear must go down before he can accept that he no longer has the power of a king," Lisa commented. "But eventually he learns. 'They flattered me like a dog,' he says. 'They told me I was everything.' But after the night on the heath he learns that he, like all other men, is 'not ague-proof.'"

"It's through his experiences that he learns he is simply a man, one with no position or title," Dave said, steering the discussion into another important area. "Through his suffering on the heath, be begins to learn what it means to be a man, to be a *mere* man in a harsh world. 'Thou art the thing itself,' he says to himself in a famous passage, 'unaccommodated man is no more but a poor, bare, forked animal.'"

Pat picked up on the theme. "Lear learns not only that a man alone is unprotected from the elements, but also that a man alone in human society, without wealth and power, is at the mercy of other people. He comes to see that the rich and powerful are as full of sin and cruelty as the poor and weak. The only difference is the finery with which their sins are covered. In another famous passage, he observes that,

> 'Through tattered clothes small vices do appear;
> Robes and furred gowns hid all. Plate sin with gold,
> And the strong lance of justice hurtles breaks;
> Arm it in rags, a pygmy's straw does pierce it.'"

"And he learns humility," Doug said. "He realizes that he himself should have taken more care in dealing with others less well off than he is, or was. In recognition of that point, he insists that the Fool go ahead of him into the hovel and out of the storm."

"Dave is right," Amelia observed. "Lear learns these things through his experiences—through his sufferings. And suffer he does—physical suffering on the heath, and emotional suffering as he thinks about his daughters' heartless abandonment of him to the storm. Filial ingratitude is sharper than a serpent's tooth, he says. The rain and wind and thunder are less unkind than his daughters, he believes, because those elements had no duty to treat him kindly."

"Our time is almost up," Alan said. "Before this session ends, it is important to note the progression of the three plays that Dave has introduced. They form a clear path from lightheartedness in *The Two Gentlemen of Verona*, to a magical play with undertones of strife, *A*

Midsummer Night's Dream, and finally to a world of decrepitude, madness and suffering in *King Lear*. Shakespeare's journey in life was one of growing disillusionment. There is so much more to say about *King Lear*. We haven't even touched yet on Gloucester and his troubles. I'll try to make time for them in one of the final sessions."

As the students were leaving the classroom, Alan overheard Doug say to the others that this session reminded him of *Scooby Doo*. "You remember the TV cartoon? Scooby Doo is a big dog. In each episode he and his human friends encounter a ghost or other mysterious happenings designed to frighten people away from a certain place. It always turns out, though, that the ghost or monster was fake. They were always created by bad guys wanting to hide their nefarious activities.

"Well, just as Scooby Doo and the others ripped through the appearance to get to the reality, so too Shakespeare has ripped through the social coverings to get at the real nature of human beings. And what he finds ain't always pretty."

107

Amelia and Alan arrived at the Cary Museum separately, but at the same time. The Museum had wings focused on the natural history and the human history of North Carolina. They walked arm in arm toward the wing showing how the first people to occupy the area lived, stopping to look closely at a diorama depicting a typical family.

"Their life was very hard," Alan observed. "Everybody is busy, even the children. They're carrying water from the river, collecting branches and leaves to reinforce the walls and roof of the hut, tending the few animals the family owned, or fishing or hunting. It was a life of constant effort to combat the elements, find food and protect themselves from wild animals and other people."

Amelia nodded, and commented on how closely the members of the family appeared to be cooperating, with each person understanding his or her responsibilities. "It was the family that enabled them to survive." And then, after a pause, she wondered aloud if she would ever have a family of her own like the one they were looking at. "I envy them," she whispered. "I don't care how primitive their living conditions are. They are a complete family." She wiped away small tears from her eyes.

Alan put his arms around her. "Amelia," he said softly, "I didn't tell you this before, but I have had a wonderful dream—the same wonderful dream several times. In it I give you a baby daughter. Together we watch your belly grow big until the day when she is born. And that dream when I am asleep matches my hopes when I'm awake. I want us to become a family."

They sat on a bench together for several minutes, nestled against each other. Finally, Amelia stood up. "Come," she said. "I have had the same dream. And it's a nice dream. But let's continue."

In the next diorama they saw the family joining with other families around a large fire. Meat was cooking, and all the children were playing together. "I'm surprised to see the women in the diorama grouped together on one side of the fire and the men grouped together on the other," Alan commented. "Surprised not that the adults are segregated by sex—something I've seen many times at receptions and dinner parties—but that the Museum curators have been bold enough to portray a scene that violates the modern pretense that men and women are identical in every way except for the shape of their genitals. I wonder how much longer this exhibition will stay up."

They wandered into a small gift shop selling replicas of items that might have been used by the people they'd seen in the dioramas. Alan saw Amelia looking carefully at a pair of earrings that resembled dolphins carved out of a brilliant dark blue stone. "I would like to get those for you, Amelia. They would look beautiful on you. Or rather you would look even more beautiful than usual when wearing them."

After he paid for them, she immediately took off the earrings she'd been wearing and put the new ones on. "I feel special. Thank you, Alan. Maybe these will bring us the luck we need to overcome the obstacles keeping us apart."

They continued through the Museum until they came to the exhibits showing local contributions to the national war efforts in World War I and World War II. Exhibits depicted not only fields of battle, but also home scenes, with women working hard at new responsibilities in place of the men who were away. Others showed women alone in the evenings, missing their husbands, brothers, sons and fathers. Most heartbreaking of all was the exhibit showing a woman receiving a telegram informing her that her husband had been killed in battle.

"Life is very difficult," he observed.

"Yes," she agreed, "difficult for different people in different ways at different times. But we must be strong to meet the challenges. Just as we must have strong muscles to survive physically, so too we must have strong spiritual sinews and tendons for our soul to survive. And, like muscles, psychic sinews must be used to remain strong. Unfortunately, difficult times are needed to stay fit. In easy times, we relax too much and they become weak. Then they aren't ready when we need them again."

Alan agreed. "We become capable by meeting challenges. We strengthen our capacity for resilience by being resilient in the face of difficulties. There is no other way."

"Look!" Amelia pointed toward the cafeteria. "They have many flavors of ice cream here. Remember when we talked of difficult times before, of the things that Viktor Frankl helped us survive? And then had ice cream to make us feel better? Life is sometimes good to us in spite of its difficulties."

FRIDAY, JULY 24

108

Why hadn't Edward de Vere's authorship been accepted by literary scholars even though continental drift has been accepted by geologists? Academia had been able to cling to belief in Shakspere's authorship, Alan concluded, because Oxfordians haven't yet definitively explained how and why de Vere's authorship could have been successfully hidden.

The usual Oxfordian explanations, he knew, were that de Vere couldn't acknowledge authorship of his literary works because of his status as a courtier, and because he'd portrayed and ridiculed prominent people in the plays. Hiding his authorship would have made identification of them less likely. But a substantial minority of Oxfordians believe that those explanations aren't emotionally weighty enough to account for the shame that de Vere repeatedly expressed in the *Sonnets*. To them, traditional explanations don't adequately explain why the effort to hide de Vere's authorship continued for decades after the deaths of de Vere and those ridiculed in the plays, or how the effort to hide his authorship could have succeeded.

The incompleteness of Looney's theory could be compared not only with the initial incompleteness of Wegener's theory, but also, Alan realized, with that of Charles Darwin's theory of the origin of species through natural selection. All three had lacked an explanation for the mechanics of how they worked. Continental movement hadn't been accepted until the development of the mechanics of plate tectonics in the 1970s. Darwin's theory of natural selection hadn't become widely accepted until the formulation in the 1920s of population genetics, which explained the mechanics of how traits were passed from one generation to the next. Perhaps Oxfordian theory remained unaccepted by academia because the second phase of its development hadn't yet been completed.

Some Oxfordians, though, had proposed a fuller explanation that answered the how and why questions: the so-called Prince Tudor theory. It was based on the idea that Edward de Vere had an affair with Queen Elizabeth that resulted in the birth of a son, who was raised as the Earl of Southampton. If so, a direct male descendant of the queen, even if illegitimate, would have been a serious threat to King James, who was only Elizabeth's half-nephew. Strong political reasons would have existed to keep Southampton's real parentage secret throughout James's reign. It was de Vere's veiled references in his plays and poems to his liaison with the queen and the birth and status of their son that provided the motive for hiding his authorship and keeping it hidden. The use of state power in the cover-up explains how it could have been successful.

Some adherents of the Prince Tudor theory also believe that Edward de Vere was Elizabeth's son as well as her lover. If so, the incestual aspects of the affair between de Vere and the queen would have been emotionally weighty enough to account for the shame de Vere describes in the *Sonnets*. Percy Allen first proposed that idea in 1933. It had been reaffirmed by Charlton Ogburn's parents, Charlton Ogburn, Sr. and Dorothy Ogburn, in *This Star of England* in 1952, and expanded more recently by Betty Sears and Charles Beauclerk. Proponents believe that it is in accordance with the facts revealed in historical documents and by Oxford himself in his plays and poems, especially the *Sonnets*. Many other Oxfordians, however, believe that all versions of the Prince Tudor theses are too speculative or are patently incorrect.

Alan drew up a chart to help make that situation clearer to himself.

Issue under examination	Initial Version of New Theory		Mechanics/motivating force added later		Complete Theory
Origin of species	Natural selection	+	Population genetics	→	New Synthesis
Features of Earth's crust	Continental drift	+	Sea floor spreading and movement of plates rather than continents per se	→	Plate Tectonics
Authorship of works attributed to Shakespeare	Edward de Vere as author	+	References to Southampton's parentage in the works is motive for hiding de Vere's authorship. Use of state power explains the mechanics.	→	Oxfordian Theory Completed

He wasn't quite ready to accept an idea as startling as the Prince Tudor theory, but still it couldn't be ignored. It wasn't any more outlandish than the idea that Shakspere wasn't Shakespeare. He would have to investigate further later. Now he had to move on to consideration of the methodology of literary studies. After lunch, of course. It was a mystery why sitting still and thinking made him hungry.

109

Putting his coffee cup down next to the mouse, Alan considered how the methodology of literary criticism had changed over the last half century. It hadn't evolved in ways supportive of the authorship question the way that changes in the methodology of geological science helped facilitate the idea of continental movement, and he wanted to know why.

In 1920 J. Thomas Looney had introduced the idea de Vere's authorship into an environment in which belief in Shakspere's authorship within academia was accompanied by growing doubts about it outside. Convinced that Shakspere's authorship had been confirmed by the First Folio, Stratfordians followed a deductive methodology as they sought to flesh out the context in which Shakspere had written his works. To them, correspondences between the works and the known life of an alternative candidate were irrelevant. With correspondences ruled out as an acceptable form of evidence by their methodology, scholars felt justified in ignoring the authorship question.

The weakness of that mindset was shown by the case of Charlotte Carmichael Stopes (1840-1929), author of several books about Shakespeare, including *The Life of Henry, Third Earl of Southampton*. Stopes had spent many years searching for evidence of ties between Shakspere and Southampton, the dedicatee of Shakespeare's two long poems. Unable to find even a single scrap of evidence to connect the two men, she regarded her search as a failure. It was too bad that she hadn't had a more open-ended methodology, Alan thought. She might have come to realize that the problem wasn't in the quality of her search but in her assumption of Shakspere's authorship.

Looney, in contrast, had investigated the authorship issue guided only by qualities he thought the author must have had, without pre-judging what he might find. Because what he was investigating took place in the past, he was conducting the work of a historian. Alan realized that he needed more information on the methodology most appropriate for historians, and turned to a book by David Hackett Fischer, *Historians' Fallacies: Toward a Logic of Historical Thought*.

"History," Fischer explained, "must begin with questions. Questions for historians are like hypotheses for scientists." Alan read further. "The logic of historical thought . . . is a process of *adductive* reasoning in the simple sense of adducing answers to specific questions, so that a satisfactory explanatory 'fit' is obtained. . . . The questions and answers are fitted to each other by a complex process of mutual adjustment. . . . Always it is articulated in the form of a reasoned argument." In asking an open-ended question and in presenting his results "in the form of a reasoned argument," Looney, it seemed to Alan, had followed the process of "adductive reasoning" fifty years before Fischer had described it.

Once Looney had uncovered de Vere authorship, Oxfordians began to follow a process resembling the Stratfordians' deductive methodology. Both sought to establish the facts of "their" candidate's life, and then to account for how he'd come to write his works. Because their activity took place within the context of the wider methodology of literary studies, Alan saw it was time to investigate that subject further.

Methodologies, he knew, must be specific to the subject being investigated. The fields of literature, geology, biology and philosophy require different methodologies because what is studied in each case is different. Works of literature differ from matter studied by science in two important ways. Each work was unique and so had to be studied individually, as opposed to matter that was studied en masse. And works of literature were man-made.

Those differences gave rise to two distinct but complementary approaches to the study of literature that were current at the time Looney introduced the idea of de Vere's authorship. One approach explained the significance of works of literature by considering them as works of art important in themselves. Practitioners of this approach, whom Alan termed literary connoisseurs, sought to understand and demonstrate the technical perfection or artistic unity of a work. They helped readers understand the genre, literary devices and rhetorical figures used, and expressed a judgment about how successfully the author had used them.

The other approach drew from information about an author's life and times to gain insights into the meaning of his works. Alan called practitioners of this approach literary historians. Their work is of greater relevance for the Shakespeare authorship question, he knew, because they seek to understand an author's intentions and how he or she was influenced by the political, economic, social and literary currents of his or her society. Because authors lived and worked in times different from our own, general readers could benefit from literary historians' expert knowledge of the author's life.

Alan had already known that the methodology that encompasses both approaches, often referred to as the humanistic tradition in literary criticism, stretched back to the earliest Western writings about the nature of literature. He had studied the works of critics such as Aristotle and Horace, and Alexander Pope, Samuel Johnson and Matthew Arnold, and Henry James, who had lived just prior to Looney's identification of de Vere as Shakespeare. The two approaches were two sides of one methodological coin because both required close readings of literary works with the goal of teasing out the author's meanings. Alan was aware that in the humanistic tradition, as Professor Jonathan Culler explained, "[T]he task was the interpretation of literary works as the achievements of their authors, and the main justification for studying literature was the special value of great works: their complexity, their beauty, their insight, their universality, and their potential benefits to the reader."

Time to call it a day, Alan thought sleepily. Tomorrow he would examine how the methodology of literary studies had changed since Looney's day.

SATURDAY, JULY 25

110

Alan woke up early, eager to continue his investigations. The more he read, the more he realized just how extensive and how negative changes in the methodology of literary criticism had been over the course of his career. He began to see that he'd been sleepwalking through changes in his own field.

The biggest change was that the humanistic tradition itself had lost favor with academic and scholarly communities. By the end of the twentieth century, that tradition—one not unfavorable to consideration of the authorship question—had been superseded by a new methodology that didn't value close readings of literary works and in which the intentions of the author were largely irrelevant.

One of the first developments in the transformation was a change in emphasis from seeking to understand those aspects of an author's society that he purposely sought to portray in his works to those that he unconsciously revealed about them. Lionel Trilling, writing in *The Liberal Imagination*, described it as a change in focus from "the explicit statements that a people makes through its art," to what lies beneath them: the "culture's hum and buzz of implication . . . the whole evanescent context in which its explicit statements are made."

The "flaw" in the older way of thinking, newer scholars believed, was summed up by W. K. Wimsatt and Monroe Beardsley as "the intentional fallacy." For them, "the design or intention of the author is neither available nor desirable as a standard for judging the success of a work of literary art." What was important was what the author had embodied in the work, not what he or she might have intended at some point during its composition. The work of literary scholars was now, Jonathan Culler explained, to "expose the unexamined assumptions on which a text may rely (political, sexual, philosophical, linguistic)."

A second development was the deliberate separation of a work from its creator. After the heyday of the New Criticism, some critics adopted its practice of deliberately separating works of literature from their authors—not in order to examine them as works of art as the New Critics had—but to examine their political and social content unencumbered by any thoughts of the author. With both new approaches focused on the content of the work rather than the author's intentions, there was, some thought, no need to consider the author at all. With this line of thinking, literary criticism reached what Roland Barthes called "the death of the author."

Alan shook his head. Examining works of literature in isolation from any consideration of their authors was not an approach favorable to the authorship question, which is intimately bound up with consideration of the life of the author and his reasons for writing. Neither factor is valued if works of literature are instead regarded as immaculately conceived and the result of virgin births.

He had already noted attempts to cut off consideration of the strongest type of support for the idea of de Vere's authorship—correspondences between his life and Shakespeare's works—by denying the validity of circumstantial evidence. The "death of the author" approach would have the same effect: denying the importance of the author also devalued the significance of any linkages between de Vere's life and Shakespeare's plays. Some Oxfordians have speculated that this approach to literary theory may have arisen as a response to the mismatch between the mundane details known of Shakspere's life and the brilliance of Shakespeare's works. Perhaps some literary academicians, convinced that the man from Stratford was Shakespeare, deliberately overstated "the death of the author" as one way of preserving their belief in his authorship.

Alan was aghast. The cumulative effect of these developments was a change from studying works of literature *through* the history of their times, to studying societies and cultures *through* works of literature. In the new methodology, literary criticism was no longer an independent field of study, but one that had become largely subsumed within the larger subject of Cultural Studies.

Rather than being the ends to be examined, literary works had become merely one means through which non-literary subjects were studied. Cultural theorists regarded all literary works as mere artifacts to be mined for data about the political, economic, social or sexual practices in the society from which they arose in the same manner that advertising or other anonymously written documents could be examined. The standard anthology in the field, *The Norton Anthology of Theory and Criticism*, declared that "Literary texts, like other artworks, are neither more nor less important than any other cultural artifact or practice. Keeping the emphasis on how cultural meanings are produced, circulated and consumed, the investigator will focus on art or literature insofar as such works connect with broader social factors, not because they possess some intrinsic interest or special aesthetic value."

Let's be clear, Alan emphasized to himself, that when the so-called "death of the author" is discussed, the death of literary criticism itself is necessarily implied. Consideration of works of literature as works of art important in themselves—the approach of literary connoisseurs—has little place in this methodology, and has largely ended within academia. Gone was any sense that literature has something meaningful to say about the larger aspects of human life on planet Earth.

He was shocked to see how completely the humanistic tradition in literary criticism seemed to have vanished from English literature programs and journals. The editors of *The Norton Anthology*, for instance, couldn't find much space in their 2,785-page volume for the giants of traditional humanistic literary criticism in the twentieth century. Lionel Trilling wasn't represented at all, and only one unrepresentative essay by Edmund Wilson was included, even though the book claims to "present a staggeringly varied collection of the most influential critical statements from the classical era to the present day."

The introduction to another book Alan hadn't previously examined—the widely used text *Cultural Studies*—advised that "although there is no prohibition against close textual readings in Cultural Studies, they are also not required." Thus, as literary critic Jonathan Culler observed, "In theory Cultural Studies is all-encompassing: Shakespeare and rap music, high culture and low, culture of the past and culture of the present" are all equally worthy of study.

Alan took note of an example that Culler provided. "Interpreting *Hamlet* is, among other things, a matter of deciding whether it should be read as talking about, say, the problems of Danish princes, or the dilemmas of men of the Renaissance experiencing changes in the conception of the self, or relations between men and their mothers in general, or the question of how representations (including literary ones) affect the problem of making sense of our experiences."

Alan noted with dismay Professor James Seaton's observation that, "in some of the most influential academic centers literary criticism has been replaced by Cultural Studies." The situation, Alan saw, isn't that Cultural Studies courses are taught alongside literature courses. It's not even that the methodology of literary studies has been expanded to include new factors. It's that a takeover has occurred in which there appears to be little room left for the traditional humanistic approach to literary studies.

Alan couldn't avoid the conclusion that the humanistic tradition, in place when Looney identified Edward de Vere as Shakespeare, had been supplanted by one in which the author was regarded as an outmoded "construct" to be bypassed in favor of cultural forces that determine the content of literary works. That the entire field of literary studies has been subsumed under the field of Cultural Studies, itself wracked by serious methodological flaws, has led to an environment in which the academic study of the authorship question couldn't easily take place.

111

It was a lazy Saturday afternoon. Alan and Amelia had worked on their academic projects in the morning, and were now idling together in her apartment, enjoying being close to each other. Amelia was reading one of the *Calvin and Hobbes* books and laughing from time to time. Alan laughed when she did even though he couldn't see which strips she was reading.

Then Alan spoke. "You know, Amelia, many people fall in love."

"Yes, and many of those who fall in love either quickly or eventually fall out of love. That is why feelings aren't reliable guides to actions."

"Exactly. I have been thinking about something I read years ago, something in a book by Walter Lippmann, *A Preface to Morals*, in 1929."

"Wow, Alan, I knew you were old, but I didn't know you were that old," she said, laughing.

"I don't mean that I read it in 1929," he said, laughing with her. "I mean he wrote it in that year. I just remembered the passage because we've had so much pleasure from sharing things that we love with each other. It's because we appreciate and even love so many of the same things that I know our relationship is built on a solid base. We don't just read the same books and listen to the same music; we have the same intellectual and emotional responses to them."

He saw Amelia looking at him, and continued.

"That we share an emotional togetherness through those things is why Lippmann's observation is such a powerful commentary on our situation. Here it is: 'Lovers must love many things together and not merely each other. Love and nothing else very soon is nothing else.'

"I have been haunted by those words ever since I read them decades ago. You are the first person I have ever shared them with, the only person I have ever wanted to share them with."

"Alan—"

"Wait, there's more. All of this is apart from our similar experiences, from the difficult times we faced in the past, from what we learned from them, from the strength of soul we demonstrated in overcoming them. Even though there are still so many things we don't yet know about each other, from all the things I do know about you, I can't help but think of you not as Amelia, but as my soulmate."

"Alan—" she said, a bit more strongly this time, but he continued quickly.

"I have always laughed at people who talked about searching for their soulmate. I didn't think that any such person existed, and that they should instead be looking for 'Mr. or Ms. Good Enough.' But I'm not laughing any more, because I have found my soulmate. I've found the person I want to spend the rest of my life with."

"Alan," Amelia said even more forcefully, "before you say anything else, listen to me. Everything you feel—everything you have just described—I feel, too, just as strongly as you do. But there is one factor you are overlooking. You are married."

"Amelia—" Alan started to say.

"Let me continue. I already know your feelings because you have understood me like no one else ever has. We truly are soulmates, and it's a miracle we met, in this world of so many billions of people.

"But I want to talk about 'The Rules.' Not the rules that describe how young women should act if they want to test the strength of the desires of the young men courting them. There are other rules—rules more important in our particular situation—and violating them is inevitably a source of pain and suffering. One rule is that women shouldn't get involved with men who are married. I have already violated that rule, and the stronger our feelings for each other become the greater my suffering will be."

Alan again started to speak, but she continued.

"Another rule is that married men shouldn't fall in love with other women. In Vietnam we have a saying, '101 percent of Vietnamese men have affairs.' Vietnamese wives don't like the fact that their husband might sometimes have sex with other women, but we accept that. We know that men have a desire for a variety of sexual partners that women don't share.

"But 'affairs' refers to the physical act of sex only. It doesn't refer to love affairs. It doesn't refer to husbands developing feelings for other women. That is where Vietnamese women draw the line. And that is the important rule you have broken. Not that you've had sex with a woman who isn't your wife, but that you've fallen in love with her. The penalty for breaking that rule will be pain and suffering. It is unavoidable."

Alan once again started to speak, but Amelia continued quickly.

"I know what you are going to say, that you will end your marriage so that you can marry me. If you do that, then the pain and suffering will be extended to a third person—your wife—and to a fourth and fifth—your daughter and son—and to others. Have you thought about all that?

"And that leads to another rule that I haven't yet broken. The rule is that a woman should never allow herself to be the cause of the disintegration of a marriage. If that happens, I would feel such a strong sense of guilt for the pain I would have caused other people that it would color our relationship.

"There is still another aspect of the situation to consider, Alan. If you end your marriage for me, you will have demonstrated that you are the type of man who would leave his wife for another woman. Even though we are soulmates, even though I know the depth of your love for me, even though I know that we are the ideal companions for each other, I would also know that you are a man who has demonstrated the capacity for leaving his wife for another woman. So we are caught. There is no easy way forward in our situation, and it is our own fault because we have broken the rules."

Neither spoke after she finished. Then Alan, took her hand and led her to the sofa. They sat down, looking at each other.

"Amelia, I have thought of all of these things. They are practically all I have thought of for weeks."

"Those things and the Shakespeare authorship question," she added. They both laughed.

"Yes, and the authorship question, too. That is yet another interest that binds us together. I hadn't thought of our situation in terms of rules, as you have. But I've been obsessed with these things for weeks, going round and round in my mind, looking for a solution.

"Here is what I think: If I were to end my marriage, I'd be doing it for my own reasons, not because of you. Through knowing you I've realized that I'd been a sleepwalker for years. Because of you I have now woken up to a fuller life. But I would be leaving my marriage to escape a suffocating situation that has nothing to do with you. The reason would be to end the frustration that anyone who owns 8,000 books would feel if married to someone who has never read a book in her life. It's the same frustration that someone who is very religious might feel if married to someone who sees no value in religion. It's a case of basic incompatibility that has nothing to do with anyone else.

"Only after I am free would I be able to turn to someone new. I hope that relieves your feelings of guilt at being the cause of the end of a marriage. You wouldn't be the cause, but only a partial catalyst for my recognizing what I must do for my own health.

"There is a question that I have been wanting to ask you, one that has been burning inside me for weeks, but it's a question that must be asked in a direct way, not a conditional way. So I cannot ask it now; I must free myself first."

Amelia suddenly stood up. "My brain is tired from so much talking. You know I am a very physical person. I need some movement, some exercise to relieve the tension."

"Let's go swim some laps," Alan suggested.

"No, I have a better idea," she said, taking his hand and leading him toward the bedroom. "You have said you love me. I want you to prove it, physically."

SUNDAY, JULY 26

112

They woke up at the same time, early, looking into each other's eyes.

Alan shook his head in disbelief, as best he could while it was resting on a pillow. "When we are apart for more than a couple of days, I sometimes have the thought that you couldn't possibly have the effect on me that you do, that I must be exaggerating it or remembering wrong. But once I see you, I'm again staggered by the effect the mere sight of you has on me."

Amelia lay still, listening, watching him with her brown eyes.

"It's not merely that we both enjoy, or even love, so many different intellectual subjects. It's not even that you have awakened my need for a close companion to share those things with, something I had forgotten or suppressed. It's more than that. I can't begin to explain it. Seeing you is like a key turning in a lock. The fit between us just feels so right."

"It is the same for me, too, Alan. I had often imagined that there must be someone in the world who I felt at home with, who I could relax with. You are that person. But there is more to life than feelings, no matter how strong they are. There are obligations and duties to other people. Commitments that, having been made, must be kept."

She paused before continuing. "I know from my own experience that the effort to end one set of commitments is an unbearably painful and lengthy process. No one can know in advance if he or she has the strength and courage to go through with it. No one can understand in advance just how painful it will be to see the suffering one is causing someone he or she loves, or had loved and still cares about."

Rising from the bed, she changed the subject. "Come on, Alan. In spite of exercising on the bed for half the night, I need still more physical movement. Let's go to the pool to swim those laps."

113

Back home in the afternoon, Alan thought about Amelia, wondering how this was all going to turn out. He'd had the same thoughts about his efforts to promote Edward de Vere's authorship. It was to the latter subject that he now turned his attention.

He understood that the most critical factor affecting acceptance or rejection of new theories is methodology, the process through which scientific or academic communities pursue new knowledge and evaluate new ideas and data. One mistake academia was making in its refusal to consider the authorship question was its reliance on an overly deductive methodology. The appropriate methodology would combine the "adductive reasoning" that Fischer had determined was best for historians with the two approaches of traditional literary criticism—those practiced by literary connoisseurs and by literary historians. But none of those three practices were valued in literary studies today.

Another mistake was blindly adhering to *any* methodology rather than focusing on substantive accomplishments. Theories, like data, must be considered separately from the methodology that was in place when they were formulated. American geologists had made the mistake of rejecting Wegener's theory because it hadn't been formed through "correct" methodological procedures. Stratfordians were making the same mistake today.

Their rejection of circumstantial evidence was particularly unfortunate, Alan thought. He was convinced that circumstantial evidence was as legitimate in historical investigations as it was in courtrooms. Correspondences between events and characters in a literary work and events and people in the life of an author are indeed legitimate grounds for establishing a relationship between the two. What is important is the quality and quantity of the correspondences, as both Looney and Wegener had argued.

The longer a methodological practice continues unchanged the more firmly it becomes entrenched, he realized. In order for independent and creative thought to take place, it is necessary to resist bureaucratic pressures to regard adherence to methodology as an accomplishment in itself.

So what would have to happen for the current methodology to be overthrown? A starting point, Alan saw, would be restoring the relevance of the author in literary criticism. The so-called "death of the author" must be replaced by the "resurrection of the author" if literature is again to be studied as works of art created by individuals with specific intentions. Circumstantial evidence could be recognized as a legitimate analytical tool only if the author was recognized as having an essential role in the creation of works of literature.

The healthy study of literature under a new methodology could take place only if literature shakes off the shackles placed on it by Cultural Studies. The health of both fields requires that they be separated. The two study different things and so require different methodologies. They need to be housed in different departments dedicated to maintaining high standards in their own distinct methodological areas.

Once truly independent literary studies departments are established, safe havens would exist in which literary scholars would be free to cultivate what one historian described as "the ability to enter imaginatively into the life of a society remote in time or place, and produce a plausible explanation of why its inhabitants thought and behaved as they did." With this imaginative understanding, scholars would be able "to make the great works of literature more consequentially available not only to academics but to general readers without any special intellectual equipment beyond the educated good sense of their time," as James Seaton phrased it. In such an environment the Shakespeare authorship question could finally receive a fair hearing.

But I've only kicked the can down the road, not solved the problem,

Alan recognized. I've imagined only what changes need to take place, not how to enact them. So how are new methodological practices and independent literature departments to be established?

He had an idea. It could be that the authorship question will be the catalyst leading to the return of genuine literature programs in our universities. If a significant impetus toward the "death of the author" had been the desire to avoid considering the lack of correspondences between the life of the man from Stratford and the works of Shakespeare, then serious academic study of the authorship question could lead to the "resurrection of the author."

Building on this, he envisioned a scenario for the implementation of a new methodology and acceptance of the legitimacy of the authorship question that mirrored geologists' path from fieldwork to laboratory work, from geology to geophysics. The initial step would be a few literary scholars beginning to use the new technique of establishing links between author and literary works in order to strengthen the case for their existing belief in Shakspere's authorship. As they became more comfortable with the new method, they could begin to accept conclusions it supported even when they conflicted with conclusions supported by other methods.

From there it would be only a short leap to the resurrection of the author, because an author was necessary if correspondences were to be established. With that step, the new methodology would be largely in place and the authorship question well on the way to being resolved.

MONDAY, JULY 27

114

"Stormy weather predicted by the end of the week." The weather report was on the radio playing in the coffee shop as Alan passed through it on his way to class. That's crazy, he thought as he walked out the glass door and onto the campus grounds. He saw perfectly clear blue skies overhead as he continued to the seminar room.

"Today," Pat began, "we continue our examination of the theme of appearance versus reality. We'll examine only one play, *Hamlet*, in both sessions. In the first we'll look at how confusion between appearance and reality in Hamlet's world drives the plot forward in ways we haven't previously considered. After the break we'll look at Hamlet's efforts to sort through appearances to get at the reality of himself, to understand himself better.

"On the first subject, I want to note how hard it is to get an accurate, objective picture of the world from other people. It's especially difficult if you are a prince, because people tell you what they think you want to hear. Here's an example. When Hamlet compares the shape of a cloud to a camel, Polonius agrees, saying 'By th' mass and 'tis like a camel indeed.' When Hamlet then says it is like a weasel, Polonius again agrees, saying 'It is backed like a weasel.' Polonius also agrees when Hamlet says it looks like a whale.

"Now consider Hamlet's penchant for observing things and making notes. He compares his brain to a notebook in which things can be written and from which they can be erased. He tells his father's ghost that of course he'll remember him. 'Remember thee?' he asks. 'I'll wipe away all trivial fond records . . . And thy commandment all alone shall live / Within the book and volume of my brain.'

"Then comes Hamlet's famous observation of appearance versus reality, one that he will record in his notebook.

> 'O villain, villain, smiling, damnèd villain!
> My tables – meet it is I set it down
> That one may smile, and smile, and be a villain.
> At least I am sure it may be so in Denmark.'"

"You know," Dave said. "That observation reminds me of Octavius's in *Julius Caesar*: 'And some that smile have in their hearts, I fear, / Millions of mischiefs.'"

"Yeah, that is similar," Pat agreed. "And Shakespeare has presented many other distinctions between appearance and reality in *Hamlet*. Let's turn to those you think are most important."

"One of the most interesting is the distinction between Hamlet's sanity and supposed madness," Lisa said. "After he saw the ghost he wasn't sure how to proceed, yet he felt it couldn't be business as usual. So he decides to pretend to be mad—'To put an antic disposition on,' is how he describes it—and he swears Horatio and the others to secrecy. He appears before Ophelia in his mad guise, and his behavior is so extraordinary that I'm sure you all recall the passage—the one where Ophelia is set out as bait and their conversation is heard by the king and Polonius."

"But here's the thing," Nancy offered. "I'm not sure whether in that scene Hamlet is merely putting 'an antic disposition on,' or whether he's trying to see deep into Ophelia's soul, or whether he really is a bit crazy. After all, he had reason to be confused, because Ophelia wouldn't see him and had returned all the things he'd given her, without providing any explanation."

"How about this?" Doug asked. "Maybe Hamlet is someone who is mad pretending to be someone who is sane pretending to be mad."

"Doug," Alan commented. "In all my years of studying and teaching *Hamlet* I have never heard anyone propose that particular idea."

"So it really is possible for there to be something new under the sun," Amelia observed.

Everyone laughed, and the discussion continued.

"Here's another instance of confusion between appearance and reality," Dave said. "Hamlet thinks he sees Claudius at prayer. He doesn't kill him then because he doesn't want to send his soul to heaven. But Hamlet doesn't know that Claudius isn't really praying. He isn't asking God for forgiveness for his sins; he's having an internal conversation with himself about whether asking forgiveness would be effective when he is unwilling to give up what he gained by murdering his brother—the crown and the queen.

"It's a powerful scene because the audience knows the real situation. Hamlet could have achieved his goal of revenge for both his father's murder and the torment of his soul, but, guided by appearances, he doesn't know that. That was the last opportunity he had, because Claudius, increasingly suspicious of Hamlet, never again puts himself into a vulnerable position."

"Here's another example," Nancy said. "It's a deception organized by the king. We know that he is worried about how popular Hamlet and Laertes are with the people. He knows that Laertes wants to avenge his father's death by killing Hamlet, but restrains him from any rash act. Instead, he designs a way that Laertes could kill Hamlet in a fencing match so that he, the king, would be free of any hint of involvement in his death. And, if things go right, Laertes might also die in the game, thus eliminating two political rivals at once.

"The match isn't a fight to the death, but one in which points are scored for each hit or nick. The king and Laertes arrange for the tip of Laertes's sword to be poisoned, so that a slight prick will kill Hamlet. The king also arranges for poisoned wine to be served just in case the poisoned sword doesn't do the trick."

"Of course everything goes wrong," Doug observed. "Laertes nicks Hamlet, but then the swords get switched and Laertes himself is nicked. Then the queen accidentally drinks the poisoned wine. Laertes, dying, reveals the plot to Hamlet, who then stabs the king. In only ten minutes four people have died. Add in the deaths of Polonius and Ophelia, and six major characters are dead. With six deaths and no marriages, *Hamlet* is truly a tragedy in every sense of the word."

"And then, with appearances not being clear," Amelia said, "Hamlet with his dying breath urges Horatio to make the reality known. 'Report me and my cause aright / To the unsatisfied,' he commands. 'If thou didst ever hold me in thy heart, / Absent thee from felicity awhile, / And in this harsh world draw thy breath in pain, / to tell my story.'

"It's often the case that the truth needs a spokesperson. It isn't enough for the truth to be true. It needs to be pointed out and supported by someone that people respect. In this case, Horatio promises to fulfill that role. He then blesses Hamlet as his spirit leaves his body. 'Now cracks a noble heart. Good night, sweet prince, / And flights of angels sing thee to thy rest!'"

After a moment of silence in honor of the exquisiteness of Hamlet's passing and Horatio's tribute, Pat turned to another point of confusion between appearance and reality.

"We know that Hamlet is upset by his mother's 'o'erhasty' marriage to her dead husband's brother because he tells us so. In his first soliloquy, he tells us two things. First, his mother had been in love with his father. He even describes his mother's sexual desire for him."

"Do you want to read that one?" Pat asked Lisa. "Sure," she said, blushing slightly. "'Must I remember? Why, she would hang on him / As if increase of appetite had grown / By what it fed on.'"

Amelia glanced at Alan, thinking of a similar passage in *Antony and Cleopatra*, and he caught her eye briefly.

"And second," Pat continued, "Hamlet describes his distress at his mother's sudden marriage to Claudius." He glanced at Lisa, who read the appropriate passage. "'and yet within a month . . . / O God, a beast that wants discourse of reason / Would have mourned longer – married with my uncle . . . / . . . O, most wicked speed, to post / With such dexterity to incestuous sheets!'"

"So it's not only the speed with which his mother remarried that is so upsetting to Hamlet," Pat informed them. "It's also the speed with which she changed her affections and even the person for whom she felt sexual desire."

"Oh! I think I see where you are going with this, Pat," Amelia said. "May I jump in?"

"Please do."

"Hamlet is confused by the appearance. He wouldn't be upset by that if he understood the reality. But the reality would have made him even more upset, although for a different reason. Oh, this is brilliant!

"Hamlet has been away for several years, at school in Wittenberg. The images he has of his mother hanging on his father 'as if the increase of appetite had grown by what it fed on' weren't recent. They were perhaps two years old. So the speed with which his mother changed from the images in Hamlet's mind to what he sees now wasn't one month, as he thought, but somewhere between one month and two years. If Hamlet had understood that his mother's feelings had changed over a longer period of time, he wouldn't have been upset by the 'wicked speed' of her change of heart."

"But if Hamlet had thought further," Pat said, jumping back in, "he would have asked himself when during that two-year period his mother's feelings and allegiance began to change. The only possible answer would have been during the time she was still married to Hamlet's father. And recognition of *that* reality would have been even more upsetting than the earlier false appearance of an 'o'erhasty marriage.'"

"It gets worse," Amelia said, continuing the explanation. "Hamlet would have asked himself not only when his mother changed her feelings, but when she began sleeping with Claudius. The answer, given to us by the ghost, is that she began sleeping with him while still married to Hamlet's father. Here's the ghost's words.

> 'Ay, that incestuous, that adulterate beast . . .
> . . . won to his shameful lust
> The will of my most seeming-virtuous queen.
> O Hamlet, what a falling off was there
> From me, whose love was of that dignity
> That it went hand in hand even with the vow
> I made to her in marriage, and to decline
> Upon a wretch whose natural gifts were poor
> To those of mine!'

"It's very clear. The ghost tells us three times that his wife began sleeping with Claudius while he was still alive. First, by the use of the phrase 'that incestuous, that adulterate beast.' 'Incestuous' is ambiguous; sleeping with a brother-in-law was considered incest in those days, but it could have happened before or after the king's death. 'Adulterate' is not ambiguous at all. They clearly slept together while she was still married to the king.

"Second, that Claudius 'won the will of my most seeming-virtuous queen.' That had to refer to a time when she was still married to Hamlet's father, because she wasn't his queen after his death. She was only his widow. 'Seeming-virtuous' tells us the same thing.

"Third is the phrase 'what a falling off there was from me.' A falling off could have happened only while the king was still alive."

"So," Pat concluded, "Hamlet would have been even more upset if he'd listened closely to the ghost and considered the timing of his mother's actions while he was away studying."

"If that's true," Doug said, thinking like a lawyer, "if Gertrude slept with the king's brother while still married to the king, then she and Claudius are guilty not just of immorality but also of treason. As we have seen, illicit sex with a female member of the royal family, who might bear an offspring with a claim to the throne, was treason."

<h2 style="text-align:center">115</h2>

After the break, Pat introduced the second topic. "Shakespeare had Hamlet seek not only knowledge about the reality of the world around him, but also the reality within himself. He gave Hamlet the desire, one that perhaps he himself shared, to understand the nature of his own being. Who has some thoughts on this idea?"

"I do," Nancy said. "Right from the beginning of the play, Hamlet examines himself, cataloguing his feelings and thoughts. He is inward-focused. He has what the psychologist Howard Gardner calls 'Intra-Personal Intelligence,' which is knowledge of oneself, as opposed to 'Inter-Personal Intelligence,' which is facility in developing relationships with others.

"Hamlet describes his ideal man to Horatio, saying that such a man would take what comes with equanimity, almost with Brutus's stoicism. Such a man would have an even disposition, an inner emotional balance during stressful times. It's important to note his exact words.

> 'For thou hast been
> As one in suff'ring all that suffers nothing,
> A man that Fortune's buffets and rewards
> Hast ta'en with equal thanks; and blessed are those
> Whose blood and judgment are so well commedled
> That they are not a pipe for fortune's finger
> To sound what stop she please. Give me that man
> That is not passion's slave, and I will wear him
> In my heart's core, ay, in my heart of heart,
> As I do thee.'

"Later he describes human nature, which would include his own nature, in exalted terms.

> 'What piece of work is a man, how noble in reason; how
> infinite in faculties; in form and moving how express and
> admirable, in action how like an angel, in apprehension how
> like a god: the beauty of the world, the paragon of animals!'

"Glorious, right? But then Hamlet immediately adds, 'And yet to me what is this quintessence of dust? Man delights not me—nor woman neither.'"

"That's a rather shocking juxtaposition," Dave said. "But then maybe it is explained somewhat by statements Hamlet made just a few moments earlier.

> 'I have of late – but wherefore I know not – lost all my mirth,
> forgone all custom of exercises; and indeed, it goes so
> heavily with my disposition that this goodly frame the earth
> seems . . . nothing to me but a foul and pestilent congregation
> of vapors.'"

"Perhaps Hamlet's loss of mirth," Lisa suggested, "is due in part to the flawed nature of the people around him. Even before his first contact with the ghost, he muses on the imperfections of human beings. 'Some vicious mole of nature in them,' he says, overshadows even the greatest of their virtues. 'The dram of evil / Doth all the noble substance often dout, / to his own scandal.'"

"And then we come to a key statement," Amelia declared. "After Hamlet sets up a description of the ideal man, and after he notes that all people are flawed, he describes himself as among the most flawed. 'I could accuse me of such things that it were better my mother had not borne me,' he says. 'I am very proud, vengeful, ambitious, with more offenses at my beck than I have thoughts to put them in, imagination to give them shape, or time to act them in.'"

"And then," Doug said, "Hamlet calls for pity for all of us flawed creatures. When Polonius proposes to use the players 'according to their desert,' Hamlet replies with a reaction that is out of place in that situation but that would describe his compassion for all of God's flawed creatures. He tells Polonius to give the players better than they deserve.

> 'God's bodkin, man, much better! Use every man after his
> desert, and who shall scape whipping? Use them after your
> own honor and dignity. The less they deserve, the more merit
> is in your bounty.'"

"So," Pat summed up, "we have seen Hamlet describe the ideal man, note that individual men, not least himself, fall short of that ideal, and conclude that they should nevertheless be treated with honor and dignity."

"I'm afraid we're out of time," Alan said gently.

"Might we continue for another ten minutes?" Pat asked. "We're coming to another critical point. The six of us go to lunch together after class, so I think we all have time to continue a bit longer?" He phrased it as a question, and the other students all assented.

"Thanks, everyone. If we could back up to Hamlet's first soliloquy, we'll see that he was melancholy long before he saw the ghost. He already had thoughts of suicide before he was was informed that his uncle might have murdered his father or that love had faded from his parents' marriage. 'O that this too too sullied flesh would melt, / Thaw, and resolve itself into a dew,' he says, regretting that God had fixed 'His canon 'gainst self-slaughter.'

"The only reason Hamlet cites for thinking that 'things rank and gross in nature' possess the world is that his mother married his uncle too soon after her husband's death. Now, thoughts of suicide by a man approximately our age," Pat said, looking at Doug and Dave, "is a gross overreaction to his mother's getting remarried so quickly. How are we to explain it?"

"That's a key question," Alan affirmed. "If I might offer an additional piece of information on this point, the poet and critic T.S. Eliot—I hope you have all heard of him—thought that *Hamlet* the play was an 'artistic failure' for just this point—because the events of the play were insufficient to explain the nature and intensity of Hamlet the character's feelings—his melancholy and thoughts of suicide."

"Well, if T.S. Eliot and I agree on that point, maybe I'm smarter than I thought I was," Pat said. "Hamlet, in his melancholy mood and his statements about his mother's 'o'er hasty marriage,' sounds not like a son concerned about the slight to his dead father's honor, but like a jilted lover."

"But that can't be," Lisa interjected. "Hamlet was away from Elsinore, studying in Wittenberg for the past few years. He hadn't even seen Gertrude for a long time, and in any event, she was his mother, not his lover. Further, Hamlet specifically lists the three grudges he holds against his uncle, and marrying the woman he desired wasn't one of them. The first two are that 'He . . . hath killed my king and whored my mother,' and the third is that he has 'Popped in between th' election and my hopes.'"

"On the other hand," Pat continued, "some interesting things are said when Hamlet confronts his mother in her closet—the scene in which Hamlet stabs Polonius, who is hiding behind the arras. After Hamlet begins berating his mother, she says 'Have you forgot me?' meaning 'Have you forgotten your place relative to me? That I am your mother, that you are my son and so owe me a certain degree of respect?' Hamlet responds with another comment that doesn't quite make sense in the context of that scene. 'You are the queen, your husband's brother's wife, and (would it were not so) you are my mother.'

"What an extraordinary statement that is. It could be interpreted in two ways. It could mean, 'You have so disgraced yourself and so dishonored my father by your quick marriage—and by marrying the man who murdered your husband—that I wish you weren't my mother.' Or it could be interpreted to mean 'I wish you weren't my mother because then *I* could have married you.'

"That's all I have," Pat concluded. "A puzzle, not a solution."

"I think we'll have time to pick this issue up again in one of the final class sessions," Alan told them. "Perhaps by then one of us will have solved the puzzle."

"You know," Alan overheard Doug say to the others as they were leaving, "this discussion of *Hamlet* reminds me of an episode of *Gilligan's Island.* Remember the one where a theater director is stranded on the island, and the castaways perform *Hamlet* for him, hoping that he will be so impressed with their acting that he will rescue them? But instead of speaking the lines from the play, they sing them to melodies from Bizet's opera *Carmen.* It was pretty funny!"

"Doug," Alan heard Pat say as they walked away," it's amazing that you have actually read any of the plays, given how much time you spend watching movies and TV reruns."

116

Elvin turned to the subject of why so many people believe, or profess to believe, that human activities significantly affect the Earth's climate in spite of so much evidence to the contrary. This time he would be straying from "The Contrarian's" scientific focus. But, he reasoned, the entire field of global warming had become so politicized that it is no longer possible to write about it solely as a scientific issue.

He had found that global warming is big business. By one estimate $300 billion was being spent on the issue by governments every year. Another estimate was $1.5 trillion. It's just common sense, he thought, that everybody would want a piece of the action. Even those whose activities aren't directly related to global warming would brand themselves with it in order to steer funds their way. In doing so they increased the number of those with a financial interest in keeping the global warming myth alive.

The fact that the government was the predominant funder reminded Elvin of the military-industrial complex that many had worried about in the early 1960s, as he'd mentioned to Alan Fernwood. He'd use that as the hook for this week's columns.

But there must be more to it than merely keeping money flowing, Elvin thought, and he turned to the idea of groupthink. Scientists, even if they managed to shield themselves from external influences, still faced pressures from within the scientific community. They conducted research not in isolation, but as members of a community with established beliefs and methodologies, and with pressures to accept both. Scientists had to free themselves from blind conformity to those beliefs and methodologies even as they were guided by them.

As Elvin saw it, climate scientists were investigating a subject about which little is really known. He recalled that American geologists, setting out to explore an unknown continent in the 19th century, had carefully distinguished between fact and theory, and adhered to a strictly inductive methodology that required determining what the facts were before forming theories to try to explain them. It was disappointing that climate scientists weren't following a similar methodology.

Having finished reviewing his notes, Elvin began to write his next column.

The Military-Industrial Complex Redux? Part I

In his Farewell Address in January 1961, President Dwight D. Eisenhower urged the American public to "guard against the acquisition of unwarranted influence, whether sought or unsought, by the military-industrial complex." His concern was that the military and the companies and contractors funded by it would exert a combined influence on the political system strong enough to keep funds flowing their way at a level higher than was justified by the interests of the country as a whole.

One doesn't need to look hard to see something similar occurring today—except that now government funds are flowing to environmental contractors. By some accounts more than $300 billion is spent by governments on global warming research and remediation every year, giving the departments through which the funds are channeled and the scientific and environmental organizations that receive them a joint interest in keeping the funding flowing.

The problem isn't that governments provide funding for scientific research; that's a good thing. The problem is that government funding for climate change is such a huge percentage of all funds supporting research into the issue that it gives the recipients—scientists, environmental organizations, the media—incentives to push the idea of global warming forward. That is bound to be the result whenever one entity provides the bulk of funding for research—regardless of who the funder is, the field being studied, or the goals of the recipients.

Science, however, must aim at the unbiased pursuit of knowledge if it is to remain science. Scientists must retain their independence of mind. Aaron Wildavsky explained it best: "The integrity of science as a process of seeking knowledge . . . depends on institutions that maintain competition among scientists and scientific groups who are numerous, dispersed, and independent."

Independence of mind in both individuals and institutions is likely to become compromised when the large majority of total funding comes from a single source. Add to that situation the fact that the dominant source of funding is government, which wields enormous political power as well, and the problem begins to emerge. Combine those two factors with government leaders making repeated and forceful statements in support of the theory of human-caused global warming and the danger of corruption of the scientific process becomes clear. Recipients of global warming funding can easily see the need to show results not inconsistent with the beliefs of political leaders if they want funds to continue to flow their way.

Environmental organizations aren't shy about charging that conclusions reached by scientists funded by industry are tainted and should be ignored. But they fail to realize that the same charge could be made against their own findings. If industry-sponsored research is likely to underestimate global warming, then government-funded research is likely to overestimate it. That environmentalists fail to recognize this point reminds us of Upton Sinclair's observation that "It is difficult to get a man to understand something, when his salary depends upon his not understanding it."

The way to guard against the danger of bias is strict adherence to the scientific method; that is, to determining the accuracy or falsity of a theory based on the evidence for or against it regardless of who proposed it, who is funding the research, or what results anyone might want to see from it.

That task will be harder for government-funded institutions than for those funded by industry because government funding for global warming research outweighs industry funding by a factor of ten thousand to one. Even the largest skeptical organization—the Heartland Institute—has an annual budget of only $7 million—small potatoes compared with the global warming industry's $300 billion. And, it should be noted, the Heartland Institute has never accepted more than five percent of its annual funding from industry.

Ideally, in a field such as climate change in which so little is known, an inductive methodology would be followed—one in which explanations are formulated *after* data have been uncovered. But that isn't how things work in climate studies, in which investigations appear to be biased in favor of the theory of human-caused global warming as though the theory is already a fact and all that is needed is stronger justification for it.

As we see it, the major effort on the subject of the Earth's climate, coordinated under the IPCC umbrella, is dedicated not to understanding the science of weather and climate and temperature, but rather to promoting only one theory of why the planet is warming. As

Robert Carter, Science Policy Advisor at the Institute of Public Affairs, concluded, "The IPCC charter requires that the organization investigates not climate change in the round, but solely global warming caused by human greenhouse emissions, a blinkered approach that consistently damages all IPCC pronouncements."

The problem, ultimately, is that the IPCC, as a branch of the United Nations, is itself an intensely political body, not a scientific body. As its chairman, Dr. Rajendra Pachauri, admits, "We are an intergovernmental body and we do what the governments of the world want us to do. If the governments decide we should do things differently and come up with a vastly different set of products we would be at their beck and call."

The core of the problem is that a political effort, backed by hundreds of billions of dollars a year, is geared toward establishing the validity of a theory that has failed practically every test applied to it.

"The central lesson to be learned from this episode in scientific history," independent scientist Willie Soon concluded, "is that to create an organization financially and ideologically dependent upon coming to a single, aprioristic viewpoint, regardless of the objective truth, is to create a monster that ignores the truth. Regrettably, the cumulative effect of the IPCC's conduct over the last 25 years has inflicted severe and long-term damage on the reputation of science and of scientists everywhere."

Sadly, the entire field of global warming science has become thoroughly politicized. The corruption of politics has seeped into it through every pore.

TUESDAY, JULY 28

117

Happy to resume work on his Shakespeare projects, Alan was examining the process through which academic or scientific communities change their beliefs. Fortune smiled on him, as he recalled a book on the subject he'd read years earlier, Thomas Kuhn's *The Structure of Scientific Revolutions*.

In a simplified version of Kuhn's model, change occurs through a process with several identifiable phases. In the first, scientists or scholars work within an existing paradigm or model to solve puzzles that haven't yet been explained. If puzzles continue to resist explanation, a new phase begins, the "growing-sense-of-crisis phase," in which the unsolved puzzles are regarded as anomalies that challenge the legitimacy of the existing paradigm. Eventually a true moment of crisis might be reached if a new paradigm is introduced that can explain the anomalies. If the community accepts the new paradigm, then the process begins anew.

Applying Kuhn's model to Stratfordians, Alan could see that they had reached the growing-sense-of-crisis phase, as their paradigm of authorship by William Shakspere was increasingly unable to explain anomalies resulting from the mismatch between the mundane known details of his life and the learned nature of the works.

It was clear to Alan that Oxfordians must work to increase Stratfordians' sense of crisis by pushing for more widespread awareness of just how severe the anomalies are. They must present them with information documenting the disconnect between the biography of their man and the qualities and experiences that the author of Shakespeare's works must have had. He needed a document summarizing that disconnect and got to work to create one. By the end of the day he had produced a list of 108 items showing the weakness of the Stratfordian claim. Of the items on the list, Shakspere got 2 yes's, 1 maybe, and 105 no's.

Supportive of William Shakspere?	**Criteria**
	FACTORS TO CONSIDER CONCERNING SHAKSPERE'S AUTHORSHIP OF SHAKESPEARE'S WORKS
1/9	J. Thomas Looney's General Characteristics
1-2 /9	J. Thomas Looney's Special Characteristics
0/10	Diana Price's 10 types of evidence in a literary paper trail
0/10	Ramon Jiménez's ten witnesses who knew Shakspere but did not comment on any literary activities by him
0/21	Katherine Chiljan's list of plays written too early for Shakspere, born in 1564, to have been the author
0/4	Links to important people depicted in the plays
0/21	Links to other writers
0/13	Experiences to acquire substantive knowledge
0/4	Works that most influenced Shakespeare
0/7	Psychologists' understanding of the nature of genius and creativity
Yes – 2 Maybe – 1 No – 105	**TOTALS**

Alan expected that Stratfordians would continue to explain away the anomalies by proposing *ad hoc* explanations for them, but Oxfordians can't let them get away with it. Oxfordians must continually highlight weaknesses in the evidence supporting Shakspere's authorship so that problems are seen for what they really are—not mere puzzles that haven't yet been worked out, but true anomalies so severe that the inability to explain them challenges the entire Stratfordian paradigm. One of the most effective ways to do that, he thought, would be by distributing copies of *Shakespeare Beyond Doubt?* as widely as possible.

But Oxfordians must do more than that, he realized. Because it's not only intellectual recognition that anomalies exist that will result in change, but also the emotional discomfort that accompanies the rising sense of crisis, we must do all we can to increase Stratfordians' nagging feeling that something isn't right. We must work to vex them: to increase the stress and tension they feel, to heighten their agitation and anxiety. We must generate the emotional pressure that will push Stratfordians forward through the succeeding stages of the transition to the Oxfordian paradigm.

118

So why do so many people continue to believe in a theory that has been repeatedly shown to be false? Elvin needed an explanation other than witchcraft or groupthink. He began to see that many people believe in the validity of human-caused global warming with an almost religious zeal. Political and scientific processes had been captured and corrupted by zealots. It was unfortunate that the scientific method, one of mankind's greatest achievements, had become debased by weaknesses in human nature.

He then noticed something interesting. The latest IPCC report, *Climate Change 2013: The Physical Science Basis*, contained more modest predictions about the planet's warming than earlier IPCC reports, and it forecast only small economic impact from that warming through the rest of the century. Yet the IPCC, and politicians influenced by it, continued to call for the same extreme measures as before to combat global warming—measures that would, Nigel Lawson calculated, "be far worse than any adverse impact from global warming."

Politicians themselves were as caught up in the global warming embroilment as everybody else, Elvin now realized. If they opposed funding for global warming research, or suggested channeling funding toward other urgent problems, they would be pilloried as enemies of the climate. It was the same for every other group involved—environmental organizations, scientific institutes, the media. They were, he thought, like the coyote in the Road Runner cartoons who has run off a cliff but hasn't noticed it yet. When they do, their journey will be just like the coyote's: straight down.

Elvin felt he had enough information, and began to put together his next column.

The Military-Industrial Complex Redux? Part II

It's natural for employees to want to please their employers. Non-governmental organizations and scientific institutes similarly want to please their sponsors. But why do so many in the sponsoring organizations continue to believe in a theory that has repeatedly been shown to be false? Why do they ignore the evidence? "The Contrarian" seeks an explanation other than witchcraft.

Some believers in the idea of human-caused global warming resemble religious zealots. They show the same blind belief in the validity of their creed, the same sense that something valuable is in danger, and the same intolerance for dissenting views.

The problem is not that zealots in power have examined the data contradicting the theory of human-caused global warming and found it to be flawed. It's that their blind belief in the theory leads them to conclude that all data that conflicts with it *must* be flawed. And because it is flawed, there is no need to examine it. How's that for circular reasoning?

Their attitude reminds us of the priests who refused to look through Galileo's telescope 400 years ago. There is no need to look, they told him. They would not see the moons orbiting other planets that Galileo said were there (and whose existence would justify the heliocentric view of the universe), because they weren't there. And even if they did see them, they told him, that would only be because the devil had placed the images there to mislead them.

Want another example of blind belief? The president of the Sierra Club recently testified before a Senate Judiciary subcommittee that "our planet is cooking up and heating and warming." When confronted by a senator with data from NOAA and NASA satellites documenting that the global climate trend over the past several decades was only .11° C per decade, or only 1.21 degrees per century—a fraction of the amount of warming claimed by the Sierra Club and other environmental organizations—he asserted that the data were incorrect. The senator was incredulous. "I'm curious," he said. At "the Sierra Club, is this a frequent practice to declare areas of science not up for debate, not up for consideration of what the evidence and data show? . . . How do you address the fact that in the last 18 years, the satellite data show no demonstrable warming whatsoever?"

The Sierra Club president had no response except to blindly repeat the claim that the planet was heating and warming. Even "The Contrarian" knows that repeating a statement doesn't make it true. But what can one say to him? As Jonathan Swift noted long ago, "It is useless to attempt to reason a man out of a thing he was never reasoned into."

Some zealots go beyond refusing to examine the evidence; they also try to block others from doing so. Recall, for instance, the scandal from 2009, in which thousands of leaked e-mails from the Climate Research Unit at the University of East Anglia showed that "senior members were quite happy to discuss ways and means of controlling the research journals so as to deny publication of any material that goes against the orthodox dogma. The ways and means included the sacking of recalcitrant editors."

Gosh! First they refuse to publish scientific studies with results that contradict the theory of human-caused global warming, then they turn to others, point to the journals, and say "See, the doubters' work isn't published in the most important journals. If it was real science, it would be published there."

These are leading climate *scientists*? They seem more like shills, engaging in deceptive practices to support positions determined in advance by blind faith.

Is "The Contrarian" alone in recalling H. L. Mencken's observation that "The whole aim of practical politics is to keep the populace alarmed (and hence clamorous to be led to safety) by menacing it with an endless series of hobgoblins, all of them imaginary"?

Are we alone in our dismay at seeing scare tactics in the media? Images abound of retreating glaciers, floods, hurricanes—even heavy snowstorms—attributed to global warming. Few are accompanied by information or analysis that would enable readers or viewers to place the images in the proper context. Such reports are only propaganda designed to stir up emotions.

Are we alone in our disgust at seeing smear tactics used against those who challenge the validity of human-caused global warming? We can't help recalling a comment by Nigel Lawson, who has spoken against global warming theory. Although Lawson had spent his career in the rough-and-tumble world of politics, he writes that "I have never in my life experienced the extremes of personal hostility, vituperation and vilification which I—along with other dissenters, of course—have received for my views on global warming and global warming policies."

Perhaps the most bizarre term of abuse we have seen applied to dissenters is that of "climate deniers." We're a bit puzzled by that one. How can one deny that climate exists? It's like denying that air exists. People who think logically don't use such absurd phrases.

In sum, we can't help but agree with geologist Ian Plimer's

conclusion that "Climate change catastrophism is the biggest scientific fraud that has ever occurred. Much climate 'science' is political ideology dressed up as science."

It is indeed a mess, with the dangerous combination of government money and zealots in high positions keeping the whole rotten global warming enterprise afloat.

Is there a solution? We'll have thoughts on that subject next week.

119

Delilah arrived at the restaurant first. She got a table in the dining area, and reviewed the abrupt ending to her last encounter with Elvin. After leaving the jazz club, he'd driven her back to her car at Southpoint, and then maintained radio silence for a week before calling her two nights ago.

She had expected him to call sooner or later, and felt that she had to wait for him to call first. She knew he loved her, and that he wouldn't sleep with her without marrying her because she was Alan's daughter. She also knew that for some men, marriage was like a trip to the dentist. Although feared in advance, the actual events weren't as bad as anticipated, and the aftermaths were good things to have in one's life. How to get him over the hump, she wondered. Anyway, she was glad that they'd talked at length and that things were back to normal.

"Hi, El," Delilah said, rising quickly from her seat when she saw him. She gave him a hug and they both sat down.

"Sorry I'm a bit late, Dee. I was celebrating with some of the guys from the paper and couldn't get away sooner."

"Celebrating? Then we both must have good news. You go first."

"Well, I learned this afternoon that a dozen newspapers around the country are going to pick up my column, 'The Contrarian.' My editor says that syndication could become much larger over time. So that means I am building a name for myself and will receive royalties! Of course, I have to split them with the *Cary City Herald*. This is the first time any column from the paper has become syndicated, so the editor threw an impromptu party for us."

"El, that's wonderful! I'm so happy for you."

"And what's your news, Dee? I'm sure it tops mine."

"I don't know about that, but it is exciting. You remember my telling you that I would be in another TV commercial? We filmed it today. It was even more thrilling than the first. This one was for a new whiskey, White Heron whiskey.

"In the commercial, I'm standing on a balcony, like Juliet. A young man on the ground who is in love with me begins to recite poetry to me, but the poetry is bad, and he stumbles when he says it. I like him, but it's not at all romantic, so I turn my nose up at him and close the shutters. In the next scene, the next day, he is miserable and explains why to a friend. The friend gives him a bottle of White Heron and assures him that it will make him a better poet and help him feel bolder when he sees me.

"And it works! That night, when I'm again standing on my balcony, he drinks a glass, on the rocks, looks up at me with love in his eyes, and recites beautiful poetry in a romantic manner. I then throw a rope ladder down to him and he climbs up. In the final scene, he wraps his arms around me, and the camera closes in on my face as I look directly into it and say, 'Thanks, White Heron!'

"Remember at the end of the Amway commercial, when the girl looks into the camera and says 'Thanks, Amway!'? In both commercials, the viewer has the impression that what is happening is exactly what the girl wants to have happen," she said, laughing. "Apparently saying thanks and the name of the product while looking directly into the camera as a man wraps his arms around me is what the director wants to become my trademark commercial. He also produced the Amway ad."

They both laughed.

"And I'm getting paid for both commercials! I hadn't thought of that. I had thought I was just doing them as part of my internship with the marketing company. After the filming the director gave me the bottle of White Heron that was used in the commercial. Here it is."

"And then, the handsome actor from the commercial tried to come on to me. But I blew him off. All I could think about was meeting you."

"Well, I am glad to hear that," Elvin said, with genuine relief. "Why don't we save the bottle until next week. We can open it on your birthday. Then I can recite poetry to you and wrap my arms around you."

"Okay," she agreed. "But you don't have to wait until next week to wrap your arms around me, El."

WEDNESDAY, JULY 29

120

Alan was up early. His unconscious brain had been pondering the plan for promoting de Vere's authorship while he slept, and he woke up full of ideas about how to trigger the moment of crisis that Kuhn determined was necessary for a paradigm shift to occur.

According to Kuhn, scientific communities never move from one paradigm to another until a point of crisis is reached, and that point is always generated by the introduction of a new paradigm that explains anomalies the old one couldn't. "Competition between segments of the scientific community is the only historical process that ever actually results in the rejection of one previously accepted theory or in the adoption of another. . . . No process yet disclosed by the historical study of scientific development at all resembles the methodological stereotype of falsification by direct comparison with nature."

Applying Kuhn's conclusions to the Shakespeare authorship question, Alan saw that the moment of crisis would come only when Stratfordians recognize that the Oxfordian paradigm explains anomalies that the Stratfordian paradigm can't. But, as he knew from his own case, Stratfordians will avoid that recognition for as long as possible. As uncomfortable as the growing-sense-of-crisis phase might be, the crisis itself would be even more harrowing. They would try to muddle through by ignoring the anomalies, by providing *ad hoc* explanations for them, and by ignoring the groundswell of interest in the authorship question outside of academia.

If the move to a new paradigm required a crisis, and if crises are always generated by awareness of a new paradigm that explained anomalies that the older one couldn't, then Oxfordians had no choice but to push the Oxfordian paradigm. But if that strategy was correct, then his earlier thinking—that pushing for acceptance of the legitimacy of the authorship question would be sufficient for the paradigm shift to occur—was wrong.

And, he reasoned further, literary scholars themselves wouldn't be able to stop at the point of a neutral academic consideration of the authorship question. After all, he hadn't.

The emotional energy—the vexation that has been bottling up inside Stratfordians—wouldn't allow them to stop with a neutral "I don't know, let's examine this further" attitude. That energy would continue to build until the shock from recognition of the validity of the new paradigm pushed them into the paradigm shift. The Oxfordian paradigm will be fiercely resisted until the moment when it is accepted, he concluded. There could be no middle ground.

To underscore the importance of pushing the Oxfordian paradigm, Alan asked himself where the theory of evolution would be if Darwin had proposed it but then done nothing to promote it. He knew that Thomas Henry Huxley, an early proponent, had been known as "Darwin's Bulldog" because of the forceful way he promoted Darwin's theory. Does Oxfordian theory have a "bulldog?" he asked himself. Maybe it needs a whole pack of them.

Oxfordians, then, need clear and persuasive talking points on behalf of de Vere's authorship. A good place to start in preparing them, Alan saw, would be to modify the chart he'd prepared yesterday showing the mismatch between Shakspere's life and Shakespeare's works. He added a column to show how the same criteria supported de Vere's case for authorship.

Studying the finished chart, Alan was surprised by how clearly it illustrated the differences between the two men. Whereas the man from Stratford had 105 "no's" and only two "yes's," Oxford had 95 "yes's" and only one "no." The evidence for Oxford and against Shakspere would be overwhelming to anybody who examined it with an open mind.

Supportive of William Shakespeare?	Criteria	Supportive of Edward de Vere?
FACTORS TO CONSIDER IN DETERMINING AUTHORSHIP OF SHAKESPEARE'S WORKS		
1/9	J. Thomas Looney's General Characteristics	9/9
1-2 /9	J. Thomas Looney's Special Characteristics	9/9
0/10	Diana Price's 10 types of evidence in a literary paper trail	8-9 /10
0/10	Ramon Jiménez's ten witnesses who knew Shakspere but did not comment on any literary activities by him	--
0/21	Katherine Chiljan's list of plays written too early for Shakspere, born in 1564, to have been the author	21/21
0/4	Links to important people depicted in the plays	4/4
0/21	Links to other writers	21/21
0/13	Substantive knowledge and experience	12-13 /13
0/4	Works that most influenced Shakespeare	4/4
0/7	Psychologists' understanding of the nature of genius and creativity	7/7
Yes – 2 **Maybe – 1** **No - 105**	**TOTALS**	**Yes – 95** **Maybe – 2** **No – 1** **N/A - 10**

121

Alan joined Adelina Banduka and Sheila Anderson, two literature professors, at their table in the restaurant. A few minutes later they were joined by another colleague, Daniel Dubois. The four of them, along with Matt Harris, formed the Courses Committee that decided which literature courses would be offered and who would teach them. It wasn't yet time to make decisions about the spring term, and the four of them were meeting as colleagues and friends.

"What's this I hear about your proposing a conference on the Shakespeare authorship question, Alan?" Adelina asked.

Alan had wanted to mention his idea for a course on the issue. Now he had his opening. "I'm glad you asked about that. I have been doing some research into the issue over the past couple of months—"

Daniel interrupted. "When the cat's away the mice will play," he said, smiling. Turning to Adelina and Sheila, Daniel explained that Alan's wife was away for the summer. "Look at what kinds of mischief he gets himself into when Diana isn't around!" They all laughed.

"I'm glad to have had the time to investigate the issue," Alan continued, "because I have found that the evidence in support of Shakspere's authorship is far weaker than I'd thought. The conference I proposed would look at the issue from a scholarly point of view. But now I think it might be worth offering a course on the authorship issue as well."

That brought the conversation to a halt. They all looked at him. Sheila asked, "Why do you think that, Alan? You have always sneered at those who had doubts about Will."

"Yes, I did, but now I'm more aware of things. One factor is what I just mentioned—the weakness of the evidence in support of authorship by the man from Stratford. Equally important is the strength of the groundswell of interest in the issue outside of academia."

"Is it really that strong?"

"Yeah, it is, Sheila. The reality is that many major media publications have recognized the legitimacy and importance of the authorship question, as have five U.S. Supreme Court Justices. Dozens of prominent people have also expressed their doubts about Shakspere's authorship, including Walt Whitman, Mark Twain, and Charlie Chaplin. And Frederich Nietzsche, Sigmund Freud, and Malcolm X."

"You have certainly done some research on the issue," Daniel observed.

"I have," Alan agreed. "Another factor is that we—as literary scholars—have been lagging behind by rejecting the issue out of hand as one not worthy of academic study. Either there is something to the question or there isn't; we as a body haven't made the effort to find out. Ignoring the issue is almost an abdication of our duty, and others have noticed.

"I'm now worried that we're being left behind as people outside academia take the lead in a subject that departments of literature were created for; that is, the scholarly study of questions important to literature. If we don't examine this question seriously, we lose the chance to determine the truth for ourselves. Others will begin to define the issue without input from us. We must act now to maintain our leadership role in literary matters."

"I'm concerned that our colleagues at other universities will look askance at us if we offer a course," Adelina objected. "I'm not aware of any other universities offering similar courses."

"There's a few—but only a few," Alan replied. "That's the problem. Academia as a whole is in danger of being left behind. Here," he said, handing each of them a copy of *Shakespeare Beyond Doubt?* "This is the sort of careful examination of the issue that should be conducted within academia, but isn't. The Shakespeare Authorship Coalition is eating our lunch."

"Speaking of eating lunch, I'm hungry," Sheila said. "Let's order."

"I'll take a look at this book, Alan," Daniel said. The conversation then turned to other areas, to the relief of the other three professors. Alan, though, could have talked about the authorship issue all day.

THURSDAY, JULY 30

122

"Good morning, everyone," Alan began. "I left this session and the next one open so that we would have time to return to subjects discussed earlier if we needed it. Today I'd like to return to the subject of the political aspects of love and desire, but approach it from a slightly different angle than in the discussions that Amelia and Lisa led so well.

"In most of Shakespeare's plays, the romantic attachments that form are between young adults who are entering the game for the first time. Romeo and Juliet, for instance. In *Antony and Cleopatra* however, Shakespeare considers love the second time around.

"In that play, Antony tries to combine love and duty. But it just doesn't work, because both demand everything from him. In trying to split himself in two between his political activities in Rome and

Cleopatra in Egypt, he ends up serving neither well. The result is disaster for him and Cleopatra.

At the very opening of the play, by remaining in Egypt with Cleopatra, Antony has soiled his reputation with his own soldiers. As one of them notes, 'His Captain's heart, . . . is become the bellows and the fan / To cool a gypsy's lust. . . . The triple pillar of the world [has been] transformed / Into a strumpet's fool.'"

"Yeah," Dave agreed, shaking his head in sympathy with Antony's plight. "He also angers the other two members of the Triumvirate, Caesar Octavius and Lepidus, by failing to give them the support they expected of him. Caesar tells Lepidus that Antony's dalliance with Cleopatra would be excusable if it affected only himself. But it also affects us, he says. Antony isn't here when we need him."

Doug spoke next. "Antony realizes he must choose between Rome and Egypt, between Caesar and Cleopatra, between his public life and his private life, between duty and pleasure. But the choice is so difficult because his desire for Cleopatra is so strong. As he explains, 'Let Rome in Tiber melt and the wide arch / Of the ranged empire fall! Here is my space.' Finally he hears the call of duty. 'These strong Egyptian fetters I must break / Or lose myself in dotage.'"

"In leaving for Rome in an effort to reconcile with Caesar, Antony alienates Cleopatra," Lisa noted. "She charges that 'O thou, the greatest soldier in the world, / Are turned the greatest liar.'"

"It was a difficult choice for him. I can see that," Amelia observed. "But here's the thing. Antony really had no choice. He had to go. The reason is that Cleopatra, as pharaoh, was regal through and through. She was political in her very bones, as head of the Ptolemy lineage. She wouldn't have been satisfied with an ordinary man, no matter how illustrious his past. If Antony had stayed in Egypt and turned his back on Rome, Cleopatra would eventually have turned her back on him. His being a member of the Triumvirate was an essential part of why she desired him."

"He does promise to return," Nancy recalled. "While he is away, Cleopatra lovingly recalls times she and Antony had spent together. These are delightful scenes, wonderfully depicted by Shakespeare at the height of his literary powers. In one of them, Charmian recalls the time Cleopatra had a diver hang a salted fish on Antony's hook. Cleopatra responds with,

'That time – O times! –
I laughed him out of patience; and that night
I laughed him into patience; and next morn

Ere the ninth hour I drunk him to his bed;
Then put my tires and mantles on him, whilst
I wore his sword Philippan.'

"I'm not an overly romantic person, but those scenes affect even me. They were beautifully done in the performance we saw."

"So," Alan said, "we have seen the problems that arise when Antony tries to split himself between Rome and Cleopatra. But what happens after he returns to Egypt? Not all is well even then."

"That's right," Pat said. "Angered at Antony's return to Egypt, Caesar sets out to fight and defeat him. Antony, the world's premier soldier, begins to make mistakes. He allows Cleopatra, someone with no battle experience, to influence his military decisions. Following her preference, he moves to fight Caesar at sea, where Caesar is strongest, rather than on land, where Antony has never been defeated."

"Then he makes another mistake," Doug pointed out. "He allows Cleopatra to be present at the naval battle, on a ship near his that will be exposed to the fighting. It's kind of like John Lennon having Yoko Ono sitting next to him in the studio while the Beatles recorded their final albums. Not only does it distract his attention from where it needs to be, on the other navy that is trying to kill him, but it also irritates his naval officers."

"And worse was to follow," Dave noted. "When the inevitable happens—the battle heats up and Cleopatra and her ships flee the scene—Antony turns and flees with her. At that moment, when the battle might still have been won, his retreat seals his fate. His love for Cleopatra—his failure to keep love and politics/business/war completely separate—spells disaster for both of them. It's the beginning of the end."

"Perhaps 'all's fair in love and war,' as someone once said, but the two shouldn't be mixed," Pat observed. "When they first meet after the disaster, Cleopatra says she hadn't thought that Antony would follow her. He responds by saying that of course he had to follow, that 'My heart was to thy rudder tied by th' strings, / And thou shouldst tow me after.'"

"He then comforts her," Nancy commented, "with words of such tenderness—'Fall not a tear, I say: one of them rates / All that is won and lost. Give me a kiss; / Even this repays me.'—that they almost bring tears to my eyes. And he excuses his own weakness because of his great love for her."

"But weakness is never forgiven in the hard world of war," Amelia said. "I can't help feeling that *Antony and Cleopatra* and *Coriolanus* were written about the same time. They are, of course, very different in tone, but both are pitch-perfect in what they are. *Coriolanus* is tightly constructed—cold, hard, perfectly formed, like a diamond with no flaws. *Antony and Cleopatra* is expansive, overflowing with feeling between two lovers who are older and so experienced enough in life to recognize just how wonderful and rare their love is."

"I like that observation, Amelia," Nancy remarked. "In both plays, late in his life, Shakespeare shows us it's impossible to mix love and duty. Coriolanus spent much of the play focused only on military matters. But when love for his mother, wife and son intrudes in spite of his best efforts to push it away, he is overwhelmed and abandons his military battles. That was good for Rome, which was about to be conquered, but his collapse led to his death. That didn't really help his family at all. Neither Antony nor Coriolanus found a way to combine love and duty. Is it even possible?"

After the class ended, Alan overheard Doug telling the other students that their discussion reminded him of an older movie. "I can't quite remember the title," he said, "but it starred Elizabeth Taylor and Richard Burton. In it, Elizabeth Taylor is a queen—I can't remember where—and Richard Burton is a warrior from somewhere else. They fall in love, have a great time together, and then commit suicide, just like in *Antony and Cleopatra*. In fact, I think Elizabeth Taylor dies by having an asp bite her breast, just like in the play. They must have copied that scene from Shakespeare."

Amelia opened her mouth to say something, but Dave waved her off. Both started laughing.

"What are you guys laughing about?" Doug asked.

123

Amelia and Alan lay stretched out on the bed, panting like two dogs after the rough stuff had ended. She glanced over at him and said in a sly voice, "In 'how many ages hence shall this our lofty scene be acted over, in states unborn and accents yet unknown!'?"

Alan began laughing softly but soon the laughter took over his whole body. "'So oft as that shall be, so often shall the' . . ." he tried to say, but couldn't continue. They were both laughing hard.

Finally Alan managed to regain control of himself. "We belong together, Amelia. We were made for each other. The question is how to get from here to there. Scientific paradigms change only when the reigning paradigm clashes with a new one in a moment of crisis. Maybe that is the best way for love paradigms to change, too. I'm trying to see how I might generate a crisis that could lead to a change. I will be talking to Diana on the phone later tonight."

Neither spoke. Then Amelia said softly, "Be careful, Alan. Be gentle. A clash might not be the best way in matters of the heart. It is important that all avoidable pain be avoided, because once in the heart pain never really leaves."

Later, as Alan was about to go to meet Elvin, Amelia turned to him and commented, "You know, Doug is pretty funny."

"Yeah. His comments after class are sometimes hysterical. I'm not sure he always means to be funny, and that just makes it all the funnier."

"Like today," she said. "It was hard to tell if he really knew that the movie he described was the film version of *Antony and Cleopatra* or not. I was afraid to find out."

"Sometimes," she added as Alan was leaving, "there is great uncertainty in life—about what we know and about what we should do."

124

"Hi, Elvin. I'm glad you had time to meet again so soon," Alan said as they greeted each other at the bar of the Harvest Hotel's ground floor restaurant.

"Hi, Alan. We have a lot to talk about. We need to explore further what our two battles have in common, and what strategies we have separately come up with might be effective for both of us."

"Exactly my thoughts," Alan told him. "The forces aligned against us will target us in a big way—if they haven't already—and we need to be ready. Not just with talking points, but also with a clear strategy of how to respond. We need to take the offense. We need to know what opportunities might arise and how best to take advantage of them."

"Don't have any doubts," Elvin replied. "The big guns will be used against us. Our opponents will seek to crush us by any means they can, right up until that moment when they announce they agree with our points and always have."

After being seated at their table, Alan broached a related point. "One of the comments I hear from my colleagues—at least from those who are strong Stratfordians and who just want the whole authorship issue to go away so they won't have to deal with it—is 'What difference does it make who wrote the plays? It's enough that we have them.'

"But in saying that the authorship issue doesn't matter, all they're really saying is that it doesn't matter to them. And they're being disingenuous in saying that or they wouldn't be fighting so hard against any consideration of it. Knowing something about the author of

Shakespeare's plays certainly matters to the millions of people who continue to buy biographies of Shakespeare. It's a shame that they are being misled so drastically by the so-called 'experts.'

"It also matters to people like me who want to understand the plays from a professional point of view. There are many obscure passages and references that we can't figure out if we don't have the right author and the right time frame. Beyond that—and beyond the issue of justice and recognition for the greatest literary figure in Western civilization—it's a matter of simple curiosity to want to know more about the man whose works inspired so many other creative people over the last 400 years."

"In my own STEM area," Elvin noted, "no issue is of greater importance than global warming because it is absorbing so much money that could and should be going into other areas—by some accounts up to $1.5 trillion a year. Development funds are being sucked out of all other areas—AIDS research, malaria, waterborne diseases, and so on—in order to fund yet more studies of the fantasy of human-caused global warming. In addition, the misguided laws and regulations designed to reduce mankind's carbon footprint are stifling economic activity and raising costs of all goods produced. It's a real tragedy for everybody."

Their waitress appeared.

"Oh, before I forget," Elvin said, after they ordered. "I got an e-mail from Carson." Elvin had become almost like an older brother to Alan and Diana's son, who looked up to him and was always glad when he came for dinner with the Fernwood family.

"He's really enjoying his first-hand examination of Gothic architecture in Germany, France and Belgium. He was excited to learn just how advanced the knowledge of structural engineering was 500 years ago. It's giving him a new perspective on what he learned in his classes."

"Yeah, I got a message from him, too," Alan said. "He went on and on about how he's had to revise his thinking. Before the trip he thought the cathedrals had been built using principles discovered through the scientific method. Now he's come to realize that wasn't the case at all. The great Gothic cathedrals were built hundreds of years before Bacon, Descartes, Newton and others created the scientific method. And he has found that the builders of the cathedrals weren't interested in truth—scientific truth, I mean; they were very interested in religious truth. When it came to building, they were interested in technology, in knowing what worked. In fact, he is now writing a paper on the distinction between science and technology."

"I think he must have sent us similar messages," Elvin said. "Did he mention to you books by Lewis Wolpert and Alan Cromer?"

"Yeah, he did." They were silent, recalling the ideas that Carson had mentioned in his messages.

"The creation and use of technology seems to be a far more natural activity for human beings than the pursuit of scientific knowledge," Carson had written to them both. "We are naturally good at technology, at using our minds to design and create tools to accomplish practical tasks, but not too inclined to search for theoretical explanations for why things work.

"As Lewis Wolpert concludes," Carson had continued, "'The use of tools and the development of technologies such as metalworking and agriculture do not require scientific thinking. But to do science it is necessary to be rigorous and to break out of many of the modes of thought imposed by the natural thinking associated with 'common sense.'

"Alan Cromer similarly notes that science did not arise naturally from man's innate intelligence and curiosity, and that it is not a natural part of human development. Rather, 'scientific thinking, which is analytic and objective, goes against the grain of traditional human thinking, which is associative and subjective. Far from being a natural part of human development, science arose from unique historical factors.'

"Isn't that amazing? The beautiful Gothic cathedrals were built not only without modern machinery, but also without modern science. Becoming aware of this has changed my whole view of human beings in previous times and places."

Alan broke the silence. "I'm glad Carson is having such an interesting time and learning so much. It is indeed surprising to realize just how unusual the thought processes necessary for science are. Carson's distinction between science and technology is relevant to what we are trying to do as well. Even today, most people are not interested in seeking truth, but only in knowing what works. They want only that knowledge that will help them reach their immediate goals."

"Yeah," Elvin said. "The distinction between technology and science is reflected in the difference between 'climate studies' and 'climate science.' Climate studies is any discussion that touches on climate. To many people, it almost doesn't seem to matter whether what is being discussed is true or not. As long as somebody said it, it's accepted as legitimate information, as valid as any other statement. 'Climate science,' on the other hand, is the dedicated effort to find out the truth about which factors affect the climate.

"You and I seem to be in the small minority of people who have a dedication to truth, to seeking out what really is the case, whether in the area of the Earth's climate or the authorship of Shakespeare's works. We want to know the reality of our subject areas, not just what others say it is. That's a problem for us. Going beyond the level of knowledge needed to reach everyday practical goals makes us different from most people around us. Other people sense that we are different and respond to that difference negatively.

"You remember what happened to a couple of other guys who were different—Socrates and Jesus. How people respond to those who seek truth rather than consensus is something that we must understand well so that we can take it into account in planning our strategies. But as Carson reminds us, that won't be at all easy because most people are satisfied with what works. They want consensus and harmony. Truth is third on their list, if it's on the list at all. They get irritated when people pursuing truth interfere with their pursuit of consensus."

125

"The funny thing," Alan observed, after they ordered dessert, "is that if we could just get people to look at the evidence, convincing them of the reality of the situation isn't all that hard. The difficult part is getting them to open their minds enough to look at evidence objectively in the first place. I know because I myself rejected the authorship question out of hand for decades."

Alan paused, wondering whether he would have launched such an intensive effort into investigating the issue if Amelia hadn't mentioned *Anonymous* and her interest in the authorship question on the first day of class. That got him thinking about the scholars in *Love's Labor's Lost* and their recognition of what they could gain from the eyes of beautiful women—not only a type of knowledge not found in books, but also inspiration to make the effort to seek out that knowledge.

"What? What did you say?" Alan suddenly asked. "I was lost in thought. Could you repeat that?"

"I was just saying that I had blindly accepted the reality of human-generated global warming for years without ever making the effort to examine the evidence for myself. We need to figure out a way to get others to make the same effort to examine the issues that we did."

"Oh, that reminds me," Alan said. "I think I have found a way to do just that. In rereading Thomas Kuhn's *The Structure of Scientific Revolutions*, I think I have discovered an effective way to engage people who believe in false paradigms. Alan recited Kuhn's conclusion that change in a community's beliefs happens only when a moment of crisis occurs, only when the reigning paradigm clashes with a new paradigm that has greater explanatory power.

"We must push our paradigms in ways that clash with the existing widely accepted but false beliefs. In the authorship issue, that means pushing the Oxfordian thesis hard so that the idea of de Vere's authorship will continually be on Stratfordians' minds. We must show them as often as possible how de Vere's authorship solves the anomalies that bedevil Shakespeare studies."

"Well, that makes a lot of sense," Elvin responded. "From what I recall from classes on the history of science, Kuhn is right. Scientific revolutions occurred only when one belief was challenged by another. But what would be the new paradigm to pose against that of human caused global warming? Oh, of course! The new paradigm is the one that everybody believed before the global warming nonsense was proposed. It's the idea that changes in climate occur naturally.

"For that belief to have been supplanted, evidence should have been provided showing that it was false. But that didn't happen. Somehow it got pushed aside by political forces without ever having been shown to be false, and replaced by a belief that nobody has ever proved to be true and that contradicts the data we have. What a crazy situation!

"Of course, belief that natural forces cause changes in the climate wasn't the earliest explanation. It supplanted supernatural explanations, in which storms were caused by the gods, who could be appeased by human prayer and sacrifice. But that gave way to belief in natural cases after the onset of the scientific revolution. That was a move toward greater rationality in our understanding of how the universe functions.

"How odd, then, that that extraordinarily powerful understanding of nature—and of the tiny place of human beings in the cosmos—could have been replaced by an oversized opinion of the magnitude of human beings' power. It's as though the dethroning of human beings from the central place in the universe that occurred as a result of the scientific revolution has been reversed. But this time we're at the center not because God placed us there, but because we have such an inflated vision of our own power as to believe that our actions are the determining cause of the planet's weather and climate. Talk about hubris!"

Alan refilled their wine glasses.

"I couldn't agree more," he said. "But we need to do one more thing. The clash is fine but by itself it's not enough. To get the believers in the older paradigm across the gulf to the new one—or over the mountain, if you prefer that analogy—we have to provide something more attractive than what they'd be leaving behind.

"For the authorship question, that is the chance for research and writing and publishing. Changing the paradigm opens up many new fields of investigation. Professors exist to write and publish, something that has become harder and harder to do because so many aspects of the Stratfordian paradigm have already been investigated. So, once they stop to think about it, they will see that moving to the Oxfordian paradigm has many professional advantages for them."

"Hmm," Elvin thought out loud. "Off the top of my head, I can't think of a comparable advantage for scientists who investigate climate issues. I wonder what could be offered them that would outweigh the huge levels of government funding corrupting the process. I expect that mere appeals to their professional consciences won't be enough."

"The problem wouldn't exist if people could just accept the power of zero," Alan lamented. "But they can't."

"The power of zero?"

"People just can't accept that they don't know something. Human beings are programmed to want explanations for everything they see. It's unnatural not to have an explanation. If one isn't readily at hand, the mind will make one up. We form rationalizations not just about our own motives, but also about the operations of the natural environment. In efforts to understand the world, 'I don't know' is the equivalent of 'zero' in mathematics. It's a place-holder until better explanations are found. But it's not one that most people are willing to accept. So if the place holder isn't present—if there's no conscious recognition of that spot for which no knowledge yet exists—then wrong knowledge gets put there.

"Aristotle began his *Metaphysics* by noting that 'All men by nature desire to know.' But he was mistaken. It's not that people desire to know what's *true*, it's that they desire to have *explanations*. Those explanations don't have to be correct; people just don't want blanks, uncertainties. They would rather be wrong than say 'I don't know.'"

They both pondered the issues they'd been discussing as Alan signaled for the check.

"I was talking to Delilah recently," Elvin said, moving to a different subject. "She misses her mother. Has Diana set a date to return yet?"

"I'm not sure," Alan replied. "But I'll be talking to her later this evening. That's one of the questions I have for her."

126
Alan sighed after he hung up. He hadn't said what he'd intended to.

Diana was such a good person that he hadn't been able to say anything that would cause her pain. She is a wonderful person, he thought again, just not the right person for me.

He recalled the many times he'd tried to tell her of his literary ideas and of her inability to understand them. He shook his head as he recalled how Shakespeare had expressed a similar situation in *As You Like It*.

> When a man's verses cannot be understood, nor a man's good wit seconded with the forward child Understanding, it strikes a man more dead than a great reckoning in a little room. Truly I wish the gods had made thee poetical.

Now that he had met someone with whom he could share parts of his life so important to him, what was the point of staying married to Diana? They lived in different worlds anyway, even though they shared the same house and bed, especially now that the kids no longer lived at home. A perfect example had occurred shortly before Diana left on her trip. While he was listening to a marvelous recording of Beethoven's *Spring Sonata* on the car radio, she had interrupted several times to show him pictures on her friends' Facebook pages of scarves they'd just purchased. They simply lived in different universes.

His inability to say what he had intended to say on the phone reminded him of a passage from *Julius Caesar*.

> Between the acting of a dreadful thing
> And the first motion, all the interim is
> Like a phantasma or a hideous dream.
> The genius and the mortal instruments
> Are then in counsel, and the state of man,
> Like to a little kingdom, suffers then
> The nature of an insurrection.

Maybe that is the chief value of Shakespeare and other writers, he thought, that they help us understand ourselves better by portraying situations similar to those we face in our own lives. But it was still disappointing that he hadn't been able to do what he knew he had to do.

FRIDAY, JULY 31

127

Moving Stratfordians across the paradigm abyss would involve emphasizing the emotional and the practical benefits of the move, Alan knew. Today's task was figuring out exactly how to do that.

Oxfordians must show Stratfordians that acceptance of the Oxfordian paradigm would provide relief from the emotional tension they have experienced throughout the increasing-sense-of-crisis phase and during the crisis itself. At the moment of crisis, Oxfordians should move from pushing to pulling, from vexing to soothing, from pointing out flaws in the old paradigm to describing the benefits of the new one. They should show Stratfordians how the Oxfordian paradigm solves the anomalies that are plaguing them. They should show them that Oxfordians regard Shakespeare's works as literary treasures just as they do, and, perhaps most importantly, they should show them that the Oxfordian paradigm would offer them many new opportunities for fruitful research and publishing because so much still remains unknown about de Vere's authorship.

But all the talking points in the world wouldn't be enough, he realized. Oxfordians can't convince Stratfordians of the validity of de Vere's authorship of Shakespeare's work; they have to do that for themselves. And it's almost equally true that they can't convince themselves, either. A change in viewpoint of this magnitude isn't a matter of logic or reasoning, but of insight—and insights can't be forced.

Alan recalled Kuhn's recognition that the moment of insight occurred within individual minds not by "deliberation and interpretation, but by a relatively sudden and unstructured event like the gestalt switch. . . . because it is a transition between incommensurables, the transition between competing paradigms cannot be made a step at a time, forced by logic and neutral experience. . . . [I]t must occur all at once (though not necessarily in an instant) or not at all."

Stratfordians, Alan saw, will become convinced of the validity of the Oxfordian paradigm at different rates, in response to different types of evidence. Some will never be convinced. That's okay, he thought. Oxfordians will have reached their goal if a substantial number of scholars accept Oxford's authorship.

Alan envisioned the battles to come within departments of literature, with neither side entirely understanding the other. Stratfordians, of course, wouldn't understand the new converts to the Oxfordian paradigm. New Oxfordians, also, he realized, wouldn't understand why Stratfordians couldn't see what they now saw.

He then had a surprising idea. He had first concluded that it wasn't necessary for Oxfordians to push for academia's recognition of de Vere's authorship, that they needed only to push for recognition that the authorship question was one worthy of academic study. Then he had concluded just the opposite, that Oxfordians had to push hard for recognition of de Vere's authorship, because doing so was the only way to generate the crisis necessary for Stratfordians to break free from the older paradigm.

The new surprising idea was that although Oxfordians must push for acceptance of the Oxfordian paradigm, they should be satisfied if Stratfordians decide to take the face-saving step of introducing authorship studies, instead of de Vere studies, into their curricula. *Acceptance of the legitimacy of the authorship question is all that needs to happen, even though that cannot be the goal that Oxfordians push for.*

With his thoughts on that final step in the paradigm shift completed, Alan decided to grab a quick bite to eat before going to tell Matt about his latest idea for the authorship conference.

He wished he could devote all his time in the coming year to the game plan and further investigations into the reasons for de Vere's having hidden his authorship. But the fall term would begin in only a few weeks, and he would once again have a heavy teaching load. Well, he sighed, I'll try to get as much work done as I can before then.

128

"Hi, Matt. Thanks for finding time for me to drop in. I know that you're busy."

"I'm glad you came by, Alan. I was going to call you to ask you to stop in anyway."

"Matt, I have a new idea for a Shakespeare conference. Forget about *William Shakespeare: Did He or Didn't He?* and forget about *The Shakespeare Hoax*. The new idea is *William Shakespeare, Glover, vs. Edward de Vere, Earl of Oxford: The Trial of the Millennium*. The idea, which I read about in *Shakespeare Beyond Doubt?*, is to treat the authorship of the literary works as a crime and to present evidence as to which of the two principal suspects is guilty. Isn't that brilliant?"

"Yes, that's quite an idea, Alan. But I need to talk to you about something else. Take a seat." Alan sat down, looking at Matt expectantly.

"As you know, the School of Arts and Humanities is under pressure from the Dean to move from being a net consumer of funds to a net producer of funds for the University."

"Yeah," Alan said. "I can't imagine a more ridiculous goal. What's the latest on that, by the way?"

"The other department Chairs and I came up with a plan to increase revenue by offering an Asian Studies program geared toward Asian students. We have already presented it to the Dean, who has accepted it.

"Every department in the School will be adding Asian Studies courses. You might wonder, as I did at first, why students from Asia would want to come to the United States to study their own culture. The answer is that we can offer students a broader, if not deeper, study of Asian literature, art, music and society than almost any university in Asia. Universities there tend to focus on their own country only; Asia-wide courses are rare. Our program, with the cachet of an American degree, should enable us to bring in hundreds of additional Asian students each year, all of them paying full tuition."

Alan tilted his head in admiration. "That's truly brilliant. I didn't know that we—humanities professors—had it in us to come up with an entrepreneurial plan like this. My hat is off to you and the other Chairs."

"Well, actually," Matt said, with some embarrassment, "we didn't come up with it totally by ourselves. It came from somebody who, ah, isn't a member of the faculty. Someone who heard about the Dean's priorities and our consternation over how to meet them. She proposed the plan. All our hats are off to her."

"Well, however it happened, it looks like the problem is solved."

Matt paused, dreading the next part of the conversation.

"Alan, that's only half the plan, the half about raising additional revenue. The other half involves reducing expenses. In order to create the positions for faculty teaching Asian literature in this department, and other Asian Studies courses in other departments, we need to reduce faculty positions in other areas."

Matt paused again to look at Alan, who nodded and waited for him to continue. "We have looked carefully at the courses that could most easily be cut—those that have the fewest numbers of students—and determined which existing faculty positions could most easily be eliminated to create room for the new Asian Studies positions. We have determined, Alan, that your position of Shakespeare Specialist is one of those that will be eliminated."

"Oh, I see now what you have been leading up to. If the number of courses in Shakespeare is to be reduced, I'll have to teach more courses in non-Shakespeare literature subjects. It's been a while, but I can dust off my old lecture notes and move into other areas."

"I'm afraid that isn't quite what we have in mind, Alan. The plan is to have certain courses now taught by professors taught by part-time lecturers at a fraction of their salaries. We envision eliminating your position entirely. It's not a matter of having you teach non-Shakespeare courses, but of your university employment ending completely."

Alan was speechless for a moment before replying. "Perhaps you have forgotten that I have tenure. I am Associate Professor with tenure at this university."

"We know that, Alan. But under the rules here at Cary, you should realize that tenure only protects you and your teaching in the classroom. It doesn't protect your position if the university decides to eliminate it entirely."

Alan started to speak, but Matt went on. "I know what you are going to say. That the union will fight this move. Actually, we—the Dean—has already discussed this plan with the union because it involves eliminating faculty positions within practically every department of the School of Arts and Humanities. The union has said it won't oppose the plan because challenges to similar moves at other universities over the past few years have been defeated in the courts."

Alan reminded Matt of the three large conferences he'd organized on behalf of the Department and the University over the past ten years, the most recent one drawing more than 600 academics from across the country. "You are aware, Matt, that those events significantly raised the national profile of this Department. This Department is on the map because of me.

"Look," he continued, pointing to the wall. "You have a framed poster from the third conference hanging right there. This is a hell of a way to show gratitude to someone whose work has had such benefits for the Department. There are other professors whose contributions have been far less significant. Why not move out one of them instead of someone with my record of accomplishment?"

"Alan, you're right about the effectiveness of your work here, not just your teaching and publishing but also those wonderful conferences. But you also reaped benefits from those events. They led directly to your promotion to Associate Professor only six years after you joined the faculty—half the time it usually takes.

"The reality is that times have changed. The new Dean has new priorities, and every department is adapting to them. As central as you and I know Shakespeare is not just to British literature but to Western civilization, the fact is that the School's move toward greater emphasis on Asian Studies means that a position dedicated to Shakespeare is no longer needed."

By now, Alan's sense of alarm had reached a high pitch. "Matt, you can't do this to me! I have two children studying at private universities. If I don't have a job, I have no way to pay their tuition and other school costs. You can't just toss me out. You know I am a fighter. I will fight this with every means at my disposal."

"I know, Alan. Here's the final part of the plan. A small number of faculty whose positions are being eliminated will be offered buyout packages. You're one of them.

"I had to fight hard to get that package approved. Initially the Dean didn't want to offer any buyouts. But the Chairs pushed back and convinced her that some people had made such significant contributions that the University couldn't simply end their employment without providing a benefits package of some sort. In the end, she finally agreed to one buyout per Department. You are receiving the only one in the Literature Department. But part of the agreement is that you agree to keep it confidential. You can't mention it to anybody else."

"What's in the buyout package?" Alan asked.

"It has two parts," Matt explained. "The first is that you immediately qualify for a pension based on the number of years you have taught here. Granted, it will be smaller than the pension you would receive if your employment had continued until the usual retirement age. Second, you will receive a cash payment equal to six months' salary to tide you over until you find other employment. Here is a packet of information and a letter for you to sign stating that you are leaving Cary University voluntarily."

Silence reigned until Alan said, "This is happening because of my promotion of Edward de Vere, Earl of Oxford, as the real author behind the pen name William Shakespeare, isn't it?"

Matt thought carefully before responding. "Alan, the Dean is a complicated woman. On one hand, she hates controversy and publicity. To her the truth or falsity of the authorship question is irrelevant. What matters to her is that your position is controversial and your activism is generating considerable publicity within the academic community. Most comments, as you know, are negative.

"At the same time, the Dean is launching a plan to reorient the School in ways that are controversial and are also going to generate considerable publicity, much of it negative. So apparently she doesn't mind publicity when she is at the center of it.

"She did not support offering the buyout to you because of your Oxfordian activities. She wanted me to give it to someone else, someone less controversial even though that person's contributions have been much less substantial than yours. I had to push hard to get her approval, and my guess is that if you push back—if you do not accept the package within a few days—she will retract it and give it to somebody else."

After an awkward silence, Alan stood up and looked at Matt. He couldn't think of anything else to say, so he picked up the envelope and left the office.

PART III

SATURDAY, AUGUST 1

129

Alan woke up in the middle of the night still in shock. He hadn't seen that coming, not at all. Even in modern society with all its protections and safeguards it's still possible to have the rug pulled out from under us, he thought. We think we're so well protected that bad things can't happen, but we have fooled ourselves. We are as vulnerable to surprises, shocks and disasters as our distant ancestors. Only the nature of the danger has changed.

Because disasters happen less often, we are less prepared for them, physically and mentally. It takes us longer to get over the surprise. Perhaps this is a sign that we have become too prosperous. When faced with adversity, we find that we have become like tamed animals suddenly released into the wild, unused to caring for ourselves.

We are still subject to ingratitude, betrayal, and banishment. The University is continuing to benefit from the national reputation that my conferences earned for it. But I've been banished from the place that has been my intellectual home for more than a decade. What a difference a day makes.

Alan recalled the initial shock he felt as he left Matt's office. His feelings over the following hours had swung wildly up and down. In exulted moments he cheered the fact that the buyout package would enable him to pay his kids' tuition while enjoying what was, in effect, a year's sabbatical—a year that he could devote to developing and implementing his game plan to promote academia's acceptance of de Vere's authorship. That part was a dream come true.

But in other moments, meekly accepting the buyout seemed cowardly. He was a tenured professor with a strong record of accomplishment that redounded to the credit of the University. How could he accept such treatment? At those times he felt sure he would contest the elimination of his position and teaching responsibilities. Surely his being a tenured Associate Professor would enable him to continue in his present status.

But what if he challenged his ouster and lost? Then he'd lose the buyout package, too. He would be in a much worse situation, with Delilah and Carson perhaps having to drop out of school. But can I simply walk away—or allow myself to be pushed out—he asked himself. The scales seemed so evenly balanced.

I must not lose sight of one key fact, he reminded himself. The University would prefer not to pay the buyout package. It's doing so only to make my departure uncomplicated and uncontested. If it finds out about my relationship with Amelia it will dismiss me without a second thought and without the package. So I really don't have a choice: I must accept the buyout package now, before the relationship is discovered.

It was true, he knew, that the University turns a blind eye to relationships between professors and students—when it wants to. But when it has other reasons for wanting to move a professor out, it could use the relationship as a pretext. There had even been rumors that the University sometimes set up faculty members by arranging for female students to indicate their availability and then waiting for professors to take the bait. He wouldn't put it past the University to have done that to him. But no, he told himself, that can't be the case. Amelia is a Fulbright student who has been in the United States only two months. And besides, if the University had set me up, it wouldn't be offering me the buyout.

After leaving Matt's office, Alan had tried calling Amelia, but she hadn't answered. It was late Friday afternoon, and she was probably out with other Fulbright students. He had thought of calling Diana in Taiwan, but it was the middle of the night there. So he'd sent her an e-mail laying out the situation and asking her to call him.

Diana had called a couple of hours later. She was as shocked by the development as he was, but seemed to recover from it more quickly. She reminded him that he'd wanted to leave the University to be able to devote his time to literary projects. She also pointed out that there was no need for financial panic because the buyout package would cover Delilah's and Carson's tuitions for the coming year. She really is very level headed, he thought. It's good to have such a person to talk this through with.

But Diana could tell that Alan was very upset. She asked if she should return home now rather than in two weeks as planned. Her father still wasn't completely well and it would be good if she could stay for a while longer, but if Alan needed her she would leave immediately.

"No, no, I am okay," he'd said. "Today has probably been the worst day, and I'll adjust to the new situation little by little."

"Don't worry about things too much," she'd responded. "I will love you just as much whether you are a tenured professor or not. I didn't marry you because you were a professor. In fact, you weren't a professor in a suit when I married you. You were an untenured assistant professor with an untucked shirt. I loved you then and I love you now. We will get through this."

"I love you, too," Alan had said, wondering at first if he really did, and then realizing that, yes, he did. No amount of money could buy Diana's love and support. She was a truly wonderful person. That was why he'd married her. She was the real deal. He knew how rare such loving and supportive people are in the world.

He recalled their conversation, two months ago, when she told him that her father was ill. "I must go," she'd said. "You can go with me or stay here, but I must go even if you do not. He is my father. He cared for me when I was sick as a little girl, and he supported me when I was a university student when he had so little money. Everything he had he used to ensure that I would be able to continue studying. So I must go now. He needs me. I must take care of him."

After hanging up, Alan suddenly shuddered when he thought of how close he'd come the day before to telling Diana that he wanted out of their marriage. What a disaster it would have been to have broken her heart one day before he lost his job.

SUNDAY, AUGUST 2

130

Amelia lay awake. It was almost midnight, but she hadn't been able to sleep since Alan had stopped by to tell her about the loss of his teaching position. She'd realized immediately that her offhand remarks to the department Chairs had, in fact, been developed and implemented. Was she somehow responsible for Alan's losing his job? No, she told herself, she'd proposed only an Asian Studies program, not the idea of eliminating faculty positions. She hadn't told Alan that she was the one who'd proposed the idea of the new program. It seemed better to wait. Now it might be better not to mention it at all.

What she had done after Alan explained the situation was to lead him into the bedroom. They both needed the comfort and the physical release of making love. This time it was pure animal rutting. No talk of his being an android, or of the shape of her shadow on the bed. Just him pounding into her again and again and again, giving them both the release from the tension that the new situation had generated.

They were exhausted afterwards, and she was glad that Alan had gone home. She needed to think. She decided first to think like an Asian, like the person she'd been before coming to America. Alan was no longer the best fit for the sponsor box at the University because he wouldn't be working there. As for the spouse box, that was now problematic, too. A man with a wife and family and no job already has two strikes against him, a phrase she'd learned from Alan.

She also recalled the times Matt Harris had looked at her when she proposed the idea of the Asian Studies program, when they saw the play in the park, and when she'd been in the Department office. As the Chair of the Department, Matt would be an even better traditional sponsor than Alan. He had a higher position, and there was no chance of her falling in love with him. She could have the traditional sponsor-with-sex relationships she'd had in Vietnam. But no, she told herself, she was too old to need a sponsor. And besides, she is now in America and did not need to be bound by Asian practices.

On the other hand, she thought, Matt is unmarried, and thus a potential spouse. But he didn't have Alan's intellect or life of the mind. She'd already been through one marriage with a man like that. Being with Alan had spoiled her; she would have to share both a physical and an intellectual companionship with whomever she married. She wondered how Matt, with his seemingly minimal intellectual interests, could have become Chair of the Department of *Literature*. But then, she reasoned, it was probably his political skills that put him there. Alan would never want such a position, and his interests in literature and other intellectual subjects would make him a less than ideal Chair even if he somehow ended up in the position.

It was the combination of kindness and toughness, along with the intellectual life of the mind, that made Alan so different from most other men. Many men seemed to have kindness to a degree, but it was often just marshmallow softness. True kindness needs to be accompanied by the toughness that can come only from having survived difficult experiences without becoming embittered. Alan had that.

Matt had the toughness, too, but it was touched with bitterness. That, along with his limited life of the mind, removed him from consideration for the spouse box. Still, his position as Chair, his toughness, and his physical qualities would make him a suitable sponsor-with-sex if it ever came to that.

MONDAY, AUGUST 3

131

"Good morning, everyone," Alan said in his usual greeting, though a perceptive observer might have discerned a tougher, edgier aspect than usual to his manner. Amelia did.

"Today's session is on Shakespeare's portrayal of ingratitude, betrayal, and banishment. Ingratitude for one's accomplishments, sacrifices, or support given freely to the person or institution showing the ingratitude. Betrayal of other people, or of justice or duty, or of ideals of courage and honor.

"And banishment, which Shakespeare was particularly obsessed with. The number of banished characters in his plays is remarkable. Romeo in *Romeo and Juliet*; Bolingbroke in *Richard II*; Coriolanus in *Coriolanus*; Prospero in *The Tempest*; Alcibiades and Timon in *Timon of Athens*; Cordelia, Kent and Edgar, and Lear and Gloucester, in *King Lear*; Belarius, Morgan and Posthumus in *Cymbeline*; Valentine in *The Two Gentlemen of Verona*; other characters in *The Winter's Tale* and *Henry VI*; and Orlando, Oliver, Rosalind's father and Rosalind herself in *As You Like It*.

"Ingratitude, betrayal, banishment—these are all situations that Shakespeare portrayed repeatedly in his plays. Perhaps he had personal experience with them—in both directions—that generated almost an emotional fixation on them.

"But what Shakespeare was really depicting in these instances—and in so many others where characters suffer the loss of loved ones killed in war or by ambitious politicians—was pain. Shakespeare was able to translate the pain he felt in his own life into stage productions with plots, developments and scenes showing how pain is generated and how characters deal with it.

"I now want to call your attention to the distinction between *tragedy* and *tragic*. Getting hit by a speeding car or developing leukemia—things like that are tragic, but they're not the subject of tragedy. They're accidents. We might say, 'What a tragedy,' but if we do, we are using the word only metaphorically because the events—the tragic events—reminds us of the painful ends in tragedies.

"Tragedies are a form of literature or drama in which the outcomes are indeed tragic, but they're not the result of chance or accident. What distinguishes a tragedy from a play with a sad ending is that the outcomes flow directly from the characters' nature, decisions or actions. Usually the choice results in a fall from a height, which means that only those at the top of society—those who have a long way to fall—can be the subject of tragedies.

"I want to discuss a tragedy not on our reading list, *Romeo and Juliet*. Romeo is so shocked by his banishment that he says the word 'banished' or 'banishment' fourteen times in the space of forty-two lines. He doesn't just rage against the sentence and bemoan his fate; he throws himself on the floor, weeping, and rejects the good advice that Friar Laurence gives him. He's a poster child for how not to handle setbacks."

"Professor Fernwood?" Lisa said, tentatively. "I have the text here, if you would like me to read that part of that scene, since the play wasn't on our reading list. I brought in the complete works of Shakespeare today. It's really heavy, but Pat was kind enough to carry it for me."

Amelia glanced at Pat, wondering how he'd happened to be at Lisa's apartment so early in the morning. No one else seemed to catch the subtext of Lisa's remark.

"Sure, Lisa. That would be helpful. I can then comment on certain lines as you read them."

"Maybe Pat would like to help me by reading Friar Laurence's lines. Start here, Pat."

FRIAR [Pat]
> Hence from Verona art thou **banishèd**.
> Be patient, for the world is broad and wide.

ROMEO [Lisa]
> There is no world without Verona walls,
> But purgatory, torture, hell itself.
> Hence **banishèd** is **banished** from the world,
> And world's exile is death. Then **"banishèd"**
> Is death mistermed. Calling death **"banishèd,"**
> Thou cut'st my head off with a golden ax
> And smilest upon the stroke that murders me.
> . . .
> O friar, the damnèd use that word in hell;
> Howling attends it! How hast thou the heart,
> Being a divine, a ghostly confessor,
> A sin absolver, and my friend professed,
> To mangle me with the word **"banishèd?"**

"So you hear Romeo say the word six times in those few lines," Alan pointed out. "You hear him 'psych himself out,' as we might say, rather than 'buck himself up,' by equating 'banished' with 'death' and 'execution' and 'hell.'" He motioned for the readers to continue.

FRIAR
Thou [foolish] mad man, hear me a little speak.

ROMEO
O, thou wilt speak again of **banishment**.
FRIAR
I'll give thee armor to keep off that word;
Adversity's sweet milk, philosophy,
To comfort thee, though thou art **banishèd**.

ROMEO
Yet **'banishèd'**? hang up philosophy!
Unless philosophy can make a Juliet,
Displant a town, reverse a prince's doom,
It helps not, it prevails not. Talk no more.

"Romeo here is rejecting philosophy and the Friar's efforts to find a way forward. Soon after this he throws himself on the floor and won't get up even when somebody knocks at the door. The Friar tells him to hide in his study, but he won't move, potentially making his situation even worse when the visitor enters. It happens to be Juliet's nurse, and she asks where Romeo is. Pointing to him, the Friar says 'There on the ground, with his own tears made drunk.'

"This is only one of the many ways that Shakespeare's characters respond to adversity. Quite a different response was Brutus's to news of the death of his wife in what might have been suicide. As a follower of Stoicism, Brutus had trained himself to handle pain so well that hearing painful news would not disrupt him from whatever activities he was involved in when he heard it. So, Shakespeare constructs situations in which characters feel pain, and he shows us how they respond to it. But he also does something more important; he shows us how they should respond.

"In play after play, Shakespeare portrays the silver lining in the cloud of adversity. He shows us how terrible losses can draw forth from us the very qualities needed to overcome them, and how they give us the chance to show the world what we are made of."

"Nestor, in *Troilus and Cressida*, observes that 'In the reproof of chance / Lies the true proof of men.' He describes how when the seas are calm, strong-ribbed barks and shallow bauble boats may both sail. But when storms hit, that's when the more powerful ship proves its worth and the bauble boat reveals how flimsy it is. 'Even so / Doth valor's show and valor's worth divine / In storms of fortune,' he concludes.

"Shakespeare also shows one more advantage of adversity. It can pull us out of everydayness. It can enable us to see the world from new vantage points, with deeper insight. So, the silver lining is twofold. By encountering disasters, we can strengthen important qualities, and we can gain deeper insights into the nature of human beings and human life. Both our vision and our character can be strengthened through adversity."

The class then turned to several other plays to examine how characters respond to a world full of slights, wrongs, slander, madness and worse. Searching for models to follow or avoid beyond those of Romeo's adolescent meltdown and Brutus's stoical passive acceptance, they found that admirable qualities or responses were rare among Shakespeare's characters. Just as adversity could bring out hidden noble qualities such as determination and perseverance, so too it could reveal hidden character flaws that weren't visible during ordinary times.

They found Timon's withdrawal into physical isolation and hatred of all mankind a model of how not to respond to difficulties and betrayals. Alcibiades in the same play, like Coriolanus, actively sought to conquer and destroy the society that had, he believed, wronged him. That response was also not one to be emulated.

Nor was Richard the Second a model to copy, though some students thought his passive acceptance, and even eagerness, to abdicate was a positive step because it enabled him to move to a situation better suited to his poetical temperament. They all praised Prospero because he forgave those who asked for forgiveness as he reclaimed his dukedom from his brother. Lisa read out Prospero's key statement.

> "'Though with their high wrongs I am struck to th' quick,
> Yet with my nobler reason 'gainst my fury
> Do I take part. The rarer action is
> In virtue than in vengeance. They being penitent,
> The sole drift of my purpose doth extend
> Not a frown further.'"

The higher emotions of love, kindness, sympathy and forgiveness, they agreed, were the only antidote to tragedy, betrayal, slander and other forms of adversity, whether caused by human or natural forces.

132

After the break, Alan moved the conversation along. "So far, we have seen Shakespeare depict three things: the onset of loss or adversity, characters' expression of their pain, and steps they take in response to the challenges they face. I now want to add a fourth subject, one that is

speculation on my part. It's difficult to explain, but I'll try to find the right words to make it clear to you.

"We have seen characters such as King Lear who suffer because of their own actions, and characters such as Anne in *Richard III* who suffer because of actions taken by other characters. In all those cases, Shakespeare has portrayed individuals suffering as the result of actions taken by other individuals. "Individuals" is the key word here. But I have come to think that at some point something drastic happened in Shakespeare's life. A major shift occurred in his thinking, in his attitude toward human nature and human life. He no longer saw human suffering as the result of actions taken by individuals. Rather, he saw it rising from human nature itself, with that fundamental force acting *through* individuals. In other words, yes, Richard III did terrible things, but it wasn't Richard acting merely as an individual. He was a tool that human nature itself used to cause those terrible things.

"In an analogous situation, Hamlet begs forgiveness from Laertes for having killed his father, Polonius. He says it wasn't himself, but his madness that was the cause.

> Was't Hamlet wronged Laertes? Never Hamlet.
> If Hamlet from himself be ta'en away,
> And when he's not himself does wrong Laertes,
> Then Hamlet does it not, Hamlet denies it.
> Who does it then? His madness.

"In other words, Shakespeare came to believe that the entire human species is mad, insane, diseased. The continual stream of lies, slander, betrayals, murders and other horrific events that comprise much of human life is just what is to be expected because all of it arises from corrupted human nature.

"We sometimes speak of disillusionment, of the scales falling from our eyes, of a new profound awareness of reality. Shakespeare as a young man might have absorbed the medieval view of the great chain of being with man somewhere in the middle, below the angels and above the animals. But something happened in his life that not only shook his faith in that construct, but also led him to expect the worst of people. This extreme demoralization is what resulted in *Timon of Athens* and *Troilus and Cressida*, which, remember, is part of *The Iliad* told from Thersites's sordid perspective.

"The reason I have come to believe all this is *King Lear*. Recall that Lear repeatedly expressed the fear that he is going mad or will go mad. Here's one of the times: 'O, let me not be mad, not mad, sweet heaven! / Keep me in temper; I would not be mad!'

"And recall Hamlet's madness and the question of whether it was real or feigned. Maybe Doug was more accurate than he knew when he proposed that Hamlet is someone who is mad pretending to be someone who is sane pretending to be mad.

"But it's not Lear's fear of madness, or even his real madness, that leads me to believe that something profound happened to Shakespeare. It is, rather, the suffering that he portrays in *King Lear*—suffering far beyond what's called for by the plot of the play, suffering far more intense and far more real than has ever been presented on the stage in any other play before or since.

"Torture is not too strong a word. There is the physical torment of Lear on the heath and of Gloucester's eyes being gouged out. There is the mental torment that both men feel because they think their children have been ungrateful and betrayed them. There is the emotional torment that Edgar feels when he has been wronged by his father, and later when he sees his blinded father wandering the heath aimlessly. There is the horror that Gloucester feels when he learns that he has wronged his faithful son, Edgar, and doubts he will ever be able to see him again— well, not see him, exactly—but communicate to him his awareness of his, Edgar's, innocence and of how terribly he regrets his cruel mistreatment of him.

"There is the bittersweet wonderfulness Edgar feels on hearing that his father now knows of his innocence. But he is full of pain, too, because his empathy and love for his father forces him to feel his father's pain as intensely as his father does. Worst of all is the self-torture that Gloucester feels when he learns that the man who has been caring for him is his son, Edgar. The waves of emotion are too much for him. 'His flawed heart - / Alack, too weak the conflict to support - / 'Twixt two extremes of passion, joy and grief, / Burst smilingly,' and he dies.

"Lear's and Cordelia's pain is even more extreme, ending with Lear holding the dead Cordelia in his arms. But I'm not going to talk of it. It's too intense.

"My conclusion is that the pain and suffering in *Lear* is so far out of bounds, so far beyond what is necessary in the play, that something had to have happened in Shakespeare's life—something so overwhelmingly painful that it made him capable of writing the play. Something compelled him to portray suffering so intense that it bordered on madness—and maybe crossed the border. What could possibly have happened in Shakespeare's life that affected him so deeply that he wrote—that he became capable of writing—that he was compelled to write—*King Lear*? That is the mystery I want to leave you with today."

For the first time, Alan left the room before the students, so he did not hear Doug say that this discussion reminded him of *You've Got Mail.* "In the movie, Kathleen Kelly is put out of business by Joe Fox at just that moment when she breaks up with her b.f. She faces double adversity, but she finds the strength to overcome it. She gets a new job as a children's book editor, something she is good at and enjoys, and best of all, she gets revenge on Joe Fox by marrying him!"

Once again, Amelia was about to say something to Doug, but again Dave caught her eye, and she didn't say anything. They both shook their heads and smiled.

133

Johan Meer waved Alan over to a table in the area of the coffee shop informally reserved for faculty from the humanities departments. They were long-time colleagues in the Literature Department. "Alan, you know Alastair and Ella, from the art and music departments, don't you?"

He nodded. "Hi, guys, good to see you again."

"They have just been telling me a most interesting story," Johan said. "I know you are aware of the plan to emphasize greater Asian Studies components in all departments in the School of Arts and Humanities."

"Yeah, I have heard about it." Alan purposely didn't mention the elimination of his position. "It's all built around the desire to increase revenue by appealing to Asian students paying full tuition, isn't it? I'm still amazed that professors in the arts and humanities—even department Chairs—had the entrepreneurial thinking to come up with a plan like this."

"But that's just it," Johan exclaimed. "We didn't. Alastair and Ella have just been telling me the behind-the-scenes story. It isn't what you might think."

"It's quite interesting," Alastair said. "It's true that the idea was proposed to the Dean by Matt Harris, the Chair of your Department. But he didn't think of it himself. It actually came from a student in the Literature Department. As I understand it, the student is an Asian foreign student."

"What?" Alan was unable to contain his surprise. "The idea originated with an Asian student in my department?"

"That's right," said Ella. "She is reportedly quite brilliant—and quite beautiful. You have probably seen her around."

Alan swallowed and found it hard to speak. He finally asked, "Do you know her name?"

Alastair replied. "Well, I don't know her real name, but she has an American nickname, Amelia."

"Oh, yes, she is in my summer Shakespeare seminar," Alan told them, with some difficulty. "You're right, Amelia is both brilliant and charming. But you say she proposed the idea to Matt, who then proposed it to the Dean? How could she even know about the Dean's priorities and the difficulties of the School in meeting them? And how could she know Matt well enough to be able to propose the idea to him?"

"We were just wondering the same thing," Ella said. "We just suggested several ideas to each other."

"None of them suitable for children's ears," Alastair added.

That was about all that Alan could listen to. First the shock of realizing that a core belief in his professional area was wrong; then the shock of having his position eliminated. And now finding out that the plan resulting in the elimination of his position had come from Amelia. The combination of the three blows was disorienting him. He felt dizzy.

Alan stood up slowly, holding on to the table. "Well, that's all very interesting. But I've got to get moving." And then, after a pause, "You're sure it was Amelia who came up with the plan?"

"Yep, no doubt about it," Johan confirmed. "I wish she was in one of my classes. Beautiful, smart, bold in her thinking. She sounds like someone I would like to know."

134

Amelia was already at the restaurant when Alan arrived. He had asked her to meet him there, but hadn't told her why. She'd been able to tell from the sound of his voice, though, that something was wrong.

"It's been quite a week. First the news from Matt that my position will be eliminated. That was quite a shock, though the buyout lessens it somewhat. But I got another surprise today. I just learned that the idea for establishing the Asian Studies program and eliminating many positions in the Humanities Departments came from you, of all people, Amelia." He looked at her not in an accusing way, but with his head tilted, inviting her comment, as though he couldn't understand how her involvement could have been possible.

"No, no. I did not propose that your position be eliminated. I only proposed the part about offering Asian Studies courses to attract more Asian students paying full tuition. I have often heard students in Asia complain about the lack of such courses in their own universities. I was as shocked as you were to learn about your position. I'm sorry I didn't tell you about my suggestion for the program before, but you were so upset that it seemed best not to then."

"But, Amelia, how could you possibly have known about the Dean's priorities?"

She explained that she'd overheard the Chairs discussing the situation in the coffee shop back in June, that their idea of selling trinkets to raise money was so weak that she had jumped into their discussion. She had just blurted her idea out without thinking, and hadn't thought of it since. She had no idea that her proposal had been taken seriously until he told her.

They finished eating. Amelia could see that Alan was still saddened by the situation. And she could see that although he held her blameless, he wanted to go home rather than back to her apartment.

TUESDAY, AUGUST 4

135

"Okay, Matt, I'm ready to do this," Alan told him. He hadn't been yesterday, and even this morning he was unsure if he would sign.

They were in Matt's office, and had been reminiscing about the ways that the study of literature had changed since they began their undergraduate studies close to thirty years ago.

"Things aren't what they were, are they, Matt? Not so long ago Shakespeare was the pride of the English Department. Now, comic books are taught as literature, and those courses are worth as many credits as Shakespeare."

"Yes, times have changed, perhaps more than you have realized, Alan. You are one of the few—maybe the only professor remaining in the Literature Department—still teaching literature in your courses. Everybody else, to one degree or another, has followed the trends toward teaching sociology or Cultural Studies or other non-literary subjects through literature."

"Yes, I was only vaguely aware of those changes as they occurred. I had thought that those changes, which are harmful to the study of literature, would have their day and blow over. But now I see that it's the study of literature that is being blown away.

"I thought of proposing to you and the Dean the alternative idea of cutting out all programs with the word 'studies' in the title to make room for the new courses on Asia. Women's Studies, Environmental Studies, Black Studies, and so on—everybody knows those aren't real academic subjects. I have known that since they tried to teach me Social Studies instead of history in primary school. But then I recalled that the word 'studies' appears in the Dean's precious Asian Studies program. It was that realization that led me, finally, to agree to sign."

Matt slid the final version of the agreement across the table to Alan, who checked it over and signed it. Matt then signed, and it was done. There was nothing left to say. Alan stood up, shook hands with his college friend, and left.

Once outside, he felt relieved. So this is how a career ends, he thought. At the end of the summer term, with few colleagues around to share the occasion. Still, he reasoned, it had to happen sooner or later. Better now with the buyout than later without it. Matt is suited to the new conditions; I'm not. Better to devote my energy to writings justifying the study of literature as literature, not as mere printed copy to be mined in support of biased cultural theories. Better not to waste my energy fighting to stay in a position that I don't want to be in anyway.

136

Elvin wanted to write a column or two to advise his readers on how to investigate scientific issues for themselves so that they wouldn't be at the mercy of visceral responses triggered by images in the media.

Understanding how to sort through the welter of conflicting reports would also make them better citizens, he thought. In a democracy or a republic like the United States, the people are, to use a business analogy, the "owners" of the state. The federal and state legislative bodies are the equivalent of the Board of Directors appointed by the owners to oversee the enterprise. The president and state governors are the chief executive officers appointed to manage the day-to-day operations.

As owners, citizens need to understand the major issues of the day in order to practice good stewardship. Becoming better informed was so important, he wanted to tell his readers, because the costs of not being informed were so high, with hundreds of billions of dollars of "their" money being spent on scientific, technological, environmental and medical issues every year.

So, what could he tell his readers that might help them understand those issues? First, a general principle: "Demand evidence and think critically"—guidance he heard from Alan Fernwood, who had picked it up from Tom Regnier, an Oxfordian. If everyone did that, Elvin thought, they would be manipulated less often and more problems would be solved. And second, he could lay out a four-step process through which issues could be mastered.

A few hours later Elvin finished the first of the two columns urging his readers to investigate issues for themselves.

What's a Girl to Do? Part I

"Salt is a killer." "Salt is harmless." "The climate is warming." "The climate is cooling." "GMOs will kill mankind." "GMOs are a blessing for mankind." "The ozone hole is expanding." "There is no ozone hole." "William Shakspere wrote Shakespeare." "Edward de Vere, Earl of Oxford, wrote Shakespeare." "He wants your heart." "He only wants your body."

How is one to know what's true? In short, what's a girl to do?

The answer is, of course, "Use your assets!" No, not that pair, girl. The lobes in your head—your frontal cortex and one behind it. The left side of your brain and the right.

It's been said that those with a human brain who don't use it are no better off than those without one. So think or sink. Either educate yourself to elevate yourself, or descend to the level of the animals. If sinking is what you're thinking, choose which animal you'd like to be.

Sheep appear to be a popular choice. It's so easy to blindly follow direction from the sheepdog as it herds you down one path or another. Others have apparently chosen to be mice, happy for the pellet they get at the end of the maze, without having to think about where it comes from. Others seem to be like tamed lions, unable to fend for themselves when released into the wild. At the lowest end are the birds who have become brainwashed into believing that the experts who lectured them on how to fly actually gave them their flying abilities.

So if you don't want to become a sheep, a mouse, a tamed lion or a brainwashed bird—if you want to use your brain and so become fully human—what do you do? How do you educate yourself about the major scientific, technological, environmental and medical (STEM) issues of the day? How can you become knowledgeable enough not to be at the mercy of the visceral responses that images in the media trigger in you?

Here's a general principle: "Demand evidence and think critically." And here's a four-step process to follow: 1) investigate the scientific basis of the issue, 2) assess the net impact of human activity, 3) determine the most cost-effective way to alleviate a problem (if one exists), and 4) compare the benefits of responding to one problem with the benefits of responding to others.

In the first step, make it your business to understand the physical processes at work in the natural world apart from any consideration of human activities. Read the scientific reports, not just the articles about them in the media. Skim through half a dozen or so, until you get a clear picture of the overall issue. Then go back to the hard parts. Chances are they will have become clear without your realizing it.

Read critically and ask questions. How does the writer know that what he says is true? Are claims well-founded, or merely stated without justification?

If your subject is global warming, ask how much warming has occurred and when. Ask why temperatures peaked in the 1930s, then cooled until the 1970s, then rose again until the late 1990s, then remained steady or declined. Ask how, if CO_2 was such a minuscule percentage of the atmosphere—1/36th of one percent—a doubling of it could have such drastic effects on the planet's climate. Ask what factors other than CO_2 might affect warming and cooling. Ask how today's temperatures and CO_2 levels compare with those in the past. Ask whether real world data support or contradict the models' projections.

Most importantly, read a variety of viewpoints. Note where reports or articles differ. Compare not just their conclusions, but also their evidence, logic and reasoning. The mind by itself is lazy. It's passive and will unthinkingly accept any idea, no matter how ridiculous, if other people also accept it. It's the existence of rival views—discrepancies, conflicts and contradictions—that spurs the mind into thinking.

In step two, examine the net effect that human activities have on the environment (if a problem exists). Consider beneficial as well as harmful effects so that both sides of the scale are weighed.

If the issue is global warming, ask what actions by human beings affect the climate in either direction. Perhaps toasters and CO_2 emissions warm the atmosphere, but activities that produce smoke, sulfuric acid and other aerosols cool it. The point is to find the net effect of all human activities.

Then consider how the environment responds. Might it adjust on its own, as plants absorb more carbon dioxide from the atmosphere when concentrations are higher? Might additional clouds form when temperatures rise, blocking heat from the sun? What is most important is not the gross effect of human actions, but the net effect after the environment has adjusted.

Remember that human beings are more important than things—and that the environment is a thing. To retain that perspective, keep in mind the guidance that some primary schools give their students: "Take care of yourself. Take care of each other. Take care of this place." It's simple, easy to understand, and in the right order. It places human beings first and the non-human environment last.

If you disagree with this order, ask yourself this question: If you are speeding down a steep hill in San Francisco because the brakes on your car have failed and you must choose between crashing into a tree or hitting a human being, what would you do? If after considering this question you disagree with the order in the guidance simple enough for primary school children to understand, "The Contrarian" would be happy to recommend a mental health specialist for you.

Step three: if human activities will have, or are having, a net harmful effect—not just a net change, but a net effect that is harmful for human beings—then consider what measures might be taken to improve the situation. The best responses would be those that alleviate the worst aspects of the problem at the lowest cost and disruption to other aspects of human life. The benefits from any proposed measures must be weighed against their cost.

If the issue is global warming, and if warming is harmful to human beings, and if that warming is caused by human-generated CO_2, then the solution might be steps to reduce the amount of CO_2 generated by human activity. Or it might be best to remove the CO_2 from the atmosphere later, perhaps by planting more trees. The goal must always be to identify the remedial effort providing the greatest benefit at the least cost.

The less severe a problem is found to be, the less extreme the remedy needs to be. That's why it's so important to understand the net harm that human activity might cause before determining what remedial measures might be required. Solutions must be judged by how well they actually solve a problem, not by how good they look on paper.

With these three steps taken, only one remains to be discussed. We'll examine it next time.

137

Something more is needed, Elvin felt. He wanted to help his readers—and himself—overcome the sense of demoralization they might feel on seeing the world's leaders invest huge amounts of money in unproductive ways. He knew of many misguided policies through which governments, ignoring the beneficial aspects of higher levels of carbon dioxide, sought to reduce their country's carbon footprint.

How are we to combat what has been described as an army of bureaucrats, politicians, scientists and businesses that live off the climate catastrophe scare? Is there any solution at all? It would take an individual—a movement—of extraordinary political will and courage to challenge and overcome the political, financial and bureaucratic forces supporting such wasteful measures to deal with a nonexistent problem when so many real problems cried out for attention.

Turning to write the second column, Elvin didn't want to leave his readers with a sense of futility. Or himself, either. He'd have to find a way to provide them with a ray of hope, then he'd go see Delilah. She always knew how to buck up his spirits when the ways of those crazy creatures called human beings got him down. He hoped his readers had a lifeline as effective as his.

What's a Girl to Do? Part II

Owners of human brains can increase their understanding of STEM (scientific, technological, environmental, medical) issues by following a four-step process. We considered the first three steps last time: 1) investigate the scientific basis of the issue, 2) assess the net impact of human activity, and 3) determine the most cost-effective ways to alleviate the problem (if there is one).

We now turn to the fourth and final step. Alleviation measures that pass the cost-benefit test (step three) must still pass one more test before being enacted. The net benefits of a measure proposed to address one problem must be compared with the benefits of addressing other problems. Given that resources are finite, problems must be prioritized and those most urgent dealt with first.

A decade ago, Bjorn Lomborg set out to identify which problems are most worth being addressed. The result was The Copenhagen Consensus 2004, which included an expert panel of eight top economists who sought to answer the question "What would be the best ways of advancing global welfare, and particularly the welfare of developing countries, supposing that an additional $50 billion of resources were at governments' disposal?"

The panel heard presentations by eight distinguished economists on nine challenging global problems, and also considered critiques from twenty prominent researchers who opposed the solutions proposed by the economists. It then prioritized the solutions to use the $50 billion as effectively as possible.

Surprisingly, the panel came to a near unanimous agreement. "First and foremost the world ought to concentrate on controlling HIV/AIDS. At a cost of $27 billion . . . The benefit-cost ratio is predicted to be 40 times that figure." Malnutrition and hunger were number two on the list, and the panel also saw big benefits from the elimination of trade barriers, control and treatment of malaria, and incentives to ensure clean drinking water. The panel found that all these problems, which affect billions of people worldwide, could be effectively solved.

Global warming finished dead last in the panel's list of priorities. "The experts were not unaware that climate change is important," Lomborg explained, "but, for some of the world's poorest countries, which will be adversely affected by climate change, problems like HIV/AIDS, hunger, and malaria are more pressing and can be solved with more efficacy."

Lomborg explained further that "It is unethical not to take into account knowledge that indicates where we can do the most good. The Copenhagen Consensus constitutes the cold, rational approach. Instead of intending to do good, isn't it better to actually *do* good?"

So there it is: four simple, clear steps to follow to become masters of the universe, or at least masters of STEM subjects. Who knew it would be so easy to become less naïve, gullible and innocent, and so perhaps be a bit less often conned, fooled and hoaxed by the rest of the world?

So what are we to think when we see how unwisely governments—who control the resources needed to solve big problems—use them?

What are we to think when we see a proposal in Australia that would reduce CO_2 emissions by five percent by 2020 when the climactic benefits of the measures being considered—assuming a reduction in temperature to be a benefit—would be a "cooling of between 0.0007 and 0.00007 degrees Celsius," and when, by one estimate, the economic effects of the measure would be so large that "Australia would suffer an alarming fall in its standard of living," with "the economically vulnerable . . . pushed into fuel poverty"? How could such a large cost possibly be justified by the vanishingly small benefit to be received?

What are we to think when we see in the United States that the EPA's Clean Power Plan requires "that states reduce their electric utility sector carbon dioxide emissions an average of 32% below 2005 levels by 2030,"—a goal that would "dictate returning CO_2 emissions almost to 1975 levels" even though the country's population has increased by 40 million—a policy that would cause electricity rates to rise from "8-9 cents to 36-40 cents" per kilowatt hour, all in order to "prevent less than 0.03° F of global warming 85 years from now"?

What are we to think when we see World Bank President Jim Yong Kim pledging to spend $29 billion of the Bank's money on climate related projects by 2020, and the leaders of China, the United States, the United Kingdom, France and the Asian African Development Bank pledging to spend another $100 billion?

We could, like Bjorn Lomborg, regard these developments as "deeply troubling" because "aid is being diverted to climate-related matters at the expense of improved public health, education and economic development" at a time when "malnourishment continues to claim at least 1.4 million children's lives each year, 1.2 billion people live in extreme poverty, and 2.6 billion lack clean drinking water and sanitation." The divergence of funds is, he concludes, "immoral."

Who can see this absurd misallocation of resources, this almost criminal negligence by our political leadership, and not agree with Friedrich Schiller that "Against stupidity, the gods themselves contend in vain"?

But all is not lost. It was also Schiller who overcame awareness of human stupidity to write his "Ode an die Freude" or "Ode to Joy," his paean to human brotherhood that inspired Beethoven to write the finale of his Ninth Symphony. We are indeed a flawed species. But, somehow, perhaps keeping in our thoughts the angelic heights to which the human mind and heart can ascend more than compensates for awareness of the brainless sub-animal depths to which we can also descend.

WEDNESDAY, AUGUST 5

138

All six students were already at Amelia's apartment when Alan arrived at seven p.m., the agreed upon meeting time for a showing of *Anonymous*. The apartment smelled like a movie theater because so many bags of microwave popcorn had already been popped.

Alan smiled at seeing what good friends the students had become. At the same time, he also realized more deeply that he was truly of a different generation from them. Amelia was somewhat in the middle. Returning to the living room with a Coke, Alan saw that Amelia had gathered the students together on and near the sofa. "Dr. Fernwood," she asked, "would you like to say a few words to introduce the film?"

"Oh, sure, Amelia," he said. "You're all aware that over the past couple of months I have become convinced that Edward de Vere, Earl of Oxford, wrote the works attributed to William Shakespeare. This film, *Anonymous*, presents that idea by portraying William Shakspere as a front for Oxford, the real author. But it also presents ideas even more controversial—that the Earl of Southampton and Edward de Vere himself were sons of Queen Elizabeth. Those ideas are highly speculative, so just remember that *Anonymous* is only a movie, not a documentary.

"The director, Roland Emmerich, is known for box office blockbusters such as *The Patriot* and *Independence Day*. *Anonymous* was a very different type of film for him, and one he felt so strongly about that he put $20 million of his own money into funding it.

"I saw the movie twice in public theaters, and both times witnessed audience responses different from any I have ever seen for any other movie. At the first showing, everybody applauded at the end as if they had just witnessed a live performance. It was an extraordinary moment. At the second showing the reaction was even more moving. The entire audience sat through all of the final credits as though they were completely caught up in the profundity of the experience and didn't want it to end. Not a single person left. I was amazed. So, I'm looking forward to seeing if you will be equally impressed by it."

Amelia then started the movie. The students appeared to enjoy it. Some of them booed when William Shakspere appeared on the screen, and Doug threw popcorn at the TV when Shakspere was trying to blackmail Edward de Vere.

After the movie ended, everyone wanted to talk about it. Those who'd seen it before liked it much more than those who hadn't. Those seeing it for the first time found it confusing, with so many characters to keep track of and with the scenes jumping backward and forward in time. "I had the same reaction the first time I saw it," Alan said. "Even though I knew the names of all the major historical figures in advance, I still had a hard time keeping them straight. That problem tends to disappear with the second or third viewing."

Dave and Lisa were a bit angry, saying that Shakespeare had been slandered. "I thought so too at first," Alan responded. "Throughout my entire life I thought that those who doubted Shakspere's authorship were nuts. But now I have become one of them. I now have no doubt that Shakspere of Stratford did not write Shakespeare's works."

While the students discussed the movie further among themselves, Alan went to the kitchen to get a Coke, then to the balcony to drink it. When he returned to the living room, he found that the students had already left. Amelia was sitting alone on the sofa, and he sat down close to her. This was the first time they'd been alone together since he had learned of her inadvertent role in the creation of the Asian Studies program. They were both feeling uneasy, with Alan wondering if the loss of his job had affected her feelings for him, and Amelia wondering whether his feelings for her had changed.

"Do you remember when we met again for the first time after we made love?" he asked. "On that Monday? And we were both a bit shy, wondering how the other felt?"

"Yes, I do. I had to show you the shadow of my profile on the bed to break the shyness that had overcome us." She laughed as she spoke.

"Well, I think we are both feeling somewhat the same way now. Since it's night and there is no sun to cast shadows, here is what we will do. Do you remember the scene in *Anonymous* where the queen asks Oxford what he liked best about Italy, and he says 'their theater . . . and their women—'"

"Yes, I do," she said, starting to smile again.

"'—because when they see something they want they take it. They don't wait to be taken?' Let's reverse the roles. I'm seeing something I want, and I'm going to take it."

Then they were in each other's arms. "Oh, Alan. I have felt so bad, both for you and your situation, and because I didn't know if you still wanted me, still loved me."

"Both of the above," he said as he picked her up and carried her into the bedroom. "I will want you and love you till the day I die."

THURSDAY, AUGUST 6

139

"Good morning, everyone," Alan greeted his students as the final regular class meeting began.

"This summer, in Shakespeare in His Own Words, we've spent a lot of time discussing themes, situations or personality types of greatest interest to Shakespeare—the things he returns to again and again in his plays. Among those subjects were the distinction between an individual and his position and his title; the political aspects of love and desire; and the distinction between appearance and reality. Today we have a chance to continue our discussions of ideas or plays that we didn't have enough time for earlier. Are there any particular subjects that any of you would like to discuss?"

Amelia, knowing that she was speaking on behalf of everyone, said that she wanted to discuss further the puzzle they noted in *Hamlet* and the mystery related to the intensity of the suffering in *King Lear*.

Alan nodded. "I thought you would. I also wanted to return to those two topics today. But we must first turn to the authorship question.

"It wasn't easy for me to reach the conclusion that Shakespeare's works had been written by Edward de Vere, Earl of Oxford, because it was so difficult to force myself even to examine the issue. Until two months ago, I was a lifelong believer in Shakspere's authorship, and considered those who doubted it lacking in reason and maybe even sanity. But once I examined the evidence, the conclusion that de Vere was the author was pretty easy to reach. The evidence supporting his authorship is overwhelming and the evidence for authorship by William Shakspere of Stratford-upon-Avon is becoming weaker all the time."

Alan cited the example he'd given Matt: Alexander Waugh's discovery that Hampton Court, the royal palace in which theatrical performances were given for Queen Elizabeth and other members of the court, was known among the nobility of the time as "the Avon." "The phrase 'sweet swan of Avon' in the First Folio, therefore, didn't necessarily refer to the Avon River that flowed by Stratford. It could just as easily be used to support de Vere's authorship as Shakspere's. It's already firmly established that Oxford managed a theater group that performed at court."

"Waugh's finding undercuts one of the most powerful pieces of evidence in support of Shakspere's authorship," Nancy observed.

"And does so very cleverly," Dave added. "It's clear that whoever put the First Folio together was making a deliberate effort to say things that could be interpreted in more than one way."

"I agree," Alan said. "That's only one way that the Folio is deliberately ambiguous, but we don't have time to go into that now. When I put this course together, I believed that Shakspere was the author. Or, rather, I didn't pay any attention to the authorship question. My focus was on the issues and themes in Shakespeare's plays that we have been discussing. But now, looking back on the subjects we tackled with my new understanding of who wrote Shakespeare's works, I can see clearly the almost total disconnect between those issues and Shakspere's life, and I can see how interest in them would have grown naturally out of Edward de Vere's.

"I have created a chart showing how those themes relate to the lives of the two purported authors," he said, handing out copies. He gave them several minutes to look over the handout. During that time, he considered just what to say to answer the questions posed about *Hamlet* and *Lear*.

SUMMER SHAKESPEARE SEMINAR		
Issues discussed in this course:	Connections to William Shakspere	Connections to Edward de Vere, Earl of Oxford
Themes addresses in the first half of the term: The importance of decisions; Clashes in values; Politics		
Plays as political in nature, how power is wielded, transferred, legitimized (*Coriolanus, Henry V, Richard II*)	?	Lord Great Chamberlain of England
Plays reflect political issues and developments important in Queen Elizabeth's court and government (*Richard II, King John*)	?	Lord Great Chamberlain of England
Characters act within political settings; little is totally private (*Measure for Measure*, others)	?	Lord Great Chamberlain of England
Moments of decision: plays built around major characters' moments of decision	?	Major decisions of his documented

Clash between values: pagan Roman vs. Medieval Christian society and values; revenge	?	Lived in Italy for one year, brought Renaissance culture to England
Clash between values: Medieval idea of honor vs. values of the burgeoning commercial economy	Small time businessman, money lender, grain merchant	Prime example of a nobleman affected by the new commercial developments
Knowledge in decision making: Hamlet's efforts to confirm uncle's guilt (*Hamlet*)	?	Lived in similar court setting
Knowledge in decision making: conflict between head and heart (*Love's Labor's Lost*)	?	Had at least one extramarital affair
Knowledge of human nature: changes in animals humans are compared to (various)	?	Tutored by Thomas Smith, England's premier naturalist
Knowledge of human nature: extremes, need for middle ground (*Timon*)	?	Wildly extreme personality
Valuing people and things: Helen and Achilles (*Troilus and Cressida*)	?	?
Major Theme I: Distinction between Individual, Title, Position		
Relationships on basis of title or position (*King Lear*)	?	Had title and senior position in government/court
Primogeniture and place of bastards (*King Lear, King John*)	?	Was eldest son of nobleman, and fathered an illegitimate son
Unsuitability of poets for political positions (*Richard II*)	?	Was a poet in a high position in the court
Unsuitability of military men for political positions (*Coriolanus*)	?	Had military exp. in Scotland, Low countries, Armada
Major Theme II: Political Aspects of Love and Desire		
Helen and Cressida as political pawns ((*Troilus and Cressida*)	?	High-level political experience
Arranged marriages and opposition to them (*Midsummer Night's Dream*)	?	First marriage was arranged and he initially opposed it
Complications of mixing political and romantic activities	?	Details of his complicated love life

(*Antony and Cleopatra*)		are known
Strength of desires and need to control them (*Measure for Measure*)	?	Fathered an illegitimate son
Major Theme III: Appearance and Reality		
How easily appearance and reality are confused (*Midsummer Night's Dream, Troilus and Cressida*)	?	The appearance of Shakspere as author and the reality of Oxford's authorship
Need for experience to distinguish between them (*King Lear*)	?	Had a wide variety of experiences similar to those depicted in the plays
Hamlet's efforts to know the reality of the world (*Hamlet*)	?	
Hamlet's efforts to know the reality of himself (*Hamlet*)	?	Surviving letters show insight into his nature
General Subjects Depicted in the Plays		
Ingratitude, betrayal, banishment	?	Banished from court in 1581
Knowledge of politics, diplomacy, high level developments	?	Lord Great Chamberlain of England
Knowledge of War	?	Participated in campaigns in Scotland, Low Countries, Armada
Knowledge of life at court	?	Was a courtier
Knowledge of Italy	?	Lived in Italy for more than 6 months; visited all Italian cities where Shakespeare's plays are set
Knowledge of law	?	Studied law at Gray's Inn
Knowledge of plants, animals, etc.	?	Tutored by Thomas Smith, England's foremost naturalist
Knowledge of literature, languages	?	Tutored in these subjects, purchased books on them, and lived in a house with one of largest libraries in England

"Okay," Pat said, "I'm intrigued by the authorship issue. But I want to learn more about it before accepting that de Vere was the author."

"Seeing this list," Lisa sighed, "my head tells me there are good reasons for concluding that Shakspere was not Shakespeare. But at the same time, it's hard for my heart to accept that the image of the author that I've had for my entire life is false. It's very disconcerting. I'm not sure that I could ever totally accept that the man from Stratford wasn't the author."

"That's fine, Lisa. Different people look at the same evidence and reach different conclusions," Alan replied. "The majority, who haven't yet examined the issue, believe that the man from Stratford was Shakespeare. Their numbers, though, are in decline. After all, a hundred years ago nobody thought de Vere was the author. Most people who move to the new view don't do so overnight. It takes time to become familiar and comfortable with it.

"With this background on the authorship question out of the way, let's turn to the *Hamlet* puzzle and the *Lear* mystery. But keep in mind that everything I am about to say on these subjects is speculative. It's one interpretation of the facts, and one that not many people agree with—yet.

"We ended our discussion of *Hamlet* with a puzzle—the mismatch noted by T.S. Eliot and Pat between the fact of the 'o'er hasty' marriage by Hamlet's mother to Hamlet's uncle on one hand, and Hamlet's emotional responses on the other. Although Hamlet claims that his concern was only with the speed with which the marriage occurred, his reaction at times seems to be those of a jilted lover rather than a son.

"And we ended our discussion of *King Lear* by noting the mismatch between the situations called for by the plot and the intensity of the suffering of so many of the characters. That suffering is so intense that I speculated that it must come from outside the play, from an unknown event in the life of the author—an event of such intense suffering and pain that it resulted in de Vere's re-evaluating human nature—a downward revision, a dispelling of all illusions and hopes, into a deep certainty about the evil nature of human beings, coupled with its opposite, a grasping belief in love as the only way out of the depths.

"So, how are we to explain these two mismatches—one regarding sexual feelings and the other suffering? Nothing known about the life of William Shakspere of Stratford-upon-Avon explains either of them. But if Edward de Vere, Earl of Oxford, is considered to be the author, the two puzzles, taken together, solve each other. An event might have occurred in the life of the Earl of Oxford that caused such an extraordinary depth of suffering and pain that it explains *King Lear*.

"I'm going to offer you three speculations—three ideas that I haven't yet accepted as true—that go right to the heart of these two mysteries, and also explain a third mystery—why Oxford's authorship of Shakespeare's works was hidden during his lifetime and after his death.

"Speculation Number One is that the Earl of Southampton, who was sentenced to death in 1601 for his role in the Essex Rebellion, was actually the son of Edward de Vere. Southampton wasn't just the dedicatee of Shakespeare's *Venus and Adonis* and *Lucrece*; he was also the author's son. He wasn't a nobleman patron of a commoner playwright, nor was he the author's homosexual lover. He was his son.

"Now, as Elizabeth's Lord Great Chamberlain and as the most senior earl in the kingdom, Oxford was head of the jury of twenty-five noblemen that considered the fate of the those involved in the Essex Rebellion. That jury found them guilty of treason, and the penalty for treason was death. So, if Southampton was Oxford's son and if Oxford was Shakespeare, then Shakespeare was head of the jury that sentenced his own son to death.

"If we are looking for an experience of deep and profound mental torture, this is it. This event would explain Shakespeare's darkening view of human nature and the source of the intense suffering that he portrayed in *King Lear*."

Alan paused for a moment before continuing.

"Speculation Number Two is that Southampton was Oxford's son by Queen Elizabeth. Queen Elizabeth and Oxford had an affair in the early 1570s from which an illegitimate son resulted. The child was placed in the Southampton household and raised as the ostensible son of the Second Earl and his wife. Perhaps that explains the portrayal of so many bastards in Shakespeare's plays. It could be that Oxford had hoped, even expected at one point, that his son by the queen, the Third Earl of Southampton, would, somehow, eventually be acknowledged as her heir and become King of England. The death sentence in 1601 pretty much ended that possibility, adding to the depth of Oxford's suffering."

He paused again, giving that possibility time to sink in.

"Speculation Number Three is that Oxford himself not only had an affair with Queen Elizabeth, but was also her eldest son. He was born to her when she was a teenager, long before it appeared likely that she'd ever become queen—her brother Edward was king and her sister Mary was ahead of her in the line of succession. If de Vere was Elizabeth's son—and if de Vere and Queen Elizabeth were represented as Hamlet and his mother, then the puzzle in *Hamlet* is explained. If Hamlet sounded like a jilted lover, maybe that's because he was. If Hamlet tells his mother that he wished she wasn't his mother, maybe that was because he wished that obstacle to their marriage could be removed.

"Introducing the element of incest also provides an answer to the nature of the 'vulgar scandal' that generated feelings of 'shame' that Shakespeare referred to in his *Sonnets*.

"Now let's turn to the third mystery, the Shakespeare authorship question. If Southampton was Oxford's son and also Queen Elizabeth's son, and if Oxford himself was Queen Elizabeth's son, these would have been three of the deepest, darkest secrets of Elizabeth's reign.

"And yet here's Oxford broadcasting them to all the world in his plays and *Sonnets* and other poems. Not openly, of course, but to those already in the know his references to them were easily recognized. I'll give you a list later of books that identify those references.

"The question that the political powers faced was how to keep those secrets secret. They couldn't suppress the plays themselves because they were too popular. But they could sever the connection between the plays and the author and put up a new one. If the author was made to be a country bumpkin who wasn't even in London much of the time, then the public would be more likely to see the plays as works of imagination and fantasy, and less likely to connect them to real events or real people.

"Oxford's authorship of the plays had to be kept hidden in order to protect Elizabeth's reputation as the virgin queen. It had to be kept hidden even after her death as part of the effort to hide her illegitimate son or sons so that no challenges to the legitimacy of King James's reign would arise. So there you have it. All three mysteries solved at once."

The students were quiet. Alan couldn't tell if they were stunned by the explanatory power of the three speculations, if they were still trying to absorb such new ideas, or whether they disagreed with the interpretation but were too polite to say anything.

In any event, he wouldn't have gone into any of these authorship subjects, and certainly not into the speculations, if this hadn't been the last day of class of his final term of teaching at Cary University.

Alan then called for the break.

"And now on to the final exam," he said, once everyone returned. "It's in two parts. Each has three questions; you are to select and write on one—and only one—question from each part. Each essay should be about 800 to 1,000 words long. These are open-book, take-home exams, similar to the midterm. You can turn them in electronically any time up through the end of the scheduled test period on Monday.

"I will be here during the test period, and hope you will stop by to say goodbye. I just might have a bottle of champagne on hand to celebrate the end of the term and to thank you for all of your hard work. I know that Shakespeare isn't easy, especially on the first reading or two. But you have all done marvelously well in overcoming the difficulties. You now have a solid grounding in many of the themes and subjects of most interest in Shakespeare, and I hope you will build on this base by returning to the plays for enjoyment and inspiration over the course of your lives. Believe me, you will always find new things in them."

"Well, I'll certainly be here if champagne is being served," Doug responded.

"I look forward to seeing your essays, and to seeing you on Monday. But if you can't make it, I wish you a wonderful rest of the summer."

"And so ended the final regular class meeting of the final term of Dr. Alan Fernwood's teaching career at Cary University," Alan said out loud after the students had left the room.

140

Amelia had, as usual, gone for lunch with the other students. That suited Alan fine, because he needed to think through why he'd been unable to tell Diana about wanting to end their marriage. What he wanted—or thought he wanted—was to put everything else in the world aside and move into Amelia's apartment with her. Well, maybe not that apartment. It was too small. Another apartment, a bigger one. A house would be even better, one with space for his large library. What he actually wanted was to live with her in the house where he was now living with Diana. But that was impossible. So what was possible?

For weeks Alan had tried to sort through the possibilities, but his thoughts had always come out jumbled. They were becoming clearer now, though. He began to see four factors that needed to be considered. Two principal reasons supported his spending the rest of his life with Amelia, and two showed why that was impossible. He needed to state each clearly to himself and then weigh them against each other.

On the side for Amelia, we share many interests together, he began. Not just literature and the authorship question, but so many others, too. Anytime I read something or hear a piece of music that catches my attention, I know I can share it with her and that she will catch the very aspect of it that gave me pleasure. Our minds work the same way and appreciate the same things.

A second reason in support of Amelia is the wonderful life we could build together. She is such an interesting person in her own right—

accomplished, and with a mixture of charm and playfulness as well as an edginess that makes her endlessly fascinating.

So why don't I move on, he asked himself. Why wasn't I able to raise the subject with Diana? He turned to the other two factors. The first was the pain he would have to inflict on himself and his family. There was also the likely loss of his house and the sudden meaninglessness of all the belongings and memories that he and Diana had accumulated over more than twenty years of marriage. The practical and emotional difficulties of trying to sort through all those belongings was more than he could bear to think about.

The other reason was, paradoxically, the loss of his freedom to read, think and write. I have finally reached a point where I don't have to work for others, at least for a year, he reminded himself. I finally have control over my time and can use it to think and write about the subjects of most interest to me. But that freedom would vanish if I married Amelia because my savings and small pension wouldn't be enough to support two households. I'd have to find work, probably teaching at another university.

Two factors pulled him in one direction and two in the other. The balance was a feather's weight heavier on the side that enabled him to engage in the work he'd wanted to do his entire professional life. But a life without Amelia was unacceptable. He would have to rethink everything again later.

141

This is a very pleasant place, quiet and peaceful, Amelia said to herself. I can see why Alan likes it so much. She was in the large lobby of the Harvest Hotel, a few blocks from campus. After he had introduced her to it, she sometimes came here to read and think. Today she had a book with her, but she really wanted to think about the change in Alan's situation and what it might mean for her.

She looked up as a couple came in and sat down on a sofa not far from her chair. That girl is beautiful, but she's upset about something, Amelia thought, and the man looks capable and concerned about her.

"It's just not fair," the girl said. "After all he has done for the University. Dad is putting up a brave front, saying that he will be glad to have more time for his literary projects, which is what he loves most. But I can see that he is very upset about losing his teaching position. The University has been his whole life for more than a decade."

Oh, Amelia realized, the girl's father must be one of the professors whose positions have been eliminated to make room for the Asian

Studies program. She listened more carefully, while pretending to read.

"One thing that has him particularly worried is how he will pay for my tuition for my final year. It's frightfully expensive. He says he'll manage, somehow, but I know it will be very difficult for him. We might have to borrow money. Maybe I should go to work without graduating. The company where I'm working this summer as an intern wants to hire me, but I told them that I have to return to school."

She was quiet for a moment, and her friend tried to console her. "Everything will work out, dear. You won't have to drop out of school. You know that your father has received some sort of buyout that will help him pay for your final year."

"But you know, Elvin, even though my father is very worried now—and my mother is, too—I talked with her on the phone last night—I know they will be fine. There have been problems in the past, difficulties in his career before coming to Cary University. I was too young to know the details. But I remember very clearly my mother supporting him, the two of them supporting each other at that difficult time, talking together, working it out. I could see that they loved each other very much."

"Alan is a strong man, and your mother is a brave woman," the man said. "They will get through this difficult time, too."

Amelia's head jerked up and she stared at the couple. If that girl's father is Alan, she must be Delilah.

"When I get married," the girl continued, "I want it to be to a man with whom I can share my life as deeply as my parents have shared theirs. I know there will always be problems, but I want a man I can share them with, and that together we can overcome them.

"It's funny. My father owns 8,000 books and is so absorbed in his reading, thinking, writing and teaching all the time, and my mother has no such interests. But there is a connection between them—love is what I suppose you would call it—at a deeper level than my father's intellectual life."

Amelia's mind was racing. She loved Alan more than anyone she had ever known outside of her family, and she knew that he loved her. She knew they would have a wonderful life, if they could only get together. But, but, but. She didn't want to see a marriage such as this one destroyed. She didn't want to be the cause of its destruction. Hearing what Delilah said, Amelia knew with even more certainty than before that Alan would be a good husband for her. But she now knew that he was already a good husband for another woman. Their marriage would not fall apart easily. It might not collapse at all, no matter how much he loved her.

She put those thoughts aside and thought about Delilah. She was such a pretty girl; young, but also perceptive, intelligent, caring. I don't want to do anything that might hurt her, she said to herself, almost out loud. She remained deep in thought long after the couple had left.

142

With some food now in her, Delilah's mood had brightened considerably since she and Elvin had discussed her father's situation in the lobby downstairs an hour earlier. They were seated at a table in the outdoor part of the Harvest Hotel's rooftop restaurant, where she and Elvin were celebrating her twenty-second birthday, just as they'd planned a week ago.

She had been thinking a lot about what her future with Elvin might be. Is it really necessary to wait until after beginning a career to get married? Elvin is very special to me. I don't know that I could ever meet anyone that I like more—that I love more. It was the recognition that she both liked and loved him that made her question her decision to postpone marriage.

She'd also considered Elvin and his position. He was thirty years old and his career appeared to be on the rise, especially since his column had become syndicated. She knew he loved her, and that he was in a position to get married if he chose to. Together they would have a wonderful life. But she also knew that men were hesitant to take the leap across the abyss to married life. How might she put that idea into his mind, she'd wondered. Then she had an idea.

Her father's news had almost upset her plans, though. But now everything was back on track. Better than on track, she felt, because her heartfelt remarks downstairs about her parents' marriage and on the type of man she hoped to marry had led her to indirectly broach the subject of marriage.

It was time to launch the next step in the process, the one she'd envisioned earlier in the week. "Oh," she lamented, after they had ordered dessert. "I forgot to bring the bottle of White Heron whiskey with me. But," she then added with an air of cool nonchalance, "we can go back to my apartment to open it after we finish dessert."

Elvin looked at her oddly, trying to determine if she was really so naïve as to think that a healthy young man and a healthy young woman who were in love with each other could go back to her apartment and open a bottle of whiskey together without the inevitable happening. Was she inviting him into such a situation for just that reason? Or was she just incredibly innocent? He didn't know.

"Oh, that's a good idea," he agreed, just managing to say it with an equally nonchalant air.

Once they were inside Delilah's apartment, Elvin opened the bottle.

"Happy twenty-second, delightful Delilah," he said with a smile, as their glasses touched in a toast. They had a few sips.

"Elvin, am I as beautiful as a white heron?" She looked directly into his eyes as she spoke.

"Well, do you remember that I once told you that all parts of a woman's body are usually as beautiful as her hands are, and that you have beautiful hands?"

"Yes, I do," she replied, smiling at him.

"I think the time has come to see if that theory holds true for you."

"Does your theory hold true for men as well as woman? Are all parts of your body as powerful as your hands?" she asked, lifting her head.

"Let's find out," he replied, just able to get the words out before their lips met and the fire, multiplied a thousand times in intensity by the White Heron, burned through them.

FRIDAY, AUGUST 7

143

Alan knew it was time to consider the most controversial issues within the Oxfordian movement—why and how Oxford's authorship had been hidden.

Although he'd told his students of the three speculations that form the fullest version of the Prince Tudor theory—the idea that the effort to hide Oxford's authorship was somehow related to his direct involvement in the succession to Queen Elizabeth—he still wasn't quite sure what to make of it. He now had three books with more information: Hank Whittemore's *The Monument*, Charles Beauclerk's *Shakespeare's Lost Kingdom*, and Peter Rush's *Hidden in Plain Sight*. He needed to study them carefully.

SATURDAY, AUGUST 8

144

"Alan, is that you?" Amelia whispered to the lump in bed next to her, wondering if it was him or only her pillow. It was almost dawn.

"Huh?" the lump said. "No, this isn't Alan. This is Matt Harris." He quickly turned on the light and looked at her. "So you have been sleeping with Alan Fernwood?"

Amelia knew immediately she'd made a big mistake. A big mistake in addition to the smaller one. The smaller one had been in agreeing to go home with Matt. She'd run into him in the lobby of the Harvest Hotel, where she'd gone with a few friends. She'd probably had one mojito too many as they'd celebrated the end of the term. After the others had left, she stayed in the lobby to think about how much her life had changed over the past two months. She especially wanted to think about the complications with Alan—about his finding out that it was her idea that had snowballed into his losing his job, and about the conversation she'd overheard between Delilah and her friend.

What she needed was a good hard workout in the pool. She was, she knew, a very physical person. She was just realizing that the pool was probably closed at that hour when Matt Harris sat down next to her. With the pool closed, perhaps what she needed was a night of vigorous, uncomplicated sex. So when Matt asked her to go home with him, she accepted with hardly another thought.

The other mistake—the bigger one—was letting Matt know about her relationship with Alan. Matt appeared to be dancing around the bed, gleeful that he had found a way to impress the Dean. "If Alan has slept with one of his students, he could be fired for cause. It would no longer be necessary to pay his buyout package. I will be able to impress Dean Wolpuff by reducing expenses much more than expected. This is very good news."

Amelia was shocked. From the way Alan had talked about Matt, she had assumed that they'd been friends as well as colleagues for many years.

"I'm going to take a shower," he announced.

This can't be happening, she said to herself. I must find a way to stop Matt from doing this. Then she had an idea.

145

Alan woke up early thinking about Isaac Asimov. That's odd, he thought. I haven't read anything by him in years. Perhaps it's because Asimov once wrote that "Of all the books I have ever worked on, I think *Asimov's Guide to Shakespeare* gave me the most pleasure, day in, day out. For months and months I lived and thought Shakespeare, and I don't see how there can be any greater pleasure in the world—any pleasure, that is, that one can indulge in for as much as ten hours without pause, day after day indefinitely."

Well, I can certainly understand that, Alan thought, as he continued to lie in bed. And yet, there was something else, some other thought about Asimov, that was slowly pushing its way into his consciousness.

Suddenly he had it. Asimov had once found himself in a situation similar to Alan's. His university had tried to take his teaching position away from him because the dean objected to his science writing. Asimov had pushed back, using the fact that he had tenure to keep his position, though in a non-teaching, unpaid status.

That's just what I'll try to do, Alan said to himself, studying the buyout agreement he'd signed. Yes! The agreement had only specified that he would no longer *teach* at the university. It didn't say anything about his position as a tenured Associate Professor. Thus, he reasoned, I could insist on retaining the tenured position even if I don't teach and am not paid. It'll be like taking an extended sabbatical.

This is exciting, he thought. I would no longer have an office on campus, but would still have the title and the use of the library and other resources. I should present this scenario to Matt right away. Now that the agreement is signed, I no longer have to fear losing the buyout. I can fight to maintain my position.

146

Alan reached Matt's house and jogged up the few steps to the porch. He was just about to ring the doorbell when he happened to look in the window. There was Amelia, wearing a robe, engaged in a conversation of some importance with Matt.

He moved away from the window so that he wouldn't be seen. No, that can't be Amelia. It must be somebody else, he told himself. He looked in again. Yes, it is her. He thought of Troilus observing Cressida with Diomedes, of his disbelief at what he was seeing. That is and is not Cressida, Troilus had said. That was what Alan felt now. He decided not to ring the bell. It would be better to see each of them separately.

Alan waited for Amelia a block away, on the way back toward her apartment, guessing that she would pass by on her way home. He sat on a low brick wall, just around a corner, so that the sight of him would catch her by surprise. Half an hour later, Amelia came around the corner. She saw Alan and stopped. She didn't say anything.

"Hello, Amelia. How are you this morning?"

She didn't answer at first, then finally uttered a weak "Hi, Alan. What are you doing here?"

"Waiting for you. What were you doing here?"

"I'm just on my way home," she said before realizing that that was probably not the best response.

"Home from where, Amelia? From Matt Harris's house? I'm wondering why you might have been at Matt's house, wearing his bathrobe, so early in the morning."

"Alan, this isn't what it looks like." Her mind was spinning as she considered how best to explain things.

"The situation isn't what it looks like, Alan," she began again. "Yes, I spent the night with Matt, but I did it in order to blackmail him to protect you. He found out about our relationship and he's planning to use that knowledge to impress the Dean. On Monday morning he's going to have your buyout package canceled to cut the department's expenses because the University can now fire you for cause.

"The only thing I could think of so quickly to help you was sleeping with Matt so that I could blackmail him. Look, I took photos of him with my phone when he was in the shower to use as evidence that he seduced one of the students in his Department."

Alan pushed her hand away. "Photos of Matt Harris naked are the last thing I want to look at."

"Then look at these," she urged him. "I even took pictures of myself crying in his bed while he was in the shower."

Alan glanced at the phone. "You are beautiful even when you are crying. How did you learn that he had found out about us?"

"I was at the lobby of the Harvest Hotel with some other students. When I went to the restroom I had to pass by the bar area. Matt was there with some other men, and I overheard him telling them about his plan. I was horrified. I had to do something quickly to stop him. I have noticed the way he has looked at me, and I had to use his interest to trap him. After all, if Alan Fernwood could be fired for sleeping with a student, so could Matt Harris."

That sounds plausible, he thought. "How did he find out about us?"

"I don't know. I didn't think to ask him that. Maybe he or someone else saw us together. We have been rather careless in public lately."

Neither of them said anything for a minute. Then Alan asked if she had been planning to tell him about all this.

"Yes, of course I would have, Alan. Or maybe not. It all happened so quickly last night; I haven't had time to think about it."

Alan considered the situation for a while. "I'm amazed," he finally said. "I knew you were brilliant, I knew you were audacious, I knew you could think fast on your feet. But I never knew you could come up with such a plan on the spur of the moment. I didn't know that your love was deep enough that you would sacrifice yourself for me in this way. I'm sorry I doubted you."

Amelia didn't say anything as she squeezed his arm and rested her head on his shoulder.

"I'm going to go see Matt," he told her. "This is just the leverage I need to push him to act." He explained his idea to her and then headed toward Matt's house.

As Amelia walked home she hoped that Matt wouldn't say anything that contradicted her story. Luckily, she'd had the foresight to take the photos of herself pretending to cry. Actually, she'd been so upset that it hadn't been all pretense.

147

Hearing the doorbell, Matt saw Alan through the window. Alan was the last person in the world he wanted to see right now. Thank God Amelia has already left, he thought as he opened the door.

"What brings you over here so early in the morning, Alan?"

"Whoa, it looks like you had quite a time here last night, Matt," Alan observed, looking past him into the living room.

"Oh, I had a few friends over. I'm just now cleaning the mess up. We had too much to drink to take care of it last night."

A few friends or only one? Alan was about to ask. But he stopped himself in time.

After Alan explained his idea of retaining his professorship but in a non-teaching capacity, Matt shook his head. "It's a brilliant idea, but Dean Wolpuff would never go for it. She particularly wants you out because of the waves you are making with this Shakespeare authorship thing of yours. You know how domineering she is. Or maybe you don't. But either way, take my word for it. She is as imperious as they come. Once she has made up her mind about something, she doesn't listen to anybody. I can't push her on this point, Alan. I can't even raise the issue with her."

"But that is just what you are going to do, Matt," Alan told him, stiffening his tone. "On Monday morning you are going to see Dean Wolpuff and tell her that Dr. Alan Fernwood will retain his professorship, but in a non-teaching, non-salaried capacity."

Matt looked at him. "You must be crazy, Alan. Why would I take a career-damaging step like that?"

"You will do it, Matt, because if you don't you will face a career-ending situation. I will inform the University that you have been sleeping with a student in your own Department. Not just any student, but a Fulbright student who turned to you for assistance. Instead of helping her, you lured her back to your house, got her drunk, and fucked her."

"How did you—" Matt started to say. "That's crazy. You have no evidence that any of that took place."

"Actually, I do," Alan said. "Amelia took pictures with her phone. She even took pictures of herself crying while you were in the shower."

"What? Why would she do that? Alan, look, you and I are friends. We have been friends for decades. Why are you putting me into this difficult position?" The thought flashed through Matt's mind that Amelia might not have told Alan the full story, but he quickly pushed it away so that he could focus on Alan's threat.

Alan had a look of disgust on his face as he replied. "To answer your second question first, yes, I had thought we were friends. But when I heard how gleeful you were about finding out about my relationship with Amelia because you could make points with the Dean by getting my buyout package canceled, I realized just how hollow our friendship is. Or rather how little it means to you if you're willing to throw it overboard to raise your balloon a few inches with the Dean. Do you really think she cares at all about this?

"And to answer your first question, Amelia actually cares about me. She was shocked to see you dancing around with job about taking an action that would harm someone she cares about. But she is a good enough actress to hide her feelings then and later in your bed in order to do something to save someone she loves. You didn't actually think she enjoyed being with you, did you? Or that it would ever happen again?"

"You know, I thought I saw flashes of light when I was showering, but then dismissed them as my imagination," Matt said. "Okay, Alan, I will raise the issue with the Dean on Monday."

"You will do more than that, Matt," Alan said stiffly. "You will make sure that she signs off on my maintaining my position as Associate Professor in an unpaid non-teaching status. There are no points for trying here. You will succeed or I'll inform the University about your seduction of Amelia."

SUNDAY, AUGUST 9

148

Amelia stared at the wall. The situation is getting too complicated, she thought. She needed to figure out what to do, but didn't know if she could sort out it all out by herself. She needed to talk to Phuong.

Between the two of them they should be able to figure out what she should do.

An hour later Amelia found herself at Phuong's house. They were seated at a table on the patio, looking out on the garden. Tom wasn't home, fortunately, so they could speak freely. She explained the situation, with all its intricate details.

"Well, Amelia, when you called I thought the problem might involve Alan, as I suppose we should call him from now on. But it's a bigger mess than I anticipated."

Amelia looked at her, and sniffed a few times. Her tears appeared to be stopping, at least for now.

"Let me summarize, as best I can, what you have just told me. First, you are in love with Alan and he is in love with you." Amelia nodded.

"Second, Alan is married."

"Yes."

"Third, you slept with Alan's boss in order to blackmail him, to stop him from doing something bad to Alan, and he found out about it."

Amelia nodded again. There was no need to explain to Phuong that she'd actually slept with Matt in a moment of weakness. Or that Matt had found out about her and Alan because of a mistake she'd made while in bed with him. Or, for that matter, that her comments to the Department Chairs about an Asian Studies program had started the ball rolling in the first place.

"Fourth, Alan knows why you slept with his boss, that you sacrificed yourself for his sake. Yes, I can see that would be a problem. Even if Alan understands intellectually why you slept with his boss, he will still feel emotionally that you wronged him."

"That's the biggest problem," Amelia confirmed. "I don't know how to square things with Alan. But there is more. His wife returns home next week. Alan says he will end the marriage then, but can he? I know he loves me, but divorce is such a painful process. Alan is a strong man, but is he strong enough to go through with it? So there is the possibility that he will not leave his wife, with all the pain that will mean for me.

"Even if he decides to get a divorce, I don't know if I am strong enough to go through the process with him. The year leading up to my own divorce two years ago was so painful that it almost killed me. I don't know if I can go through that again, even though I would not be one of the two directly involved."

The two women continued to ponder the situation silently. Then Amelia spoke. "There are a few more pieces that might or might not fit into this puzzle. One is that I have other options. The Fulbright program placed me into three universities. One of them I didn't want to attend at all. But the other one was as good as Cary University in nearly every way. I went back and forth before deciding to come here.

"That other university still wants me, and has even offered me a full tuition waiver. The Chair of the Literature Department contacted me just a few days ago to say he is holding a place open for me. Because it would be much cheaper than Cary University, I'm sure that the Fulbright program would approve my changing universities even at this late stage. It's not uncommon for Fulbright students to attend their summer orientation program and academic program at different universities."

Sharing her situation with Phuong had been just what she'd needed, Amelia thought during the bus ride back to her apartment. She felt relieved and even managed a small smile. Her emotions were once again well ordered. From having overcome so many difficulties in the past, she knew that she had the internal strength to do what needed to be done.

149

"Hello," Alan said, answering his phone in an emotionless tone. It was dark out, but it was too early to go to bed. He had no energy to work on any of his literary projects, not even enough to balance the checkbook.

"Alan, it's me," Amelia said. "Might you be able to come over?"

"Um—"

"Alan, I want you. I need you. Please come over."

"Okay. I will be right there," he told her, hanging up the phone.

He was relieved that she had called and wanted to see him, but unnerved about sleeping with her after she had slept with Matt. He understood her reasons, but somehow it left him feeling soiled. He imagined that she felt even worse.

"Come in, Alan," Amelia said with a tight smile as she opened the door. "I am so glad you are here. I'm so worried about you and about us. I spent much of the day crying."

He looked at her red and swollen eyes. "I know, Amelia. I'm sure you feel even worse than I do. I feel uneasy, unsettled. I know that tomorrow or someday soon I will feel grateful to you for having stopped Matt from cancelling my buyout package. But right now, the way it had to be done is too distressing to think about.

"I had thought Matt was a friend, and that as Department Chair he had reasons to be grateful to me for the conferences I organized that gave this department a national reputation. 'I have done the state some service, and they know it,' as Othello once said. But nothing can stop a man of ambition from using every means to advance himself."

"Alan, hold me. Hold me like you will never let me go." She pressed herself against him. They held each other silently for a long time.

Finally she spoke. "Alan, do you remember that I told you that 101 percent of Vietnamese men have affairs, and that their wives accept that as long as they are matters of the body only and not of the heart? And that the reason they tolerate them is because they know that men and women have different desires?"

He nodded.

"But there are three factors in the equation, and all three must be acknowledged. The first is that men and women sometimes have sex together for love; they make love. The second is that men sometimes have sex with women not for love, but only for physical pleasure. The third factor is less widely recognized. It is that women also sometimes have sex with men not for love. But when they do, it's usually not for physical pleasure but to accomplish other non-sexual goals."

"The reason I had sex with Matt was to help you, to save your buyout package because I know how important that is. I did it for your daughter, because I know you need the buyout to pay her university tuition."

"Well, when you put it like that, it doesn't seem quite so bad."

"If you cannot accept my sacrifice then you are a smaller man than I thought you were." Then she added, "However small you might have been a moment ago, I can feel that you are getting bigger by the second."

"Yes, I can feel my desire returning like the tide coming in at the beach. But much quicker." And with that, they kissed with the most heartfelt kisses either of them had ever given or received. An instant later they were in the bedroom.

Late that night Amelia watched from her balcony as Alan walked through the parking lot to the street. Seeing her looking at him, Alan recalled the scene in *Cymbeline* in which Imogen watches Posthumus's departing ship until it could no longer be seen. He waved good night before turning the corner, and walked slowly back to his house.

Just as he turned the corner, Amelia waved goodbye. She then sighed and sat down at the table to write the letter to Alan that she knew had to be written. She hoped she could finish it before the tears came again.

MONDAY, AUGUST 10

150

It had been a good term, Alan felt as he waited for the final class session to begin. All six students had been interested in Shakespeare, and had given up a significant part of their summer to participate in an intense seminar on his plays. They couldn't have found a better way to spend their summer, he thought.

The students arrived one by one, rather than in small groups as they usually did. Fifteen minutes into the hour, though, Amelia still hadn't arrived. Alan decided not to wait any longer. He took the first bottle of champagne out of the ice and gave it to Dave to open. Lisa handed out the plastic cups. They toasted each other for having survived such a demanding course.

Alan then made a few remarks. "This class might be the one and only time in your lives that you will have the chance to immerse yourself in the works of the writer widely regarded as the greatest in the English language and in fact in all of Western civilization. In the cultural area, that civilization at its peak includes Mozart and Beethoven and Stravinsky. And Rembrandt and Cezanne, and Rodin. And those who built the Gothic cathedrals. But topping them all is Shakespeare. Unlike all the others I mentioned, he uses words. He speaks directly to our intelligence without the need for specialized musical or artistic knowledge. He helps us, more than any other writer, to understand ourselves and the world around us.

"This course was designed to show you the subjects of most interest to Shakespeare. I hope it will serve as a foundation for a lifelong effort to learn from him and his work. For more than for any other writer, experience is needed to appreciate Shakespeare. Younger students might enjoy love stories like *Romeo and Juliet*. But for most people, decades of involvement with the issues of adult life are needed to understand the nuances of Shakespeare's portrayals. I hope you will continue to read and reread his works over the course of your lives. You will get more out of each play with each reading as your experience in life becomes wider and deeper. I guarantee it."

Alan then offered a toast, and brought out another bottle of champagne. Amelia still hadn't arrived, so Nancy made a few remarks on behalf of the class. She revealed that they'd learned from Amelia, who'd overheard a comment made in the Department office, that this was Alan's last term teaching at Cary University. They all wanted him to remember them, his final class, and had a small present for him.

Alan felt grateful. They were doing more for him than the University was at the end of a dozen years of distinguished achievements. He unwrapped the present and laughed. "An Edward de Vere coffee mug! Wherever did you get it?" he asked, smiling at each of them in turn.

"Oh, we found it on e-Bay," Pat told him.

"We're just glad it arrived in time," Lisa added.

"This is the nicest gift I have ever received," Alan said. "And it is from the most enjoyable group of students I have ever taught. Thank you, one and all. And I have something for you, too." He handed each of them a copy of *Shakespeare Beyond Doubt?*

Word that this was Alan's final term had somehow gotten out. As the students from his final class began to drift away, a few students from previous classes and several faculty colleagues wandered in. Whether to say goodbye to him or to have some free champagne, it wasn't entirely clear. He opened the final bottle, and with one conversation after another taking place, it was close to noon before he was alone.

After the room had cleared, Alan thought a bit about each of his last six students. They'd all shown up for all class meetings, prepared for them, and participated in the discussions. If only all classes were as enjoyable as this one, he thought, teaching would be heaven on Earth.

Dave, more than the others, had regard for power, authority, order, and probably the ability to get things done through a chain of command. He enjoyed his life, and so others enjoyed having him as a friend.

Doug was quieter, but observant of everything going on around him. He certainly had an extensive knowledge of TV shows and movies. At the same time, his comments showed he could draw connections between disparate subjects. That would be useful in legal work, Alan thought. He also had a good sense of humor that was unexpected.

Pat had the good cheer and camaraderie that would make him popular in whatever group he found himself. He'll probably end up in a career that combines a specialized ability with the need to engage other people easily.

Nancy was smart, no doubt about that. She also had a lot of business sense, and the ability to use her intelligence to manage organizations, or to figure out how best to manage the people in them.

Lisa has strong beliefs, which she backed up by careful attention to detail. She'll keep any group focused on its goals, he thought. She also had a good sense of humor, though it didn't come out as often as Doug's or Pat's.

Alan kept his impressions of Amelia limited to what he knew from the class meetings. She brought a non-American perspective to many of the discussions, which was very useful. She was probably the most brilliant of all of them, and had read more widely in literature and philosophy than the others. She had a playful side, but at the same time seemed to be a very private person.

I will wonder what has become of them, Alan thought. That's one of the downfalls of being a professor. So many interesting people pass through and then disappear. Except, of course, the one who'd become a lifelong soulmate.

As he walked over to the Department office, Alan thought it odd that Amelia hadn't been at the final class meeting, even though it was optional. The other students were disappointed, too, he could tell. She had been an integral part of their discussions, and, as she'd explained to him, they regarded her as a big sister. With her brilliance, insights, and ability to bring people together, she was a natural leader.

Oh, well, he thought to himself, I'll see her later today.

151

Matt entered Dean Wolpuff's office hoping he would have the fortitude and craftiness to get her authorization for Alan's unpaid non-teaching status while still keeping his own position as Department Chair.

But the Dean was having none of it. "What? Why are you bringing this outrageous plan to me? You know I will never approve it." Matt was silent, trying to decide just how hard to push on behalf of Alan's request.

"And that reminds me," she said, changing the subject. "I have been looking over the numbers. Eliminating Fernwood's and the other positions we discussed and farming their courses out to part-time teaching staff won't save enough money to fund the Asian Studies literature courses. Let's also eliminate the courses on science fiction."

To that proposal Matt didn't need any time to think. "Science fiction is important," he argued. "It brings in new perspectives on human life, perspectives that don't arise in literature written from more usual points of view. Isaac Asimov, Robert Heinlein, Ray Bradbury—these writers are important. We can't possibly eliminate those courses." He didn't add that he himself taught all science fiction courses.

"What difference does it make, Matt? So we move the perspective from outer space to Asia. It's still an unusual point from which to view human life. And besides, everybody knows that sci fi isn't real literature. Not like Mark Twain's works."

Matt was angry now. He stood up and spoke without thinking.

"Dean Wolpuff, Mark Twain's novel *A Connecticut Yankee in Sir Arthur's Court* is a marvelous book, set in the past. Isaac Asimov's

Foundation Trilogy is a marvelous series, set in the future. If I had to choose between them, I would say that Asimov's is the more valuable contribution to American literature. The Literature Department will not eliminate its science fiction courses. And further, Alan Fernwood has made major contributions to the Literature Department over the past decade. I urge you to approve his retaining his professorship, though in a non-paid, non-teaching capacity."

"Matt," Dean Wolpuff responded, rising angrily from her chair, "if you continue to push for Fernwood's position, you will be gone. Maybe not from the University, but from your position as Department Chair."

Her face was red as she leaned over her desk toward Matt, and Matt's was equally heated as he leaned forward toward her.

"Actually, Dean Wolpuff, you don't have the power to do that. Department Chairs are elected by the faculty. Faculty throughout the School of Arts and Humanities are furious over the elimination of positions and the loss of some of their most senior and accomplished professors. They will back me 100 percent on this. If a new election is called regarding the Chairmanship of the Literature Department, even those who didn't vote for me before would vote for me now as a sign of their opposition to you and your actions.

"So, you can approve this unpaid non-teaching status for Fernwood quietly, or I'll pass the idea on to the other Department Chairs, who will, I'm sure, demand similar status for the other professors who received buyouts. Do your worst, Dean Wolpuff. If you don't sign off on Fernwood's new status, I expect that your tenure at Cary University will be rather short."

For the first time in her professional life, Mary Wolpuff found nothing to say.

Walking out of the building, Matt began shaking. He was amazed that he'd been courageous enough to stand up for Alan and terrified that the whole situation would blow up in his face. Perhaps I wouldn't have been so outspoken if she hadn't insulted science fiction again, he thought. But mostly he was relieved that the conversation was over. Come what may, he was proud that he'd done everything he could to right things with Alan. The Dean was a bully, he reasoned, and like all bullies would back down when faced with strength. Time will tell if I have analyzed the situation correctly or not. Anyway, it's now outside my hands.

There was no reason why Cary University couldn't host Alan's conference on the Shakespeare authorship question, Matt thought. Alan might not be teaching any longer, but with luck he would remain a tenured professor. And, he reasoned, if the authorship issue should catch fire within academia, it would be good to be on the right side of history.

152

Alan walked into the Literature Department office to check his mailbox. Not much of importance today, he saw. There was an envelope, though, with no marking on it except his name. Inside he found a handwritten letter; how odd, he thought before recognizing Amelia's handwriting. The first sentence alone jolted him. He stopped reading and staggered into the nearest chair. I can't read this here, he realized, and forced himself to get up and leave the office.

Somehow he managed to walk to a bench under the elms, the same bench where he had sat with Amelia when he described the scene from *Pillow Talk*. He started the letter again, reading from the top of the page.

10 August

Dear Alan,

Writing this letter is the hardest thing I have ever had to do in my life.

I have loved every minute that we have spent together because I have loved you. I love you still. But the time has come for me to begin a life apart from you. We are the right people for each other, but the circumstances are not right for us to establish a life together.

You know that I am a realist, that I always try to adapt myself to reality. The reality now is that if I stay at Cary University the pain of seeing you, the man I love, married to someone else, would be too great. The only way I can avoid it is by leaving.

You know how painful my divorce was for me. I cannot go through another one, not even one in which I am not a direct party. Because you would be directly involved, I would inevitably feel your pain during that long difficult process.

I also could not handle the guilt I would feel by being the cause of the pain that the divorce would bring to your wife and children. I have always tried to act properly and being the cause of a divorce would not be a proper way to act.

But there is another aspect of the situation, Alan. I think that you probably love your wife far more than you realize. You have spent so many years together and overcome so many difficult times together. Even if she cannot share your intellectual interests, you have a life together, a marriage together, and it is a good marriage. I could not bear to be the cause of it breaking apart.

I know that I could not remain at this university, so close to you, and stay away from you. Trying to do so would tear me apart. The only solution is for me to leave.

I will remember you with love, Alan, every time I read a book of literature and every time I see a romantic scene in a movie.

My grandfather was right; it will be hard for me to find a man of my own. I will always remember you as the first man I ever truly wanted. But you are not free, and I must try to find one who is.

I must move on quickly to minimize the pain that the break with you will cause me. I am convinced that this is the best way for you, too, Alan.

The previous two times I backed away, in June and early July, you were a gentleman. You let me go. Please do the same now.

Amelia Mai

153

Thank God the sun has gone down and this day will soon end, Alan thought. He was at home, having a glass or two or three of Riesling, and listening to music. Sometimes the only solace for pain is music, he thought. Classical music. Beethoven. Beethoven and wine are a good combination.

Alan was in torment. He'd experienced hard times before, like everybody else, but it had usually been possible to see those times coming and to prepare for them. Not this time.

Listening to the music kept his mind focused on something other than the developments that were causing him such pain. He considered how music could mirror the emotional contours of thought by rising and falling in intensity as tempos, volume, or keys changed; or as tone colors varied or textures thickened beneath the melody. Those changes could happen in smooth or jarring ways. They could occur to a greater or lesser degree, and the rate at which they occured could itself vary, all of which mirrors, somehow, our fluid emotional states.

Alan had put together an all-Beethoven play-list of pieces that matched his state of mind. He had already listened to the funeral march from the *Eroica Symphony*, the slow movement of the *Seventh*

Symphony, the entire *Tempest Sonata*, the Adagio of the *Pathetique Sonata* and other works that somehow embodied bearing up under pain that was unbearable but had to be borne.

He had worked himself up to the piece that he always held in reserve for the times when life was at its stormiest, the *Piano Sonata No. 31*. He didn't quite understand why, but that piece held a special ability to soothe his mind. Perhaps he would conclude with the *String Quartet in C-sharp Minor*, a work so complex that it blotted out thoughts of any other subject. Tomorrow he might turn to Shostakovich, another composer who knew something about suffering.

As he listened to Beethoven, Alan reviewed the hours after receiving Amelia's letter. He had gone straight to her apartment. There'd been no answer at her door, but he'd run into one of the other residents on her floor. She said that Amelia had left for the airport that morning, and that she was transferring to another university. Just this morning, she'd said, Amelia had given her some small pieces of furniture from her apartment.

He'd heard the same story of her departure at the International Student Office when he had checked in there, so it was probably true. It made sense. He knew that she'd been accepted at two other universities, including one that had excellent programs in linguistics and literature.

She must have dropped off the letter at the Department office while he was in the final class meeting, and then gone directly to the airport. She would have been able to take her belongings with her, as she hadn't accumulated much, only some clothes and books, most of which he'd given her.

He drifted off to sleep and didn't wake up until the sun was shining.

TUESDAY, AUGUST 11

154

Well, that was a blessing, Alan thought, sleeping through the night. His unconscious brain, though, had been working overtime while he slept, and question after question now flooded into his mind.

First those that dealt with Amelia. Was she only a fair-weather friend? Did she leave because he no longer had a job? What was her real story? Had she really loved him, or had it all been a lie? Had she merely been looking for a man with an established position to grab for a husband for herself and a father for her son? Was she only looking for a green card? Was her love of literature only a pretense? He recalled how she'd dressed and styled her hair so beautifully for their first dinner. Was it really all just a setup that fell apart when he lost his job?

What was the situation with Matt? Had she slept with him only to save his buyout package? When had she really started sleeping with him? Had she ever stopped? Then there were the questions about himself. Should he follow her? Should he forget her? Should he end his marriage? Should he bury himself in his work? It was hard to know what to do.

Alan knew he was torturing himself with these questions, but he was powerless to stop them. He wanted to believe what her letter said, that she couldn't endure the pain of staying away from him if she remained at Cary University and if he remained married. That she couldn't endure the guilt she would feel if he and Diana divorced. That she had chosen the quickest way to end the pain, that of cutting him out of her life.

He remembered the times he'd recognized that he couldn't leave Diana, that he wasn't strong enough to end it all. Amelia hadn't known that, but she'd been right. He had a real marriage, a strong one, even if Diana couldn't share his life of the mind.

But at other times he railed against the situation. How could she have left me, he asked, forgetting that he'd never asked her the question he'd wanted to ask her. Remembering that calmed him. It wasn't as if he'd asked her to marry him and she'd turned him down. He wondered what Amelia would do if she were in his situation. But he already knew the answer. She would do exactly what he would probably ending up doing, if he could. She'd adapt to the reality of the situation, get through the difficult time and move on. He had to let her go.

Should he contact her? Maybe an e-mail just to let her know that he'd received her letter, if he could hold himself back to that simple confirmation. He would send a message today. Or maybe not; he would decide later. The thought of contacting her launched another round of questions. Did she really want him to let her go? Did she want him to come after her? Did she want him to stay in touch with her?

He always came back to the same conclusions. She meant what she said in the letter. Cutting him out of her life was the decision she'd made in order to minimize the pain for both of them, though right now his pain didn't feel very minimal.

Alan tried to work on his Oxfordian game plan, but the words and thoughts wouldn't come. So he did the next best thing. He read. He needed words from books to keep the words of his questions out of his mind during the day. Music worked best after the sun had gone down.

155

"Hmm," Elvin thought. Ever since his dinners with Alan, he'd been reflecting on the similarities between how believers in human-caused global warming and believers in Shakspere's authorship of Shakespeare's works responded to their critics. Then he'd heard the distressing news of Alan's departure from the University. The idea of a "Contrarian" column addressing these issues began to form in his mind.

Those issues dovetailed with another he'd been wanting to write on—the difficulty of forming correct beliefs when external and internal pressures push the other way. The external pressures came, of course, from other people who want their beliefs to become widely held. They try to bring forceful pressures to bear on those who doubt them. That was the "logic" behind labeling those who doubted the idea of human-caused global warming "anti-climate" or even "anti-Earth," and those who doubted Shakspere's authorship "anti-Shakespeare."

The internal pressures include the human proclivity for forming emotional attachments to ideas and beliefs as well as to people and things. It was an odd human trait that those attachments remained in place even after all the original reasons for a belief had been demolished.

The situation reminded him of a story about a group of monkeys. A bunch of bananas had been hung from the top of their cage, too high for them to reach without standing on a chair. But every time one of them stood on it, the cage was sprayed with ice-cold water. The monkeys learned not to reach for the bananas. Then one of the original monkeys was replaced by a new one. When he tried to stand on the chair, the others beat him up to stop him. The same thing occurred as, one by one, each of the other original monkeys were replaced. Even after all of those who had been sprayed with cold water were gone, the new monkeys continued to stop each other from reaching for the bananas.

Elvin didn't know if such an experiment had actually been conducted. But he found it plausible, given what he'd observed of the willingness of his fellow human beings to blindly accept belief in ideas they'd never investigated for themselves. Without any further preparation he began to write the column.

Shakespeare Is Innocent!

So far, "The Contrarian" has commented almost exclusively on scientific matters. It is therefore with some amazement we note that our comment generating the most intense reader response was the brief reference to the Shakespeare authorship question—"William Shakspere wrote Shakespeare. Edward de Vere, Earl of Oxford, wrote

Shakespeare"—in last week's "What's a Girl To Do?" column.

That caught us by surprise, given the controversial nature of the other issues we've addressed. Nevertheless, we can see the reason for it. The debate between proponents of those two candidates for authorship of Shakespeare's works is hot and heavy. Few subjects in academia generate as much fire and light as the clash between supporters of William Shakspere's authorship and those of Edward de Vere's.

What has struck us most forcefully is the similarity in how holders of two dominant theories—human-caused global warming and Shakspere's authorship of Shakespeare's works—respond to those who doubt them. In both cases, the primary response hasn't been to point out doubters' mistakes in evidence, interpretation of evidence or flaws in logic, but instead to attack them personally. Doubters have been subjected to attacks on their sanity, their personalities, their morality—even their table manners!—but rarely on their evidence or logic. Something strange is afoot when that is the principal reaction.

Without daring to take sides on the authorship issue, it's interesting to note that several people with no skin in the game who initially believed that Shakspere was the author changed their minds after investigating the subject. One was Michael H. Hart, author of of *The 100: A Ranking of the Most Influential Persons in History: Revised and Updated for the Nineties.* Hart carefully examined the arguments on both sides while preparing the second edition of his book, and concluded that "the skeptics have much the better of the argument and have reasonably established their case." He then changed his Entry 31 from "William Shakespeare" in the first edition to "Edward de Vere" in the second.

Two others who changed their minds are James F. Broderick and Darren W. Miller, authors of *Web of Conspiracy: A Guide to Conspiracy Theory Sites on the Internet,* published in 2008. As Broderick explained, "What I discovered is that most [conspiracy theories] do not hold up under scrutiny. The more one digs, the shakier and less credible they become. The Authorship Question was different. The more I dug, the more credible it seemed, until I became fully convinced of its validity. What I had set out expecting to debunk turned out to be the most compelling, fact-based 'conspiracy' I had ever researched."

The latest battle in the Authorship War was just fought right here, at Cary University. Literature Professor Alan Fernwood, a lifelong believer in Shakspere's authorship, was bitten by the Oxfordian bug a couple of months ago. The disease spread quickly, leaving him a complete convert to Edward de Vere's authorship. Enraged by his heresy and his efforts to promote it, his colleagues prevailed upon the university to have his position abolished, thus ending his teaching career there. Tenure apparently means nothing when one's crime is challenging authorship by the beloved Mr. Shakspere, a known moneylender and grainhoarder.

What is especially galling about this development is that Fernwood's was the sole remaining position specializing on the greatest master of the English language. His departure leaves the University not only with no requirement that its English majors take a course on Shakespeare's works, but also without a scholar with a national reputation on the greatest works written in the language.

It's shameful that Fernwood's position will be replaced by one specializing in Asian literature. We have nothing against literary works from across the Pacific and have enjoyed reading Asian authors over the years. But was it really necessary to eliminate the sole remaining Shakespeare position to make room for an Asian literature specialist?

Readers might recall our earlier distinction between professors (who seek the truth) and politicians (who seek personal gain). Fernwood is clearly one of the professors. He remains uncowed by recent developments, and is determined to spread the word of Oxford's authorship far and wide. Whether this Intellectual Warrior is courageous or foolhardy we don't dare to say, but we can't help admiring his willingness to fight to reclaim territory in academia lost over recent decades to philistines smugly indifferent to cultural values, intellectual pursuits and aesthetic refinement.

We wish Fernwood the best of luck in this uphill challenge to bring to his blinkered (former) colleagues the enlightenment on the authorship issue that exists in so much of the world outside academia.

156

Intellectually, Alan knew that Amelia's decision was best for both of them. Or was it? How could he possibly know something like that for sure? He wondered if he would ever have answers to his questions. Would he have to live the rest of his life not knowing if acquiescing in her departure had been the best thing to do?

He turned to a related issue. Assuming Amelia was gone for good, at some point the pain of her departure would lessen. But how long would it take to get to that point? It takes ten minutes to get over the impulse to buy junk food, he had heard. How long does it take to get over the loss of a soulmate? Ten days? Ten weeks? Does it ever happen? How would he get to that point, assuming it ever occurred? How would he survive with his mind intact from now until then?

Alan then remembered the book that Amelia had given him, Aldous Huxley's *Island*. He decided to read it now after recalling her description of how it had helped her get through difficult times. He saw that one of its messages was that everybody has painful memories—of abusive people, of hurts and slights, of losses and regrets. None of these things can be changed, and nothing positive can be gained by dwelling on them even if that is what our minds want to do.

The people on Huxley's fictional island taught themselves from childhood onwards to avoid the downward emotional pull from painful memories by focusing on the present and the future. Whenever someone succumbed to painful thoughts of the past, a friend or relative was at hand to pull him or her back to the present. "Here and now!" and "Pay attention!" were catch phrases with them. They had even taught parrots to say these two phrases, and as a result heard them repeated at odd moments throughout the day. By the end of the book, a newcomer had absorbed that way of thinking, and so could pull back one of his island friends who was sinking into a cesspool of emotion.

The book had helped Amelia, Alan recalled, by encouraging her to pay attention to the world around her in two ways. One was to seek out enjoyment and meaning in whatever situation she found herself. The world was full of people and books and music to be explored and enjoyed. The point was to focus on things outside of herself, something that couldn't happen if she became mired in thoughts of the past.

The other way was by working to become the fullest person she could be. That required focusing on the present and the future, on working to acquire the skills and abilities she would need to take advantage of future opportunities. Alan knew that the person he was meant to be was a researcher and writer, and the subject that absorbed his interest now was the Shakespeare authorship question. Delving into it, designing his game plan and working to carry it out was what interested him most. What goal could possibly be more important than helping to garner rightful recognition for Edward de Vere as the author of the greatest literary creations in human history?

He recalled Amelia's comment that Huxley had written *Island* in his mid-sixties, shortly before his death. He could see that the book couldn't have been written by a young man, but only by someone who had suffered many hurts—mostly received, but also some given and regretted—and who had to find a way to live without being overly burdened by memories of the past.

WEDNESDAY, AUGUST 12

157

In the morning it occurred to Alan that Amelia was trying to "wash that man right out of her hair and send him on his way." He regretted that he wouldn't have the chance to share that moment from *South Pacific* with her.

But then another thought occurred to him. Does "Here and Now," and "Pay Attention" and washing him out of her hair mean that Amelia is trying to erase him out of her memory as well as her present? That thought depressed him almost as much as her departure had. I was her soulmate as much as she was mine, he thought. Or was I? Are her memories of me as precious as mine are of her?

Does it really have to be all or nothing, black or white, he wondered. Is there a way we could maintain some kind of friendship, perhaps the literary one that we enjoyed so much? Suddenly he heard the young Frank Sinatra in his head singing "All or Nothing At All." Does it have to be that way? Maybe after the pain of the separation had eased a bit, if that ever happens, their friendship could be resumed.

Alan recalled two things indicating that probably wasn't possible. One was the advice Amelia mentioned she'd received from a friend. "The quickest way to lose a friend is to sleep with him." The other was when they'd watched *When Harry Met Sally* together. That scene after Harry and Sally had finally slept together and realized that having done so was destroying their relationship. Harry says to Sally something like, "I'm not saying that sex doesn't mean anything, but why does it have to mean everything?" Her response had been unanswerable: "Because it does." Amelia had nodded in agreement with Sally, and repeated those words later when they discussed the movie.

Alan then remembered Amelia's description of the categories, positions and boxes that people occupied, and the pre-set relations among them. Intellectually, he'd understood what she was talking about, but it had never occurred to him that she'd placed him in one of her boxes and herself in another.

That realization came as a shock. To him, what had happened between them was personal, between the two of them only. But apparently not to her. Could it be, he wondered, that because I no longer fit into any of her boxes I no longer exist for her? He no longer fit into the sponsor/mentor box, he could see, because he didn't have a position at the University. He didn't fit into the spousal box because he was married. He wasn't in the lover box, because lovers shared only their bodies, not their minds. That left only friends. But one didn't sleep with friends. There was no other box. She didn't know what to do with him, so she'd had to cut him out. Was that the right explanation?

If there is any accuracy to this analysis, Amelia is far more tough minded than I am, Alan thought, and more than most Americans are. We don't think like this. He knew that her adherence to the rules was an Asian way of thinking. And yet he didn't know any other Asians, even among his in-laws, who adhered so strictly to it.

Maybe that was one of the reasons he loved her. She'd found a way to deal with the pain of the awful situations she had faced when young, and later, during her divorce. To cut the pain—present and future—out of her life, she'd been forced to cut him out of her life. Perhaps she was like a wild animal caught in a trap that must chew off its own paw to escape. If so, he again admired her acute sense of reality and her toughness in adapting to it. She would have been one of the survivors of the death camps.

What hurt the most—no, he couldn't say "the most" because so many aspects of the situation hurt him—was that she had left without even saying goodbye in person. He realized with a jolt that on Sunday night when he had waved good-night to her and she had waved back, she'd been waving goodbye. She had known then that she'd be leaving the next day.

Alan sensed that he was calming down because his unconscious brain was beginning to provide answers to his questions. He knew that Amelia wasn't a fair-weather friend and that she suffered as much as he did. He knew she had a deep love of literature and a life of the mind. It wasn't merely a pretense.

He also found that he couldn't disagree with anything she'd said in her letter. She had covered all the bases. It's not enough to meet the right person, to fall in love with the right person. One must also meet that person at the right time. If one has already assumed obligations to other people and formed emotional ties with them, then breaking those obligations and ties has costs—costs that would inevitably color the relationship with the new person even if she was a soulmate.

He grudgingly accepted that her departure had saved both of them a lot of pain over an extended period of time, with unknown results at the end of it. He knew that her strong-mindedness was a benefit to them both, thought it didn't quite feel that way now. Amelia's letter had boxed him in. She had asked him to let her go, to be the gentleman that he'd already shown himself to be. He couldn't be less of a gentleman now. She had trapped him into doing what she wanted. He was still her android.

158

"Ed needs to see you right away!" Elvin heard that from at least three people in the time it took to walk from the lobby to his desk. He had just dropped his bag on his chair when Jennifer appeared. "He's in Ted Torres's office."

Elvin headed over to the Editor in Chief's office with a rising sense of concern. This can't be *good* news, he thought. I hope this isn't about the column on Alan Fernwood and the authorship question.

A dozen people were seated at the conference table in Ted's office. Elvin paused in the doorway, unsure whether to enter until Ted waved him in. He took a seat near the end of the table.

"This is potentially a very serious matter," said Jackson Sloan, who covered legal issues for the *Herald*.

His comment was immediately countered by Jordan Williams, the *Herald's* legal counsel. "Well, by itself, this letter from the Planet Earth Coalition is not all that serious. It's an attempt to silence us. It isn't notice of a lawsuit, only the threat to take legal action against the *Herald* if the paper doesn't disavow the anti-global warming ideas expressed in 'The Contrarian.' The Coalition is demanding public retractions by Elvin Alvarez, 'The Contrarian,' and the *Herald*."

Elvin froze at hearing his name mentioned in connection with possible legal action against the *Herald*. How did they learn my name, he wondered. The column is unsigned. He began tapping his foot with increasing speed.

Jordan continued. "My impression is that the Coalition sent the letter to us because "The Contrarian" has become syndicated and appears in a dozen papers across the country."

"Twenty-two," Ed said. "Syndication is growing weekly. There is apparently increasing interest in the anti-global warming side of the climate issue."

"Okay, twenty-two. My point is that syndication is the problem. Without that, the Planet Earth Coalition would probably have ignored us."

"It's true," Jackson responded, "that the letter isn't legal action, that it's only the threat of it. The problem is the climate—no pun intended— in which the letter was sent. Climatologist Michael Mann has sued *The National Review* and is trying to put the magazine out of business because of its coverage of Mann's pro-global warming activities. U.S. Senator Sheldon Whitehouse has urged the Justice Department to launch RICO investigations of climate skeptics."

Elvin froze again, even more solidly. "The Contrarian" hadn't been merely skeptical, but had confidently stated that little or no warming had been caused by human production of carbon dioxide, and that increased levels of the gas and higher temperatures would both be beneficial for the biosphere.

Jackson went on. "Senators Edward Markey and Barbara Boxer sent letters to a hundred organizations, including private companies and policy institutes, demanding that they turn over information about funding and research related to climate issues. Twenty state attorneys general have formed a coalition to investigate and prosecute companies that deny the threat of carbon emissions. The Coalition's letter to the *Herald* is not an isolated event, but part of a coordinated effort to silence those who publicly express doubt that human activities are changing the Earth's climate.

"The letter also states that several large foundations, including the Rockefeller Family Fund, are financing legal action against doubters. The implication is that the Coalition has adequate funding to carry through on its threat."

Ted Torres turned to the legal counsel. "How do you propose that we respond, Jordan?"

"I have two suggestions. First, I propose that we ignore the letter. It isn't a legal notice. The Coalition hopes to scare us into a retraction and an apology because it knows it has no other way to stop the paper from stating its views. But it has no case. 'The Contrarian' has stated facts and expressed opinions on a scientific theory that is still unproved, and for which no consensus yet exists, despite what its supporters claim.

"Second, in the unlikely event that it did file against us, the *Herald's* liability insurance would cover all legal costs. We're covered for defense against any legal action arising from anything printed in the paper—facts and opinions; articles, columns and editorials."

Everyone was quiet when Jordan finished speaking, waiting to see what Ted Torres would say. Ted looked at Elvin. "Elvin, how accurate are the facts you have cited in 'The Contrarian?' Are scientists quoted accurately? Do their statements have the same meaning in 'The Contrarian' that they did in their original context?"

With everyone staring at him, Elvin looked as tense as he felt. "Yes, sir. All quotes are accurate and not taken out of context. A far larger number of scientists have doubts about human-generated global warming than most media ever acknowledge. Our paper has been one of the few brave enough to state what it believes to be the truth."

Ted smiled. Then he laughed, and much of the tension in the room evaporated. "What we wrote was true. But it doesn't matter if it was true or not. This is still a free country where opinions can be expressed. The syndication of the column must have them especially worried, because it shows that others are becoming braver, more willing to run reports that counter the dominant view that human actions are destroying the planet. The letter is simply an attempt at intimidation, one that won't work. Elvin, good work on 'The Contrarian.' Let's keep hitting this issue again and again. There is still much more to be said—on both the science and the politics of the issue."

Elvin had never felt so relieved.

159

"Ted and I were discussing your latest column when the letter from the Planet Earth Coalition arrived, Elvin," Ed said. They were sitting in Ed's office after the meeting in Ted's had broken up. "It's on a very controversial subject, the Shakespeare authorship question."

"Yeah," Elvin replied. "I know it's a bit different from 'The Contrarian's' usual scientific focus, but we got so many reader responses to my brief reference to the authorship question last week that I thought it would be a good subject to write about."

"Ted and I had similar thoughts. We liked the column on the authorship question, but we've got to remain focused on scientific issues, particularly global warming, now that the column is syndicated. So we decided to run the Shakespeare piece as a special 'Contrarian' column, and have you write another on scientific issues.

"Then the letter arrived. Ted's decision to ignore it gives us another reason for needing a new column on global warming. We need to show the Coalition that the *Herald* isn't intimidated by its threat. So even if we had thoughts about moving occasionally to other STEM issues, we can't do that now."

"I agree," Elvin said. "But how did they know that I write the column? Can they sue me individually?"

"Don't worry, Elvin. They can't sue you unless they also sue the *Herald*. We printed the columns. You can say anything you want in your columns, legally. Whether it's true or not. Whether you believe it to be true or not. And in the unlikely event of a lawsuit, you would be covered by the *Herald's* insurance policy. So, we need another column on global warming right away. Can you write one quickly?"

"Yes, I can," Elvin answered confidently.

"What's the new angle?" Ed asked.

"It was actually discussions with Alan Fernwood on the Shakespeare authorship question that gave me the idea. On *that* issue, there are two clear sides: authorship by Shakspere and authorship by Oxford. A clear choice can be made on the basis of the evidence.

"But when we come to the issue of global warming, there is only one side in the public mind—that of human-caused warming. We need another side to put up against it, so that a clear choice can be made between them. The opposite side—the side that needs to be framed as the alternative—is simply that changes in weather and climate have been occurring since the planet was formed. They are simply part of nature. They have natural causes.

"The new column could mention some dramatic facts—such as that New York City was under ice two miles thick 12,000 years ago, and sea levels were 400 feet lower than they are today. If changes that dramatic occurred naturally in what was only the blink of an eye in geological time, what reason is there for concluding that any changes occurring today aren't also caused by the same natural forces?

"The idea that natural processes are causing changes in the Earth's climate today has never been disproved. It should have been shown to be false before any other theory replaced it. Instead it got pushed aside by political forces and has been supplanted by a belief in human-caused global warming, a theory that nobody has ever proved to be true and that conflicts with real world data. I have more details to add, but that's the gist of it."

"Yes, that would work fine," Ed said. "Can I have it first thing tomorrow?"

160

In the evening, it occurred to Alan that there were two types of pain, good and bad, just like there are two types of cholesterol. The good type was the pain one endures voluntarily in order to reach important goals— the kind of pain one feels when running a marathon, swimming laps, or learning to play the piano. The other kind was harmful. It arose from being caught in situations that couldn't be avoided. In the worst situations, one could see no end to the suffering and no benefit from it.

Alan knew of some of the difficult times Amelia had faced, and knew there had been others. Perhaps, he thought, there was a lifetime limit to how much pain one could endure, and Amelia had reached hers.

Several more thoughts occurred to him. One was that he should distinguish between pain and suffering, and get them in the right order. It was not that pain caused suffering, but that suffering caused pain. A second thought was that suffering caused not only pain but also damage. The pain is felt instantly; the damage is more long-term and could even be permanent. Suffering damaged the nervous system, the emotional system, even the soul.

Suffering at too young an age harmed the development of the nervous system, damaging one's ability to respond to challenges later. Alan recalled the manic-depressive woman he had known. She had suffered repeated traumas early in life from which she'd had no chance of escape. The suffering from those events had damaged her irreparably. Amelia was made of stronger material. She had been able to handle the suffering and overcome the hardships she'd faced. He admired her hardiness and toughness of spirit, and knew she'd be able to adapt to any reality by accepting pain now in order to avoid suffering later.

Perhaps Amelia's need to cut him out of her life was the result of damage caused by previous suffering. Perhaps her way of keeping people in boxes and of adhering to preset relationships between them was a successful strategy for dealing with suffering and adversity. But perhaps it was also a form of damage, a loss of flexibility that held her back during good times.

Alan also wondered about himself. If the suffering that Amelia had endured in the past had damaged her, then maybe the suffering he had experienced had also damaged him. True, his suffering had occurred later in life than hers and not been as intense, but it had likely left its mark on him. Perhaps everybody is damaged to some extent, and we're all just trying to get through life as best we can.

THURSDAY, AUGUST 13

161

Alan woke up thinking about how fortunate he was to be getting out of the academic racket. Shakespeare studies, in fact all of literary criticism, wasn't what it used to be. The whole field had changed, and it had taken his investigations into the Shakespeare authorship question to understand just how much. He had liked Amelia's calling him a scientist of literature. That was as good a definition of "scholar" as any he'd ever heard. Scholars were scientists seeking truths within works of literature, not advocates for particular points of view, as in Cultural Studies. But in the eyes of so many of his colleagues, great works of literature, once considered important in themselves, had become mere texts to be mined for evidence in support of cultural theories.

He took another look at *The Unkindest Cut: Shakespeare in Exile 2015*, a report by the American Council of Trustees and Alumni that documented the shrinking number of universities requiring English majors to take a course on Shakespeare. He'd hoped that the elimination of the Shakespeare requirement at Cary University a few years ago would lead to a rise in the quality of the students in his courses, because only those with a real interest in the subject would enroll. But that hadn't happened.

Most students enrolled because they were attracted by Shakespeare's famous name. That wasn't a bad thing. The real problem was that students were unprepared for the demanding work required of them. They no longer had the frames of reference from the Bible and from Shakespeare himself that would provide a foundation. They were starting almost from scratch, and many didn't have the English language skills needed for study at the tertiary level. Teaching had become more a matter of providing basic knowledge that students should have acquired in high school.

Moreover, today's students had absorbed the values of the new approaches, and regarded works of literature as no more important than any other form of writing. In recent years he'd had to spend class time trying to get students to appreciate the value of seeing things from another perspective, and to stop them from forcing a modern interpretation on works of literature written in different times and different circumstances. Not only is classroom work becoming more difficult and less rewarding, he thought, but he was having less success in convincing the students of the value of literature itself.

Alan brightened up as he realized that he no longer had to deal with those issues. The University had actually done him a favor. He would now be free to pursue the activities he enjoyed most. He hadn't liked the way the school had gone about making the change, but he knew it was good for him. And he was grateful to Matt for pushing for the buyout.

The more he thought about it, the more he realized just how fortunate he was. He recalled something Theodore Roosevelt had once said: "Far and away the best prize that life offers is the chance to work hard at work worth doing." It's true for me, he thought. His priorities would now be preparing a game plan for Oxfordian engagement with Stratfordians and working to implement it. That, and further research into the question of why Oxford hid his authorship and the mechanics of how the effort to hide it had been successful. And, of course, his book *Shakespeare's Journey*, now focused on Oxford, rather than Shakspere.

162

Waking up from a nap after lunch—another benefit of the buyout!— Alan decided to take a look at *Shakespeare's Journey*. He hadn't worked on it seriously since being overwhelmed by the authorship question more than two months ago. Before that happened, he'd identified the issues, themes, character types and situations of greatest interest to Shakespeare—those he'd returned to again and again in his plays. They were the things he'd had his students examine during the summer term.

His original plan for the book had been to show how those issues had changed over the course of Shakespeare's life as a result of his experiences. Because the issues had been drawn from the plays and not the life of the author, they wouldn't change even with a "new" author—Oxford—in mind. Alan now understood why the authorship issue was so important to him. The change to de Vere resolved the difficulty that had made it so hard to write *Shakespeare's Journey*. Now, with de Vere as the author, the fit between the life and his works was so tight that it would be an exciting adventure to write the book.

In writing about Shakespeare from this perspective, Alan knew he had one advantage that Shakespeare hadn't had when writing his plays. He knew how things turned out, at least in the larger details. De Vere, of course, could not have known what steps would be taken to hide his authorship after his death. He had no knowledge of the First Folio and the later Folios, the Jubilee, and so many other developments.

Alan had another advantage, too—the summer seminar discussions. He knew that authors sometimes thanked their students in the acknowledgment sections of their books. Now he had first-hand experience in how a remarkable class could contribute to a professor's writings. So, for those two reasons—the work he'd done on the authorship issue, and the classroom discussions—he now realized that he had been working on *Shakespeare's Journey* throughout the summer without even knowing it.

163

As he refilled his Edward de Vere coffee mug, Alan sensed another idea coming up from his subconscious. He closed his eyes, trying to grasp it. Then he had it.

The themes in the plays he'd identified as of special importance to Shakespeare were also of special importance in his own life. He was astonished at the overlap. The distinction between an individual and his title and position. Yes, that was important to Shakespeare—and it was also important to him. He'd lost the position on the teaching faculty, but he'd fought hard to keep his title of Associate Professor. He was still an individual, so he had two out of three—the two that were most important to him.

Like Shakespeare's characters, he had also worked in a politicized environment. There were similarities between the closed, hierarchical world of the court and the university environment. Shakespeare had lived in a center of intrigue where courtiers competed in underhanded ways for advancement—and so did professors. He recalled the contrast in *As You Like It* between the pompous and envious nature of life in the court and the peaceful nature of life in the forest. As a professor of literature focused on his work, he hadn't been a player in the political games going on in the Department. He wasn't, like Matt, suited for political positions such as Department Chair. He was more like Prospero, Richard II and other characters who wanted a private life.

Like Prospero, he had been taken advantage of by more politicized colleagues eager to push him out in order to create new opportunities for themselves. They—he had a good idea who they were—had used his dedication to teaching literature rather than Cultural Studies, and his interest in the authorship question, to present a distorted version of his work to the Dean. He'd been banished, just like so many of Shakespeare's characters, and even like de Vere himself. Ah well, he thought, the joke's on them. I now have what I want most—the chance to work on my literary projects free from the burden of having to teach.

Alan saw similarities, too, in how his life had been affected by the political aspects of love and desire. His ability to fight back against the effort to push him out of the University had been hampered by his relationship with Amelia. He had needed to move quickly to secure the pension and buyout before their relationship became known. It wasn't Amelia's fault, just like it wasn't Cleopatra's fault that Antony had abandoned the field of battle. But her presence had been a distraction and a complication in Alan's efforts to defend himself, just as Cleopatra's had been for Antony.

He then thought of the similarity between the giddiness he'd felt as he walked to Amelia's apartment for the first time and that felt by Troilus as he walked to meet Cressida at her room for the first time. And like Troilus seeing Cressida in Diomedes's tent, he had been incredulous at seeing Amelia in Matt's house. He also recognized that Cressida and Amelia had good reasons for doing what they did. Cressida had to find a protector to save herself from being used in sexual common by the Greeks, and Amelia had acted to save his buyout package. Still, he and Troilus had been devastated by what they'd seen.

Alan was struck by another thought. Isabella had refused to sacrifice her body to save her brother's life in *Measure for Measure*. Amelia, though, had been willing to sacrifice hers to save his buyout. He was filled with awe and gratitude that she had done so, and regretted that he hadn't thanked her properly for her sacrifice. He'd been too upset at the time, and now he might never be able to.

Alan also saw that he had faced a series of shocks, just like Hamlet and so many other Shakespeare characters. There was the shock of realizing that his lifelong belief in Shakspere's authorship had been wrong, the shock of losing his job, and, worst of all, the shock of Amelia's sudden departure. Occurring one on top of the other, the three events formed a major turning point in his life. He now had to show himself and the world that he could make good decisions, that he had control over himself, that he would not let inappropriate desires and emotions overwhelm him.

But it was all so uncertain. Was he the strong-ribbed bark cited by Nestor, or only the bauble boat tossed about by the waves? Would he prove himself capable of surviving this difficult time? He would try to become the ideal man that Hamlet had described, a man who "in suffering all suffers nothing," one who "takes Fortune's buffets and rewards with equal thanks," one who is not "passion's slave," one whose "blood and judgment are so well commedled that they are not a pipe for fortune's finger to sound what stop she please."

Another thought occurred to Alan. Not only had his journey been similar to Shakespeare's, but so is everybody else's. Each one of us has to make decisions on the basis of incomplete information. Everyone experiences disillusionment. We all suffer and feel pain.

None more so than Amelia. She, too, had had tough decisions to make, and she'd made them. What she'd most wanted, whatever the cost, was to avoid suffering. To avoid it she'd walked away from what she'd wanted second most: a man to share her life with. He knew she was suffering as much or more than he was. And he knew that she'd done what had to be done to limit that suffering.

Alan looked out the window, trying to clear his mind. He wanted to consider the process through which authors choose what to write about. He had always heard that writers write about what they know about. Joseph Conrad's writing about sailors after spending half a lifetime at sea was only the most striking example. Shakespeare, Alan was sure, had done the same thing.

Writers write not only about what they know about, but also about what they care about. He recalled Doris Alexander's observation, in her book *Creating Literature Out of Life*, that writers are impelled to write particular works by the urgent life problems they face. "They were able to resolve the problem [in their life] through the resolution they found for the problems of their characters in their story."

Yes, Alan confirmed to himself, that is exactly what Shakespeare did. What makes his works so absorbing is that, through them, he was working out problems important in his own life. So, writing *Shakespeare's Journey* will be a fascinating experience. If he could capture the essence of Shakespeare's mental or emotional journey, the book would be as enjoyable for others to read as it would be for him to write.

Then it struck him that in writing *Shakespeare's Journey* he was doing exactly what Shakespeare had done in his plays—writing about issues important to himself—important not just in the past two months, but over the course of his whole life.

FRIDAY, AUGUST 14

164

Alan began the new day considering how his relationship with Amelia had changed him. He wasn't the same person he'd been two months ago. The intensity of his recent experiences had been like a bend in a river, making it harder to see the route he had traveled before the bend. He knew that future events—new bends in the river—would make it equally difficult to see the last two months.

That brought up another thought—that he might lose his memories of Amelia. That was yet another possibility that must be accepted. He had learned from her that we must do all we can to determine the reality of a situation and then adapt ourselves—our lives—to it. He then realized that Shakespeare had told him the same thing. As Henry V had phrased it, "What is't to me, when you yourselves are [the] cause" by not adapting yourselves to the reality of the situation?

That Amelia was gone was the hardest reality to adapt to because so many questions remained unanswered. How can I adapt myself to reality, he asked himself, when I don't know what that reality is? He accepted that he sometimes had to make decisions on the basis of incomplete information. But it was harder to accept the growing recognition that he might never have answers to his questions. He might never know if he'd acted for the best.

If knowledge was to be ever incomplete, maybe what is needed is not more knowledge, but a greater awareness of what was most important for him as an individual. With that, he could adapt himself to any set of circumstances. "Connoisseurship"—perhaps that is what he could call the ability to know what would be best for himself. He would need to become a connoisseur of his own life. He smiled to think that the word was as difficult for him to spell now as "Renaissance" had been thirty years earlier. He wondered if Amelia knew how to spell it. That was yet one more thing he'd probably never know.

Connoisseurship in wine tasting, he knew, developed over time as one's palate became more discerning. Maybe it was the same in the connoisseurship of life. It wasn't a natural activity. It certainly required experience, but reaching the higher levels wasn't possible without the focused effort that was rarely possible when caught up in the day-to-day activities of living. Perhaps that was why his appreciation of Shakespeare's works had developed slowly over many years and hadn't taken off until he had begun studying them intensely.

Alan saw a similarity between everyday activities and connoisseurship on one hand, and Carson's distinction between technology and scientific knowledge on the other. Many people want technological knowledge and the knowledge needed in day-to-day living, but only a few seek scientific knowledge and connoisseurship. But for those that pursued it, connoisseurship could shine a light on all aspects of their lives. It could help him organize his day-to-day activities in the most enlightened way.

So he could see that one of his goals, along with his Shakespeare projects, must be cultivating his . . . his what? His mind? His heart? His spirit? His soul? What is it exactly that becomes cultivated as one becomes a connoisseur of life? He was a true beginner in this field, but it suddenly fascinated him. He was again grateful that for the first time in his life he had the time to pursue subjects like this one.

165

Alan went to bed early. As he waited for sleep to come, he juggled several ideas. One was that life is more important than literature, more important than his life of the mind, than his books, than his absorption in all his intellectual activities combined. Those things, he saw, were important for what they could tell him about how to cultivate connoisseurship.

But if a life of the mind was only a supporting activity for living a good life, was the study of literature any different from other supporting activities such as vacuuming and dusting? He rejected that comparison outright. Thinking and housekeeping were differences of kind, not differences of degree, just as animals and plants were differences of kind even though both were forms of life.

Perhaps he could draw on the phrase "part and parcel" that John

Stuart Mill had used to describe things so important for happiness that they are part of it, not just contributors to it. His intellectual activities were so important that they were "part and parcel" of his very life. Only in the most extreme situations could a division between his life and his life of the mind be contemplated. Living in a concentration camp, perhaps, and maybe not even then. Many people in history died for their beliefs, for the intangible things they loved, when they could have saved their lives by renouncing or abandoning them.

The best life of all, he concluded, would be spent with someone with whom he could share the things that mattered most to him. He'd met such a person, but now she was gone. At the same time, he recognized more clearly that he had a wife with a true heart. Even if Diana couldn't be an intellectual companion, she didn't get in the way of his work, and that, he thought, is not a small thing. Trying to live with Amelia would have meant a year or more of emotional heartache, which surely would have affected work on his literary projects.

He sighed, recalling how close he'd come to losing Diana forever. Had he not seen Amelia through Matt's window, he might have walked away from Diana. If he had taken that irrevocable step just before losing his job, he would have been out in the cold. Amelia might have left anyway, and then he would have lost her, his job and Diana. Miraculously, that worst possible scenario had been avoided. Maybe he should be relieved that his relationship with Amelia had ended as cleanly as it had, something due to her intelligence and strength of character, not his own.

He had no doubt that Amelia would be fine after a period of adjustment. She would prosper wherever she was. She was too tough-minded not to—too intelligent, too witty, too beautiful, too playful, too captivating to be alone for long. He knew that she would find someone who had many of his own qualities, but who wasn't married. Probably someone more accomplished, smarter, younger. If he ever learned of it, he would rejoice in her happiness.

166

Elvin kissed Delilah's neck as he stood behind her in the kitchen of her apartment. They had just finished eating dinner.

He had gone directly to meet her after leaving the *Herald* on Wednesday. They had been together practically every moment since, except when they had reluctantly parted to go to work.

"Do you mind if I jot down some thoughts?" he asked. "I want to get started on the next column."

"Not at all, dear," she said, turning around and kissing him.

Elvin walked into the living room, pulled out his laptop and began organizing his notes. The Earth's climate had been far hotter in the past without grave dangers for the biosphere, he noted, trying to stay focused on what he was doing. The Medieval Warm Period, when the climate was warmer than today, was a time of growing prosperity in Europe that reached its peak in the 12th and 13th centuries. During that time Greenland was settled by the Vikings, and "cows grazed and willows grew in Greenland and seals basked on the shores of Antarctica."

Those colonies had been abandoned during the Little Ice Age of the 14th and 15th centuries. Temperatures had recovered from that low point, but, he had learned, are still a little below the average for the past 3,000 years. Another report showed that the late twentieth century peak is just about at the average temperature for the last 10,000 years, and yet another found that temperatures during the Holocene Climatic Optimum, 8,000 years ago were as much as two full degrees warmer than today.

Elvin found it hard to stay focused on writing. His fear of a lawsuit had passed as he realized that the *Herald* was led by people with courage, but his relief was now turning to anger at the Coalition that had tried to silence him and the paper. If his column was inaccurate, let him know, he thought. If he had misinterpreted data or if his logic was faulty, show him where. There was no need for an underhanded effort to intimidate him.

He turned back to his column. He had found that CO_2 levels expected by midcentury shouldn't be a cause for alarm because levels had been as high as forty times the current level in the past. In fact, he learned, "all six of the great ice ages were initiated when atmospheric CO_2 was far higher than at present and, with the first two great ice ages, up to a thousand times higher than the current atmospheric CO_2 content."

Elvin stopped work again. He recalled how supportive Delilah had been on Wednesday night, as he described the threat of the lawsuit. Her warmth and concern and reassurance were just what he'd needed, and had helped relieve his intermittent bouts of fear since then.

He now knew that he wanted—needed—her with him always. He had to do something to ensure that they would always be together. He had to make their togetherness permanent.

If, he reasoned, the Earth could remain the Earth even as its climate changed so radically over the billions of years of its existence, then surely he would still be Elvin even if his marital status changed. He could marry Delilah without losing his identity. He had to nail it down now. He couldn't take a chance on ever losing her. He went to find her, to ask her a question that simply had to be asked.

SATURDAY, AUGUST 15

167

Alan was in good spirits as he ate lunch before driving to the airport to pick up Diana. He reviewed the changes in his life over the past twelve weeks as he ate. He had begun the summer term as Associate Professor with a full teaching load, and ended with the freedom to think and write that he'd wanted for so long. With the buyout, he wouldn't have to go back to work for at least a year, and with a bit of luck he might never have to work for a paycheck again. He would never be rich, but he'd have the tradeoff between money and time that he would have chosen even if it hadn't been forced on him.

He'd begun the summer with the Shakespeare authorship question not even on his radar, and ended consumed by it. That fascination had the added benefit of solving the problems that had blocked his progress on *Shakespeare's Journey*.

And he'd begun the summer unaware of just how much he hungered for an intellectual companion. Meeting Amelia had shown him how powerful that hidden desire had been, and the disastrous ending to their relationship had revealed other realities of his life that he hadn't been fully aware of. Among them were that the vines tying him to Diana were too thick to cut, and that spending his life with someone with a true heart wasn't something to be lightly dismissed. He might not have everything, but he had enough. He had, he told himself, more than anyone had any right to expect from life.

168

"Hello," Alan said, having run to the phone, hoping against hope that it might be Amelia. He knew he should be doing the tough-minded thing, which he was sure she was doing, that of moving their relationship from the present tense to the past.

"Dad? It's Delilah. Are you okay? You sound out of breath."

"I'm fine. You sound bright and cheerful this morning, Delilah."

"Well, that's exactly how I'm feeling. I'm calling with some wonderful news. Elvin and I have decided to get married."

Short of a call from Amelia, which would have been a mixed

blessing anyway, he couldn't think of anything that would have made him happier. "That's wonderful news. I'm so happy for both of you. When did you make the decision?"

"Last night. Mom comes back today, right? Can you give her the news when you pick her up at the airport? I'd call her myself but she's on the plane." Before Alan could say anything, Delilah continued, talking at the speed of her mother's airplane. "I've got to go now, Dad, we have a million things to do, even though we haven't yet set a date. Can you and Mom meet me and Elvin for dinner tonight? We can give you details then."

"Your mother will be so excited, Delilah. You know she and I both have the highest opinion of Elvin."

"I know. And he, you. See you tonight!" And then she was gone, off on the start of one of the biggest adventures of her life.

169

Alan caught himself humming an old Sinatra tune, "I've Got the World on a String," as he drove to the airport. I must be happy, he thought. I don't know if I should be, but I am. Looking out the window, he noticed what a clear day it was, with not a cloud in the sky.

AFTERWORD

WEDNESDAY, DECEMBER 23

170

"I'm dreaming of a white Christmas, just like the ones I used to know." Alan was singing along with the holiday songs playing at the Southpoint Mall. It was almost Christmas, and he and Diana were out for some last minute shopping. They enjoyed walking around in the cold air, being among the crowds, and occasionally looking up to see if any snow was on the way.

"Professor Fernwood!"

He stopped singing and turned around.

"Oh, hi, Lisa! It's good to see you again. This is my wife, Diana."

They greeted each other, and then suddenly there was Pat, slipping his arm around Lisa.

"Pat and I are kind of together, now," she told him, smiling.

"And we owe it all to you and your Shakespeare Summer Seminar," Pat said. "We would never have met if we hadn't taken your course."

"And you know what is even more amazing?" Lisa asked, laughing. "Nancy and Dave are now a couple, too."

"Well, that's doubly amazing," Alan responded.

"You know what I think did it?" Pat asked. "Those intense discussions about *Troilus and Cressida*, *Antony and Cleopatra*, *Hamlet*, and *King Lear* in the second half of the course. Somehow the magic from those plays affected everyone in the classroom."

"Do you know what happened to the others, Doug and Amelia?" he asked.

"Well, no one has heard from Amelia since she left the school," Lisa said. "I guess she doesn't like to keep in touch."

"But Doug is doing well," Pat added. "He is actually transferring to another university, the one in Charlotte, and has already left Cary."

My God, Alan thought. Amelia transferred to Charlotte. Could it be that she and Doug have hooked up? "Well, I hope he does well there," he said.

"Merry Christmas to both of you," Lisa and Pat said at the same time to Alan and Diana.

"And Happy New Year to all of us," Alan replied with a wave, as the two couples headed in different directions.

• • • • •

APPENDICES

SUGGESTED READING

NOTES

APPENDIX 1: CLASSROOM MATERIALS

			SHAKESPEARE SUMMER SEMINAR SESSIONS	
	Date	**Moderator**	**Plays discussed**	**Topic**
1	Monday, June 1	Alan Fernwood		Shakespeare in His Own Words
2	Thursday, June 4	Alan Fernwood	*Julius Caesar*	Importance of decision points in the plays: a) Brutus in *Julius Caesar*
3	Monday, June 8	Alan Fernwood	*Hamlet, Julius Caesar; Merchant of Venice*	Clashes of values in Elizabethan society: a) revenge in pagan vs. Christian societies b) honor vs. commercial values
4	Thursday, June 11	Nancy Kramer and Doug Jordan	*Hamlet; Timon, King Lear, others*	Importance of knowledge in making decisions: a) Nancy: verifying the validity of knowledge b) Doug: human nature and animal nature
5	Monday, June 15	Amelia Mai and Pat Compton	*Love's Labor's Lost; Timon of Athens*	Conflicts between sources or types of knowledge: a) Amelia: conflicts between head vs. heart b) Pat: Timon's extremes, lack of middle ground
6	Thursday, June 18	Dave Camacho and Lisa Newton	*Troilus and Cressida*	Valuing things and people: a) Dave: Subjective and objective views of Helen b) Lisa: Subjective and objectives views of Achilles
7	Monday, June 22	Alan Fernwood	*Henry V, Richard II*	Plays as political in nature; not Merry Olde Englande: a) Divine right of kings, Tudor politics b) Marriage issue, War with Spain
8	Thursday, June 25	Alan Fernwood	*Henry V*	More political issues in the plays: a) The succession to Queen Elizabeth b) Political considerations affect all characters
9	Monday, June 29	Alan Fernwood		Review: a) Review, authorship question b) Midterm essay topics
10	**Thursday, July 2**			**Midterm Exam**

11	Thursday, July 9	Nancy Kramer	*King Lear; King John*	Individual vs. title vs. position, Part 1: a) Interaction on basis of positions, titles b) Primogeniture and the place of bastards
12	Monday, July 13	Doug Jordan	*Richard II, The Tempest; Julius Caesar, Coriolanus*	Individual vs. title vs. position, Part 2: a) Intellectuals unsuited for political positions b) warriors unsuited for political positions
13	Thursday, July 16	Amelia Mai	*Troilus and Cressida; Midsummer Night's Dream*	Political aspects of love and desire, Part 1: a) Helen and Cressida as political pawns b) Arranged marriages and opposition to them
14	Monday, July 20	Lisa Newton	*Richard III Measure for Measure*	Political aspects of love and desire, Part 2: a) Intertwining of political and sexual desires b) Strength of desires, need for control over them
15	Thursday, July 23	Dave Camacho	*Midsummer Night's Dream, King Lear*	Appearance and reality, Part 1: a) Appearance and reality in *MSND* and *King Lear* b) *King Lear* and the value for experience
16	Monday, July 27	Pat Compton	*Hamlet*	Appearance and reality, Part 2: a) Appearance and reality in the world b) Hamlet's efforts to know himself
17	Thursday, July 30	Alan Fernwood	*Antony & Cleopatra*	Political aspects of love and desire, Part 3: a) Intertwining of politics and love
18	Monday, Aug. 3	Alan Fernwood	*Romeo and Juliet; King Lear*	Open (Ingratitude, betrayal, banishment)
19	Thursday, Aug. 6	Alan Fernwood	*Hamlet, King Lear*	Summing up of themes discussed. a) The authorship question and solving the *Hamlet* puzzle and the *Lear* mystery b) Final exam topics
20	**Monday, Aug. 10**			**Final Exam Due**

APPENDIX 2:
BOOKS, MOVIES AND MUSIC MENTIONED IN
CONVERSATIONS BETWEEN CHARACTERS IN *SUMMER STORM*

NONFICTION BOOKS

Althen, Gary	*American Ways: A Guide for Foreigners in the United States* (2003) (Scenes 4, 10)
Datesman, Maryanne	*American Ways: An Introduction to American Culture* (2005) (Scene 4)
Duggan, William	*The Art of What Works: How Success Really Happens* (2003) (Scene 21)
Frankl, Viktor E.	*Man's Search for Meaning: An Introduction To Logotherapy* (1959) (Scene 30)
Lippmann, Walter	*A Preface to Morals* (1929) (Scene 111)
Young, R. V.	*A Student's Guide to Literature* (2000) (Scene 10)

NOVELS AND OTHER FICTION

Asimov, Isaac	*Foundation Trilogy* (1942-1950) (Scene 151)
Huxley, Aldous	*Island* (1962) (Scenes 43, 156)
McInerney, Jay	*Story of My Life* (1988) (Scene 92)
Parish, Peggy	*Amelia Bedelia* (1999) (Scene 80)
Twain, Mark	*A Connecticut Yankee in King Arthur's Court* (1889) (Scene 151)
Watterson, Bill	*The Essential Calvin and Hobbes* (1988) (Scene 80)
—	*The Indispensable Calvin and Hobbes* (1992) (Scene 80)
Wodehouse, P. G.	*Right Ho, Jeeves* (1934) Scenes 43, 54)
Wolfe, Tom	*Back to Blood: A Novel* (2012) Scene 17)

MOVIES AND OTHER VIDEO

The Americanization of Emily (1964) (Scene 76)
Anonymous (2011) (Scenes 3, 53, 138)
Bambi (1942) (Scene 96)
Blast from the Past (1999) (Scene 75)
Born Free (1966) (Scene 76)
Casper (1950-1959) (Scene 20)
Cleopatra (1963) (Scene 122)
The Dick Van Dyke Show (1961-1966) (Scene 18)
Fiddler on the Roof (Scenes 74, 89)

Gilligan's Island (1964-1967) (Scene 115)
Good Morning, Vietnam (1988) (Scene 67)
The Horse's Mouth (1958) (Scene 43)
Here's Lucy (Scene 16)
A Midsummer Night's Sex Comedy (1982) (Scene 89)
Moonstruck (1987) (Scene 63)
Pillow Talk (1959) (Scenes 58, 61)
Scooby Doo (1969-1972) (Scene 106)
The Sound of Music (1965) (Scene 76)
South Pacific (1949) (Scene 157)
Top Hat (1935) (Scene 43)
When Harry Met Sally (1989) (Scene 157)
You've Got Mail (1998) (Scene 132)

CLASSICAL MUSIC

Beethoven, Ludwig van	*Piano Sonata #8 in C Minor, Op. 13 "Adagio cantabile," (Pathetique)* (Scene 153)
—	*Piano Sonata #17 in D Minor, Op. 31 #2 (Tempest)* (Scene 153)
—	*Piano Sonata #31 in A flat Major, Op. 110* (Scene 153)
—	*Sonata for Violin and Piano No. 5 in F Major, Op. 24 (Spring)* (Scene 126)
—	*String Quartet in C-sharp Minor, Op. 131* (Scene 153)
—	*Symphony No. 3 (Eroica)* (Scene 7)
—	*Symphony No. 7* (Scene 153)
Puccini, Giacomo	*La Boheme* (Scene 63)

POPULAR MUSIC

Fred Astaire	*Isn't This a Lovely Day (To Be Caught In the Rain)* (Irving Berlin) (Scene 43)
Beach Boys	*Surfer Girl* (Brian Wilson) (Scene 23)
—	*The Warmth of the Sun* (Brian Wilson and Mike Love) (Scene 73)
Antonio Carlos Jobim	*The Girl from Ipanema* (Jobim) (Scene 23)
Four Seasons	*Big Girls Don't Cry* (Bob Crewe/Bob Gaudio) (Scene 23)
The Guess Who	*American Woman* (Randy Bachman/Burton Cummings/Garry Peterson/Jim Kale) (Scene 23)
Art Pepper	*You'd Be So Nice To Come Home To* (Cole

Porter) (Scene 101)

Kenny Rogers	*The Gambler* (Don Schlitz) (Scene 30)
Nina Simone	*You'd Be So Nice To Come Home To* (Cole Porter) (Scene 101)
Frank Sinatra	*All or Nothing At All* (Arthur Altman/Jack Lawrence) (Scene 157)
—	*I've Got the World On a String* (Harold Arlen/Ted Koehler) (Scene 167)
—	*Just the Way You Look Tonight* (Dorothy Field, Jerome Kern) (Scene 99)
—	*Witchcraft* (Cy Coleman/Carolyn Leigh) (Scene 99)
—	*You'd Be So Nice To Come Home To* (Cole Porter) (Scene 101)

◆ ◆ ◆ ◆ ◆

APPENDIX 3:
"THE CONTRARIAN" COLUMNS

37,000 Scientists Can't Be Wrong! (Scene 39)
"The Science Is Settled"? (Scene 56)
The Warmth of the Sun (Scene 73)
The Heart of the Matter (Scene 86)
Witchcraft, Part 1 (Scene 97)
Witchcraft, Part 2 (Scene 98)
The Military-Industrial Complex Redux?, Part 1 (Scene 116)
The Military-Industrial Complex Redux?, Part 2 (Scene 118)
What's a Girl to Do?, Part 1 (Scene 136)
What's a Girl to Do?, Part 2 (Scene 137)
Shakespeare Is Innocent! (Scene 155)

◆ ◆ ◆ ◆ ◆

APPENDIX 4:
READING LISTS

THE SHAKESPEARE AUTHORSHIP QUESTION

Anderson, Mark
  2005   *"Shakespeare" By Another Name: The Life of Edward de
          Vere, Earl of Oxford, The Man Who Was
          Shakespeare* (New York: Gotham Books)
Beauclerk, Charles
  2010   *Shakespeare's Lost Kingdom: The True History of
          Shakespeare and Elizabeth* (New York: Grove Press)
Boyle, William E. (editor)
  2013   *A Poet's Rage: Understanding Shakespeare Through
          Authorship Studies* (Somerville, MA: Forever Press)
Chiljan, Katherine
  2011   *Shakespeare Suppressed: The Uncensored Truth about
          Shakespeare and His Works* (San Francisco: Faire
          Editions)
Crinkley, Richmond
  1985   "New Perspectives on The Authorship Question,"
          Shakespeare Quarterly, Vol. 36, No. 4 (Winter, 1985),
          pp. 515-522.
De Vere Society Newsletter
  2013   "Royal Shakespeare Company's Psychological Aberration?"
          Vol. 20/3 (October, 2013), p. 27.
Edmonson, Paul and Stanley Wells (editors)
  2013   *Shakespeare Beyond Doubt: Evidence, Argument,
          Controversy* (Cambridge: Cambridge University Press)
Gore-Langton, Robert
  2014   "Could the Real Mr. Shakespeare Please Stand Up?" *The
          Daily Express* (27 October 2014), p. 13. (reprinted in *The
          De Vere Society Newsletter*, Vol. 21/3 (October 2014), p.
          3-5.)
  2014   "The Campaign to Prove Shakespeare Didn't Exist,"
          Newsweek, 29 December 2014, accessed at
          http://www.newsweek.com/2014/12/26/
          campaign-prove-shakespeare-didn't-exist-293243.htm.
Hope, Warren and Kim Holston
  2009   *The Shakespeare Controversy: An Analysis of the
          Authorship Theories, Second Edition* (Jefferson, North
          Carolina: McFarland & Company, Inc., Publishers)
Hughes, Stephanie Hopkins
  2007   "Hide Fox and All After: The Search for Shakespeare,"
          Shakespeare Oxford Newsletter, Vol. 43, No. 1
          (Winter, 2007), pp. 1, 5-11.
Jiménez, Ramon

2007   "Shakespeare in Stratford and London: Ten Eyewitnesses
         Who Saw Nothing," *Report My Cause Aright: The
         Shakespeare Oxford Society Fiftieth Anniversary
         Anthology, 1957-2007* (The Shakespeare Oxford Society)

Leahy, William
2007   "Two Households, Both Alike in Dignity:' the Authorship
         Question and Academia," *The De Vere Society Newsletter*
         (February 2007), p. 4-11.

Looney, J. Thomas
1920   *"Shakespeare" Identified in Edward de Vere* (London:
         Cecil Palmer)
1922   "The Earl of Oxford as 'Shakespeare:' New Evidence," *The
         Golden Hind*, Vol. 1, No. 1 (October 1922), p. 23-30.

New York Times
2007   "Did He or Didn't He? That Is the Question," 22 April 2007.

Ogburn, Sr., Charlton and Dorothy Ogburn
1952   *This Star of England: "William Shakespeare" Man of the
         Renaissance* (New York: Coward-McCann, Inc.)

Ogburn, Charlton
1992   *The Mysterious William Shakespeare, Second Edition*
         (McLean, VAEPM Publications, Inc.)

Price, Diana
2012   *Shakespeare's Unorthodox Biography: New Evidence of an
         Authorship Problem*. Published in paperback with
         corrections, revisions, and additions. (Shakespeare-
         authorship.com) (First published by Greenwood Press,
         Westport, CT, 2001)

Rush, Peter
2015   *Hidden in Plain Sight: The True History Revealed in Shake-
         speares Sonnets* (Leesburg, VA: Real Deal
         Publications)

Sears, Elizabeth
2003   *Shakespeare and the Tudor Rose* (Marshfield Hills, MA:
         Meadow Geese Press)

Shahan, John M. and Alexander Waugh (editors)
2013   *Shakespeare Beyond Doubt?: Exposing an Industry in
         Denial* (Tamarac, Florida: Llumina Press)

Shapiro, James
2010   *Contested Will: Who Wrote Shakespeare?* (New York:
         Simon & Schuster)
2011   "Hollywood Dishonors the Bard," *New York Times*, October
         16, 2011.

Singleton, Esther
1929   *Shakespearian Fantasias: Adventures in the Fourth
         Dimension* (New York: William Farquhar Payson)
1940   "Was Edward de Vere Shakespeare? *Shakespeare*

Fellowship Newsletter (American Branch), Vol. 1/4 (June/July 1940), pp. 9-10.

Stritmatter, Roger A.
  2003   *The Marginalia of Edward de Vere's Geneva Bible: Providential Discovery, Literary Reasoning, and Historical Consequence* (Northampton, MA: Oxenford Press)
  2006   "What's In a Name? Everything, Apparently . . .." *Rocky Mountain E-Review of Language and Literature*, Vol. 60, No. 2, pp. 37-49.

Ward, Colonel B. R.
  1929   "Queen Elizabeth's 'Patrimony,'" *Shakespeare Pictorial*, June 1929, p. 20.

Warren, James A.
  2015a   *An Index to Oxfordian Publications, Third Edition* (Somerville, MA: Forever Press)
  2015b   "The Use of State Power in the Effort to Hide Edward de Vere's Authorship of the Works of 'William Shakespeare,'" *Brief Chronicles VI*, pp. 59-81.
  2015c   "Oxfordian Theory, Continental Drift and the Importance of Methodology," *The Oxfordian XVII*, pp. 193-221.

Waugh, Alexander
  2014   *Shakespeare in Court* (Kindle single, available at Amazon.com)

Whittemore, Hank
  2005   *The Monument.* (Marshfield Hills, MA: Meadow Geese Press)

Wright, Dan
  2013   "'I am I, howe'er I was begot'" *A Poet's Rage*, edited by William E. Boyle (Somerville, MA: Forever Press)
  2000   "Ver-y Interesting: Shakespeare's Treatment of the Earls of Oxford in the History Plays," *Shakespeare Oxford Newsletter*, Vol. 36/1 (Spring, 2000): 1, 14-21).

Wright, Louis Booker
  1959   "The Anti-Shakespeare Industry and the Growth of Cults," *The Virginia Quarterly Review*, Vol. 35, No. 2 (Spring 1959). (reprinted in *We Write for Our Own Time: Selected Essays from 75 Years of the Virginia Quarterly Review*, edited by Alexander Burnham. Charlottesville: University of Virginia Press, 2000, pp. 105-115.)

GENERAL SHAKESPEAREAN STUDIES

Alvis, John
  1981   "Introductory: Shakespearean Poetry and Politics," *Shakespeare as Political Thinker*, edited by John Alvis and Thomas G. West (Durham, North Carolina: Carolina

Academic Press)

Alvis, John and Thomas G. West
    1981   *Shakespeare as Political Thinker* (Durham, North Carolina:
           Carolina Academic Press)

American Council of Trustees and Alumni (ACTA)
    2007   *The Vanishing Shakespeare* (Washington, D.C.: ACTA)
    2015   *The Unkindest Cut: Shakespeare in Exile 2015*
           (Washington, D.C.: ACTA)

Asimov, Isaac
    1978   *Asimov's Guide to Shakespeare* (New York: Avenel Books)

Bloom, Alan, with Harry V. Jaffa
    1964   *Shakespeare's Politics* (Chicago: The University of Chicago
           Press)

Campbell, Lily B.
    1968   *Shakespeare's "Histories:" Mirrors of Elizabethan Policy*
           (San Marino, CA: The Huntington Library)

Cowan, Louise
    1981   "God Will Save the King: Shakespeare's *Richard II*,"
           Shakespeare as Political Thinker, edited by John Alvis
           and Thomas G. West (Durham, North Carolina: Carolina
           Academic Press)

Eliot, T. S.
    1928   "Hamlet and His Problems" *The Sacred Wood, second*
           edition (New York: Barnes and Noble)

Flannery, Christopher
    1981   "*Troilus and Cressida*: Poetry or Philosophy?" *Shakespeare*
           as Political thinker, edited by John Alvis and Thomas G.
           West (Durham, North Carolina: Carolina Academic
           Press)

Hart, Alfred
    1934   *Shakespeare and the Homilies* (New York: Octagon Books)

Jaffa, Harry V.
    1964   "The Limits of Politics: *King Lear*, Act I, scene I,"
           Shakespeare's Politics, by Allan Bloom with Harry V.
           Jaffa (Chicago: The University of Chicago Press), p.
           113-138.
    1981a "Chastity as a Political Principle: An Interpretation of
           Shakespeare's *Measure for Measure*," *Shakespeare as*
           Political Thinker, edited by John Alvis and Thomas G.
           West (Durham, North Carolina: Carolina Academic
           Press)
    1981b "The Unity of Tragedy, Comedy, and History: An
           Interpretation of the Shakespearean Universe,"
           Shakespeare as Political Thinker, edited by John Alvis
           and Thomas G. West (Durham, North Carolina: Carolina
           Academic Press)

McCarthy, Penny
> 2006   *Pseudonymous Shakespeare* (Burlington, VT: Ashgate
>   Publishing Company)

Spurgeon, Caroline
> 1935   *Shakespeare's Imagery and What It Tells Us.* (Cambridge,
>   UK: Cambridge University Press)

Starner, Janet Wright and Barbara Howard Traister
> 2011   *Anonymity in Early Modern England: What's In a Name*
>   (Burlington, VT: Ashgate Publishing Company)

Tillyard, E.M.W.
> 1959   *The Elizabethan World Picture* (New York: Vintage)

West, Thomas G.
> 1981   "The Two Truths of *Troilus and Cressida*," *Shakespeare as
>   Political Thinker*, edited by John Alvis and Thomas G.
>   West (Durham, North Carolina: Carolina Academic
>   Press)

GLOBAL WARMING AND CLIMATE CHANGE

Bolt, Andrew
> 2015   "False Prophets Unveiled," *Climate Change: The Facts*,
>   Edited by Alan Moran (Woodville, NH: Stockdale
>   Books)

Bethel, Tom
> 2005   "The False Alert of Global Warming," *The American
>   Spectator*, May, 2005.

Carter, Robert M.
> 2015a   "The Scientific Context," *Climate Change: The Facts*, edited
>   by Alan Moran (Woodville, NH: Stockdale Books) CNS
>   News (http://cnsnews.com)
> 2015b   "Sierra Club President Says Satellites Are Wrong: 'Our
>   Planet is Cooking Up'"
>   http://www.cnsnews.com/news/article/barbara-
>   hollingsworth/sierra-club-president-says-satellites-are-
>   wrong-our-planet-0. (accessed October 28, 2015)

Goklany, Indur M. (Foreword by Freeman Dyson)
> 2015   *Carbon Dioxide: The Good News* (The Global Warming
>   Policy Foundation)

Greene, Kestern; and J. Scott Armstrong
> 2015   "Forecasting Global Climate Change," *Climate Change:
>   The Facts*, edited by Alan Moran (Woodville, NH:
>   Stockdale Books)

Intergovernmental Panel on Climate Change
> 1990   *First Assessment Report*
> 2014   *Climate Change 2013: The Physical Science Basis* (Working
>   Group 1 Contribution to the Fifth Assessment Report of
>   the Intergovernmental Panel on Climate Change, co-

chaired by Thomas F. Stocker and Dahe Qin) (New York: Cambridge University Press)

Lawson, Nigel
  2015   "Cool It: An Essay on Climate Change," *Climate Change: The Facts*, edited by Alan Moran (Woodville, NH: Stockdale Books)

Lindzen, Richard S.
  2015   "Global Warming, Models and Language," *Climate Change: The Facts*, edited by Alan Moran (Woodville, NH: Stockdale Books)

Lomborg, Bjorn
  2006   *How to Spend $50 Billion to Make the World a Better Place* (New York: Cambridge University Press)
  2015   "Trade-Offs for Global Do-Gooders," *The Wall Street Journal*, September 18, 2015.
  2016   "The White House launches a scary campaign about deadly heat. Guess what: Cold kills more people." *The Wall Street Journal*, April 6, 2016.

Michaels, Patrick J.
  2015a   "Why Climate Models Are Failing," *Climate Change: The Facts*, edited by Alan Moran (Woodville, NH: Stockdale Books)
  2015b   "When Will Climate Scientists Say They Were Wrong?" *Townhall.com*, May 29, 2015.

Michaels, Patrick J. (editor)
  2011   *Climate Coup: Global Warming's Invasion of Our government and Our Lives* (Washington, D.C.: Cato Institute)

Michaels, Patrick J. and Robert C. Balling, Jr.
  2009   *Climate of Extremes: Global Warming Science They Don't Want You to Know* (Washington, D.C.: Cato Institute)

Moran, Alan (editor)
  2015   *Climate Change: The Facts* (Woodville, NH: Stockade Books)

Nongovernmental International Panel on Climate Change (NIPCC)
  2013   *Climate Change Reconsidered II: Biological Impacts*
  2014   *Climate Change Reconsidered II: Physical Science*

Nova, Jo
  2015   "The Trillion Dollar Guess and the Zombie Theory," *Climate Change: The Facts*, edited by Alan Moran (Woodville, NH: Stockdale Books)

Paltridge, Garth W.
  2015   "Uncertainty, Skepticism and the Climate Issue," *Climate Change: The Facts*, edited by Alan Moran (Woodville, NH: Stockdale Books)

Plimer, Ian
    2015   "The Science and Politics of Climate Change," *Climate Change: The Facts*, edited by Alan Moran (Woodville, NH: Stockdale Books)

Reuters
    2015   "American Cancer Society Eases Mammogram Recommendations" (accessed October 21, 2015)

Ridley, Matt
    2014   "Whatever Happened to Global Warming?" *Wall Street Journal*, September 4, 2014.

Robinson, Arthur B., Noah E. Robinson and Willie Soon
    2015   "Over 37,000 Scientists Sign On Against Man-Made Global Warming Fraud!" Oregon Institute of Science and Medicine. http:www.kickthemallout.com/article .php/story-the+petition+project. (accessed August 15, 2015).

Soon, Willie
    2015   "Sun Shunned," *Climate Change: The Facts*, edited by Alan Moran (Woodville, NH: Stockdale Books)

Spencer, Roy W.
    2012   *The Great Global Warming Blunder: How Mother Nature Fooled the World's Top Climate Scientists* (New York: Encounter Books)

Wildavsky, Aaron
    1997   *But Is It True?: A Citizen's Guide to Environmental Health and Safety Issues* (Cambridge: Harvard University Press)

OTHER NONFICTION WORKS

Alexander, Doris
    1996   *Creating Literature Out of Life: The Making of Four Masterpieces* "University Park: Pennsylvania State University Press)

Althen, Gary (with Amanda, R. Doran and Susan J. Szmania)
    2003   *American Ways: A Guide for Foreigners in the United States, second edition.* (Yarmouth, Maine: Intercultural Press, Inc.) [original published in 1988]

Anonymous
    1954   *A Woman in Berlin* (New York: Ballantine Books)

Asimov, Isaac
    1980   *In Joy Still Felt: The Autobiography of Isaac Asimov, 1954-1978* (New York: Avon Books)

Broderick, James F. and Darren W. Miller
    2011   *Web of Conspiracy: A Guide to Conspiracy Theory Sites on the Internet* (Medford, NJ: Information Today)

Cerf, Christopher and Victor Navasky
    1998   *The Experts Speak: The Definitive Compendium of*
            Authoritative Misinformation, Expanded and Updated
            (New York: Villard)
Christian, David
    2011   *Maps of Time: An Introduction to Big History* (Berkeley:
            University of California Press)
Cromer, Alan
    1993   *Uncommon Sense: The Heretical Nature of Science* (New
            York: Oxford University Press)
Culler, Jonathan
    2009   *Literary Theory: A Very Short Introduction.* (New York:
            Oxford University Press)
Datesman, Maryanne Kearny, JoAnn Crandall, Edward N. Kearny
    2005   *American Ways: An Introduction to American Culture, third*
            edition (White Plains, NY: Pearson Education, Inc.)
Duggan, William
    2003   *The Art of What Works: How Success Really Happens* (New
            York: McGraw Hill)
Fischer, David Hackett
    1970   *Historians' Fallacies: Toward a Logic of Historical*
            Thought. (New York: HarperCollins)
Fish, Stanley
    2008   *Save the World on Your Own Time* (New York: Oxford
            University Press)
Frankl, Viktor E.
    1992   *Man's Search for Meaning: An Introduction to*
            Logotherapy, fourth edition. (Boston: Beacon Press)
            [originally published in 1959]
Geoffrey, Norman
    2015   "Do I Dare to Eat an Egg?" *The Weekly Standard*, 16 March
            2015.
Grossberg, Lawrence, and Cary Nelson and Paula Treichler (editors)
    1992   *Cultural Studies* (New York: Routledge)
Hart, Michael H.
    1992   *The 100: A Ranking of the Most Influential Persons in*
            History, Revised and Updated for the Nineties. New
            York: Citadel Press.
Johnson, Paul
    1974   *Elizabeth: A Study in Intellect & Power* (London:
            Weidenfeld and Nicolson)
Kuhn, Thomas S.
    2012   *The Structure of Scientific Revolutions, Fourth Edition*
            (Chicago: University of Chicago Press) [originally
            published in 1962]

Leitch, Vincent B. and William E. Cain (General Editors)
  2010   *The Norton Anthology of Theory and Criticism, 2ⁿᵈ Edition.*
          (New York: Norton)
Lippmann, Walter
  1929   *A Preface to Morals* (New York: First Edition)
Murray, Charles
  2003   *Human Accomplishment: The Pursuit of Excellence in the
          Arts and Sciences, 800 B.C. to 1950* (New York:
          Harper Collins)
Oreskes, Naomi
  1999   *The Rejection of Continental Drift* (New York: Oxford
          University Press)
Popper, Karl
  1962   *Conjectures and Refutations* (New York: Basic Books)
Seaton, James
  2014   *Literary Criticism from Plato to Postmodernism: The
          Humanistic Alternative* (New York: Cambridge
          University Press)
Simonton, Dean Keith
  1994   *Greatness: Who Makes History and Why* (New York: The
          Guilford Press)
  1999   *Origins of Genius: Darwinian Perspectives on Creativity*
          (New York: Oxford University Press)
Toye, Francis
  1987   *Rossini: The Man and His Music* (New York: Dover
          Publications, Inc.)
Trilling, Lionel
  2008   *The Liberal Imagination: Essays on Literature and Society.*
          (New York: New York Review of Books) [originally
          published in 1950]
Wall Street Journal, The
  2014   "The Salt Libel: Another Example that Scientific Debates
          are Rarely 'Settled'," 18 August 2014.
Weekly Standard, The
  2015a   "Caffinated Confusion," 16 March 2015.
  2015b   "The Scrapbook: How About Rights for Trans Fats?" 20
          July 2015.
  2016   "A Bathroom of One's Own," 6 June 2016, pp. 8-9.
Wolpert, Lewis
  1993   *The Unnatural Nature of Scien*ce (Cambridge: Harvard
          University Press)
Young, R. V.
  2000   *A Student's Guide to Literature* (Wilmington, Delaware: ISI
          Books)

◆ ◆ ◆ ◆ ◆

SHAKESPEARE PLAYS QUOTED
(all are from the Pelican series of individual plays)

SCENES 8
Will not let you eat . . .   *Julius Caesar*, II.i 251-254
Et tu, brute?   *Julius Caesar*, III.i 76
Let him be Caesar . . .   *Julius Caesar*, III.ii 46
Do not consent that Antony . . .   *Julius Caesar*, III.i 234-237

SCENE 9
So Caesar may . . .   *Julius Caesar*, II.i 27-28

SCENE 16
I'll not be juggled with . . .   *Hamlet*, IV.v 130-136
Cut his throat . . .   *Hamlet* IV.vii 124
If thou didst ever the dear father . . .   *Hamlet*, I.v 23-25
I, with wings as swift . . .   *Hamlet*, I.v 29-31
Doomed for a certain term . . .   *Hamlet*, I.v 2-13
Taint not thy mind . . .   *Hamlet* I.v 85-88
Am I a coward? . . .   *Hamlet*, II.ii 210

SCENE 20
Indeed it is strange-disposèd time . . .   *Julius Caesar*, I.iii 33-35
And it is very much lamented . . .   *Julius Caesar*, I.ii 59-72
Be thou a spirit of health . . .   *Hamlet*, I.iv 40-45
I have heard that guilty . . .   *Hamlet*, II.ii 528-531
Love? his affections do not . . .   *Hamlet*, III.i 162-167

SCENE 23
Necessity will make us all . . .   *Love's Labor's Lost (LLL)*, I.i
                                               146-151
What? I love, I sue . . .   *LLL*, III.i 186-194
I will not love . . .   *LLL*, IV.iii 7-17
From women's eyes . . .   *LLL*, IV.iii 324-330
Is ebony like her? . . .   *LLL*, IV.iii 244-250

SCENE 28
Nay, if we talk of reason . . .   *Troilus &Cressida*, II.ii 46-50
What's aught but . . .   *Troilus & Cressida*, II.ii 52
Witness this army of such mass . . .   *Hamlet*, IV.iv 47-56
Here is such patchery . . .   *Troilus & Cressida*, II.iii 70-73

SCENE 36
Every subject's duty . . .   *Henry V*, IV.i 172-173

SCENE 41
    Not all the water . . .   *Richard II*, III.ii 55-58

SCENE 67
    Age cannot wither her . . .   *Antony and Cleopatra*, II.ii 45-50

SCENE 75
    And I am I . . .   *King John*, I.i 174
    the very spirit of Plantagenet . . .   *King John*, I.i 167
    Old Sir Robert . . .   *King John*, I.i 82-83
    With all my heart I thank thee . . .   *King John*, I.i 260-70
    Why, what a madcap . . .   *King John*, I.i 84
    fits the mounting spirit like myself   *King John*, I.i 206-208
    in the lusty stealth of nature . . .   *King Lear*, I.ii 11

SCENE 82
    What light is light . . .   *Two Gentlemen of Verona*, III.i
                                  174-188

SCENE 83
    I weep for joy . . .   *Richard II*, III.ii 4-10
    Let's talk of graves . . .   *Richard II*, III.ii 145-171
    My lord, wise men . . .   *Richard II*, III.ii 178-179
    Yet looks he like a king . . .   *Richard II*, III.iii 68-71
    No lord of thine . . .   *Richard II*, IV.i 253-259
    How soon my sorrow . . .   *Richard II,* IV.i 289-298

SCENE 84
    I know he will not . . .   *Julius Caesar*, I.iii 103-105
    Stoop, Romans, stoop . . .   *Julius Caesar*, III.i 106-111
    Where gentry, title, wisdom . . .   *Coriolanus*, III.i 143-148

SCENE 88
    I take today a wife . . .   *Troilus & Cressida*, II.ii 61-68
    Why should I war . . .   *Troilus & Cressida*, I.i 1-4
    Prithee, tarry . . .   *Troilus & Cressida*, IV.ii 16-18
    Before you tumbled me . . .   *Hamlet*, IV.v 62-65

SCENE 89
    Perhaps he loves you now . . .   *Hamlet*, I.iii 14-23
    I beg the ancient privilege . . .   *Midsummer Night's Dream*
                                    (MSND), I.i 41-42
    Be advised, fair maid . . .   *MSND*, I.i 46-51
    Is it excepted . . .   *Julius Caesar*, II.i 280-286

SCENE 91
the fleshed soldier . . .   *Henry V*, III.iii 11-43

SCENE 95
O thou foul thief . . .   *Othello*, I.iii 60-64
O most disastrous chances . . .   *Othello*, I.iii 95-169
I think this tale . . .   *Othello*, I.iii 171
Thou, thou, Lysander . . .   *Midsummer Night's Dream*, I.i
                                              28-38

And thou unfit for any place . . .   *Richard III*, I.ii 109-201
Was ever woman in this humour . . .   *Richard III*, I.ii 227-237

SCENE 96
Rather wishing for a more . . .   *Measure for Measure (MM)*, I.iv
                                             3-5

Hail, virgin   *MM*, I.iv 16-17
Lord Angelo, . . .   *MM*, I.iv 57-61
Go to your bosom . . .   *MM*, II.ii 136-141
Dost thou desire her . . .   *MM*, II.iii 167-186

SCENE 105
I account of her beauty . . .   *Two Gentlemen of Verona*, II.i
                                             60-75

to say the truth . . .   *Midsummer Night's Dream*, III.i
                                             137-138

hath ever but slenderly . . .   *King Lear*, I.i 298-299
Time shall unfold   *King Lear*, I.i 286
Fortune [will] turn . . .   *King Lear*, II.ii 172-173
I love you more than word . . .   *King Lear*, I.i 55-56
I profess myself an enemy . . .   *King Lear*, I.i 72-76
I love your majesty . . .   *King Lear*, I.i 92-93
I will have such revenges . . .   *King Lear*, II.iv 279-282

SCENE 106
I do invest you jointly . . .   *King Lear*, I.i 131-140
Idle old man . . .   *King Lear*, I.iii 16-18
Who am I, sir? . . .   *King Lear*, I.iv 77-78
All thy other titles . . .   *King Lear*, I.iv 145-148
Does any here know me?   *King Lear*, I.iv 230-235
This is not Cressida . . .   *Troilus & Cressida*, V.ii 117
The shadow of your sorrow . . .   *Richard II*, IV.i 292-293
The king would speak . . .   *King Lear*, II.iv 99-117
They flattered me like a dog . . .   *King Lear*, IV.vi 96-105
Thou art the thing itself . . .   *King Lear*, III.iv 102-108
Through tattered clothes . . .   *King Lear*, IV.vi 164-167

SCENE 114

By th' mass . . .	*Hamlet*, III.ii 369-375
Remember thee? . . .	*Hamlet*, I.v 95-103
O villain, villain . . .	*Hamlet*, I.v 106-108
And some that smile . . .	*Julius Caesar*, IV.i 50-51
To put an antic disposition on . . .	*Hamlet*, I.v 175
Report me and my cause . . .	*Hamlet*, V.ii 322-332
Now cracks a noble heart . . .	*Hamlet*, V.ii 342-343
Must I remember? . . .	*Hamlet*, I.ii 143-145
and yet within a month . . .	*Hamlet*, I.ii 143-159
Ay, that incestuous . . .	*Hamlet*, I.v 42-57

SCENE 115

For thou hast been . . .	*Hamlet*, III.ii 65-73
What piece of work . . .	*Hamlet*, II.ii 273-277
And yet to me . . .	*Hamlet*, II.ii 277-279
I have of late . . .	*Hamlet*, II.ii 265-273
Some vicious mole . . .	*Hamlet*, I.iv 23-38
I am myself indifferent honest . . .	*Hamlet*, III.i 122-129
My lord, I will use them . . .	*Hamlet*, II.ii 468-473
O that this too too sullied . . .	*Hamlet*, I.ii 129-137
He . . . hath killed my king . . .	*Hamlet*, V.ii 62-66
You are the queen . . .	*Hamlet*, III.iv 15-16

SCENE 122

His Captain's heart . . .	*Antony & Cleopatra*, I.i 6-13
Let Rome in Tiber melt . . .	*Antony & Cleopatra*, I.i 33-40
These strong Egyptian fetters . . .	*Antony & Cleopatra*, I.ii 114-116
O thou . . .	*Antony & Cleopatra*, I.iii 32-39
That time – O times! . . .	*Antony & Cleopatra*, II.v 15-23
My heart was to thy rudder,	*Antony & Cleopatra*, III.xi 57-61
Fall not a tear, I say . . .	*Antony & Cleopatra*, III.xi 69-71

SCENE 126

When a man's verses . . .	*As You Like It*, III.iii 10-14
Between the acting . . .	*Julius Caesar*, II.i 61-69

SCENE 131

Hence from Verona art thou . . .	*Romeo and Juliet*, III.iii 15-60
There on the ground . . .	*Romeo and Juliet*, III.iii 83
In the reproof of chance	*Troilus and Cressida*, I.iii 33-47
Though with their high wrongs . . .	*The Tempest*, V.i 25-27
What I have done . . .	*Hamlet*, V.ii 209-216
O, let me not be made . . .	*King Lear*, I.v 41-44
His flawed heart . . .	*King Lear*, V.iii 189-192

OTHER SOURCES QUOTED

SCENE 8
"The subject which for Shakespeare . . ." Alvis, 1981a, p. 6.

SCENE 10
"the reader or theatrical spectator . . ." Young, p. 14.

SCENE 14
Louis P. Bénézet's poem . . . Ogburn, p. 393-97.

SCENE 22
"adhered to the orthodox view . . ." Crinkley, p. 515.
"the work of Ogburn's parents . . ." Crinkley, p. 515.
"I was enormously surprised . . ." Crinkley, p. 518.
"rightly, in my opinion . . ." Crinkley, p. 515.
"is the first time in my memory . . ." Crinkley, p. 519-20.
"Shakespeare scholarship owes an enormous . . ." Crinkley, p. 522.
"93 instances of 'too early' . . ." Chiljan, p. 343.
"either the great author was a serial plagiarist . . ." Chiljan, p. 343.

SCENE 26
"resembled the experience of Hamlet . . ." Stritmatter, 2006.
"a prolific correspondent . . ." Stritmatter, 2006.
"had been known as . . ." Stritmatter, 2006.

SCENE 28
"may be called the Eastern . . ." West, p. 127.
"discover truth in the knowledge . . ." West, p. 127.

SCENE 31
"It is made as clear as anything can be . . ." Looney, 1920, p. 174.
"When, therefore, he . . ." Looney, 1920, p. 175.
"highly implausible . . . its implausibility . . ." Ogburn, 1992, p. 198.
Galsworthy's description Ogburn, 1992, p. 146.
Freud's comment Ogburn, 1992, p. 146.
Gellett Burgess's comment Ogburn, 1992, p. 146.

SCENE 32
For the text of the letter and information about it, see Robinson, Robinson and Soon.

SCENE 33
"produced at the age of twenty-nine . . ." Looney, 1920, p. 36.
"If, after having performed so miraculous . . ." Looney, 1920, p. 36.
"It is difficult to believe . . ." Looney, 1920, p. 36-37.

"The exceptional character of . . ." Looney, 1920, p. 72-73.
"the Shakespearean dramas, as we have . . ." Looney, 1920, p. 310.

SCENE 35
For Singleton Letter, see Singleton, 1940.
"the best trained and most highly . . ." Hope and Halston, p. 88.

SCENE 36
"put into the form of sermons . . ." Alfred Hart, p. 27-28.
"What is peculiar to Shakespeare . . ." Alfred Hart, p. 28.

SCENE 39
"Many of the 3,000 members of this . . ." Robinson, Robinson, Soon.
"Contrary to reports of a 97 percent consensus . . ." Soon, p. 65.

THE CONTRARIAN #1: 37,000 SCIENTISTS CAN'T BE WRONG!
For the text of the letter and descriptions of it and the letter signers,
   see Robinson, Robinson and Soon.
Gandhi quote is readily at many places on the Internet.
Einstein quote, Bolt, p. 276.
Samuel Johnson quote, see Fischer, p. 282.
"To access . . . the scientific basis" Soon, p. 58.
"Use all best endeavors . . ." Soon, p. 58.

SCENE 42
"the preferred gender pronoun . . ." *Weekly Standard*, 2016, p. 8.

SCENE 48
"'disciples of cults,' that 'have all the fervor of religion,' . . ."
   Louis Booker Wright, "The Anti-Shakespeare Industry and the
   Growth of Cults," quoted in Ogburn, 1992, p. 154.

SCENE 55
"the weight of the evidence . . ." Michael Hart, p. 155.
"what I discovered is that most do not hold up under scrutiny . . ."
   Shahan, 2013, p. 212-13.

SCENE 56

THE CONTRARIAN #2: THE SCIENCE IS SETTLED
The examples of experts having been wrong are drawn from Cerf
   and Navasky, 1998.
"Salt . . ." *The Wall Street Journal*, August 18, 2014.
"Cholesterol . . ." Norman, March 16, 2015.
"Coffee . . ." *The Weekly Standard*, March 16, 2015.
"Trans fats . . ." Norman, March 16, 2015.

"**Mammograms . . .**" Reuters, October 21, 2015.
"**unrelated to the accuracy . . .**" Green and Armstrong, p. 171.
"**the clean bill of health given to salt . . .**" *The Wall Street Journal*, August 18, 2014
"**a study that had already . . .**" Norman, March 16, 2015.
"**a *New York Times* headline . . .**" Wildavsky, p. 370.
"**a *Newsweek* article was even scarier . . .**" Bethell, 2005.
"**. . . a new Ice Age.**" Bethell, 2005.

SCENE 59
"**No one expressed doubt . . .**" Shanan and Waugh, p. iii.
"**alleging that authorship doubters . . .**" Shahan and Waugh, p. vii.
"**a psychological aberration . . .**" De Vere Society Newsletter, October, 2013, p. 27.

SCENE 60
"**to imply that Looney's later criticism . . .**" Shapiro, 2010, pp. 180-182.
"**had a secret 'agenda' . . .**" Shapiro, 2010, pp. 180-182.

SCENE 62
"**the zeal and intensity by which believers . . .**" Crinkley, p. 518.
"**There would seem . . . to be no mystery -. . .**" Ogburn, 1992, p. 162.

SCENE 73
"**near-perfect correlation of 95 percent . . .**" Wildavsky, p. 363.
"**There is widespread agreement . . .**" Wildavsky, p. 358.

THE CONTRARIAN #3: THE WARMTH OF THE SUN
"**near-perfect level of 95 percent . . .**" Wildavsky, p. 363.
"**we have to change our view . . .**" Keith Shine, in Wildavsky, p. 363.
"**the sea temperature increases . . .**" Wildavsky, p. 359.
"**neither a consensus nor an authoritative review . . .**" Soon, p. 58.
"**incorrect representation of the solar zenith . . .**" Soon, p. 60-61.
"**persistent and systematic failure . . .**" Soon, p. 60-61.
"**the effect of minimizing the role of the sun . . .**" Soon, p. 65.

SCENE 77
"**the conversion of academics . . .**" Leahy, p. 7.
"**the core of a college or university experience . . .**" Fish, p. 21.
"**should be discussed in academic sense . . .**" Fish, p. 25-26.

SCENE 81
"**50,000 chunks or patterns of . . .**" Simonton, 1994, p. 67.
"**unwittingly lays bare his own innermost likes . . .**" Spurgeon, p. 4.
"**They deeply love what they do . . .**" Simonton, 1999, p. 87-88.

SCENE 86
"Each doubling of CO_2 in the atmosphere . . ." Carter, 2015a, p. 71-72.

THE CONTRARIAN #4: THE HEART OF THE MATTER
"have grown faster and more solidly . . ." Goklany, p. xi.
"the optimal percentage . . . is 900 ppm" Goklany, p. 4.
"the increased value of crops . . ." Goklany, p. 7.
"for the 45 crops that account for 95% . . ." Goklany, p. 5.
"human burning of biomass . . ." Wildavsky, p. 367.
". . . two-thirds of it exists in the oceans . . ."
   http://www.skepticalscience.com/human-co2-smaller-than
   natural-emissions.htm (accessed October 26, 2015).
"for less than a decade." Wildavsky, p. 372.
"Only one molecule of every 85,000 . . ." Plimer, p. 12.
"kelp fields expand . . . and plankton prosper . . ." Wildavsky, 366.
"carbon storage in terrestrial reservoirs . . ." Wildavsky, p. 361.
"The first 100 parts per million . . ." Plimer, p. 12; Carter, p. 71.
"a rapid saturation of its effect . . ." Carter, 2015a, p. 72.
"no warming . . . for the past 18 years . . ." Ridley, 2014.

SCENE 87
"they are often very aggressive . . ." Leahy, p. 7.
"17 percent of professors . . ." *NYTimes*, April 22, 2007.

SCENE 91
"if he threatens to expose . . ." Ogburn, 1992, p. 162.
"There is, of course, a price to be paid . . ." Stritmatter, 2006, p. 38.

SCENE 97
"because the flux is small . . ." Lindzen, p. 41.

THE CONTRARIAN #5: WITCHCRAFT, PART I
"The pause has now lasted . . ." Ridley, p. 2014.
"more than one million readings . . ." Wildavsky, p. 347.
"downward trend . . . of minus 0.07° C . . ." Robinson, Robinson,
   Soon.
"predictions of 102 models . . ." Michaels, May 29, 2015.
"the destruction of science . . ." Michaels, May 29, 2015.
"the entire north polar ice cap will be gone . . ." Bolt, p. 282.
"we'll have an ice-free (summer) Arctic . . ." Bolt, p. 283.
"still covered by six million square kilometers . . ." Bolt, p. 283.
"NASA says sea ice cover in Antarctica has grown . . ." Bolt, p. 282.
"global sea ice area is the largest in has been in 25 years . . ."
   Brown, December 17, 2013.
"Sea levels have slowly risen since 1880 . . ." Bolt, p. 281.
"the rate of sea level rise has decreased . . ." Plimer, p. 14.

"the sea level for the Tarawa atoll showed no rise . . ." Bolt, p. 282.
"The Maldives is now 70 centimeters higher . . ." Plimer, p. 15.
"a success rate of only 8 percent . . ." Wildavsky, p. 350.
"Their models cannot even 'predict' past . . ." Wildavsky, p. 353.
"a massive, unexplainable, and persistent . . ." Michaels, p. 30.

SCENE 98
"even the most comprehensive . . . models . . ." Wildavsky, p. 353.

THE CONTRARIAN #6: WITCHCRAFT, PART II
"changes in temperature preceded increased . . ." Plimer, p. 12.
"were premised on the supposition . . ." Wildavsky, p. 357.
"half will be reabsorbed . . . within ten years." Wildavsky, p. 372.
"thin layer near the top of the troposphere . . ." Nova, p. 157.
"the trend up there is . . ." Nova, p. 157.
"The tropical troposphere had actually cooled . . ." Nova, p. 157.
"the IPCC followed only 17 of 89 . . ." Green and Armstrong, p. 173.
"The models are consistent. They're bad at . . ." Nova, p. 159.
". . . 37 consecutive years of . . . model failure." Michaels, p. 31.
"mostly at night, mostly in the winter . . ." Wildavsky, p. 347.
"higher minimums during the days . . ." Wildavsky, p. 347.
"about 9,000 people die from heat each year . . ." Lomborg, 2016.

SCENE 100
"Taken individually . . ." Oreskes, p. 57.
"The predominating element . . ." Looney, 1920, p. 80.
"Once any theory is held in a preferred position . . ." Oreskes, p. 139.
"Wegener's book gave the impression . . ." Oreskes, p. 126.
"a now-sunken continent that he called . . ." Oreskes, 56-57.
"no independent evidence . . ." Oreskes, p. 218.
"that evidence from mammalian evolution . . ." Oreskes, p. 295
"written after his death . . ." See, for example, Shapiro, 2011: "Perhaps
    the greatest obstacle facing de Vere's supporters is that he died in
    1604, before ten or so of Shakespeare's plays were written."
"in the 1920s or early 1930s . . ." Oreskes, p. 6.
"if continental drift were true . . ." Oreskes, p. 313.
"Very naturally . . ." Oreskes, p. 156.

SCENE 102
"the man who saw the significance . . ." Oreskes, p. 260.
"what he had 'proved' . . ." Oreskes, p. 260-61.

SCENE 109
"History must begin with questions . . ." Fischer, pp. xx, 4.
"The logic of historical thought . . ." Fischer, p. xv.
"the task was the interpretation of literary works . . ." Culler, p. 47.

SCENE 110
"the explicit statements . . ." Trilling, p. 205.
"the dim mental region . . ." Trilling, p. 206-07.
"the intentional fallacy . . ." Wimsatt and Beardsley, p. 1.
"the meaning of a work . . ." Culler, p. 67.
"reconstruct the original context . . ." Culler, p. 68-69.
"Literary texts . . ." *Norton Anthology*, quoted in Seaton, p. 20.
"although there is no prohibition . . ." quoted in Culler, p. 50.
"In theory Cultural Studies is all-encompassing . . ." Culler, p. 47.
"Freed from the principle . . ." Culler, p. 50-51.
"Interpreting *Hamlet* . . ." Culler, p. 33.
"in some of the most influential academic centers . . ." Seaton, p. 1.
"present a staggeringly varied collection . . ." quoted in Seaton, p. 20.

SCENE 113
"the ability to enter imaginatively . . ." Elliott, p. xi.
"to make the great works . . ." Seaton, p. 10.

SCENE 116
"Over $300 billion . . ." Nova, p. 162.

THE CONTRARIAN #7: THE MILITARY-INDUSTRIAL COMPLEX REDUX?, PART I
"Wildavsky explained it best . . ." Wildavsky, p. 9.
"The Heartland Institute . . ." Nova, p. 162.
"The IPCC charter requires . . ." Carter, p. 75.
"We are an intergovernmental body . . ." Carter, p. 75.
The central lesson . . ." Soon, p. 65.

SCENE 117

CHART OF FACTORS
"J. Thomas Looney's . . ." Looney, 1920, p. 109-133.
"Price's 10 types of evidence . . ." Price, pp. 310-313.
"Jiménez's ten witnesses . . ." Jiménez, p. 74-85.
"Chiljan's list of plays . . ." Chiljan, see especially pp. 343-381.

SCENE 118
"by far worse than any . . ." Lawson, p. 105, 110.

THE CONTRARIAN #8: THE MILITARY-INDUSTRIAL COMPLEX REDUX?, PART II
"Sierra Club . . ." NCS News accessed in October, 2015:
    http://www.cnsnews.com/news/article/barbara-hollingsworth/sierra-club-president-says-satellites-are-wrong-our-planet-0)
"senior members were quite happy . . ." Paltridge, p. 153.

"I have never in my life . . ." Lawson,p. 94.
"Climate change catastrophism . . ." Plimer, p. 24.

SCENE 120
"Competition between segments . . ." Kuhn, p. 8.
"Once it has achieved the status of a paradigm . . ." Kuhn, p. 77.

CHART OF FACTORS
"J. Thomas Looney's . . . Characteristics . . ." Looney, 1920, p. 109-133.
"Price's 10 types of evidence . . ." Price, pp. 310-313.
"Jiménez's ten witnesses . . ." Jiménez, p. 74-85.
"Chiljan's list of plays . . ." Chiljan, see especially pp. 343-381.

SCENE 124
"The use of tools and the development of . . ." Wolpert, p. 24.
"scientific thinking, which is analytic and . . ." Cromer, p. 3-4.

SCENE 127
"deliberation and interpretation . . ." Kuhn, p. 122.
"Just because it is a transition . . ." Kuhn, p. 149.

SCENE 138
"How are we to combat . . ." Plimer, p. 24-25.

THE CONTRARIAN #10: WHAT'S A GIRL TO DO?, PART II
"What would be the best way . . ." Lomborg, p. 166.
"First and foremost . . ." Lomborg, p. xv.
"The experts were not unaware . . ." Lomborg, p. xvii.
"It is unethical . . ." Lomborg, p. xx.
"cooling of between . . ." Plimer, p. 8-19.
"Australia would suffer . . ." Plimer, p. 19.
"that states reduce . . ." Driessen, Aug. 8, 2015.
"World Bank President . . ." Lomborg, 2015.
"deeply troubling . . ." Lomborg, 2015.

SCENE 145
"Of all the books I have ever worked on . . ." Asimov, p. 464-65.

SCENE 155

THE CONTRARIAN #11: SHAKESPEARE IS INNOCENT!
"the skeptics have much . . ." Hart, 1992, p. 155.
"What I discovered . . ." Shahan, 2013, 212-13.

SCENE 166

"cows grazed and willows grew . . ." Nova, p. 180.

"they are still a little below . . ." Robinson, Robinson, Soon.

"the late twentieth century peak . . ." Carter, 2015a, p. 70.

"all six of the great ice ages . . ." Plimer, p. 12.

Made in the USA
Middletown, DE
05 October 2022

11966463R00225